# THE UGLY DUCHESS

*Translated from the German by*
WILLA AND EDWIN MUIR

# THE UGLY DUCHESS

*A Historical Romance*

*by*

LION
FEUCHTWANGER

*SECOND PRINTING*

*London:*
MARTIN SECKER
*Number Five John Street*
*Adelphi*

Die hässliche Herzogin : Margarete Maultasch

*Copyright*

POTSDAM : GUSTAV KIEPENHEUER VERLAG A.G., 1926
LONDON : MARTIN SECKER LTD., 1927

*First published in England   November 1927*

*Reprinted   November 1927*

# CONTENTS

# BOOK ONE

# CHAPTER I

BETWEEN the town of Innsbruck and the Monastery of Wilten a large open piece of level ground was covered with tents and flag-poles ; wooden galleries had been erected and a kind of arena staked out for jousting and other chivalrous sports. There was accommodation for thousands of spectators, and all was ready for their comfort and amusement. But these tents had covered the level fields of Wilten for nearly two years, waiting for the great and magnificent wedding-feast which Heinrich, Duke of Carinthia, Count of Tyrol, and King of Bohemia, wished to celebrate. The brothers of the Monastery saw to it that the wind did not damage the tents, that the tilting ground was not overgrown, and that the galleries did not fall to pieces. But still the festival was postponed ; the second matrimonial project seemed to be as great a failure as the first. The citizens of Innsbruck and the monks of Wilten sniggered ; the mountains looked down with indifference. The housewives of Innsbruck strolled down the fine gay canvas alleys, their children played tag over the benches, and lovers used the tents as convenient hiding-places.

The ageing King Heinrich—the whole of Europe good-humouredly and without irony allowed him the royal title, although he had long since lost his kingdom of Bohemia and had nothing left but the Earldom of Tyrol and the Duchy of Carinthia—rode peevishly among the tents. He had had

3

a light breakfast in the Abbey of Wilten ; baked trout
spiced with ginger, capons stewed in milk of almonds,
followed by grace after meat and comfits.   But in Wilten
they did not understand really choice eating ;  the delicate
nuances were missing.   The Abbot was a shrewd, stout
fellow and a useful diplomat, but he knew nothing about
the finer shades of cookery.   At least he, the King, had not
relished his food, and his temper, which was usually much
improved after a meal, was even gloomier than before.   He
was riding the short distance to Innsbruck without his
armour.   His tight fashionable clothing constricted him ;
it could not be denied that he was growing fatter from month
to month.   But he was a fine gentleman ;  he sat magnificently upon his noble horse with its rich trappings, and did
not allow himself to be hampered by his immoderately long
and wide sleeves.

A light wind blew, fanning the snow into flakes, bellying
the canvas of the tents so that they flapped and cracked.
Leaving his small escort behind, the King rode alone and
lazily, with an ill-humoured eye on the widespread festive
arrangements.   His smooth-shaven cheeks were fat and
flabby, his mouth, large and ugly, jutted out, with a pendulous
underlip.   His light watery eyes strayed angrily over the
canvas town, over the wooden galleries and the palisades of
the arena.   He was assuredly a long-suffering man.   But
there were limits even to his patience.   And now John,
the Luxemburger, had made a fool of him for the second
time ;  had for the second time promised him a bride with
the most solemn assurances, and for the second time left him
in the lurch.

He snorted through his small flat nose, and his breath
hung in a cloud of vapour in the cold, misty, snowy air.

Yet in spite of everything he was not really angry with John of Luxemburg ; indeed he found it very difficult to be angry with anyone. John had driven him ignominiously from Bohemia, so that of all his kingdom nothing but the empty title remained ; and yet he had been easily drawn again into amity with the gracious and elegant man, who had offered him financial compensation and the hand of his beautiful young sister Maria. Even when the Luxemburger found himself unable to keep his promise, because his sister objected to the marriage, he, Heinrich, had not raised any difficulties, and had declared himself willing to accept the other bride suggested by John, his cousin Beatrix of Brabant. But that he should be cheated of her too was too much. St. Bartholomew's day, which had been appointed for her arrival, was long past ; John's fair cousin of Brabant had not appeared, and the gay tents on the meadows of Wilten waited for her in vain. Of course the Luxemburger would produce another finely turned excuse. Only this time King Heinrich would not let himself be so easily smoothed down. Even the patience of a much-tried Christian King can come to an end.

He gave his beautifully wrought riding-whip an angry swish. He could remember very clearly his last interview with John, in May, when everything had been arranged. The Luxemburger had worn a costume of marvellous elegance, one had to admit that. The gentlemen of his suite, like himself, were dressed in the latest fashion, which had newly appeared in Catalonia and Burgundy, and had never been seen before in Germany ; extraordinarily tight clothes, sitting so close to the body that two servants were needed to pull them on, and made of parti-coloured stuff in a chequered pattern, with wide sleeves hanging down nearly to the knees.

He himself, King Heinrich, laid great weight on a fashionable appearance, but he could not deny that the Luxemburger put him in the shade. All the Bohemian and Luxemburg gentlemen—and how they could have managed it in the time he didn't understand—had even got their hair done in the latest style, with a full beard and flowing locks instead of the clean-shaven face and the short crop which had been the fashion for cavaliers ever since he could remember. He had been really surprised and impressed at the assurance and ease with which the Luxemburger had adapted himself over-night to the new mode. And so, filled with secret admiration, he had discussed with John only matters of fashion and gossip about women, horses and sport, leaving politics and the question of the marriage settlements to his advisers. His counsellors, the cautious, devoted Abbot of Wilten, the learned and eloquent Abbot Johannes of Viktring, Volkmar, his stately Burgrave, and the shrewd and pleasant lords of Villanders and Schenna, understood these painful and boring matters of finance much better than he did himself, and in their loyal and practised hands the drawing up of the preliminary contract could be left with more security. So he had confined himself to sociable conversation, and when King John extolled the advantages of the Parisian and Burgundian ladies with whom he loved to dally, he had upheld in his turn the solid charms of the Tyrolean women, whom he knew well, very well indeed, and from continually varying standpoints. And in the end his dear secretary, the Abbot Johannes of Viktring, had laid the finished contract before him, quoting a line of Latin, " This, too, might be said to have come to a fortunate issue," and had assured him that everything was well and truly settled, and that on St. Bartholomew's Day he would certainly receive his bride and thirty thousand marks of Veronese silver. And now here he was, riding about his festival ground. The tents were there, the flag-poles, the lists for jousting—but no bride, and no money.

A small boy appeared in the King's path. He had not heard the horse coming ; he was squatting with earnest absorption in a corner beside a tent, and had lifted up his skirts to relieve himself. The King, infuriated by such profanation of his nuptial grounds, aimed a blow at him. But as soon as the boy howled, he was sorry for him, and in repentance threw him a coin.

No, it really could not go on any longer. It was not befitting his kingly dignity to have the tents standing waiting like that. He would finish with the Luxemburger and his windy projects. In Innsbruck he would find the Austrian Duke, Albert the Lame, and make a contract with him, and take a bride from his hands. Was he to be dependent on Luxemburg ? Zounds ! What Luxemburg could not or would not procure for him, Habsburg would.

He was not the man to nurse ill-humour for long. When he had made his decision, he piped his wrath away into the cold and joyous air of heaven, and looked round with changed and merry eyes at the festal structures. Let people laugh! These tents would soon justify themselves. He sat more upright in the saddle, whistled a short and saucy tune, and spurred on his horse, so that his gentlemen had to put on speed to make up on him.

§ 2

THE five gentlemen of his personal retinue had been exchanging witty, allusive remarks about the King's delayed wedding as they rode through the wide-spreading town of tents. They were, all five of them, much cleverer than their overlord ; they squeezed him, especially the brutal Burgrave Volkmar, as much as they could, continually extorting from him new fiefs and reversions of taxes. But with it all they were faithful in their own fashion to their genial and accommodating prince. He was a generous man, he was pious, a good boon companion, given to sport and merry-making, and devoted to gallantry ; he loved fashionable clothes, and all kinds of comfort ; he had, too, a touch of imagination and was easily won over to any undertaking, although he was apt to tire of it as quickly. In a time when politics were completely determined by the personal influence of princes, such a man had not the best of prospects, and after the Bohemian affair he had been dropped out of all important European issues for ever. He suspected this as little as his advisers were fully aware of it. They knew that he was merely a pawn, and not a player.

From this esoteric standpoint they too surveyed Heinrich's matrimonial plans, and the waiting tents had a far different and more ironical significance for them than for the good King.

The fortunes of the Holy Roman Empire were directed by three princes, the quick, glittering, brilliant John of Luxemburg and Bohemia, the slow, hesitating Ludwig of Wittelsbach, and the tough, far-seeing Albert of Habsburg, whose lameness had made him hard, and the leader among his brothers. These three princes, equals in power, each aiming at the over-lordship of the Empire and of Christendom, crouched in wary readiness, and watched each other. Cast their eyes upon the mountain lands of Carinthia and Tyrol where Heinrich sat, an elderly widower without a male heir. Here was a possibility, the only one, indeed, of increas-

ing decisively one's possessions and power. The land in
the mountains, the rich, fertile, storied land stretched clear
from the borders of Burgundy to the Adriatic, from the
Bavarian plateau down into Lombardy. It was the bridge
from the Austrian to the Swabian possessions of the
Habsburgs, from Germany to Italy; the key to the
Empire.

To win over its ruler, the good-natured elderly epicurean,
and to secure his inheritance, seemed feasible to each of the
three princes. They took into account his longing for
a legitimate male heir in addition to his many bastard sons
and two legitimate daughters, and they angled for him with
tempting offers of marriage.

The five gentlemen, the three soldiers in full armour
and the two Abbots in travelling clothes of a very worldly
cut, smiled when they thought of King Heinrich's unwilling-
ness to recognise these facts. He pretended that it was only
out of princely kindness and devotion, out of pure friendship,
that Luxemburg, Wittelsbach and Habsburg were exerting
themselves to find him a fitting bride. But it was unthinkable
that John of Luxemburg's actions could be construed in this
manner. First he had offered Heinrich his beautiful young
sister Maria, together with twenty thousand marks of
Veronese silver, demanding in return the marriage of one
of Heinrich's daughters to one of the little Luxemburg
princes. He had inflamed the lustful old widower by showing him portraits of Maria, without troubling to mention
the matter even casually to the fair princess. It was not
difficult to understand that the young beauty, the daughter
of an Emperor, objected strenuously to marriage with such
an old and worn-out gallant. She took a vow of perpetual
virginity, but the vow—and the gentlemen grinned as they

slyly alluded to it—had not prevented her from marrying the King of France a few months later.

It was probable that John, knowing well beforehand that he could never persuade his sister to accept the Carinthian, had only wanted to keep the old King dangling, childishly delighted with the prospect of a handsome prince as the issue of the marriage. It was certain, however, that in the second affair with Beatrix of Brabant he was trifling unscrupulously with the old man. By promising him an even fatter dowry he had beguiled a contract out of him which pledged Hein-rich's small daughter Margarete to one of John's small sons, and named her as heiress of his lands in default of a male heir. If the old King died without a son this gave John an excuse for laying hands on Carinthia, Görz and Tyrol. True, he had painstakingly tracked down all Heinrich's innumerable love-affairs, and had discovered that during the last four or five years the quickly ageing King had had no children by any of his mistresses ; but still no doctor, and no man of the world, however experienced, could prophesy with cer-tainty in such a matter ; and so the longer he put off the King's wedding, the more all prospect of a male heir for Heinrich disappeared, the stronger grew his own hopes of seizing through his little son the mountain lands and in consequence the Holy Roman Empire.

This train of thought was very patent to the five gentle-men ; they knew very clearly that this was the real cause which kept the festal tents so empty and forlorn. If the Luxemburger's dear cousin of Brabant, daughter of the Sire of Louvain and Gaesbecke, niece of the late Emperor Heinrich the Seventh, still hesitated, if she protested that she was the only solace of her parents and that she did not want to exchange her beloved Flanders for the alien and terrifying

mountains, well, John had certainly not tried very hard to
bring her round

The gentlemen were uneasy and divided in their minds
over the whole project of the marriage, which was the very
kernel of Tyrolean policy. The Burgrave Volkmar, brutal
and heavy in his massive armour, did say in his gruff voice
that, Luxemburg or Habsburg, it was all one, if only the
King got his bride in bed beside him ; for these eternal
hindrances made a laughing stock of His Majesty from
Sicily to the far north, and of His Majesty's advisers too.
But that sounded somewhat constrained and insincere, and
both the sly, taciturn Tägen of Villanders and Jakob of
Schenna, a lean, subtle gentleman who was the youngest
among the counsellors, pulled wry faces. King Heinrich
was so pleasantly ignorant of finance ; he left its management entirely to his advisers, and when they submitted accounts to him and complained of the labour involved and their
out-of-pocket expenses, thanked them with many friendly
words, and was never sparing with enfeoffments, privileges
and tax monopolies, although his purse was always empty.
It was beautifully easy to grow fat comfortably in his service,
and to enrich one's coffers and estates. But now—the
gentlemen sighed—if a stranger got his fingers into this
convenient pie, they would by no means find life so easy,
whatever precautions they might take.

The two prelates were quite pleased, the wily, haggard
Abbot of Wilten, and the garrulous, bustling Johannes of
Viktring. " Good and of profit it is to observe the actions
of princes," the latter quoted from an ancient classic, and
they both relished with quiet and sportsmanlike appreciation
the Luxemburger's diplomacy. They were not unreasonable ; whether it was from Heinrich, or Luxemburg, or

B

Habsburg, they would know how to obtain all they needed for their rich and kindly abbeys.   So with almost impartial curiosity they awaited the outcome of the struggle between Albert of Austria and John of Bohemia, and regarded with benevolence the stout, pious, good-natured, jovial figure of King Heinrich, the pawn in the great game played by the three mightiest German princes.

The gentlemen overtook the King, who sat more jauntily upon his horse, observed how his mood had lightened, and guessed his decision to leave the choice of his bride to the Habsburger, happen what might.   Well, in one way or another, the affair would have to come to a head some time.   Very good, then, they would attach themselves to the Habsburger.

Yet when a few months later the tents of Wilten were at last actually thronged with wedding guests (although the bride was indeed a different Beatrix, one whom Albert had proposed, Beatrix of Savoy) John of Luxemburg had none the less elbowed his way into the affair ; it was John of Luxemburg who arranged the marriage, signed and sponsored the preliminary contract, paid the dowry, or, at least, promised to pay it, and it was John's small son Johann who was to be the bridegroom of Margarete of Carinthia and the heir to the mountain land.

# CHAPTER II

THE twelve-year-old Margarete, Princess of Carinthia and Tyrol, was travelling from her seat near Meran to Innsbruck for her wedding with the ten-year-old Prince Johann of Bohemia. Her father, King Heinrich, had suggested her taking the nearest way over the Jaufen Pass, but she preferred the long detour by Bozen and Brixen, for she wanted to sun herself in the homage of the populous settlements lying along that route.

She journeyed with a large retinue. The gentlemen rode at a foot pace ; the gaily-decorated tilt-carts for the ladies creaked and bumped up and down the rocky roads, jolting wretchedly. Many of the ladies took to mules, although that was scarcely fitting, or rode pillion behind the gentlemen for short stretches of the way.

The little Princess sat in a horse-litter with her Mistress of the Household, Frau von Lodrone, and her Lady-in-waiting, Hildegard von Rottenburg, a withered, insignificant-looking, boundlessly devoted creature. The two ladies kept on sighing and lamenting over the dust of the badly-made road, the smell of the horses, the continual shaking ; but the Princess endured these discomforts without the slightest complaint.

Still and serious she sat, in ceremonial pomp. Her bodice was so tight that she had had to be laced into it ; her sleeves of heavy green satin, in the very extreme of fashion, fell to her feet ; she wore one of the new jewelled hair-nets

which an express courier had had to bring from Flanders,
where they had recently appeared.  A heavy necklace
sparkled on her bosom, and large rings on her fingers.  So
she sat, serious and perspiring, weighed down with magnificence, between the peevish, grumbling women.

She looked older than her twelve years.  Her thick-set
body with its short limbs supported a massive misshapen
head.  The forehead, indeed, was clear and candid, the
eyes quick and shrewd, penetrating and sagacious ; but below
the small flat nose an ape-like mouth thrust forward its
enormous jaws and pendulous underlip.  Her copper-
coloured hair was coarse, wiry and dull, her skin patchy and
of a dull greyish pallor.

So the daughter of Carinthia journeyed through the land
under a brilliant September sky.  Cornets and trumpets
saluted her wherever she went, bells rang and banners waved.
In Brixen the Bishop and Chapter came out in stately procession to greet their suzerain's daughter and heiress.  Great
feudal lords received her at the boundaries of their fiefs ;
on the outskirts of the towns she was attended by the
magistrates.

In clear and flowing Latin, with authority and self-
possession, Margarete replied to the submissive words of her
loyal subjects.  The people stared at her respectfully, and
greeted her as if she were the Sacrament, lifting their children
high to catch a glimpse of their future duchess.  But once
she was past they looked at each other and grinned.  " What
a snout she has !   Like an ape ! " sneered the plain and
shabby women.  The handsome ones were sorry for her :
" The poor creature !   How ugly she is ! "

And so the child fared through the land, pale, livid,
thick-set, serious, heavy with pomp like a heathen image.

§ 2

IN the great reception tent of the canvas town at Wilten
priceless gobelins and carpets were spread, banners rustled
solemnly, and in formal rows were ranked the escutcheons
of Luxemberg, Carinthia, Carniola, Görz and Tyrol.
The ten-year-old Prince Johann stood awaiting the bride
who was to be given him.   He was slender and tall for his
years, with a fine, long head which was passably handsome ;
but his deep-set eyes were small and malicious.   He fidgeted
uneasily in his tight fashionable clothes ;  his narrow chest
was painfully cramped in a purely ornamental breastplate
which he wore on this occasion for the first time.   So he
fretted, sweating and nervous, among the fifteen lords from
Bohemia and Luxemburg who had accompanied him.

A fanfare of trumpets, lowered banners.   The Princess
had arrived.   On behalf of the Prince the Archbishop of
Olmütz stepped forward and welcomed her in rounded and
resonant phrases.   Then the two children stood face to face,
the boy decked out in his garish armour, the girl weighed
down with magnificence.   They examined each other
critically.   Shy and sulky, Johann blinked uneasily with
small malicious eyes at his ugly bride ;  coolly and almost
contemptuously Margarete stared at the tall, lanky, nervous
boy.   Then with timid formality they took each other by
the hand.

Their fathers came in.   Margarete looked up in astonishment at the brilliant and imposing bulk of King John.   What
a man !   And the Luxemburger, who was a skilled diplo-
matist, controlled himself and did not shrink from her.   High
in his strong arms he swung the hideous child who was bringing his son Carinthia, Carniola, Tyrol and Görz, and kissed

her before them all on her broad, ape-like mouth, while limp
with ecstasy she gazed deep into his eyes.   The ageing King
Heinrich, pleased and touched, stood by, his pale eyes watering
more than usual.   With his fleshy hand, which trembled
perpetually as a result of his excesses, he shook the cold,
sweating, nerveless, bony hand of his little son-in-law, and
spoke to him as if he were grown-up.

And the horns blew, the drums rolled, the banquet began.
The pavilion, in which the children had their own high
table, glittered with scarlet and gold.   Three groaning
tables sagged under their loads of splendid vessels.   The
Bishoprics of Trent and Brixen had lent their costly plate,
the towns of Bozen, Meran, Sterzing and Innsbruck their
ceremonial dinner services.   Behind the heads of the bridal
couple gleamed the heavy folds of their standards with the
stiff heraldic animals.   High on their powerful and gaily-
decked chargers the chief lords of Bohemia, Carinthia and
Tyrol, preceded by musicians, served up the dishes for the
princely children.   After each course knights brought water
and napkins, poured out wine, and carved the meat.   The
children sat enthroned amid gold and scarlet, with old and
serious faces.

Good King Heinrich swam in a sea of happiness.   He
went over to his new spouse, presiding over the ladies' table,
the young, shy, anæmic Beatrix of Savoy who was always
shivering, pressed her hand and drank her health ;  then
hurried back again to John, the first knight and the most
proficient gallant in Christendom.   It did him good to sit
shoulder to shoulder with a man like that and to feel himself
at one with him.   He was of a different breed from the dull
and serious Bavarian, the Emperor Ludwig, who spoke of
nothing but politics and soldiering.   This was a man after

his own heart, of his own kind.    He, Heinrich, enjoyed life
round about his own castles of Zenoberg, Gries, and Trent,
and in the fortresses of his barons, whose ladies were honoured
and delighted to show their devotion to their sovereign.
Nor did he avoid adventures when on his travels, and was
always pleased if the magistrate of a town gave him a formal
invitation to the brothel.    But this man John—by the
nine-tailed devil and the sacrament !—this John was still
a better man than he.    There was not a town from the
Spanish border right into the wilds of Hungary, from Sicily
to Sweden, where he had not disported himself.    He prowled
at night in disguise through the streets, questing like a tom-
cat, skirmishing with the citizens' wives and exchanging
blows with jealous lovers.    The whole of Europe rang with
his impudent, gay, extraordinary and brilliant adventures.
Already overcome with wine and blissfully happy, Heinrich
hitched himself still closer to the Luxemburger ; he was
his devoted admirer, and quite without envy.    True, he
was somewhat older, a little more mature ; but taking all in
all he saw in John only his own counterpart, something like
a younger brother of the same temperament.    Suspecting
nothing, he cheerfully believed that the world saw him in
the same light as he saw John.

He drank deeply, hiccuped, and his eyes swimming, poked
the Luxemburger in the ribs with sniggering conviviality,
whispering and stuttering ribald secrets in his ear.    The
shrewd and elegant John met with perfect friendliness the
senile and garrulous confidences of the Carinthian, and not by
the smallest gesture betrayed that he thought him an old
fool.    The two Kings laid their heads together, wound their
arms round each other's shoulders, exchanged knowing
whispers and burst out laughing.    The other gentlemen

grew merry too, and their faces flushed. The nobles from
Bohemia, Luxemburg and Tyrol understood each other
either with difficulty or not at all, which gave rise to innumerable jests. And above all the rest was heard always the
resounding laughter of the King's two natural brothers,
Heinrich of Eschenloh, and Albrecht of Camian.

The child Margarete looked at her jovial uncles with large,
shrewd eyes. Her ladies, Frau von Lodrone and Fräulein
von Rottenburg, were ashamed, and begged the gentlemen
not to tell their risky stories so loudly before the children.
Both the fading Court ladies had been drinking sweet wine ;
they had flushed patches on their cheeks, smiled sourly, and
were excited.

At the ladies' table there sat also Margarete's younger
sister, the sickly and lame Adelheid. The shrinking child
would much rather have stayed in her convent among the
nuns of Frauenchiemsee. But Margarete had insisted on
her sister's presence at the wedding. So there she sat at the
noisy feast, surrounded by roaring knights, banners, and
ceremonial plate, the granddaughter of the mighty conqueror
of the land, pale, deformed and suffering, very like the Court
dwarfs who tumbled before her making rude, sardonic jests.
Her gentle stepmother, Beatrix of Savoy, smiled to her, and
stroked her hand.

The bridegroom, little Prince Johann, was gloomy,
cramped, and stiff on his seat of honour. The two children
had hardly exchanged a word. From time to time he cast
an oblique glance at his bride, who sat beside him with easy
assurance. To help himself over his embarrassment he ate
a great deal, quickly and promiscuously, and drank spiced
wine. At length he felt sick ; he set his teeth grimly and
kept down the nausea, but finally it was too much for him.

The Archbishop of Olmütz had to take him out. Everybody laughed with delight and made good-natured jokes. Margarete, cool and contemptuous, stared straight in front of her.

When he came back he had taken off his breastplate and felt much relieved. With a sulky, sinister expression he attacked the pistachio nuts, figs, gingerbread, electuaries and sweets. This whole journey, the ugly, haughty girl who was his bride, the banquet, his father, the fat old man who was now his father-in-law—all these were distasteful to him. He would much rather have been left in the dirty Bohemian village belonging to his mother's castle ; he would much rather have been ranging round with the peasant children, with Wenceslas, Bogislav, and Prokop. He was tall, strong, and cowardly. He was in the habit of beating and biting his playfellows without mercy. If they defended themselves he took it at first in good part. But if he was in danger of being overpowered he suddenly showed his other side and became the King's son, foamed with rage, laid information against them and had them severely punished. He had been reared by his mother, the Bohemian Elizabeth, who had brought the kingdom to the House of Luxemburg. She was a hysterical woman, besottedly in love with her brilliant husband, and wildly jealous of his innumerable mistresses. Above all, she hated passionately the widow of the late king, Rudolf, who queened it in Graz, and whose incestuous relations with John had plunged the land into civil war and wasted it miserably. In such abrupt fluctuations of feeling, now clinging ecstatically to her husband and now hating and cursing him violently, she educated her son also. He could hardly come to an understanding with his father, who spoke no Bohemian as he spoke no French ;

they had to speak to one another in German, which neither
of them knew well. The boy, too, saw his father only on
the rare occasions when the latter swept tempestuously, for
a short round of festivities, into the kingdom which he
detested, which served only to provide him with money, and
to which he far preferred his smiling Rhenish possessions in
Luxemburg. According to her mood then, the mother
compelled the boy to feign love or hatred for his father. So
the child was prematurely reserved, repressed, sulky, and shy.

He did not care for the sunlit heights of Tyrol, where
everything had such clear, sharp outlines. He was homesick
for the mists and clouds of his own Bohemia. His eyes
blinked ; he had had enough of it. The wine stimulated
him ; he wanted to do something, to give orders, to torment
somebody.

His page stood behind him, and poured water over his
hands from a golden jug. Johann rounded on him, bidding
him be more careful, for he was spilling water over his
sleeves. The page flushed, bit his short lips, made as if to
answer, but controlled himself and said nothing.

Margarete turned her head, and ran her quick eyes over
the page. The boy was three or four years older than
Johann, thin, keen and brown of face, with a strong nose
and full, short lips ; his chestnut hair was long and flowing.

"What is the name of Your Highness's page ? " she asked,
in her clear, warm voice.

Johann looked at her askance, mistrustfully. " Chretien
de Laferte," he answered in a surly tone.

Chretien had been selected about a year before from his
father's court to be his older comrade and playfellow, to do
him all courtly services and to instruct him in the customs
of polite French and Burgundian society.

" Give me some of the comfit, Chretien ! " said Margarete slowly and calmly, looking full at him.

Chretien assiduously handed her the bowl of sweetmeats. With great unconcern she broke a piece into three parts, kept one for herself, gave the second to Johann, and the third to the embarrassed Chretien.

At the gentlemen's table this by-play was observed, and they jested at the childish imitation of grown-up gallantry. Little by little the jests grew more biting ; the gentlemen jeered at the unusual ugliness of the bride.

" Poor boy ! " said one of the Bohemians. " He has to pay a bitter price for his lands."

" I would rather win mine by the sword," said another. " Before one could relish a mouth like that," said a third, " it would have to be well gilded." The Tyrolese barons hung back at first ; but in the end, half unwillingly, they joined in too. The child Margarete looked across at them. She could not possibly have overheard, but her large, serious eyes seemed so full of understanding that the gentlemen broke off almost with embarrassment.

Jakob of Schenna sat among them, the youngest of King Heinrich's counsellors and intimates. He was often a guest at the King's castles. The child Margarete saw him frequently. He was the only one whom she liked and trusted. He did not speak to her with that tone of foolish condescension, that constrained childishness, which other adults adopted, and which irked her grievously ; he treated her as an equal.

He saw her sitting there in formal splendour ; he saw the raw little Bohemian Prince, with whom she had nothing in common ; he saw how she tried to establish a connection with the page Chretien. He listened to the stupid witticisms about her unfortunate appearance. Then he got up and

strode across the room, stood before her with his usual indifferent slouch, and surveyed her courteously with grey,
kindly, and very old eyes, making meanwhile sedate and
serious conversation with her.   How her father-in-law, His
Majesty of Bohemia, looked very well, and how he bore no
marks of his fatiguing campaigns.   And that the said King's
plans for a stay in Southern Tyrol would certainly involve
a good deal of trouble for Margarete, since he would likely
quarter his escort and soldiers on all her castles.   And how
much money a possible campaign in Lombardy would cost.
Little Johann shot a furtive glance at Margarete ; he was
taken aback by the sagacity of her conversation.

Soon afterwards the table was removed.   Margarete
exchanged a few formal words of farewell with her husband
before she withdrew.   She asked him what impressions he
had of Tyrol and of her father's court ; if he were looking
forward to the coming tournament ; and hoped that he
would soon feel at home.   The boy answered awkwardly
and sheepishly, a look of dislike and a kind of obstinate
stupidity on his not unattractive face.   As she went out
the page. Chretien stood beside her and swept aside the tent
curtains for her to pass.   She thanked him with composure,
cool, distant, and dignified.

Then she had herself taken to her tent ; by this time she
was thoroughly weary.   Her women undressed her with
much gossip and giggling, turning over again particular
guests and occurrences at the banquet.   She was already in
bed, but her women still chattered.   At last they went away.
She stretched herself out, her limbs freed from the heavy
oppression of her finery.   Now she would have a good sleep.
She deserved it.   She was pleased with herself.   She had
borne herself well, quite like a grown-up woman, very

royally ; she had given the lords from Luxemburg and
Bohemia no handle against her.   Johann, all the same, was
nothing to be proud of.

"Your prince isn't anything to boast of," remarked the
maid outside, who was clearing up, carefully lowering her
coarse sniggering voice.

"Compared with your princess," jeered the Bohemian
serving-man who was helping her and making love to her,
"he's an angel of light.   What a creature !   That face !
And those teeth !   In our country we'd drown anything
like that when it was born, like a kitten."

Meanwhile King Heinrich paid the bills for the wedding.
It had been a very grand wedding.   He realised that it
must have cost much ;  he was no cheeseparer.   Obligingly
his gentlemen advanced the large sums needed, and obligingly,
with cheerful lavishness, he requited their kindness by
pledging them rich villages, districts, estates, taxes and
revenues.   Why should he not hand over Visiaun and
Möltern to his dear Burgrave Volkmar ?   He gave him
Rattenberg as well.   And it was only fair that the Abbot
of Wilten, who had had to look after the fine canvas wedding
town for so long, should have the lake between Igls and Vill.
But then the monastery of Viktring had to get something
too.   For if only Wilten were to benefit, his good secretary
Johann would be justly aggrieved.   So Viktring received
its share of farms and rents.    "Nothing more gladdens the
heart than gifts bestowed upon comrades," said the eloquent
Abbot, thanking him, quoting from an ancient classic.

John was present when King Heinrich, well soused in
wine, jovial, gracious, careless and informal, signed away
these colossal gifts and mortgages.   He was generous too ;
but his barons would never have dared to approach him with

such ingenuous shamelessness. It would be a good thing
to make the merry old gentleman draw in his horns a little.
Otherwise he would give away the whole of the land and
thank people for taking it ; and in the end his little son would
have nothing left but the princess, and a fine legacy that
would be ! King Heinrich's young wife, too, the pale,
gentle Beatrix, was shocked to see her husband playing ducks
and drakes with his rich possessions. All her life she had
been accustomed to thrifty and anxious housekeeping ; and
she feared that with Heinrich's methods the very shifts
would soon be pawned off her maids' backs. She decided
to take the finances into her own control ; her pale, timid
face all at once showed a trait of shrewishness.

The next few days were set aside for jousting. On this
occasion several young squires were to be dubbed knights.
Of her own accord Margarete begged her boy husband to
have his page Chretien de Laferte made a knight too.
Johann's eyes became even smaller and sulkier ; he muttered
something. Margarete repeated her request more insistently. Prince Johann in a stifled, snappish voice said he
didn't want to. He thumped the page in the ribs with all
the force of his small, bony fist. " That's all the dubbing
he'll get," he sneered, twisting up his long face spitefully.

" I thank your Highness a thousand times for the favour,"
said Chretien, red as fire, to the Princess, " but since he is
unwilling——" " But I want him to ! " insisted Margarete, in her full, deep voice. She ran to her father and
King John. Smiling, they granted her request. Chretien,
torn this way and that, thanked the Princess. His comrades
had already teased him unmercifully about his dainty lady-
love.

On the appointed day the brilliant tournament began, to

which the whole of Tyrol had looked forward for years.
It was a noble entertainment. Four knights were run
through the body, and seven mortally wounded. Everybody
agreed that it was the most successful diversion they had had
for a long time.

King John, too, took part in the jousting. But since he
could not help knowing that knights often put up only a sham
fight with him for fear of overcoming a king, he assumed the
arms of a certain Schilthart of Rechberg. There had been
already many little outbursts of jealousy between the high-
landers and the strangers ; the Tyrolean and Carinthian
knights were afraid also that John's influence would imperil
their financial relations with good King Heinrich. So the
merry sport masked a very serious and bitter rivalry, and
men were not at all ill-pleased to see one or other of their
opponents with his ribs broken. Whether by mere chance,
or because his disguise had been betrayed, at all events
John soon found himself engaged by the heaviest and most
dangerous of the Tyrolean knights, the boorish Burgrave
Volkmar. They clashed wildly and recklessly together,
and at length the king, who had had a lively night, fell from
his horse, was dragged around in the mud, terribly trampled,
and extricated from the mellay with severe bruises. He had
to ransom his horse from the Burgrave for sixty marks of
Veronese silver. He concealed his vexation that it should
be precisely this rude, greedy, offensive fellow who had
overthrown him, bore with good grace his lameness and
injuries, and as a friend and an expert praised largely the
excellent conduct and unqualified success of the Tyrolean
sports.

At night King Heinrich sat wearily in his tent. A shadow
had crept over his delight in the fine festival ; bills kept

coming in, and still more bills. The butchers of Bozen
were asking for money ; the citizens of Innsbruck sent in
huge claims ; the good and learned Abbot of Marienberg
was at his wits' end before his creditors, whom he could
easily have satisfied had the king only repaid him a fraction
of what he had borrowed. Heinrich would gladly have
paid and paid again ; but his coffers were empty. True,
King John owed him that dowry of 40,000 marks of Veronese
silver ; and with that huge sum he could have covered
all his obligations. But it would not do to dun the king.
Not to-day, at any rate. He was finding out himself how
wretchedly such a thing spoilt a festival.

So he sat in deep perplexity. Then his gentlemen introduced three slender, shadowy figures. They were very
quiet, very humble, very insignificant. Their eyes were
quick, but could look very devoted. They were all very
like each other. The king remembered having seen them
before, but could not place them. That was natural enough;
they were so small, so unimportant. They bowed a great
deal, and spoke in low voices.

It was Messer Artese from Florence, to whom he had
mortgaged the Mint at Meran, and his two brothers. They
were very happy to have the honour on this occasion too of
assisting with a little capital such a good Christian king. They
exacted only one small condition : that his Majesty should
make over to them the revenues from the salt works at Hall.
That nice little salt mine.

King Heinrich started. The salt taxes of Hall ! The
chief source of income in the country ! It was a dear
wedding-feast he had prepared for his daughter. Even his
light-hearted counsellors looked thoughtful when they heard
of this condition. Finally they brought forward his young

wife, who managed to arrange that the salt works should be pledged for only two years. The Florentines bowed repeatedly ; paid over the money, and gathered up the documents ; glided out, shadowy, grey and insignificant, all very like one another.

Margarete said to Jakob of Schenna : " Do you think that Chretien de Laferte speaks badly of me ? Tell me honestly, Herr von Schenna, do you think that he laughs with the others because I am ugly ? "

Jakob von Schenna had heard with his own ears how the youthful Chretien, when teased by the others as the knight of the ugliest girl in Christendom, had first stuck to his guns, and then outbidden his comrades in abuse of Margarete. Jakob von Schenna saw the child's large, brimming eyes insistently questioning him. " I do not know, Princess Margarete," he replied. " I know too little about young Chretien. But I think it unlikely that he speaks badly of you." And he laid his large, thin, nerveless hand on her head, as on that of a child, and on this occasion she was thankful to be treated as a child.

C

# CHAPTER III

In the castle of Zenoberg King John was negotiating with the Tyrolese barons. As guardian of his little son he was already exacting their oaths of allegiance in case of Heinrich's death. The nobles agreed to this in principle, but demanded in return a confirmation of their privileges, and guarantees that the Luxemburger would appoint no strangers to important offices. Each man besides was playing for his own hand, openly or indirectly, asking for money, charters, estates, trade monopolies, and taxes.

John was very liberal with the guarantees and confirmations. He signed and sealed whatever they wanted. He had learned by experience in Bohemia that in the last resort everything was a question of power. If he could raise men and money, he would appoint as many representatives as he chose from France, Burgundy and the Rhine to tickle up these impudent mountaineers. If he failed to get capital and an army, then, in the name of God, he would keep his promises. Meanwhile his notaries wore their fingers out writing : "We, John, by the grace of God King of Bohemia and Poland, Margrave of Moravia, Count of Luxemburg, hereby declare, proclaim and make known, and pledge ourselves by seal and signature . . ." With money John was rather more cautious. At least he let the greedy and insatiable bargainers perceive that he saw through them. In the end he tossed them what they wanted with a fine gesture of contempt. Not in ready money, of course, for he had none, but in bills of exchange drawn for long periods. Even good King Heinrich learned to his sorrow that he would not get his 40,000 Veronese silver marks so soon as he had hoped. Gay, easy, and confidential, the Luxemburger clapped him on the shoulder and casually pledged him the administrations of Kufstein and Kitzbühel—which his son-in-law, the Duke of Lower Bavaria, had given him in exchange for others—held out hopes of payment in the spring, praised his fashionable long shoes and the pretty buxom partner he had just been dancing with. Heinrich could not bring himself to raise the question of finances again.

In the evenings King John played dice with the Carinthian and Tyrolese nobles. He staked enormous sums. Finally nobody stood out against him but the bull-necked Burgrave Volkmar. The Luxemburger hated this heavy, brutal fellow who had already overthrown him in the tournament. He increased his stake so much that even King Heinrich held his breath. Lost. Finished by remarking airily over his shoulder, that he would pay his losses sometime. The Burgrave growled and looked threatening ; with cutting courtesy John withered him into silence.

§ 2

REMARKABLY enough, although trouble had broken out in Bohemia, John did not return. His country breathed more freely. It cowered whenever he came. His stay was always brief, and meant only further extortions. It was a good thing that he kept his distance.

Yes, he remained in Tyrol. Visited the diocese of the Bishop of Trent. Sat there radiating elegance, the first knight in Christendom, idly spying and ambiguously sparkling ; not a soul knew what he was planning.

Bishop Heinrich of Trent was very discomposed by his arrival. How far could he meet his guest's advances without compromising himself with the Pope or the Emperor? There was always such a baffling obscurity around this King of Bohemia. Wherever he went there was feverish activity. Couriers from all the courts of Europe were always on his track, and never found him, for the King rarely stayed long in one place ; he went coursing over the earth as restlessly as a stream of water. Nobody ever knew the how, the whither, the why. Let him only go back to his own country, the nuisance ! But, of course, he let that go to rack and ruin. He did not love that sullen, troubled land. It was comical how obviously he preferred the sunnier West, the Rhine, his county of Luxemburg, and Paris.

The Bishop, a large, corpulent man with a strong brown Italian face, sat full of anxiety in his castle of Bonconsil, and unburdened himself to his friend, the shrewd and active Abbot of Viktring. Both ecclesiastics cursed the King vigorously. The heathen ! The Jeroboam ! He plundered his own churches and monasteries pitilessly. He had not stayed his hand even before the tomb of the blessed Albert, but had searched it for hidden treasure. The profaner of churches ! The Herod ! " Nevertheless from our bones one day will arise an avenger ! " quoted the learned Abbot from an ancient classic.

Yes, this was certainly the most dangerous and vexatious guest the Bishop had had for years. An anointed king, but —the Bishop said so frankly—a villain and a scoundrel. But for his crown he would have swung on a hundred gallows. He cheated at cards ; the Abbot confirmed it ; he had just done it again in Innsbruck. He was the most reckless spendthrift and prodigal of the century. And then,

there was the scandal of his relations with the two Bohemian
queens.    He had been well served two years ago in Prague,
when he had arranged a great tournament and made the
most exhaustive preparations, even pulling down houses in
the market-place to make room for his tents and galleries.
And of the two thousand guests invited, including Emperor
and King and princes and lords, there came but seven shabby,
questionable knights and a Genoese banker.

Unfortunately at present it was absolutely impossible to
treat him as he deserved.    That was the worst of it.    His
name and reputation changed like the moon.    He would be
shunned like a leper at one time, and in a few weeks
acclaimed as the most glorious hero of Christendom, and
even his sacked and stripped Bohemia was blinded by his
dazzling victories.

The Abbot warned the Bishop urgently against having
anything whatever to do with John's projects.    His policy
in the long run was a senseless gamble.

" Cooling waters invite with their glittering ripples the
        wanderer,
    But, if he plunges in, cruelly swallow him up,"

he quoted.    Comfortably, and with a literary pleasure in
his analysis, he dissected the Luxemburger and his nature.
His exaggerated chivalry was not content to seek out armed
men and giants in thick forests ; he loved the much more
glowing adventures of high politics.    It was not success
which attracted him, but the light-hearted dangers of complicated enterprises.    Wherever there was strife in the
troubled countries of Europe, dissension between Pope and
Emperor, between King and Pretender, France and England,

one Lombard city and another, Moors and Castilians, the Luxemburger had to have his finger in the pie. He had to be concocting treaties and alliances, arranging weddings, spinning and destroying webs of intrigue, starting wars and concluding peace, provoking or hindering battles, always in the thick of the turmoil, making friends and foes, acquiring and giving away lands and soldiers. " Everything but money," sighed the Bishop. The Abbot, delighting in his own polished eloquence, gave a final summing-up. This ingenious schemer, foreseeing the remotest possibilities, kept his hand outstretched over all the West ready to pick up or to reject. And while Bohemia suffered more and more from internal rot, he kept on gorging himself with new claims, countries and cities all over the map, inflating himself monstrously. The energetic, sociable Abbot stretched himself, and proclaimed as if from the pulpit : " But let this John career never so swiftly over the earth, smiling and elegant, for ever penniless and forsworn, carrying all before him with his impetuous charm, thus far only shall he go, and no further. What he sows shall bear no fruit, for it is sown without reason and without God. Many a time he seems to me but as a puppet, or a shadow.

' Measure there is in all things ; their bounds are fixed and established,' "

he quoted from an ancient author.

The Bishop concurred in this belief. But the end might still be a long way off. And meanwhile God had set no apparent bounds for the Bohemian, and he, the wretched Bishop, had him hanging round his neck Nor had the eloquent Abbot anything more to suggest, and the two prelates sat in thoughtful silence gazing at the glowing and wanton landscape, the undulating violet-brown hills, heavy with fruit and wine.

§ 3

No, for the present there were no bounds set for the Bohemian. On the contrary, he was serenely and firmly established in the sunny district of Trent, and spread himself at his ease, letting the pleasant zephyrs of the southern harvest fan his long hair and his handsome flowing beard, and paying court to the German and Italian ladies of the Tyrol. The news flew through Lombardy, through the rich and powerful cities, through the castles of the pampered barons : John of Bohemia is here, King John, son of the Emperor Heinrich the Seventh, John, the best knight in the West, the star of the Ghibellines. Knights and captains from Burgundy, Bohemia and the Rhine with their troops poured over the Brenner into the lovely and fruitful autumn lands. The Emperor Ludwig in Munich watched him mistrustfully. The Pope in Avignon, John XXII, became uneasy. Once more the eyes of Western Europe were turned upon this brilliant and unaccountable figure.

In the valley of the Po the barons and heads of factions outbid each other for his favour, sending him gifts and ambassadors. Two magnificent Arabian horses came from Mastino della Scala and his brother, the lord of Verona. But Brescia, through its governor, Friedrich of Castelbarco, offered him not only horses, it offered him itself, offered to make him its overlord for life. Aldrigeto of Lizzana sent four thousand Veronese silver marks to John's treasurer, praying the King—as protector of Tuscany and Lombardy— to invest him with the Brescian coast of Lake Garda. And of a sudden Messer Artese arrived from Florence, the banker, grey, insignificant and shadowy, bringing two brothers who resembled him greatly, and a huge sum of money.

And then, quietly, without much warning, John set himself in motion. Only a few thousand horsemen followed him. But they were all chosen soldiers, excellently equipped. The brilliant column glittered gaily between the ripe and laden hills. A sweet, heavy, sunny harvest. Thick clusters of grapes, swollen fruits. From the violet-brown hills the silvery stream of steel poured into the Lombard plain, which laid itself like a bride at the feet of the newcomers. Bergamo, Pavia, Cremona yielded without a single blow. Banners and bells, magistrates on their knees offering the keys of their cities. Great barons humbly imploring the confirmation of their fiefs. Novara, Vercelli, Modena, Reggio, garrisoned by his knights.

Ceremonial entries. On the balconies of the gay houses women in all their finery stared with large eyes at the conqueror who, far from being weary or covered with dust and sweat, subdued the wide, rich country as if he were treading a gallant measure. The Emperor, deeply alarmed, sent special envoys, first the Burgrave of Nürnberg and then the Count of Neissen, to find out what the Bohemian was after in Italy. John said in all innocence : he was not plotting against Ludwig at all, and everything he won he was taking over for the Empire ; he only wanted to visit his parents' tombs, that of the Emperor Heinrich the Seventh in Pisa, and his mother's tomb in Genoa, and to have their bodies carried home if possible. While in Munich at Christmas-time all the bells were silent because of the Papal interdict, and the Emperor Ludwig, as the protector of Christianity, his naked sword upright in his hand, read the evangel before a small following in his private chapel, John entered Brescia at the head of a brilliant procession. Was he come for the Emperor? For the Pope? Or only for himself? Nobody knew. Did he know himself? He called himself the Emperor's successor, the Peacemaker. The Gonzaga in Mantua, the Visconti in Milan submitted to him. A whole kingdom rounded itself for him in Lombardy, and fell into his hand like a ripe fruit detached from its bough.

He has his seat on both banks of the Po; no King of Rome has ever held more magnificent state. He receives homage from the Adriatic to Liguria. His smile is deep, satisfied, remote. Had he a fixed plan when he descended into the plains? To-day he is the most powerful man in Christendom. He has land and dominion up and down the Rhine, into the very heart of France. He has Bohemia, Moravia, Silesia, and he stretches far into Poland. He has Lower Bavaria through his daughter, Carinthia, Carniola and Tyrol through his son. He has a stranglehold on the Wittelsbachs, and surrounds the Habsburgs. And now he has the rich, sweet kingdom of Upper Italy. He stretches himself, breathes deeply, and holds high festival. Attracts the loveliest women to his court. And often, too, Messer Artese from Florence appears with his brothers, shadowy and insignificant, and stands modestly at a distance, bowing repeatedly.

# CHAPTER IV

## § 1

THE child Margarete grew up in the castles of Zenoberg, Gries and Tyrol. She liked learning, and she learned much. She asked the clever, talkative, energetic Abbot Johannes of Viktring the how and the why of everything she heard and saw. With the Abbesses of the convents at Stams and Sonnenberg she studied theology. The magnificence and solemn ceremonial of the liturgy won her admiration. She spoke and wrote fluently both Latin and German. Took a burning interest in politics and national economy. Listened attentively to the historical lectures of the learned Abbot, and while the others ridiculed and yawned over his abstract political theories could never have enough of them. From the countless strangers who visited her father she gathered a profound knowledge of the relations among other courts and countries. She sniffed contemptuously when she heard that Ludwig of Wittelsbach, the Bavarian, the elected Holy Roman Emperor, fourth of his name, could speak no Latin. She ranged through the land in coach or horse-litter. Up and down the passes, through the adjoining terraces and fruit gardens. Explored with shrewd, alert eyes the lively cities of Meran and Bozen. Observed the citizens, their stone houses, the Town Hall, the market-place, the walls, the stocks and whipping-post, the inns, the bath-houses, and the corpses of malefactors before the gates. Made quick, imperious incursions into the farms of the peasants, the watch-houses of the vintagers.

The good-natured King Heinrich troubled little about her. He left her to do as she pleased. From time to time he enquired tenderly if she had enough clothes, if she needed more jewels, horses, or servants. Asked her in passing what she thought of the new Flemish cook, or how the Genoese cloak suited him which he had just had made. He was completely absorbed in clothes, bequests to monasteries, festivals, entertainments, tournaments and women. To be sure, when she conversed with his shrewd secretary, the Abbot of Viktring, he looked at her with affection, and said to his wife Beatrix and to his guests : " My dear child ! How clever she is ! "

She had lessons in singing from the nuns. It was astonishing what a beautiful, warm, rounded voice rang out of that jutting ape-like mouth under the broad, flat nose. But although she was not reserved about her other accomplishments, and talked freely, she hardly ever sang before strangers. In the evenings, under the fruit-trees, when she was alone, she sang her songs, elaborate airs from Italy or Provence, or simple German songs which she heard on all sides among the people. Often, even when she was alone, she broke off in the middle. The gnomes might hear her. The gnomes lived in all the mountain caves. They ate and drank, played and danced with mortals. But they were invisible. Only the reigning sovereign could see them, the rightful ruler of the land in which they dwelt. Her father had seen the gnomes, and the Bishop of Brixen, too, into whose diocese they sometimes came. Jakob von Schenna had told her all about them. They could write, they had a state of their own with laws and a king, they belonged to the Catholic faith, and came by stealth into men's houses and were friendly to them. They carried precious stones which had the power of making them invisible. She asked Herr von Schenna why they made themselves invisible. Herr von Schenna evaded her question. By pure chance she discovered the reason from a serving-maid. Because they were ashamed of their ugliness. She went paler than usual and gulped.

She tended her body with the most anxious care. She took a vapour bath daily, and washed herself with oatmeal water and French soap. She rolled her tooth powder in freshly-shorn wool before brushing her large, irregularly projecting teeth. She rubbed her skin with oil of tartar, and used a red fard made from Brazilian wood and a white one of powdered cyclamen bulbs. At night she put on a wax mask to clear her muddy complexion. Anxiously and with self-denial she tried all the new prescriptions which came into fashion.

But when she could not help seeing that every buxom and unwashed peasant lass drew more appreciative glances from men than she did, she turned her thoughts abruptly from such matters, and plunged with passionate energy into study and politics. She balanced against each other for the hundredth time the possibilities and the spheres of influence attending Habsburg, Wittelsbach, and Luxemburg. Habsburg, Luxemburg, and Wittelsbach ; these were not bald political concepts for her. The men who bore these names, their colours, their lands, their coats of arms, their mountains, rivers and churches, were fused together for her into a mysterious unity. Albert of Habsburg was diabolically clever, energetic and bitter, but he limped. And with him limped his lands, the Danube, the city of Vienna, the paw of the lion on his flag. King John, the Luxemburger, was not only a cosmopolitan and gallant gentleman. His feet were Tuscany and Lombardy, the Rhine and the Elbe his blood vessels, and sunny Luxemburg his heart. And she could not think of Bavaria without calling up the long, meditative nose of the Emperor Ludwig, and his enormous, strangely blank blue eyes. When these three princes stalked and outflanked each other, made peace and war with each other, the whole world was filled with war and wrong, and in the clouds their heraldic animals carried on a mighty and mystical battle.

Her husband, Prince Johann, she did not see very often. Although he was slender and tall for his years, he appeared to be backward. His thin face, which was not badly formed, seemed to become rawer and stupider, and the small, deep-set eyes more malicious than ever. He hated books, and could barely write. What he liked was physical exercise. He romped about with other boys, with the servants' children in preference to the young nobles, and went hunting and iding. Busied himself with fowling, became not unskilled in falconry, trapped game. Tormented animals. Played evil tricks on the peasants. A peasant boy, who did not recognise him, gave him a thrashing ; was seized, put in the stocks, and flogged. The Prince eagerly watched the flogging, and egged on the officers.

He ridiculed Margarete for her silly, monkish learning, occasionally snatching her manuscripts from her, and rumpling up her hair. She endured it. It was necessary that her husband should be a Luxemburger. One had to put up with his rudeness. But she silently stored up resentment and scorn. Chretien de Laferte, the Prince's adjutant and attendant, also consigned his young master to the deepest pit of hell. Margarete hardly ever saw the slim youth, and paid little attention to him. The energetic, sceptical, garrulous Abbot of Viktring, who could not help talking about everything, teased her occasionally about the boy. She turned upon him with unusual fierceness.

She liked best of all to be with Jakob of Schenna. That slouching, lean young gentleman with the old, subtle face was always pleased to see her. She was now fourteen, and he in his thirties. But there was a delightful bond of sympathy between them. All that he said and did found its echo in her heart. She felt at home in his world. There was a barrier of coldness between her and other people ; they laughed at her, and regarded her with repugnance, or at best with pity, because she was ugly. Because she was a Princess they did not show their feelings openly ; yet she saw deep into the darkness of their hearts, she had sharp eyes, and knew what people thought of her. But Schenna radiated warmth and friendliness ; his large delicate hands and his shrewd, grey, benevolent eyes were full of respect for her, full of affection and comradeship.

Jakob von Schenna was richer and more powerful than his brothers Estlein and Petermann. He had seven strong castles, nine districts and jurisdictions, far-spreading vine-yards, prerogatives, taxes, and money. He was in the habit of speaking disdainfully and with a certain irony about his possessions. But he was attached to them, and lovingly caressed the young leaves of his vines, the sunwarmed stones of his castles. They were his vines, and his castles. Of course, possessions and influence were contemptible in themselves ; but, unfortunately, people made one's life too uncomfortable if one did not have them. He often spoke to the girl about the shamelessness with which the Tyrolean and Carinthian nobles plundered the good King Heinrich. Unfortunately he had to join in, to prevent somebody worse than he from seizing his share. So he too plundered, sceptically, with calm regret and much sympathy for His despoiled Majesty.

His castles were the finest and the best cared for in the mountains. The castles of the other nobles were built only for strength and security ; they were bleak inside, with small, damp, dark, airless rooms like cellars, and the stench of the stables everywhere. His strongholds, above all his favourite seats at Schenna and Runkelstein, were bright and sunny. They had been built by Italian architects, and they were full of lovely things, of bibelots and tapestries. While the walls of the others were barely whitewashed, and at best only the chapels were hung with holy pictures, his halls had been covered with frescoes by German and Italian masters. Even the outside south walls of his favourite castles were adorned in this manner. There strode, gay and bright, the knight with his lion ; Tristan fared upon his ship ; and Garel from the Vale of Flowers pursued his adventures.

Herr von Schenna loved the verses which recounted these tales. Margarete could make nothing of them. She understood the Latin verses which the wordy Abbot of Viktring liked to quote, she appreciated Horace and the Æneid. Those had sense, order, dignity, and a strict logic. But these German verses seemed to her sheer madness, no better than the confused improvisations of the Court dwarfs and jesters. Was it worthy of a serious man to string together in stilted words tales about things which never did and never could exist ? Herr von Schenna tried to make her comprehend that these figures, Tristan and Parsifal and Kriemhild, lived

and were real as often as one read and felt them. But this
she would not admit. His romances remained brightly-
coloured and offensive lies for her ; she did not understand
how a shrewd and serious man could find pleasure in such
empty nothings.

# CHAPTER V

§ 1

JOHN's rapid progress in Italy had made the Emperor profoundly uneasy. The head of the Habsburgs, too, the lame, clever, embittered Albert, watched with growing and consuming rage John's brilliant Kingdom of Lombardy rising out of the void. What, was the frivolous and irresponsible Luxemburger by a mere freak of fate to oust from power two serious and important men, and set himself over them ? They signalled to each other, the slow, ponderous Bavarian and the tough, bitter Habsburger. They had always hated each other, but now that the third threatened to outflank them they joined forces against him. They took counsel furtively, Ludwig, the huge, long-nosed Wittelsbacher with the bull-neck and the enormous blue eyes, and Albert the Lame with his compressed lips. They sounded each other, nodded, and came to an understanding.

Agreed that the southern kingdom must be torn from the Luxemburger's grasp. At King Heinrich's death Carinthia should fall to the Habsburgs, and Tyrol to the Wittelsbachs. The Emperor Ludwig pledged the succession in Carinthia to Albert just as solemnly as he had promised it to John the year before. And as for Lombardy, they arranged to make a concerted attack upon the Luxemburger with their allies. The Emperor called on his cousins of the Palatinate, his son-in-law of Meissen, and his two sons, Ludwig of Brandenburg and Stephan, to foment trouble for John on the

Rhine. The Duke of Austria was to invade Moravia together with the Kings of Hungary and Poland.

Meanwhile John lorded it royally in the Tuscan spring. He summoned his sons, Karl, the elder, and Johann the younger. The latter did not want to go, and Margarete offered herself in his stead.

She travelled with a small escort, led by Chretien de Laferte, into the heart of a Lombard March, by the shores of darkly gleaming lakes, where silvery olives clothed the hills, and dusky groves of orange and lemon. Meadows full of narcissus. Delicate, rosy, almond blossom. Noisy, bright-coloured cities, palaces ; quick, vivacious people. And beyond the city of Aquileia, whose Bishop acknowledged her father's suzerainty, lay the sea, on which hardy ships tossed, the illimitable, adventurous horizon.

She saw John's brilliant triumph. His celebrations, doubly joyous and full of significance under that clear sky. The resplendent, glowing, stately women. She felt very solitary and pitiable, avoided the young women, and appeared only among those who were older and less charming. But she felt herself despised even by these, or, at best, pitied. Though they were now dry and faded, they had bloomed in their time. But in the flower of her youth she was blighted and without charm. Under that sky it mattered even less than at home that she was clever, sagacious, and of the noblest blood. Under that sky people saw one thing, one thing only, that she was ugly.

She was not a coward ; she did not creep into a corner ; she drained to the dregs all the bitterness of the experience. Appeared at banquets, in her box at the tournament, and at dances. Observed how, at the first glimpse of Chretien, the young noble who walked behind her, the lips of women

parted and their eyes became deeper and more desirous ;
how next they ran their eyes over her contemptuously and
appraisingly, noting her projecting, ape-like mouth, and her
livid, repulsive skin.  She did not flinch before their scorn ;
her eyes met theirs with such composure and penetration
that they looked away, often with ashamed embarrassment.

In Brescia Margarete met for the first time Prince Karl,
John's eldest son.  The sixteen-year-old boy looked very
mature.  He had already taken an independent share in the
government of Bohemia, and was judicial and self-controlled.
From his mother he had learned not to be dazzled by his
father's brilliance.  With his calm brown eyes he looked at
Margarete, and saw that she was ugly and clever.  One
could talk to her.  And while in the palace of the Signoria
John led the dance with the lovely Giuditta of Castelbarco,
lighted by festal candles, which were so heavy that three
men could scarcely lift them, the two children, the King's
son, and the King's daughter-in-law, amid music, banners,
silver knights and adoring vassals, conversed soberly and
objectively about the effect that the events in Lombardy
would have on the Bishop of Trent's suzerainty, and about
the difficulties of the financial situation.

John's gallant sway in Italy lasted well into the month
of June.  In spite of all her critical scruples Margarete
could not tear herself away from the theatrical glitter of this
triumph.  Then the reports from Germany and Bohemia
became so threatening that John hastily departed, leaving his
son Karl behind, and hurled himself upon Bohemia.  Behind
him his adventurous Italian kingdom broke up at once of
its own accord.  With round, astonished eyes Margarete
saw, as soon as the King's back was turned, the Lombard
nobles awaken as if from a carouse, band themselves together,

intrigue with Robert of Apulia, and drive the Luxemburgers
out of the country in a few weeks, despite the valiant and
skilful resistance of Prince Karl. Broken, disappointed,
in confusion and disgrace, the silver knights fled out of
Lombardy, over which the heats of summer brooded. With
the utmost speed, in the very middle of the catastrophe,
John pledged the Italian towns he had long since lost, driving
a hard bargain with several credulous German gentlemen.
But the money he got for them covered only a small fraction
of the colossal expenses arising out of his Tuscan campaign.
And for many years afterwards, in Paris, in Prague, in
Trèves, wherever he happened to be, there appeared the
shadowy, insignificant figures of Messer Artese, the Florentine, and his two brothers, bowing repeatedly, producing
bonds and bills of exchange, the sole relics of that Lombard
kingdom.

§ 2

CURIOUSLY enough the very collapse of John's Italian
adventure made it more real and valid to Margarete. It was
now over and done with, it was history, it was a fact. It
made even Herr von Schenna's verses and improbable
romances more vivid and convincing. All King John's
feats and adventures in Lombardy sounded like one of those
fables. And yet they were real ; she had seen them with
her own eyes. From a practical standpoint it was better
to keep out of such entanglements. For if one looked
clearly and soberly at the affair, John had come to grief for
want of money. Money was not everything ; but it was
of enormous importance. It was a pity that her father
was as blind to that as her father-in-law. She often spoke
about it to Johann of Viktring. Now, the Holy Father
was of a different stamp. He sat in his palace at Avignon,

the twenty-second John, incredibly old and gnome-like, and piled up riches. Heaped it up in coin, in ingots, in silver and gold, in bills and bonds. With what a lynx-like eye did he watch everybody to see that tithes and tribute were punctually paid ! If a bishop were behindhand the Pope excommunicated him at once. Poor Bishop Heinrich of Trent ! Of what avail had been his zealous fight for the rightful Papacy ? Because he could not produce the six hundred ducats which Avignon required of him, the bull of excommunication was thundered out against him. And what cunning the Pope showed in filling the high offices of the Church ! Each newly-made bishop had to remit the whole of one year's income to the Curia. And when a bishop died, the Pope did not appoint a new prelate in his stead, no, he summoned the holder of another bishopric to the vacant see, so that every bishop's death meant a whole chain of investitures. So there was a perpetual exchange of offices among the higher ranks of the clergy, a coming and going as in an inn, and the Papal Chair gathered in the fattest first-fruits. " Keep the ball rolling ! " said the Pope and his treasurer. Pope John certainly knew his business. No wonder, for he came from Cahors, the city of bankers and stockbrokers. More than half of the money in Western Europe flowed into his coffers. The Pope clung to his wealth ; he could not bring himself to make any further use of it. He could have won back Rome and Italy with it. But he loved his gold too well, he could not be parted from it. He sat in Avignon, incredibly old and dwarf-like, bowed over his treasure, caressing the bonds and bills, and letting the gold trickle through his dry elvish fingers.

But if it was greed which ruined the policy of the clever and energetic Pope, it was irresponsibility in money matters which hampered the diplomacy of the Emperor, as of the Luxemburger and the Carinthian. Margarete listened attentively to the Abbot's exposition of the sound principles on which her grandfather Meinhard had grounded his finances. She wrinkled her forehead anxiously as she saw her good-natured father letting his whole income run away like water, and always saving a mortgage from foreclosure by contracting greater and more important ones.

Her stepmother, too, the pale, timid Beatrix of Savoy, was made wretched by King Heinrich's wild financial methods. Her excellent parents had accustomed her to thrifty housekeeping, and although she usually kept modestly and shyly in the background, she ended by constantly dinning his extravagance into her husband's ears. She was sickly, and King Heinrich perceived with resignation and senile sorrow that he could not expect an heir from her either. But she never gave up hope. She calculated, she economised, she secured taxes and revenues from her husband, and even managed with a bitter struggle to have the income from the salt works at Hall transferred to her after the withdrawal of Messer Artese, the Florentine. She became hard, grasping, and miserly, all for the sake of the son whom nobody expected but herself.

She often conferred with Margarete to see if they could straighten out here and there the embarrassed accounts. Although Margarete approved of these efforts she disliked her stepmother. How mean she was, how unlike a princess, how dry and dusty in spite of her youth ! Margarete would not admit to herself that this was not the real reason for her dislike. Beatrix was gentle and friendly to her out of sympathy for their common lot. She had no son, and Margarete, poor thing, was so ugly. God had vexed and afflicted both

of them in their most womanly attributes.    But Margarete
would make no advances, and did not return the pressure of
her hand, for Beatrix stood between her and power.
Ugly as she was, what else had she to hope for but power ?
And if after all Beatrix were to bear a son, even that last
hope would be destroyed.

King Heinrich submitted to his wife's tutelage with
a smile and a jesting assumption of defiance.    In one thing
only he brooked no interference, and even Beatrix never
attempted it :  his liberality to his countless mistresses and
their children remained unlimited.

Not only did he hold in high honour his two natural
brothers, Albrecht of Camian and Heinrich of Eschenloh,
bestowing titles, dignities, and rich fiefs upon them, but he
had natural children of his own growing up in all his castles
and estates.    He was much too good-natured to reproach
Beatrix.    Still it did him good to reflect that it was not his
fault if he had no heir ;  it was bad luck, an evil star.    And so
the old gallant moved with pride and satisfaction through his
little swarm of children, yellow-headed and dark.    He
caressed them with affection :  " This one has my eyes !
And that one my nose."    One that was shooting up had
his very walk, and would win many a prize in tournaments !
He tossed into the air a little brat which scarcely looked
human as yet, and said :  " He has my face exactly."    And he
spoilt the children, making them gifts of toys and sweets, and
also of meadows, woods and castles.

Margarete regarded her half-brothers and sisters with
sympathy.    Above all she liked Albert, who was nearly
grown-up, and whom King Heinrich had made a knight
and lord of the manor of Andrion.    This fair-haired young
man had all his father's good nature, and in addition a strong

and jovial assurance in his actions, an elastic, equable gaiety of temperament. He never showed the slightest scorn for Margarete. He himself had no gifts at all for books and theories, and he genuinely admired her cleverness and learning. She was grateful because his respect for her was not lessened by her ugliness.

Wherever her father went she met women, and always new ones ; these she looked at long. There were women of every rank and temperament, German and Italian ; some went rustling through the corridors, others walked heavily and languidly ; some laughed like clear bells, others spoke in slow, deep tones ; but all of them, when they encountered the Princess, became shy and embarrassed, hardening into a kind of hostile pity. Ah, if one could only take life easily and indolently like them ! For her it was not permitted ; she was ugly, and a Princess. She had to be severe with herself. She dared not dart about like a lizard ; she had to climb her steep and stony path without respite or diversion, like a beast of burden heavily laden with pomp and riches, bringing gifts to some great lord.

She brooded. She spoke about it to the Abbot of Viktring. Was it a punishment from God that she was so ugly ? What did God want of her ? The Abbot quoted Anselmus :

" The face of the world doth change as swiftly as fleeteth the moment ;
    Beauty on earth is naught, transient, vain and deceitful."

When he saw that this kind of comfort was unavailing, he asked whether she would rather be of humble birth, a peasant's daughter, and find favour in men's eyes. " No," she cried hastily, " not that ! Not that ! " But when she

was alone she burst out : " Yes, yes, yes ! Better to fork
dung all day and have a pretty face, than to live in a castle
with this mouth, and these teeth, and these flabby cheeks ! "

She spoke with the Abbess of Frauenchiemsee. She had
been visiting her younger sister, the ailing, crippled Adelheid.
Now she sat beside the fine, faded, gentle Abbess on the shore
of the tiny island. " My mother was not a beauty," said
the child, " but still she wasn't hideous."

The old lady laid her small, fragile hand on the mass of
coarse, copper-coloured hair. " I shall not speak of God
and of the next world," she smiled, " where it is not one's
shape that matters. But even in this world, how quickly
wrinkles line the smoothest face ! You could only have
kept a lovely face for fifteen or twenty years longer. I am
very glad to-day," she concluded, " that I was never beautiful."

Both the women gazed out over the pale, wide lake ;
there was a dull gleam of sunshine, and a seagull screamed.

A year later, without any warning, her stepmother
Beatrix took to bed and never got up again. She had always
been delicate, and now she had as well to bear her disappoint-
ment at remaining childless. After she had received extreme
unction she said to her husband that he should have his tailor
flogged and driven away, for he was embezzling a shameless
amount of the costly stuffs laid in for the King's wardrobe.
Also Heinrich should get a new leather chest to keep his
fine armour in. Then she commended her soul to God
and died.

Johann and Margarete were now the undisputed heirs
to the land in the mountains ; for nobody suspected that
there was a secret treaty between the Habsburgs and the
Wittelsbachs. As Crown Prince even the boy Johann

became more animated.    He rehearsed the titles he was to
have :  Duke of Carinthia, Görz and Carniola, Count of
Tyrol, Suzerain of the bishoprics of Chur, Brixen, Trent,
Gurk and Aquileia.    He drew himself a picture of the
remarkable old ceremony by which the succession to the
Carinthian throne is confirmed, and which pleased him
greatly.    How the prince comes dressed like a peasant, and
pushes a free-born peasant off the stone on which he is sitting ;
then, standing on the stone, flourishes his naked sword in
all directions ;   then drinks a draught of fresh water from
a peasant's bonnet.    And the boy Johann felt himself very
important.

Margarete, moved by her stepmother's death, and relieved
by the knowledge that she was now the assured heiress of
the land, found Chretien de Laferte at her side.    She spoke
to him eagerly, and with more warmth than usual.    How
grateful she would have been for a kindly, human word
from him !    But he bowed formally, and spoke to her with
great respect as to his sovereign.

The death of his wife made good King Heinrich more
pious than ever.    True, he ate and drank more abundantly
than before, and kept even more women.    But he offered
up more prayers, too, went often to confession, was in a
perpetual state of contrition, and made greater bequests
than ever to monasteries and churches.

# CHAPTER VI

## § 1

IN the Bishopric of Chur a certain Peter von Flavon held an estate as the Bishop's vassal. While still young he fell in one of King Heinrich's Italian campaigns, leaving a widow in her early thirties and three daughters. There was a doubt whether his estate descended only in the male line, or whether it was a petticoat hold. Bishop Johannes of Chur and his Chapter set about recalling the fief. Frau von Flavon came with her three infant children to implore King Heinrich's aid ; knelt before him, and wept. Her good, brave young husband ! And he had fallen in King Heinrich's service. And now the brutal Bishop of Chur was trying to rob the widow and the fatherless, and to plunge them into poverty and misery. The three pretty little daughters, rosy and dainty in their black dresses, knelt wailing beside her  Good King Heinrich was deeply touched.

He wrote to the Bishop of Chur, strongly upholding Frau von Flavon's claims. The Bishop answered curtly and peevishly, abating no jot or tittle of his pretensions. The widow, who had been received meanwhile with her daughters for a stay at Castle Zenoberg, grew daily in favour with the King. He came to high words with the Bishop, even to recriminations and blows. In the end he secured a meagre compensation for the lady.

Meanwhile she had become his avowed mistress. It

would not do to keep her on short commons. Were the poor creatures whose father had died for him to grow up like the daughters of a small country squire ? No, King Heinrich was not so mean as that. He invested them with the fiefs of Taufers and Velturn. That got him into trouble with the Bishop of Brixen, who claimed that these vacant fiefs reverted to him ; but King Heinrich held on to them grimly. In the end he had to buy off the Bishop ; but the lady remained in possession of both the estates.

She made a great show with her three daughters, feeling safe under the King's protection. She was a pretty woman with a very white skin and very fair hair, firmly made and plump. She laughed readily, and never missed a dance or a tournament. There was a continuous din of merrymaking in her castles. She always had to be up and doing ; she took part in everything, and used to retail with importance the most irrelevant trivialities, turning everything topsy-turvy. Suddenly she conceived the notion of having her husband buried in the chapel of the Castle at Taufers. For years she pursued this idea, and finally journeyed to Lombardy. There the casually interred corpse was exhumed, thrown into boiling water, as was customary, to remove the flesh from the bones, brought to Taufers and solemnly entombed amid great lamentation from the ladies von Flavon. But it was not at all certain that the remains were actually those of Herr von Flavon.

The three girls grew up without much education, wild and very spoilt. They were always at variance among themselves ; the smallest occasion gave rise to quarrels which were often serious. Whenever the good King arrived he had to smooth things over and hush things up. They defied their mother too, and often banded together against her.

The mother complained to the King about her daughters ;
the daughters about their mother. Then they would be
reconciled again, in the same senseless fashion, and make
a great parade of their harmonious family life. The children
rioted about on their wide estates, upsetting officials and
tormenting peasants, a vexation to man and beast. They
were all three very pretty, plump and fair, with smooth,
pink and white skins. The second one, Agnes von Flavon,
was the loveliest. She was taller than her sisters, her hair
darker and more lustrous, her face longer, less round, her
nose not so small and doll-like, her lips more audacious. But
all the sisters were very vain. Agnes, young as she was,
a good two years older than Princess Margarete, was hailed
unanimously as the loveliest woman between the Adige
and the Inn. Knights rode for her sake at all the tournaments ; she awarded the prizes. When any one praised
the Italian ladies, all the German gentlemen cried as if with
one voice ; " Agnes von Flavon ! " and the Italians were
silenced. In Trent, when she accompanied her mother on
estate business to the Bishop's court, the people waited in
a crowd before the palace, and cried with enthusiasm :
" An angel has come down from heaven ! Give us a
blessing, fair angel ! "

Agnes was very conscious of her beauty. She took it
for granted that the King, the knights, and the people should
fulfil her slightest wish. She considered herself queen of
Tyrol. King Heinrich, with a kind of good-natured tact,
refrained from bringing together the lovely sisters and his
daughter Margarete. But often it could not be avoided.
Agnes, with every mark of outward respect, treated Margarete
with a certain mocking condescension which infuriated the
Princess. Once, when the two girls were alone, attended

only by Chretien de Laferte, they girded at each other for nearly half an hour, and then Agnes, taking her leave, said : " Will you escort me, Herr Chretien ? "

" Herr Chretien will remain here ! " flashed Margarete, her voice unusually hard and dry.　But when Agnes had gone out with a shrug of the shoulders and a spiteful, mocking smile, " Go, Chretien !　Go ! " she said.　Upset and bewildered, the young man followed Fraülein von Flavon. The Princess, left to herself, screwed up her face, spitting hate, her bosom heaving.

With Herr von Schenna she was turning the pages of an illuminated romance.　Blanchefleur resembled Agnes, and they both gazed at the bright picture.

" Yes," said Herr von Schenna after a while, " she looks like Agnes."

" She is beautiful," said Margarete, in a stifled, curiously dead voice.

" But Fraülein von Flavon has much stupider eyes," said Herr von Schenna.

" Let's go on reading ! " said Margarete, and her voice was deep, full, and warm as usual.

§ 2

KING HEINRICH aged prematurely and went visibly to pieces. His hands trembled, he often forgot his words, and stuttered meaninglessly.　A suffocating fear of punishment in the next world overtook him.　He had seen too many pictures of the Last Judgment in galleries and at church portals, showing the pains of hell, and horrible devils grinning from the lake of brimstone ; and all this now loomed terrifyingly near.　He doubled his pious offerings and endowed Marienberg, Stams, Rotenbuch, and Benediktbeuern with rich bequests. But that availed as little to quieten him as the comforting reassurances of the Abbot of Viktring. As a penance for his sins he had a bier set up in the chapel at Zenoberg, and laid himself on it during a long winter's night. Then there came all the people whom he had caused to be plundered, tortured, or murdered ; he was a good-natured man, but none the less there were many of them. There came the women with whom he had committed adultery ; their faces were smiling, but when they turned round their backs were eaten through and through by fetid worms. The whole chapel was full of horrible devils, clawing at him. He screamed. But he had had the chapel locked, and given orders that no one was to approach, so that he would be forced to stay alone with his sins and his remorse until early mass. At last he could bear it no longer. Goaded on by fear, he clambered up the wall and sprang through the window ; crept into his bed, in a cold sweat, his teeth chattering.

From that time he pined away. He often spoke to himself, and was torn by a hollow and despairing cough. Margarete was often beside him, but was not greatly affected. He was going to die. Well, he had nothing to complain of ; he had drained life to the dregs.

He liked to have his children round him, especially the little ones. He shuffled about among the tiny, crowing creatures who stumbled and crawled on unsteady legs around him, here wiping a dirty little nose and there soothing a fat and rosy rascal who had fallen headlong and was screaming himself into a fit. He tossed the children up, sat down in the midst of them, and with many sighs held forth to his solemn and uncomprehending audience on money, church penances, and high politics.

April came    Under an azure sky the land was snowed
with almond and peach blossom.    Then he felt that his
time had come.    He had himself carried into the chapel of
Saint Pancras.    A gentle Madonna in blue smiled down
on him.    The bright stained windows glowed warmly in
the strong sunlight.    Little children stood round him with
large eyes, and the mild assiduous Abbot of Viktring was
there.    Whereat a last hemorrhage overcame him and
choked him.

The corpse was disembowelled and embalmed ;    the
heart and internal organs were to be laid in Castle Tyrol,
the other remains to be interred later with great solemnity
in the family vault in the monastery of Saint John at Stams.

The Bishop of Brixen, who had set out for Castle Tyrol
as soon as he was told the news of King Heinrich's death,
riding by night heard on the road the clatter of countless
feet.    He asked his people if they saw anything.    But
although they heard the noise too, they could perceive nothing.    As the Bishop peered more keenly through the night
he saw that it was the gnomes, who were hastily marching
north in a thick column.    But they had their precious stones
on their fingers, so that he alone could see them.    He
stopped one and asked what was afoot.    The gnome
answered that now that good King Heinrich was dead they
felt themselves no longer secure, and had to leave the country.

§ 3

ON the very same day the couriers rode through the country
carrying the death news.    One over the mountains and the
Italian plain to Verona.    There the della Scala brothers were
exultant.    Now there would be dissension in the mountain
country.    Now it would be possible to stretch a hand out

towards the north again and snatch a piece of land. One rode to Vienna. There sat the lame Duke Albert by the fire, always chilly, badly shaven, meagre, sickly. He became all attention, sent for his brother, called for his secretaries, and dictated, so engrossed by his plans and labours that he forgot his food. One rode towards Munich to Emperor Ludwig. The Emperor gazed at him over his long nose through his great frank, blue eyes, and while in fair round terms he expressed his grief at his beloved uncle's departure from this world, considered ponderously under what pretext he might most comfortably rob his little cousin of her lands.

Margarete regarded herself in the mirror. On the ivory frame into which the glass was set a bas-relief was cut in which the castle of the Queen of Love was being taken. Yes, sure enough, she, Margarete, was not like the Queen of Love in face and form. But to make up for that she was Duchess of Carinthia and Countess of Tyrol. So this was how a Duchess looked ! She examined herself with bitter humour. Show yourself ! Eyes and forehead would pass. The mouth was the worst, that out-jutting monkey jowl. Yet to make up for that, she had Carinthia. Then the hanging, flabby cheeks were a sad misfortune. But were they not outweighed by the Earldom of Tyrol ? And the grey, patchy complexion ? Add Brixen, Chur and Friuli to it, and did it not straightway become smooth and clear ? Johann, her husband, hardly knew himself. He was a Sovereign ruler now. In his exalted mood he became almost amiable. Margarete looked at him. Really he was a pretty youth ; the long, imperious face, the beautiful hair. His eyes, too, seemed freer and bolder to her now. He thought : She's not beautiful, certainly. But the lands

E

she has brought me are.  He said to her : " Well, Gretl ? "
and kissed her heartily on the ugly mouth.  He went out
of his way to tell her she must come with him sometime
hawking.

Then the two children sat together, very serious, and
considered their first administrative measures.  The situation was not easy.  The feudal barons were refractory and
would certainly exploit to the utmost the complications
brought on by the change in the administration.  Johann's
boyish, arrogant face set.  He would soon let them see.
He had mastered wild horses before.  First of all they must
send for his father, King John ; he was still in Paris at the
tournament, with his son-in-law, the King of France.  Then
embassies must go to the Emperor, and to the Dukes of
Austria.  The children commanded the Abbot of Viktring
to come, and entrusted him with the embassy, gravely but with
assumed lightness.  They set their names under the letter
giving him full powers : Johann, by the grace of God
Count of Tyrol, Margareta, Dei gratia Carinthiae dux,
Tyrolis et Goritiæ comes et ecclesiarum Aquilensis
Tridentinæ et Brixensis advocata.

But when the Abbot of Viktring delivered this letter, his
employers had already lost the greater part of their lands.
In Linz the Emperor and the lame Habsburger sat together
and discussed the treaty which divided the land in the mountains between Habsburg and Wittelsbach.  Uncouth and
bulky, the Bavarian wanted everything for himself, and
would not let the smallest village out of his fingers.  Obstinate and stiff-necked the lame Duke hung on, laying his
sharp tongue about him, and would resign nothing.  Their
thoughts only on their maps and registers, they sat and looked
over the Danube swollen with rains, clinging to their fat booty,

pulling it this way and that.    After sharp haggling they came
at last to an agreement : Carinthia, Carniola and South Tyrol
were to go to the Austrian, North Tyrol to the Bavarian.
When they had reached this stage the Abbot of Viktring
arrived with the letter and compliments of the children.    The
two princes received him with great politeness and read the
letter attentively.    Presently the Austrian responded with im-
penetrable irony that he took much to heart his uncle's death,
the noble and illustrious prince, the senior representative of
the whole line and father of them all.    He was deeply sorry
for his dear little cousin and her boy husband.    Carniola
belonged to him now.    Carinthia had been granted him by
the bounty of the Emperor : troops were already on the
way to occupy it for him.    But if in any other way he could
show his complaisance or helpfulness towards his little cousin,
he would gladly do so.    The Emperor himself spoke in
the same strain, staring at the Abbot with his great, frank
blue eyes.    Only he spoke more solemnly, more sonorously,
for he was after all the Emperor.    To his sorrow the children
had come with their requests too late ; he had already settled
everything with his dear uncle of Austria.    For the rest
he would give the matter his most gracious consideration.

When they saw how badly their affairs were going the two
children in Tyrol Castle sent express message after express
message to their father and guardian, King John.    But he had
been badly wounded in the tournament.    He lay battered and
broken, almost deprived of his eyesight, wrapped in bandages
and compresses, and could only send the feeble comfort that
the children must be of good heart ; as soon as his strength
permitted he would himself come and defend them and their
lands.    It was particularly unfortunate that he had to lie helpless in bed while the Emperor and Habsburg divided between

them the rich territories he had assured for himself by so
much wearisome and dexterous diplomacy.    But gambler
and fatalist as he was, even this catastrophe did not affect
him very deeply.    He was accustomed to sudden changes of
fortune, and at the lowest ebb, when he was helpless, showered light witticisms on the women and the lands which
escaped from his grasp in this way, and reckoned with the
indifference of the gambler on a lucky throw.

§ 4

IN the meanwhile Carinthia and Carniola were occupied
without opposition by the Habsburger.    The towns did
homage to him, the proclamation of the Emperor was
solemnly read out everywhere ;   the feudal barons accepted
the accomplished fact, and swore allegiance to the new
sovereign.    The leading barons, at their head the grave
Konrad of Auffenstein, the viceroy of the deceased King,
and by him endowed with great possessions and limitless
trust, played a very ambiguous rôle in the affair.    The
populace were reconciled to the betrayal of the two children
by Duke Otto of Austria, as representative of his lame
brother, submitting to the ancient, ceremonious, patriarchal
observance which was customary in Carinthia at a royal
investiture, and which had delighted the little Prince Johann
so much.    He put on a peasant costume, ordered the duly
appointed peasant to rise up from his stone, drank water out
of a peasant's hat, and went through a few more ceremonies
of a like traditional kind.    Duke Otto himself was an elegant, fashionable young lord ;   he was greatly amused by
his peasant garb, and for a long time afterwards he and his
noblemen made jokes about it.    But the people were extraordinarily pleased by this adherence to patriarchal usage ;

the mob were touched, and declared themselves with conviction for the new prince.

Margarete had never been of a melodramatic disposition. She had never expected that out of fidelity to the hereditary princely house Carinthia would fire up, take her part and defend her. But all the same the despicable way in which as a mere matter of course people renounced justice and ranged themselves on the side of power, in a great hurry at the same time to haggle for some small advantages for themselves, filled her with disgust and indignation. She could find no objection when Duke Johann, foaming, stamping, his voice strained to breaking point, gave orders to raze to the ground Auffenstein Castle on the Matrei, the hereditary seat of the faithless Carinthian viceroy. The acute Herr von Schenna opined, it was true, that it might be more sensible simply to confiscate it.

If Carinthia was lost, in Tyrol things developed very favourably for the children. The Tyrolean barons had comprehensive assurances from the Luxemburger that he would not appoint a foreign governor to any of the more important official posts ; in any case they would come off better with the two children than with the Wittelsbacher, hard as he was in all money-matters. So the Tyrolean lords winked at one another understandingly, decided to maintain their trusty, Tyrolean fidelity to their hereditary princess, prepared for an armed resistance, and stirred up all right-thinking people in the country.

Thus Duke Johann's elder brother, Margrave Karl, whom King John had sent provisionally to Tyrol in his stead, found that the Earldom was in a good state for defence ; and the three children were able to keep Tyrol after a short struggle, waged with the utmost incisiveness, thoroughness

and ferocity.    In this war little Duke Johann showed himsel.
of a sullen, convulsive personal bravery which was not without impression on Margarete.

Meanwhile King John also was able to rise from his sick
couch.    His eyes were really beyond remedy.    All he saw
of the world now was a feeble glimmer, and he knew that
soon he would see nothing at all.    This made him somewhat
world-weary, inclined to philosophy and quietism.    Lame
Albert of Habsburg too was weary of the war ;  he saw that
meanwhile there was nothing he could get but Carinthia,
and that, if he carried the war further, he would be really
fighting for the Emperor, who, when it came to payment,
would withdraw as usual behind his imperial dignity, taciturn,
haughty and mean.    In these circumstances Albert soon
came to an understanding with John and recognised the
Luxemburgers as rightful sovereigns of Tyrol, in return for
which John declared that he agreed to the Habsburg rule in
Carinthia ;    naturally in addition he wanted a financial
reparation ;  ten thousand silver marks of Verona.

Seeing that he was in the way of making treaties, John
flung a proposal before the Emperor too ;  Brandenburg in
exchange for Tyrol.    Ludwig, who pursued such affairs
with passion, took it up at once, and the two princes discussed with extreme vivacity the details of the scheme.    Now,
however, the devotion of the Tyroleans to their princess
broke out in raging flames—for the feudal barons would
certainly be heavily oppressed financially under the Wittelsbacher's jurisdiction.    It came to the most strongly worded
resolutions, and the popular agitation was so strong that King
John had to asseverate solemnly that he had never contemplated such an act of barter.    His son and viceroy, the
Margrave Karl, actually considered the atmosphere to be so

serious that he pressed his father to plight himself by the strongest oaths never to sell Tyrol. Which John amiably did, with a smile and a shrug of the shoulders.

But the young pair had no intention of agreeing to the settlement which John had made for Carinthia. Margarete launched forth in the most violent terms, saying that her guardian had vilely chaffered away their interests ; she and her young consort upheld to the full their demands on Carinthia and Carniola. Here young Duke Johann found a welcome pretext for the staging of a great and moving ceremony. He assembled the nobility of Tyrol around him and bade the lords, picturesquely marshalled, their swords drawn, to swear on the Cross not to rest till Carinthia was again in his and Margarete's hands.

Blind King John thought that his son was an ass. For the solitary result of this great step was that Austria did not pay the ten thousand marks of Veronese silver. In effect the Austrians remained in possession of Carinthia ; despite their vow, the dedicated Tyrolean lords stuck their swords back into their sheaths ; and through King John's chambers there glided, shadowy, insignificant, and with many obeisances, the good Messer Artese of Florence.

# CHAPTER VII

DUKE JOHANN grew riper, more manly. His face remained sullen and shrewish, but his body lost its lath-like appearance, its painfully long attentuation, and became firm, stately, not very supple, but well-knit. He was a good huntsman, had a consummate knowledge of falconry, and showed personal bravery on the battlefield. He pleased Margarete. There were handsomer men; there were cleverer, more splendid; but he had borne himself not so badly in the arduous struggle for the possession of the country; he was no longer a boy; while still very young he had grown into manhood; and he was her husband. He avoided her. Well, he was notoriously shy; only with his huntsmen was he ever communicative or confidential; he must be courted. She put herself in his way. It was of no avail; as if evading her he passed her by.

She filled the day with a thousand occupations, her toilette, affairs of government, politics and studies. But her thoughts always recurred to him. Why could she not reach him? Her nights were full of him. Almost urgently she sought his company, and whenever she knew he was at hand seized every possible pretext to break in upon him. But he was always in a hurry, and sulkily turned aside all her advances. She did not assign the reason for this to his ill-will; she was not for a moment angry with him; she found the fault in herself, in her own awkwardness.

She had to confide in someone, and obtain counsel, but from whom? Her women were dry and stupid, the good-natured Abbot of Viktring would only produce edifying saws and quotations. After a sleepless night she spoke to Herr von Schenna.

The tall nobleman sat awkwardly before her, one leg thrown over the other, his head with the somewhat faded face supported on his great hand. Through the slender pillars of the loggia they could see far into the mountains over the brightly coloured, rich, sunlit land. On the wall of the loggia walked Tristan, very gay and too slender. Isolde stood, one hand lifted high in dismissal. At the feet of Duchess Margarete the peacock strutted. In a mauve dress, her copper-coloured hair glittering in the clear light, but all the hideousness of her coarse face pitilessly revealed, Margarete spoke hesitatingly in half phrases. She had carefully prepared what she wanted to say ; but in spite of this, her sentences, usually so adroit, would not come right, and she talked in hints. After all, Johann was her husband. Someone must remind him of that. She herself—that would hardly do.

She looked at Herr von Schenna, but he sat quite still, blinked in the sun, and held his peace. Still more dejectedly she went on. In earlier times it had often been the custom for princes who had been married as children solemnly to celebrate the consummation of their nuptials at a later date. Johann was so punctilious about ceremonies. Did Herr von Schenna think it feasible for her to propose such a celebration to him ? Herr von Schenna let a moment elapse before he replied. The peacock screamed in the sunny stillness ; from below, out of the distant vineyards, very far away, sounded the shouts of children at play. Herr von Schenna was aware that the young Duke was not in the least so shy and awkward with other women as he was with

Margarete.   Slowly and very warily he began to speak at
last.   From what he knew of the young self-willed, ambitious
prince, he did not think that he would carry into effect any
idea suggested by another.   Possibly an opportunity might
come to mention the notion to him so naturally that he might
think it was his own ;  but one had to be very, very cautious.
And wait one's time.

Then, glad to turn the conversation aside, he pointed to
a gentleman who rode slowly up the path in the glittering
sunshine :  " Here comes Berchtold."

Greeting the Duchess with great respect, Berchtold of
Gufidaun approached.   This stately nobleman with the
brown, keen face, blue eyes and dark hair, was Jakob of
Schenna's best friend.   Herr von Schenna used to say :
" He is twice as stupid as I, but ten times more respectable."
Margarete was very glad to see this strong, upright and
devoted man.   Herr von Schenna sent for wine and fruit.
Evening was coming on ;  they sat and talked quietly.   During a pause in the conversation Margarete asked suddenly :
" Tell me, Herr von Gufidaun, you meet many people :
what do the people really think of me ? "   Taken by surprise
the honest man stammered uneasily that the people loved and
honoured her as was seemly, and broke into a sweat beneath
her clear and serious glance.   Schenna came to the aid of
his embarrassment.   Everywhere people knew how clever
and capable she was, and how she had saved the country
from Habsburg and Wittelsbach.

Margarete was clearly enough aware that the caution
which Herr von Schenna advised was timely, more so than
his politeness had allowed him to say ;  but she would not
admit it to herself.   She could no longer stand idle and see
how Johann eluded her.   Certainly her face was ugly, her

form ignoble and without charm ; but she was healthy,
she had noble blood, she was ready, able and entitled to receive
and bear the Prince's children.   Men were stupid, they
needed to be driven ;  that was certain.   The youth would
never do anything if he was not encouraged.

Suppressing her agitation with difficulty, she asked him
as casually as she could when and where he really thought it
advisable to celebrate the consummation of their marriage.
The Monastery of Wilten and the City of Innsbruck were
both waiting for it.   He looked her up and down, his face
twisted with jeering rage ;  his eyes became quite small.
Still another celebration ?   He had married her already ;
that had been celebration enough.   He had no intention of
figuring in a ceremonial consummation.   She would have
the goodness to wait and leave him in peace.   He screamed
till his voice broke.   Laughed discordantly and mockingly.
His eyes slid from her hard, copper-coloured hair, over her
short corpulent body, down to her feet.   He looked like
a malicious little ape.   Margarete gulped, turned her back,
and went.

Alone she raved and foamed.   Who was he, then ?   He
looked like an ill-favoured, snapping cur.   Who would
look at him if he were not a Duke ?   And she had made him
that, and now—what help was there ?—she must put up
with this insolent contempt.   Was this what she was Duchess
for ?   When had a wife ever been so scorned and insulted
as she ?   She tore her breast, and her poor, ugly face,
gnashed her teeth, snarled and groaned so that her terrified
women rushed into the room.

Next day she was encased in ice.   She threw herself into
politics.   Margrave Karl, Johann's elder brother, was
travelling on the Rhine.   The real regent of the country,

adroitly guiding Duke Johann, was Nikolaus, Bishop of
Trent, formerly the Margrave's Chancellor in Brünn,
an energetic, quick-thoughted man, and absolutely devoted
to the Luxemburgers. Now Margarete began to meddle
in even the smallest concerns, and compelled the bishop,
courteously but obstinately, to give her a share in all administrative business.

She treated Duke Johann with icy ceremony, called him
" Your Grace," and gave him all his titles. In every
political discussion he took his part, but while keeping to
all the forms of ceremonious politeness, she knew how to
expose him in front of the Tyrolean lords again and again as
a stupid, moody, petty youth. She was very dexterous at
reducing his consent to an empty formula, without his being
able, though exasperated and vexed to desperation, to prove
to the innocently astonished Margarete that she was holding
him up to contempt.

The finances of the country were better than they had
been under King Heinrich, but still by no means sound.
They exacted an endless, cautious tacking this way and that.
Weary of the strain of this petty drudgery, Duke Johann
invoked the unfailing helper whom he had come to know
through his father, Messer Artese of Florence. Insignificant,
shadowy, prodigiously ready to serve, the powerful banker
was quickly within Tyrol Castle. Of course he would
help, with all the joy in the world. He demanded in return
only a quite, quite, tiny recompense, the pledging of the
silver mines ; they were closed down in any case.

Duke Johann straightway acceded. Playing her cards
cleverly, Margarete expostulated perfunctorily and without
vigour, and let him entangle himself completely in the project.
Only when the plan was worked out in all its details did she

object unconditionally and with the utmost decision. Johann swelled with rage. His veins stood out like whip-cords. "The Italian shall have the silver mines ! " he yelled.

Quivering with triumph Margarete answered : " He shall not have them ! "

The Duke saw red. What ! He had promised the banker the silver mines and now was he not to be able to keep his promise ? Simply because the witch, the contrary, ugly slut would not allow it ? " He shall have them ! He shall have them ! " and he hurled himself upon her, struck her in the face and bit her savagely.

Happy that she had irritated him so deeply, she exulted, her full voice crying against his shrill one : " He shall not have them ! Never shall he have them ! Never ! "

Gasping, fretting with impotence, he drew away from her

Margarete sent express couriers to the Margrave Karl In an evil temper he left his important business and came back to Tyrol to arbitrate. It was clear that Margarete was in the right ; obviously the silver mines could not be surrendered to the Florentine. Margarete interposed adroitly and saved her husband from open defeat. But when they were together the elder brother dealt with the Duke so faithfully that the very marrow in his bones quivered with rage.

The sober, clear-sighted Margrave could not but recognise his young sister-in-law's talent for statesmanship. From Bohemia and Luxemburg was spread abroad to the European Courts the fame of her diplomatic ascendancy. Officially it was true all business was still transacted with Duke Johann, but in every state chancellory it was known that in reality the ugly young duchess was sole ruler of the land in the mountains.

# CHAPTER VIII

## § 1

SOON after the death of King Heinrich, Frau von Flavon, Mistress of Taufers and Velturn, died also and very suddenly while on a walk with her youngest daughter. As amid shouts and laughter she plucked the mountain flowers, the pretty plump dame slipped and fell dead. Amid universal sympathy her daughters laid her with great pomp beside the somewhat questionable remains which had been brought back from Italy as those of Peter of Flavon. The three pretty girls were in a very grave position now that their protector, good King Heinrich, was dead. The Bishop of Chur revived his old claim on their western possessions, and the Bishop of Brixen with much reason demanded that the castles and jurisdictions of Taufers and Velturn should be returned to him.

The three young ladies, fair, lovely and helpless, had to negotiate continually with the financial councillors of the Bishops. Many people were found to take their part, but it was hard to make headway against the legitimate claims of the powerful bishoprics. At last the case reached the Duke's court for final decision.

Agnes von Flavon appeared at Castle Tyrol, and fell on her knees before the young Duke. He stood, boyishly important before the kneeling lady, his lips earnestly compressed in his long, narrow face. It soothed his greed for power to see the gentle creature, beautiful and fluttering in her black robes, lie before him dissolved in tears, and gazing up at him out of her deep blue eyes. That was as it should be. Thus had God ordained it. The other ugly creature could snarl at him if she liked. This one, tender, lovely, the most beautiful woman in the country, humbled herself before him on her knees, gazed up at him devoutly, submissively, and full of trust. He was extremely gracious to her.

Agnes waited also on the Duchess. Margarete resisted gallantly the temptation to triumph over her beautiful rival, was gracious, and condoled with her in warm terms over the death of Frau von Flavon. Her father, King Heinrich, had always had a special consideration for the family, she added ambiguously. Yes, and it was very sad that the legal position from all she could hear was so unfavourable to her visitor. Of course she personally would be willing at any time to help out of her own privy purse.

Agnes had made up her mind not to exasperate Margarete, but before this enigmatic, doubly-rankling disdain she lost her self-control. What? A girl with a face and a mouth like that dared to taunt her? Even if this woman had been Empress of Rome and she herself a serf, she could not have contained herself. She looked Margarete over long and contemptuously, and said then that her case did not seem after all to be so very desperate. At least His Grace the Duke had given her very gracious and comforting assurances. Somewhat baldly Margarete concluded by saying: well, now they would hear the decision of those competent to judge and would give the affair their gracious consideration.

Before Agnes left the castle she met Chretien de Laferte also, who condoled with her in formal terms. Agnes listened to him seriously and replied with dignity. He begged to be allowed to escort her on her journey back. During that too she was suitably melancholy, but she occasionally varied the dignity of sorrow with a pert, coquettish jest, until her capriciousness threw the young lord into deep confusion.

Chretien's position in Tyrol Castle was not pleasant. So long as Prince Johann was still a boy he had had his clearly defined function as an obliging comrade, always ready to gloss over and right the countless offences of the difficult little Prince against courtly usage and good breeding. King John was convinced that no more tactful adjutant for his ill-bred son could be found than this comely, courteous and yet so unassuming youth. But Prince Johann himself had never been quite able to endure his frank, handsome friend. He had cuffed him, ill-treated him, humiliated him, watching vigilantly with his tiny wolf's eyes for his patient companion to rebel sometime, and provide an occasion for sending him away.

Chretien was a younger son of a noble French house, without property, and consequently destined to seek his fortunes at court. There was no advantage for him in being buried in Tyrol during his best years. In the armies of King John he had proved himself to be brave and gallant. An opportunity to distinguish himself strikingly, however, had not offered itself. What was he doing here with this spiteful young Duke who continually humiliated him, and at any rate was never friendly towards him ? He always nursed the thought of returning to King John's court or going to France, or better still of enlisting under the King of Castile. In the wars with the Moors gold and honour were to be had.

For a long time Margarete had ceased to give the young knight any extraordinary proofs of favour. Only when she

saw she had no means of getting into touch with Duke
Johann did she begin again to court Chretien.   She entrusted
him with little, confidential, diplomatic missions, and asked
him artless questions which acquired significance from her tone.
He was cautious, full of hesitation, and refused to understand.
It was a great piece of fortune to stand in high favour with
a lady of such rank, but there was another side to it ; it was
impossible to enter the lists for such an ugly woman.   True,
no one would dare to scorn him to his face as before ; but
his pride reared when he thought of the lewd grins, the filthy
remarks behind his back.   But then he heard again how
at all the courts they spoke with great respect of her prudence
and cleverness.   It flattered him that a lady of such judgment
should choose him, precisely him.   She impressed him greatly,
he was grateful to her, and did not try to elude her any longer.
He suited his tone to hers ; his eyes softly veiled themselves
when he looked at her ; his voice was subdued when he spoke.

Once—he had returned after a long absence—he reported
himself to the Duchess.   She was not in her room, and the
faded Fräulein von Rottenburg led him into a remote part
of the dusky garden.   From a clump of trees poured a burst
of song.   The court lady laid her fingers on her lips, signing
to him to stand still and be silent.   A warm full voice was
singing a simple song ; it mounted in exultation, sobbed out
all the sorrow of the world, yearned, gave thanks, went
through all the labyrinths of passion.   It overwhelmed the
young man as if he were in a church listening to a solemn
chant.   He took off his cap.   " The Duchess ? " he whispered incredulously.   Then she came down the avenue of
trees.   His face showed her without disguise how much he
had been moved and stirred ; she slowly reached him her
hand.   He kissed it.

F

Meanwhile the business of Frau von Flavon's estate had advanced so far that the decision could hardly be postponed any longer. Both juristic and political reasons were in favour of giving back the vacant fiefs to the bishops, who had been so useful in serving the House of Luxemburg. At the same time the judges found all sorts of threadbare pretexts which pleaded for the ladies of Flavon. Agnes had been to every one of them, and had played her cards of grief, youth, cunning and helplessness until she had sown confusion among the judges. In consequence Johann majestically decided that the ladies should keep the properties. But Margarete set herself in opposition with such good reasons and so firmly that they could not make headway against her. Finally they came to a compromise. The castle and juris- diction of Velturn should remain with the sisters ; the western properties should return to Chur, and Taufers to Brixen, but with the stipulation that the Bishop of Brixen should invest with it only a candidate nominated by Tyrol Castle.

The sisters, who had already divided their large possessions among them, had thus to content themselves with the only remaining one, Velturn. They made a great outcry, wrangled, fought each for her own hand. There was continual squabbling in Velturn Castle. It was shocking how unbelievably hard and shrill, like the screaming of pea- cocks, the pleasant voices of the young ladies became when they quarrelled. Yet in public the sisters were always a picture of unity and trust, their arms wreathed about each other, lovely, like smiling flowers.

As candidate for the vacated Castle of Taufers, Margarete proposed Chretien de Laferte. The Duke foamed with rage. What ? In this fat property should they plant that sponge, that malicious dunderhead, who always effaced himself with such false humility, and who would be certain to bite as soon as he had the power ? But Margarete remained firm. The Duke of Carinthia and Count of Tyrol could not appear in such a shabby light. He could not accept someone's service for so long and then be stingy and mean. If Chretien were to go now to another Court without reward or thanks she herself would be dishonoured by such paltry niggardliness. When Johann began to rage again she threatened to call in the Margrave Karl to decide the matter, and with a snarl Johann knuckled under.

Margarete herself imparted this decision to Chretien. "The Bishop of Brixen will invest you with the Castle and jurisdiction of Taufers. Prove yourself, Herr von Taufers ! It will be my fame if you gain honour, and my shame if you are found wanting."

Chretien's lean brown face reddened up to the roots of his wilful hair. Slowly he sank on his knee. He did not see now that her jaw jutted out like an ape's, that her skin was grey and patchy. "Your Grace ! " he stammered. "Most gracious, most beloved Duchess ! " And it was more than the usual formula that he thanked her with : "*Pour toi mon âme, pour toi ma vie !* "

§ 2

In the rude and primitive castle of the Tyrolean Military Governor, Volkmar of Burgstall, seven or eight of the most influential Tyrolean barons sat at wine. It was not often that the massive man invited guests, and when he did, it was in a brusque manner that sounded more like a command. The hall in which they sat was damp and wretched, the floor covered with a few rags, the walls quite bare. Glass windows, those fashionable vanities, were scorned by the conservative master of the house. Albert of Andrion, young and jocund, Margarete's natural brother, made merry over the planks which now, in the cold season of the year, were nailed over the open slits which let in the light. It was as if they were sitting in a cellar. Everything was covered with smoke from the fire and the candles and torches, yet in spite of this the room was not properly warmed ; the lords shifted uncomfortably to and fro ; they were roasted on one side and frozen on the other. Herr von Schenna, always nervous, coughed and sneezed ; the cheerless damp hole gave him a headache ; the odour of the stables, cold and disgusting, seemed to stand in the room. But the food —venison and fish—had been prepared with loving care and was provided in monstrous abundance ; and the wine, it was not to be denied, was excellent.

From what the lords knew of the Military Governor, he had not invited them to come for the mere pleasure of their company. But he was a man of few and rude words ; it was inadvisable to question him until he should begin to speak himself. So they drank, talked about trifling matters and waited.

Slowly, in rumbling, fragmentary phrases, Volkmar led the conversation round to politics, and drove the lords brusquely to the point he desired to reach. Yes, people were dissatisfied with the Luxemburgers. The first to say it openly was Heinrich of Rottenburg. The little nobleman with the broad, coarse, red face and the black stubbly beard grew excited, struck the table with his fist and spat out threats. Had they not—merely because he had refused to pay a few taxes—demolished his Laimburg Castle for him, his good Castle beside Kaltern, on which his father, his grandfather, and his great-grandfather had built ? It was the young Duke's work, the malignant little wolf. And the Bishop of Trent had given the order, the morose Bohemian, who was always mouthing " Authority ! " and " Obedience ! " If they had seized fields of his, vineyards, a village, or a whole district ! But to pull down a castle, a good fortress, built of good stone, in their own, not in a hostile land, and just to spite him ; that was senseless, that was sheer savagery. Lady Margarete had not approved of it either, the little Duchess. That was because she was the hereditary princess and felt with the country. But the foreigners, the Bohemians, the Luxemburgers, what did they feel ?

They wanted to extort money from Tyrol and that was all, just as the Luxemburger had done from Bohemia. And he, Heinrich of Rottenburg, would take his oath on it that King John had wanted to stake Tyrol against Brandenburg, let him deny it as much as he liked.

The others listened to this rash speech in silence. Then the prudent, elegant Tägen of Villanders began cautiously. The Luxemburgers after all had observed the strict letter of the treaty, and no foreigners had been appointed to the more important administrative posts. It could not be gainsaid, could it, that Herr von Rottenburg was High Steward, and Herr von Volkmar Military Governor ? Or could it ? The well-groomed, clean-shaven, somewhat old-fashioned gentleman stared at both of them so earnestly that they could not tell whether he was mocking them or what really he was after.

Little Rottenburg burst out : Did His Excellency take him for a fool ? Steward ? Governor ? The stupidest peasant had long since found out that these were empty titles ; but who governed in reality ? The flat-nosed

Nikolaus, Bishop of Trent, the Bohemian, who understood not a word of Tyrolese.

Berchtold of Gufidaun, the honourable man, sat sweating with raised embarrassed eyebrows. His bright blue eyes gazed disapprovingly on the contumacious, refractory barons. Such speeches against the divinely-appointed ruling house were unseemly. Young Albert of Andrion, too, became thoughtful. True, the Luxemburgers had used him ill, and had vilely curtailed good King Heinrich's rich legacies to his numerous illegitimate children. But frank young Albert was a good-natured youth, not in the least given to disloyal ideas, and full of reverence for his little sister, the Duchess. Of course anything really seditious had hardly been mentioned. Herr von Burgstall had said nothing one could lay hold on ; the adroit Herr von Villanders nothing at all ; real menaces, which one could not countenance, had only been uttered by little Rottenburg, and he was far gone in wine. All the same, the whole business smacked faintly of rebellion.

Tägen of Villanders cautiously stretched out his feelers again. Yes, that was the right sentiment. The hereditary princely house, sprung from the soil of the country, nourished on its air, was ordained by God to reign in Tyrol. Here he broke off. Rottenburg, small, vehement, with his wild, bushy beard, took up the thread. The Luxemburgers should reign where God or the devil had placed them. In Luxemburg : or if the Bohemians pleased, in Bohemia. But it was through human agency, not by God's decree, that they sat and ruled in Tyrol ; and that too had been a mistake. It had lain with them, with the nobility, to say who should be allowed into the country after King Heinrich's death The Habsburger, the Wittelsbacher, or the Luxemburger

It had been manifestly proved that in Tyrol only he could rule whom the Tyrolese themselves wanted to rule. With mountains and valleys and passes God had so disposed it that no foreign power could overrun it by violence. Let them be loyal, let them hold to Margarete. But they were not plighted to the Luxemburger by the command of God, but only by treaty. Duke Johann and the other Bohemians had abused the treaty. It was broken and did not bind them any longer.

The lords, their eyes fixed on his lips, breathed heavily. It was clear. This was sedition. It could not be argued away.

What did they think about it, then ? Herr von Villanders asked tentatively. How were they to separate Margarete and her divine right as a ruler from the Luxemburgers ?

Looking into space Schenna began to throw out vague hints ; the Duchess was not exactly happy, so far as he knew. Neither she nor the country had reason to expect an heir from Duke Johann ; that much was known to him. It might be conjectured too that the fault did not lie with her ; whereat he nodded smilingly towards Albert of Andrion, who sat among them, ruddy, fresh, laughing and flattered, the witness to King Heinrich's fruitfulness.

Herr von Villanders summed up : They had said nothing, come to no decision. One could think of a better, more popular government for the land than that of the foreign Luxemburgers. They held with absolute loyalty to the divinely-ordained Duchess Margarete. Perhaps it would be expedient to enquire what her attitude, her desire was ? In his opinion Herr Albert of Andrion was the right man for the task. They tumultuously agreed. Only the upright Berchtold of Gufidaun remained silent, torn hither and thither by indecision. Young Albert, doubtful at first, but far gone in wine and flattered by the others' entreaties, undertook and plighted himself to impart the sentiments of the lords to his sister and to sound her feelings.

### § 3

MARGARETE loved now to be much alone. Often she wore a still, secretly-pleased smile which her women could not fathom. On the slender base of her scant but real experience of love her fantasy had built a gigantic dream. Out of the little, ill-bred, unwilling youth who was her husband she made a gloomy, violent, mighty tyrant who did not understand and who from the obscurity of his overweening and ambitious soul tormented her. Young Chretien she adorned with every virtue of body and soul. He was Parsifal and Tristan, and Lancelot and the Lion Knight. Every brilliant deed that had ever been done by hero in history or song he had done, or at least could do.

It was a piece of good fortune, a great favour, that Heaven had been so severe with her and denied her any banal charm of face or form. The women, the ordinary women all round her, had their husbands and their lovers and enjoyed them in dull, animal lust in their rooms and behind bushes. Her love was entirely pure and lofty ; everything filthy, everything earthly, had been forbidden to her, barred to her from the beginning. She soared, radiant and apart, high above the petty stupefying lusts and disgusting traffic of the others. It was sweet to be pure and austere in one's own eyes and in the eyes of the world. It was sweet not to be ensnared in the bestial, unclean toils of skin and flesh.

She became morbidly sensitive to everything blatant,

coarse, physical, unclean. Contact with people disgusted her, their effluvia made her ill.

It was March. From Italy the wind came in warm, soft gusts, filling her blood with longing. Up above, the mountains lay thick in snow, but the lower slopes were covered with a tender shower of almond and peach blossom. She looked out from the loggia of Schenna Castle over the undulating bright-coloured land. Above her Lancelot and Guinevere walked, gay and too slender; Tristan fared across the sea; Dido threw herself into the flames. She was at one with them now. The verses which for so long had been empty, inaccessible and without meaning had opened to her, and she could drink now of their mysterious, solacing abundance.

Welcome, great and austere destiny! Welcome, hideousness! Welcome, princely crown and sceptre!

She was almost grateful to her harsh, tyrannical husband, for through his harshness she had found her lover. Sweet friend! He knew her! He knew that this grey, patchy, coarse skin, this horrible mouth, this dead growth of hair, were only a mask, and that within she was gentle and full of loveliness.

She seldom saw him, hardly ever spoke to him; no word ever passed between them which anyone might not have heard. Yet she never doubted even for a moment that he loved her. She had never forgotten his dark, devoted look that evening when she had sung and had come to him from among the vines. Nor the tone of his voice, and how his feelings had carried him away when she informed him of his investiture with the lordship of Taufers. This was a different love, in truth, from that she saw all around her, with its kisses and sweet nothings and trivialities. She, Margarete, had been more at one with him, and in a higher sense, through his glance that evening and his agitated words that day, than any lady had ever been with her gallant, however much he might love her. The others could possess their men physically. That possession was cheap, as common as eating and drinking. For her, the Princess, a more lofty and austere love was ordained. It was easy, too, to rekindle such a wretched love as the others knew, to warm it up again in the fire of the eyes or in the enjoyment of stupid and bestial lust. She had continually to fight against her outward form, and ever to wrest anew the love of her friend from his antipathy to her repulsive appearance.

Oh, blessed bitterness of such a fight ! She thanked God and the Virgin for a love so complicated, so difficult and so worthy of a princess.

She did not cease to endow Chretien with ever new lustre and splendour. Chretien was without ambition. She was ambitious for him. If his splendid qualities were not revealed to others, that was solely because she kept him here in Tyrol, and because here there was no opportunity for him. She, Margarete, was to blame that in the world's eyes he was insignificant and unknown. She was his debtor ; she owed him the opportunity to achieve greatness.

# CHAPTER IX

## § 1

MEANWHILE Chretien had taken over the administration of
Taufers. He owned the villages of Luttach, Sand, Kema-
ten, and the valleys of Nevestal and Reintal. All these had
deteriorated a little under the regime of the ladies of Flavon.
He looked forward with satisfaction to making them ship-
shape again.

He was filled with a great and boundless joy at being his
own master after the long years at court. The time he had
passed with Duke Johann lay behind him, empty, bright and
comfortless. The countless compulsory ceremonies, the
eternal buffets, the unwilling silences, the deep curtseys and
obeisances, the insulting comments on the top of that, the
mendacious haggling at the tourneys, all that splendid and
yet oppressive and beggarly existence, which stood constantly
in fear of the creditor. He lifted his head with the lean,
tanned face, the salient nose and the long, unbound locks,
into the air, his air. He rode around his farms ; the
peasants gazed well-pleased and full of reverence at this
slender, assured, dashing lord ; the women and girls stared
piously at him as if they were in church.

He could not have borne it any longer at the Tyrolean
court. He would have ridden away somewhere to seek
adventure, willingly and with the full sanction of his judgment. Now everything was different, and he was very content. It would satisfy to the full his thirst for enterprise

to administer his possessions here to the end of his life. Naturally he would ride to court too, take part in military expeditions, and not fail to attend the tourneys. But to go to Africa and kill Moors, or perhaps lay about him among Turks and Saracens for the Holy Sepulchre—no, thanks ! At the moment he could find no desire whatever within himself for that. Manly and content he rode about his lands and enjoyed his young authority.

One day the Duchess visited him. He was deeply and submissively devoted to Margarete. He never thought for a moment of putting his fleeting but very real connections with this or that woman in the same class as his feelings towards her. To him Margarete was an ideal, into which entered also images which he had come to know through the minstrels and wandering musicians. She was a poetical and ethereal figure who by investing him with Taufers had achieved an unexpected, fortunate, and authentic reality, but one which he did not bring into the slightest relation with the other activities of his life. He never guessed what he was for Margarete, what rôle he played in her life.

He received the Duchess with glad and devoted cordiality. His voice had that veiled and enigmatic constraint which thrilled Margarete. It was true, what he said was prosaic and practical. He spoke to her of the changes he planned for his property, of a more rational management of the lands, a more rigid supervision of the peasants. She interrupted him irrelevantly, pointing to a glacier which, solitary, clear, in mocking remoteness, ran jaggedly into the bright blue sky. " Do you never long, Chretien, to climb one of these glaciers ? "

Disconcerted, Chretien gazed at her rather foolishly. He said, and now his voice rang clear and without mystery :

" No. Why should I climb up there ? " Then he observed again how pleasant and fertile the lower slopes were.

A few days later came Agnes of Flavon. She had already visited Chretien several times at Taufers Castle. There always happened to be another little detail which had to be arranged ; Chretien too, always found—not without skill—new questions which demanded consideration and personal consultation. Agnes was fair, touching, helpless, and always took another farewell look at the castle and the mountains around with mournful eyes.

Meanwhile the elder sister, Maria of Flavon, was married to a Bavarian lord, and relinquished Velturn Castle to the two other sisters. But a considerable dowry had to be paid to the Bavarian ; the property of Velturn was itself already overburdened ; with great, candid eyes Agnes begged Chretien for advice. Chretien went to Velturn, saw the slovenly and elegant management of the sisters, recommended economies here and there which were very practical, but must change the property from a princely seat to a productive farming establishment. Agnes openly envied her sister. She was lucky ; she was out of all this misery. It was true, the Bavarian was a rough, loutish fellow, and it must be terrible to exchange this beautiful Tyrol for the tame Bavarian flats. But in the end she would probably have to suffer a similar fate. She kept her gentle and yet audacious face with the bright blue eyes turned earnestly and long on Chretien, who stood before her, slim, tanned, embarrassed, and a little foolish.

The plot against the Luxemburgers was ripe. Volkmar of Burgstall, Tägen of Villanders, Jakob of Schenna, had imperceptibly withdrawn more and more into the shade, after they had set the affair going. In the fore-front stood now the violent, little Heinrich of Rottenburg, and, half against his will, the gay and harmless Albert of Andrion, Margarete's brother. Margarete herself wove and drew closer the threads with passionate, feverish diligence. At last she saw here—at last !—her pretext to set Chretien in a place worthy of him, to create the opportunity which she owed him for great deeds.

The other lords hesitated whether to admit Chretien at all, or to entrust him with an important position. He was not a countryman of theirs, he was a Latin, and Johann's most trusted chamberlain. Margarete had to divulge in detail to what humiliations the spiteful, malicious Duke had always subjected him, and prove that Chretien had had to suffer more than anyone else from the vile temper of her tyrannical husband.

Chretien himself was somewhat surprised when Margarete spoke to him of the plot. Of course he was enough of a cavalier to join issue at once, if it was a matter of delivering out of the hand of her oppressor the lady whom he revered so deeply and to whom he was so strongly indebted. But he did not seem to be precisely enthusiastic. He was occupied with work on his estates, and it would have pleased him better if the adventure had come a little later. Apart from the self-evident, but at the moment burdensome necessity to fulfil his duty as a knight, he saw in the opportunity one rather slight advantage. Through it he would make secure his position among the native nobility ; henceforth, after taking part in this purely Tyrolean enterprise, Herr von Taufers-Laferte could hardly be regarded any longer as an alien.

Margarete burned with expectation, inflamed the others with her ardour, and spied out every contingency with her quick clever eyes. She was able to arrange that, assisted by Albert of Andrion and Heinrich of Rottenburg, Chretien should count as the real head of the affair.

Meanwhile there had arrived at Velturn Castle a certain Messer Giulio of Padua, an insignificant-looking man, slow, silent, always smiling, really a bit of an idiot. All the same his uncle held the captaincy of Padua, and he himself had rich possessions on Lake Como. He seemed to have a dog-like devotion to Agnes, and Chretien was overcome with sudden anxiety lest she might decide to follow him to Lombardy, as the year before her sister had followed the Bavarian. When he considered this, his castle of Taufers, his villages and valleys, seemed all at once to lose their dignity and splendour.

One could not speak to Agnes as one spoke to other women. One could not simply take her. She was so gentle. She might die with terror in one's arms. Very cautiously he approached her. If she was not content in the overburdened castle of Velturn, would she not live with him in Taufers ?

O, how astonished she was ! She made her eyes take on their veiled look, her lips smile timidly, her hand ward him off, modest and yet alluring. She answered in unfinished sentences filled with refusals and promises.

Undeniably he was a pretty youth, very different from the rude Tyrolean lords. The keen, thin face with the strong nose, the small, full lips. It would be pleasant to play with his flowing, long, chestnut hair. Taufers, too, was a rich property. But no ; after all, her hair, her eyes, her skin, her priceless exquisiteness and loveliness, were, by God's wounds, worth ten properties like that ! When she re-called how the Italians had stared entranced at her fair beauty, how they had turned pale on seeing her, then she was convinced that in Lombardy she could find a very different lord and master. To rule as the wife of a Visconti in Milan, of a della Scala in Verona, amid the applause and wonder of splendid cities, would be a triumph far more resounding than to be the wife of Herr von Taufers-Laferte at the Tyrolean Court.

Chretien saw that she hesitated, that she put him off. He realised that he must make himself appear more grand, more important. He initiated her into the plot against the Luxemburgers.

Agnes listened with a curious, stupid, strangely satisfied smile. She realised suddenly that it would be a far greater triumph to be Chretien's wife than that of a della Scala, or a Visconti of Milan. Was it a triumph to snatch this man from the ugly Duchess, the hideous-mouthed, patchy-skinned hag? Yes! Yes! That was triumph! Suddenly she knew that for a long time she had waited for this triumph, that she had enticed this moment to her by every means in her power. There flowed *one* stream from her to the ugly Duchess, they were balanced on *one* plank. The other was ugly, certainly; but on her ugly hair sat a princely crown, and from her ugly face looked out a pair of diabolically clever, burning, energetic eyes. To overcome her was far harder than to overcome any other merely beautiful woman. The hatred between her and that woman was a very living thing, the most important part of life, for her as for the other. How the other had fought for this man! She had robbed her, Agnes, and given him the booty; had artfully precipitated great events, in order to set him at their head and exalt him. She, Agnes, who was poor and destitute and possessed nothing but herself, had only raised her finger and this man had sprung down straightway from the mighty pedestal which the other had so painfully erected, had sprung down and was at her feet. She savoured fully this consummation, expanded, revelled in it. No, she would stay in Tyrol, would measure herself against this Duchess whom she hated, would take more from her still than her man. It was glorious to soar up on the see-saw, soar blissfully high up, and to see the other completely sunk in the depths and completely overthrown.

Chretien went into the perilous contest against the Luxemburgers as into a tournament. He was happy at having won Agnes beforehand. It never occurred to him for a moment that the Duchess could be slighted by this alliance. Margarete stood here, Agnes there ; his relation towards the one, his inclination for the other, were of very different stuff. He arranged the wedding in all haste, for events pressed. Agnes agreed warmly ; she was tickled with delight to think that Margarete would have her husband, hers, to thank for deliverance.

At the end of the week Duke Johann proposed to leave the country for several months along with Margrave Karl and the greater part of the Luxemburg and Bohemian troops, in order to assist his father in the Polish War. Agnes asked Chretien when and how the Duchess should be informed of their marriage. Chretien had planned to invite Margarete to the wedding. Under the steady, deep-blue, mocking, innocent glance of Fräulein von Flavon he grew uncertain, and postponed imparting the news to Margarete, who was completely absorbed in her plot, at first until the marriage should have been consummated, then until his final interview with the Duchess. But when he consulted with her over the final details of the enterprise, it seemed more fitting

G

to announce his marriage when the Luxemburg troops and officials had been driven out, and she was the sole sovereign of her country   However, as he parted from her, to see her next after the successful coup, there was still in his voice the same intimate, significant, veiled tone, which had filled her with such joy at the zenith of her happiness.

Shortly after Chretien had gone Duke Johann stood before Margarete in his armour, in order, he also, to take his leave.   Margrave Karl had already left with the greater part of the Luxemburg escort.   Coolly and contemptuously Margarete listened to Johann's rough instructions.   Bitingly he concluded :  "We shall have a fine regime starting now, if you rule without me.   You can see at Taufers what comes of crossing my plans."

" At Taufers ? " she could not keep herself from enquiring.

" Yes, Taufers.   Agnes has won back the castle by her own methods.   We should have left it with her at first."

Margarete did not enquire further.   Suddenly she knew all.   She controlled herself until the Duke was gone.   She did not collapse, her voice did not fail her, her gaze, calm and mocking, withstood his small, malicious, vigilant wolf's eyes

§ 2

ALONE, she burst into terrible cries.   Who had ever been so betrayed ?   He had veiled his voice, made his glance eloquent and full of deep devotion, and every gesture had spoken of understanding.   He had lulled her into the belief that he saw through her repulsive appearance into the austere, stern beauty behind it.   He had behaved as if he renounced with her in her renunciation, as if he fought in her fight, shared her painful victory ; as if he withdrew with her from the pleasant valleys of ordinary pleasure up to her cold,

solitary and savagely austere height. And he had abandoned
her in a moment for a smooth, empty mask. Who could
tell, perhaps they were sitting together now, Agnes and he,
laughing at her !

He had managed it cunningly, oh yes ! He had recouped
himself damned well for his histrionic display ; the rapt
look, the pretence of adoration. With such a prize, with
the lordship of Taufers, one could have bought all the court
dwarfs, singers, tumblers and players in the kingdom. And
now he had graciously allowed her to set him at the head of
the plot against the Luxemburgers. Had expected, no doubt,
that now he would become Burgrave, Military Governor,
the real regent of Tyrol. For that reason, too, doubtless, he had never told her till this moment of his union
with Agnes. If the coup succeeded, then he would
have all power in his hands, and would not need to fear her
anger any longer. As the deliverer of the land from the
foreign yoke he could rule even against her will.

How they must have made merry, he and she, over the
stupid, ugly Duchess, the silly goose, who thought she could
charm her hideousness away with gifts and sentimentality !
As if for a man the most resplendent soul outweighed a
blubber mouth and a hanging jowl ! She raved. She raged
against herself. With one crash the whole artificial edifice
fell, in which she had taken refuge. Oh, how deceitful
had been all those fantasies about her austere, high mission,
and her rapturous acceptance of her ugliness ! She was
ridiculous, ridiculous in the finery of her fashionable attire
and of her world-embracing feelings, she, whom God had
singled out for defeat by her repulsive form, and doubly
derided in placing her where she was.

How she had looked down from her crystalline height on

Agnes, the tiny, gay, stupid insect ! And now she lay in the mire to which she belonged, disgusting insect that she was, and Agnes smiled down on her from the sky with her delicate, red, and, oh, so finely-chiselled lips.

Did she hate Agnes ? No, she did not hate her. She was what she was. Anyone who was so beautiful had a good right to smile down on an ugly woman—why should she not ? But he, Chretien ! Oh, how he had lied ! How he had gazed at her from his keen, tanned, open face, dog-like devotion in his eyes ! How inarticulate his voice had become with emotion and desire ! Oh, that anyone with such a frank, true face could be such a liar ! How did God permit it ? How did the earth not open beneath him ! The dog ! The traitor ! The dirty liar !

In an access of unbridled fury she heaped on him all the vilest oaths and curses she knew, the most outrageous she could think of, drawn from any and every source. She raged through the room, until at last she fell exhausted on the carpet. There she lay, the thick, painted hands stretched out, unable to move, hoarse, her harsh, copper-coloured hair loosened in matted strands.

When she recovered she was much changed. She went about her affairs, icily rigid, sure of her aim, with a cold, demoniacal energy. She dictated, wrote letters herself, and despatched couriers. New letters, new sealed messages, new couriers. So it went on for two days. Then she sank into an inactivity as striking as her former restless energy had been. Nobody was admitted. She trailed up and down through her room. Gazed for hours over the country, her thick, coarse lips half-opened in a strangely lascivious, malignant smile. Waited. Ate nothing. Said nothing. Waited.

# CHAPTER X

## § 1

BEFORE Margrave Karl and Duke Johann had reached the Bohemian frontier they received an express letter from Nikolaus, Bishop of Trent, that blind adherent of the House of Luxemburg. He had received anonymous warnings from the most diverse parts of the country. The land was in a ferment. At the head of the uprising stood Chretien of Taufers, Heinrich of Rottenburg, and Albert of Andrion. He urgently counselled the princes to turn back with their troops.

The Luxemburgers returned by forced marches. They took Albert of Andrion and Chretien of Taufers in an ambush. The insurrection was a failure before it had broken out. The revolutionary feudal lords crept back into their castles ; none of them had heard even of any protest against the Luxemburg regime, let alone an armed rising. The real originators, Burgstall, Villanders, Schenna, had been too clever from the beginning to compromise themselves. Like snow in summer the rebels vanished before the Luxemburg troops. Heinrich of Rottenburg escaped : good friends, to save themselves, delivered him up.

Since the revolt had been suppressed so quickly and easily, Margrave Karl considered his further presence in Tyrol superfluous. He commanded his brother and the Bishop of Trent not to prosecute the supporters of it, but to punish the leaders without mercy. He strengthened the garrisons in Tyrol Castle and the chief strongholds and departed with the rest of the troops to help his father in Poland.

§ 2

IN the castle of Sonnenburg near Innsbruck sat Nikolaus, Bishop of Trent, and listened with morose, vigilant attention to the protocol which Duke Johann's secretary read out. Johann himself leaned against the table and stared with a faint, malicious, triumphant smile at the gloomy prelate seated near him.

Yes, now it was proved that he had been right. The Bishop had held the decision to be impolitic and had said that it would be actually harmful if nothing came of it. But he, Johann, had overridden the objection, had boldly disregarded all these scruples and qualms. The Duchess's brother, was he? Of the blood of the hereditary princely house? He was a high traitor, a perjured rebel! And he had put Albert of Andrion to the torture.

To him the fair, amiable, gay young man had always been antipathetic. Oh, he knew that Albert had always hated him and intrigued against him with Margarete. Only they had never been able to prove it. Now at last, thank God, they could convict him and make him harmless.

The Duke had stood there himself when they put the prisoner painfully to the question. He endured the first degree in stubborn silence. His feet weighted with balls of lead, they lifted him up by his hands, which were tied behind his back, lowered him, lifted him up again. His pink and white skin was covered with sweat, and swelled up. But he remained silent. He withstood the thumbscrew as well. The bones crunched, blood spurted, he vomited. But he did not give up his secret. Only when they nipped him with red hot pincers and tickled him under the armpits with burning coals did he consent to become communicative.

And so now they had the protocol. A good, invaluable protocol. True, the Bishop was of the opinion that Rottenburg was a vitriolic fool, and Chretien and Albert foolish youths ; there must be better heads concealed behind them, and these one could not reach in spite of the protocol. But in any case they now had it in black and white that the rebels had taken Margarete into their confidence ; that the Duchess had been in the plot with them.

The morose Bishop enquired ironically whether Johann had ever doubted it. The Duke responded : No, but he was glad to have the proof in his hand ; he would strike Margarete over the face with it. The Bishop asked whether he thought greater power would accrue to the house of Luxemburg from such an action.

Before he proceeded to Castle Tyrol Johann delivered final sentence on the leaders of the conspiracy. Albert, distorted and weakened by the torture, was deprived of his possessions ; and as soon as the monks of Wilten should make him in some measure capable of being moved, he was to be sent to Bohemia and kept in life-long captivity. Johann commanded little Heinrich of Rottenburg, now in rags, to be brought before him, bound and gagged ; pulled his beard, struck him on both cheeks, and then disclosed to the poor man, spluttering through the gag and rolling his eyes, that now his other two castles as well would be demolished, burned, and razed to the ground. Rottenburg himself was sent in captivity to Luxemburg ; Chretien he brought back with him to Tyrol Castle.

The Duke found Margarete not at all so despondent and contrite as he had anticipated. She crouched in a corner in a strange, deadly lassitude.   Johann had the feeling he might have had before a snake which had gorged itself, and now neither stirred nor knew hope or fear, in its apathetic, paralysed satiation.   He clanked to and fro before her, boyishly important in his armour, and blurted out menaces and lewd oaths.   She needn't think of flight ; all the exits were guarded ;   the moats, the gates and the walls trebly manned.   She should not be allowed to leave her room for months yet ;   he would consider very carefully whom he should permit her to see.   But in spite of all his great blustering words he failed in his purpose.   Margarete listened with languid, apathetic curiosity ;   he could not reach her, and it would have no sense now to strike her and spit on her, as he had pictured to himself.   He glared at her with his tiny wolf's eyes ;   but he noticed that his blustering and raging rang somewhat false and made no impression.   Disappointed, he retired at last.

She lay alone for a long time.   How empty she was, how annulled !   The day was wet and melancholy.   She froze. She wanted to warm herself, and rang.   Nobody came.   She dragged herself to the door.   Two armed men opposed her, without a word, barring her way with crossed lances.

Evening darkened in the room.   A man glided in noiselessly, set a great, flaring torch on the table, next to it something wrapped up in cloths, also a scroll, and glided out as noiselessly again.

Margarete grew chillier and chillier, blinked at the flickering torch.   Dragged herself at last to the flame, warmed her stiff hands at the torch.   The scroll consisted of chapters from the Scriptures.   From the wrapped up bundle arose a sweet, sickly odour of decay.   Against her will, as if compelled, she pulled at the wrappings ;   they fell apart.

Threads, brown threads. No, that was a human being's hair. Long, chestnut-coloured. Beneath it someone's brow. This was a severed head. She started back in horror. Chretien's face stared at her out of its glazed eyes. It lay there awry ; the strong nose was sharply outlined under the cloth ; the mouth and chin were still concealed.

Her mouth dried up. She panted, cold with icy sweat, and crouched into the farthest corner, her teeth chattering. Stared at the head, which the flickering light distorted into wayward and absurd shapes. Closed her eyes. The night danced red before her.

She felt compelled to stare at the head again. If only this torch were quenched and all its senseless flickering ! She must put it out. But she could not get up. Was she afraid ? No, she was not afraid. She was the Duchess. What if they should be watching her through a chink in the door ? She stood up. With fixed, unseeing eyes and a strangely stiff gait, she tottered to the table and dashed out the light. Fell in a heap.

She lay for a long time rigid, insensible to everything but the cold, which was almost a comfort to her. Then the darkness began to dance and jerk again. The head jerked to and fro, became infinitely long, infinitely narrow. The keen, tanned cheeks changed to a virulent, greenish yellow, and every hair in that blackened and filthy mop stabbed at her. The dead eyelids opened and snapped together in the night. They were quite without expression, like those of a dead beast. Oh, that it were day ! It would have been better not to put out the torch. Now the night lay upon her heavy and gross as a rough, smothering blanket. She lay in this night as in a coffin, and the dead Chretien kept opening his senseless eyes and snapping them together.

He was ugly.    The ugliest living being was not so ugly as the dead.

No ;  he had not gained much by his readiness to betray her.    Nor had his beautiful wife much joy of him either. With a headless man one could not make much of a show.

He had torn others down with him.    Poor Albert ! Dear, kind, good-natured brother !    He had been so harmless, such a good comrade.    He had certainly only joined in so as not to be a spoil-sport.    Now he was naked and defenceless, defaced by torture, and in prison.    The fresh, merry youth that he had been !

But Chretien was quite different.    The keen, thin, brown face.    She would not stand in fear of his dead face any longer.    She would look at it long and closely, and Chretien would belong to her, not to the beautiful one.    Now day must come, day, so that she should be able to see him !    The stupid ballads Herr von Schenna was so fond of were always singing the glory of night, which belonged to love, and execrating day, beseeching it to tarry. Folly !    Her time was the day.    Come, day !    Give me my dead friend who belongs to me, day !

But when the day crept in and the first grey light fell upon the dead face, she lay unconscious, with closed eyes, in fever.

### § 3

AFTER two months of strict surveillance she obtained permission to go for a few days to the cloister of Frauenchiemsee to see her invalid sister Adelheid.    She found the crippled girl as shy and inaccessible as ever.

Margarete was completely exhausted.    She ate, drank and went about.    Like the nuns she knelt in the chapel of the cloister, received and returned greeting and counter-greeting. She was young and old like the world. She was much older and more experienced than the mild, faded Abbess, and knew far better than her that all was vain and fleeting as wind.

The officious Abbot of Viktring came on a visit. He had never been very friendly towards the Luxemburgers; he regarded King John as a mocker and free-thinker (for that reason, too, the Lord had struck him with blindness); and he was pleased that Margarete had risen against them. In his loquacious style he conversed garrulously with her, and overwhelmed her with quotations; but she remained taciturn.

She sat for hours with the Abbess on the shore of the tiny islet, and looked over the pale, clear lake. The water lapped lazily against the reeds; it was a still, veiled day; far out on the lake a fisher sat in his rude, primitive skiff. The Abbess looked at her attentively and stroked her pudgy hands, now no longer painted. "Young Duchess!" she said in her soft, mild, understanding voice. "Young Duchess!"

"Young?" Margarete asked in response, in a tone too weary even for bitterness. "Young? You are ten times younger than I, reverend lady."

The Abbess said: "A tree is not dead, even when it stands bare and cold in winter." She said further: "There is nothing more painful, but also nothing more sweet, than after being numbed to turn back to life again." She said too: "You must sing with the nuns, young Duchess."

# CHAPTER XI

## § 1

WHEN Margarete returned to Tyrol Castle, Ludwig of Bavaria provided her with a splendid royal escort to the frontier of his territories. The first noblemen of the court of Munich led the magnificent procession ; the banner with the Wittelsbach lion waved in front ; feudal barons and courtiers stood in festive array along the route.

The Duchess thanked the lords automatically, not with her usual stately assurance. She was exhausted, indifferent, far too weary to rack her brains for the reasons which could have made the Emperor accord her such an extraordinary honour.

But the Wittelsbacher had his own good reasons. He had but now been painfully reminded again how palpably the Luxemburg regime hindered his projects. His intention to end by force of arms certain affairs in Lombardy had been baffled by the Bishop of Trent, who had coolly and point blank refused him free passage through his land. The Emperor's irritation had been cleverly utilised by the Tyrolean feudal lords. Burgstall, Villanders and Schenna, who had cunningly held themselves in the background during the first attempt against the Luxemburgers, had not by any means given up their plans. The abortive affair had taught them that it was essential to win over a great power as a guarantor. What was more obvious than to turn to the enemy of the Luxemburger, the Emperor, the Wittelsbacher ? In the last enterprise Margarete had not played a very fortunate part. It was not quite clear what had been the real stone of offence against which the revolt had stumbled. But so much was certain, that it was in particular her strange caprice to bring in Chretien of Taufers that had confused and destroyed their ingeniously-woven plans. At any rate it would be wiser this time to arrange everything over her head, and only to take her into their confidence at the last moment. Her release from Duke Johann, whatever the method of achieving it, must, as things stood now, appear like a deliverance to her.

Accordingly they sent in all secrecy an embassy to the Emperor. They represented to him that the feeling in the country against the Luxemburger was rising ; and said how much they regretted that his Italian expedition had been frustrated by the stiff-necked opposition of the Bishop of Trent, the Bohemian. Then they asked non-committally whether in any circumstances he would be agreeable to a marriage between his son, the Margrave of Brandenburg, and the Duchess of Tyrol. The Wittelsbacher, greedy for territory, tremendously attracted by the prospect of gaining Tyrol, responded as non-committally : he would talk the proposal over with his son, the Margrave ; but as long as the Luxemburgers still held the country all this could be only a dream.

This answer was quite enough for the Tyrolean lords. They knew it would never do for the prudent Wittelsbacher to explain himself more openly. His response was guarded and non-committal, but its kernel was a clear affirmative. The magnificent escort which he put at the service of the Duchess would have been answer enough. The destruction of the Rottenburg fortresses, the torture of Albert, the son of good King Heinrich, the execution of the Lord of Taufers, had stripped the Luxemburgers of all sympathy. The barons stirred up the plot, and pushed it on. And all the time without informing Margarete.

## § 2

AGNES OF FLAVON seemed to be turned to ice when she learned of the breakdown of the revolt. She saw at once what lay behind it. So dreadfully, so heavily, then, the ugly Duchess had struck back ! She stood still in horror, shrank back into herself in animal terror for her life, and thought of flight.

When she saw that no measures were being taken against her, she emerged slowly from her terror, and looked around her. She witnessed the strict measures that were being taken against Margarete and was bewildered. Was the other so stupid that she suffered the affair to turn against her ? That was certainly not the case. She was far too clever for that. It must have happened with her consent. Agnes no longer understood her enemy. Her hate grew with her fear. Certainly Margarete was planning a still more deadly blow, so that she might gloat over her destruction. Nothing happened. Nobody troubled about her. It was comprehensible that they should avoid her, the wife of a felon ignominiously executed. But why had they not confiscated her possessions ? She could not endure the silence and indifference around her. These, and her present anxiety, were only a prelude to her more complete destruction. She decided to go to Tyrol Castle. Above the city gate of Meran she saw the head of her husband, Chretien of Taufers, stuck on a pike. It gaped down at her, greenish-yellow ; the long unbound chestnut hair waved in defiled strands in the warm breeze ; flies sat on the face. She started back. Then her litter, drawn by horses, swung below the head of her executed husband into the town of Meran. Was it a bad omen ? She had no time for sentimentality. She must gather herself together for the interview with Duke Johann. That would not be easy this time. Once already she had knelt before him on the ground in her black mourning dress. Repetitions were stale. And this time the situation was against her.

Johann received her, in fact, with exacerbated mockery. He asked venomously whether she had not brought weapons with her. He would do well to be on his guard. She gazed at him with great, sorrowful eyes, rendered reproachful by this unmerited insult. Weeping bitterly, she deplored that the great-hearted young Duke, who had looked graciously on her once, should now have reason for mistrust. She asseverated that she had had no suspicion of the plots of her traitorous husband. Said it was a good thing he was dead ; for whoever betrayed his prince so insidiously would certainly not think much of betraying his wife as well. Maintained with brazen innocence that she had never loved Chretien, only married him to keep Taufers and to be able to remain near her prince. Johann listened, mistrustful and flattered. She came nearer to him, so near that he felt the odour of her flesh. He growled that he did not believe a word she had said, but that he did not fight with women ; for the time she could keep Taufers. Then while she stood there patient and watchful, with bowed head, he clapped her insultingly, roughly, lewdly, on the neck, turned rudely away and threw at her over his shoulder that he would come soon to Taufers to investigate in person whether revolt was brewing there ; but alone, for he wasn't afraid. With that he laughed loudly and unequivocally, left her standing, and went away to the hunt.

## § 3

MEANWHILE the conspiracy among the nobility had ripened. Castle Tyrol was to be occupied in the absence of Johann. They could not postpone notifying Margarete any longer. Also they had to obtain her consent to a matrimonial alliance with the Wittelsbacher. Herr von Schenna undertook to interview her.

He sat before her, lean, lazy and ungainly, and spoke to her in his weak, uneven voice of all sorts of trivialities. His old and clever eyes slid over her, looked her up and down. He alone guessed the ins and outs of the matter. With great wariness he remarked casually that she must not be alarmed if in the next few days another garrison should take possession of the castle, a strengthened garrison. Even if she should hear cries, uproar, the clashing of arms, she must just stay in her room, for she would not be in any danger. He stopped and waited. She paid no attention. After a while, gently, he enquired if she did not want to know what it was all about. But no, she did not want to know.

He changed his tactics and spoke about Agnes. Every new bereavement became her better. The last time she had been in the castle, everyone had had to remark again that black suited her best. The cunning Schenna saw that Margarete pricked up her ears ; her indifference now was only a mask. He turned aside from the theme, then came back to it again. Yes, Agnes would soon be coming here as a guest and for a long stay. In this respect Duke Johann resembled the good King Heinrich. Margarete rose savagely to the bait. Hitherto Schenna had always shown himself to be her friend. Was this true? She as a prisoner and the other as mistress; here within the same walls, breathing the same air—that was unthinkable. In the name of Christ he must tell her the truth.

Schenna responded bluntly: Yes, Johann had invited Agnes of Flavon to come, and from what he knew of the lady she would certainly accept. As Margarete shut her eyes, with a spasm of agony, he continued comfortingly that there were many ways and means, and began to speak of his plans. She signed to him to stop; she did not want to hear.

She begged Johann earnestly to come to her. Was this true? Did he really intend to do this? She flamed. To turn the castle into a brothel? He replied, yes, he would do it. He would allow himself to go so far. He saw at last that by this means he could strike her, shatter her impassivity, pierce her, gall and torment her. He regarded her with his tiny, venomous wolf's eyes, and puffed himself up. Had she the impudence? Did she forbid him to take this woman? She forbid him? She, with her looks? Margarete gulped, and, commanding herself, replied that she did not beg him to reflect what would be said among the people and at other courts if here, in the castle she had brought him, the castle of her fathers, he kept her in captivity, and the other in magnificence. But she must remind him that his mistress's husband had headed the revolt; that she had been in the plot with him, perhaps as its originator; that it was unthinkable that she had so quickly forgotten her husband's ignominious death. He must beware of her! He laughed spitefully. She need not come to him with such nonsense. She was a jealous

H

fool. He added with a swagger : What if it had been
Agnes who had warned him, and frustrated the intrigues ?

"But it was I, myself, who warned you !" she cried.
"I ! I !"

For a moment an uncomfortable feeling rose up in him ;
he saw her again as she had been, when she had lain
before him like a gorged snake ; he felt himself humiliated by his unsuccessful boast. But he recovered himself
immediately. This was obviously a transparent, sly,
impudent lie, with which she intended to bluff him.

"You can catch your Tyrolean yokels, perhaps, in such
a clumsy trap, but not me !" he said with assumed contemptuous frigidity. And, working himself up higher :
"So that brings it home at last ?  That cuts to the quick,
does it ?  The beauty must be driven out of the house ?
It hurts that she should come here ?  Just for that she'll
come !  Just for that she'll stay !  I will ride out with her !
I will ride to the hunt with her !  I will ride to Meran,
Bozen, Trent with her !  I'll teach you, you repulsive,
hideous, venomous, filthy hag !"

She sat on, stiff but resolute, after he had gone. She
had spoken so frankly and honourably, had flung open once
more the door between him and her. Anyone not deaf and
vile must have understood. He himself had chosen.

Next day Herr von Schenna came again. He laid before
her a brief letter to the Emperor, commending herself to
his protection, and sanctioning the arrangements made by her
barons. She signed it without hesitation. Schenna divulged
to her further, briefly and succinctly, that next day, when
Johann was at the chase, the castle would be occupied by
the barons' troops, and Johann refused entry. She herself
could impart the news to him if on his return he asked for

admission. They would guard against putting themselves
in the wrong by laying hands on him. They would only
deny him any shelter in the country. If in consequence
Johann forsook the country, concluded Schenna smilingly,
nobody would hinder him. For the rest, he added in a tone
of friendly devotion, this time everything was provided for.
Even if the Duke should be warned, nothing could miscarry.
He took the signed letter, bowed, and walked away with his
ungainly, unequal, hurried gait.

§ 3

NEXT day, a Friday, Johann went to hunt with a small
retinue. The weather—it was the beginning of November
—promised to be clear and bright, but presently mist came
up, along with a damp, disagreeable wind. The Duke was
in a peevish temper ; what Margarete had said to him about
Agnes had not been so easy to digest after all. Moreover,
his favourite falcon, a beautiful grey-white Norwegian
gerfalcon, had flown off, scared away by a larger bird of
prey. Now the Duke wrangled with his falconer, scolded
and screamed.

In consequence he broke up the hunt early and returned
home towards evening. He found the drawbridge up, the
gate barred. Stood in astonishment, then became furious
and cursed. Blew his horn. The sentry appeared at the
watch-tower and said he had no order to admit the gentleman. The Duke grew purple, and bellowed obscene curses
at the man. Suddenly Margarete appeared on the battle-
ment of one of the towers. She cried in her warm, deep
voice that the Prince of Luxemburg need not shout any
longer, there was no room for him there ; he must find
shelter somewhere else. At Taufers, for instance. Johann

took aim at her.    She was gone before he could unloose his arrow.

He stood there now, raging and ridiculous in his hunting attire, before the barred gate.    His attendants whispered among themselves.  ᐧ A cold wind blew ; it rained.    A few of his Bohemian followers out of the  castle crept up and related despondently and with embarrassment that the castle was occupied by an immense number of fully-armed Tyroleans, who had flung them out.

The Duke remained awhile longer before the raised drawbridge, railing vilely at the poltroonery of his followers. From the castle came laughter and ribald verses :

> " Who stands at the gate ?    Who flaps in the wind ?
> A beggar ?    A Jew ?    A vagabond hind ?
>     Oh, it's only the Count of Tyrol."

At last Johann departed cursing towards Zenoberg.    The same there.    To Greifenstein.    The same there.    It was almost midnight already.    He was weary to death, hoarse with screaming and raging, broken up.    Freezing and wretched, he passed the night in the open.

The dawn whitened faintly.    Dirty, unslept, the Duke climbed on his horse ;  his limbs pained him, his belly was hollow with hunger.    He had now only six of his followers with him ;  the others had quietly deserted.

It rained without stopping.    His attendants told him that the people showed great joy at what had happened, laughed, exulted, rejoiced, jeered.    Those verses buzzed like troublesome insects about his ears.

> " A beggar ?    A Jew ?    A vagabond hind ?
>     Oh, it's only the Count of Tyrol."

Taking by-paths he slunk to the castles of a few noblemen who lay under special obligation to him. The lords were not at home ; the castellans had no instructions ; closed doors. There were now only four of his people with him.

He wandered aimlessly through vineyards and woods. Rain, always rain. He believed he was pursued, surrounded. On the battlefield he had never known fear ; its nauseous breath crept over him now. He would not be hunted and killed like a mad dog, by a peasant or a stinking burgher ! He struck higher into the mountains. Came at last to a remote castle of Tägen of Villanders. The shrewd, cautious baron wanted, if possible, to maintain friendly relations even with the Luxemburgers, and took him in. But he could only venture to give him the respite of a lodging for a very short time, and in secrecy. Johann passed for these few days as an obscure knight Ekkehard, and did not let himself be seen. But there, too, scraps of that couplet cracked about his ears : " A vagabond hind ? Oh, it's only the Count of Tyrol ! " He let himself out during the night, trembling ; now only two servants followed him. He was still in his hunting suit. Filthy, stinking with sweat, on his overdriven, exhausted horse, which jibbed at the boggy by-paths and could not go farther, he slunk in this direction and that through his country. If only at least this cursed rain would stop ! He sold the jewels that he had with him, his weapons, his hunting-horn, at last his horse as well.

Feverish, exhausted, quite alone, he reached the Patriarch-ate of Aquileia. Came to Friuli, to the Palace of the Patriarch. The servants roared with laughter when this filthy tatter-demalion avouched that he was the Duke of Carinthia, Count of Tyrol, grandson of the Roman Emperor. The Patriarch, ever the enemy of the Tyrolean feudal lords, and owing all his power to Luxemburg, received him with deep respect and folded him in his arms.    After some days the exhausted and disordered Prince slowly came to himself. He gnashed his teeth, wove spiteful plans, brewed poison, and spat curses and menaces at the country from which his wife had driven him out.

# BOOK TWO

# CHAPTER I

In Munich the Emperor Ludwig walked up and down with his hand on the shoulder of his son, the Margrave, the Brandenburger. The Margrave was peevish and out of humour, and the Emperor spoke persuasively and kindly. Although he was now only twenty-five, the Brandenburger looked very mature, with a small blonde moustache and hard, grey-blue, somewhat piercing eyes in a tanned lean face ; he had the massive neck of the Wittelsbachers, and was tall and sinewy. But the heavy, uncouth Emperor overtopped him perceptibly. Through the pictured panes came the wan light of the snowy day. As they went to and fro, the Emperor with his arm round the shoulders of his son seemed to be dragging the hesitating, resistant youth after him.

No, no ! He could not and he would not ! He simply could not bring himself to marry the Duchess Margarete. He had five years of married life behind him already with Elisabeth, the Danish princess. She had been a modest creature, somewhat arid, perhaps. She was dead now ; God give her eternal rest. And now he would like to spend three or four years without a wife ; attend to his affairs in Brandenburg, encourage agriculture and municipal activities, and harry the Wends. Wed this Tyrolean Margarete who had got rid of her husband in such a curious way ? That monstrous creature ? No, thanks ! His royal father would always find him willing to serve him. But marry Margarete—no !

The Emperor turned his great, staring, blue eyes upon his son. His opposition did not surprise him, did not irritate him. It was hardly a pleasure to marry the Tyrolean. In the same situation he would have objected too. But he knew that his Ludwig was a good son and a sensible prince who understood that marriage was the most important of political expedients. An opportunity like this would not occur again. If the House of Wittelsbach had the Tyrol, then the realm would be invulnerable, and Wittelsbach would reign from the North Sea to the Adriatic. He understood quite well that Ludwig would have preferred to take a breathing space, and to remain a widower for a few years. But he was a prince and a Wittelsbacher. He could not allow himself such comforts.

The morose Margrave continued to bring up peevish objections. Apart from the fact that this Margarete and all about her went deeply and fundamentally against his grain, it was certain that the Pope would not dissolve her marriage with the Luxemburger. As one man the whole of Christendom would cry out, scandalised, if he wedded the wife of another. The Emperor responded coolly that all his life he had had to put up with bans and interdicts, he could not let his son dispense with them. A Wittelsbacher, unfortunately, could not make his way without them.

The Margrave shook off his father, leant against the table in vexation of spirit, and stroked mechanically his tiny moustache. The Danish Elisabeth had been no Helen ; a prince could not woo mere beauty of form ; he knew that. But this Margarete ! The clumsy figure ! " Carinthia ! " said the Emperor. The underhung jaw ! " Tyrol ! "

said the Emperor. The hanging cheeks ! The slanting, prominent teeth ! " Trent ! Brixen ! " said the Emperor.

Through Munich meanwhile rode the Tyrolean barons, who were conducting the negotiations. It was a magnificent embassy, at its head the first noblemen of the country, Burgstall, Villanders, Schenna, Eckehard of Trostberg. They were in no hurry, they were full of confidence, and regarded appreciatively and at leisure the clear, bright town, which under Ludwig had risen so fast, and the new commodious palace which he had built for himself. The Wittelsbachers were circumspect, firm princes. Only, one had to entrench oneself as securely as possible to keep them from going too far. The Tyroleans did this ; had all their bonds, charters and privileges confirmed ; raked together and seized what they could ; extorted for themselves the right of veto and control over all administrative measures. Vexed and despairing, the Brandenburger burst out : what could he do with a sovereignty that was so cribbed, cabined, and confined on every side ? The Emperor looked him full and fair in the eyes. " First put on the coat. If it is too long, you can always cut it to your measure afterwards."

After Candlemas, in mid-winter, under a radiant clear blue sky, the jingling, splendid train of the Wittelsbachers rode on horseback through the dazzling white mountains to the Castle of Tyrol. The snow crackled, weapons rattled, the trappings of gold and silver tinkled. Softly through the smoking, icy air went the long, gay procession, horses, sumpter-mules, litters, men. The Emperor in radiant spirits ; his son Ludwig, the Margrave, the Brandenburger, sulky, hesitating, but already half-tempted by the spaciousness and variety of the country ; his younger brother Stephan. Duke Konrad of Teck, the rich Swabian nobleman, the most intimate friend of the Brandenburger, gloomy, fanatical, a stern worker, an unquestioning supporter of the Wittelsbachs. The Tyrolean barons ; countless Bavarian, Swabian, Flemish and Brandenburg noblemen. The bishops of Freising, Regensburg, Augsburg. The two great theologians whom the Kaiser had attracted to his court : William of Occam and Marsilius of Padua.

During the whole journey the Emperor kept these two ecclesiastics next to him. The news of the proposed marriage of the Brandenburger with Margarete had scandalised all Europe. Not only because Margarete was the wife of another man ; but also because on the side of her grandmother, Elisabeth, she was related to the Brandenburger at the third remove. The Pope had no intention of freeing the Duchess from this obstacle to the marriage ; on the contrary he had immediately menaced her with ban and interdict. The people heard this threat with anxiety and deep uneasiness. The Emperor, however, was absolutely resolved not to give way to the Papal Court. Against the Pope he set his theologians. For himself the Emperor was without much culture and did not even speak Latin ; but he had a deep abysmal reverence for learning. He honestly deplored that his Bavarians were so dense and dull that they simply were not adapted to study. Ah, everywhere in the world, except in Bavaria alone, the voices of his great scholars, William of Occam and Marsilius of Padua, whom he had drawn to his court, could find an echo.

He was pious, he had a conscience, from his heart he revered the wise men, believed in them, and was convinced of their knowledge of God. So, staring at his theologians with his great blue eyes, he had propounded the question whether the objections of the Pope were valid.

Marsilius and William had worked out an argument to the effect that in consequence of the impotence of the husband, the marriage of Margarete with Johann the Luxemburger had never *de facto* been consummated ; thus it did not stand, and was invalid. After this, urgently implored by the Emperor, the Bishop of Freising, Ludwig of Chamstein, declared himself ready to pronounce the divorce between Margarete and Johann. For this reason, then, the Bavarian bishops accompanied the expedition over the Alps. Their mission seemed to them extremely perilous ; they themselves, very daring and important They had a strained look on their faces and sweated.

The Brandenburger rode beside Konrad of Teck. The country interested him more and more ; technical questions of administration too. Passionate economist that he was, he had no eye for the scenery or the odd customs of the people, and spoke with his hard, clear voice only of agriculture, possibilities of settlement on the soil, trade routes, the division of districts, methods of taxation. Whether Brandenburg or Tyrol—to him land was nothing more than a subject for administration. Everywhere here was rot and decay. He would assume control with a stern, capable, salutary hand.

Herr von Schenna rode beside William of Occam. Before them—the road mounted gently—towered the gigantic back and the powerful neck of the Emperor. The two noblemen spoke of him. The learned, much-travelled theologian lauded, not without a certain passion, the Emperor's leanings towards the ideal, his reverence for culture, the gay appearance of the city of Munich, the establishment of the Knightly Order of Ettal after the model of Wolfram's Parsifal. The more keen-sighted Herr von Schenna would not admit this, however ; he saw in the Wittelsbacher a much more modern type. The Emperor loved the towns more than the castles, the merchant more than the soldier, treaties more than wars, considered profit more than chivalry. Certainly he had romantic fits still ; but they were due to his traditions, not the expression of his true nature. In spite of his changeableness, King John, the Luxemburger, was much more conservative, was a knight of the old school, an adventurer. The Emperor, on the other hand, was much more like the city burghers ; he was a man of his day, a bargainer. For that reason the Luxemburger would, indeed, be able to grasp more, but he would keep less, and in the long run the Emperor would triumph ; for he was a child of his time. The theologian listened critically and unwillingly to this adroit, accurate and able summary. They saw the Wittelsbacher's broad, massive back in front of them. They both thought what neither said ; he would always work for his own advantage and for that alone, would always regard himself and the world outside frankly with his great eyes, and would always square justice, morality and the will of God with his own advantage, in all honour and with conviction.

They passed the night in Sterzing and climbed up the Jaufen Pass next day in clear, piercing, radiant frost. They had already the crest behind them and were descending into the Passeier. Here the Bishop of Freising's horse stumbled, shied, and flung its rider over its head. Very unluckily the Bishop was thrown against a rock, and broke his neck. There he lay, the active little man, on the frozen snow, under the gay, clear sky.

In defiance of the Pope's candidate he had occupied the bishop's throne at Freising ; in defiance of the Pope's will he had been about to dissolve the holy sacrament of marriage ;

now he lay yellow and stiff and dead. The gay, noisy, jingling procession came to a standstill. "The judgment of God!" someone whispered; overcome with horror the lords stood round the corpse. They wrapped the dead man in cloaks and brought him with them on a bier to Meran. Very quietly the important little man entered the city where he had intended to do the most daring and perilous deed of his life. The horror-stricken bishops of Augsburg and Regensburg refused the Emperor's request that now they should dissolve Margarete's first marriage.

All the same, the Emperor's good spirits broke out again as soon as he drew into Castle Tyrol. Avignon was far away; Benedict might launch impotent curses against him if he liked. They were mere words; he had the country. Where was another prince in Christendom as mighty as he? He had united the two Bavarias; he had Brandenburg, had the secure reversion of Holland, Friesland, Zeeland, Hainault, and now to boot the mountain land, the beautiful, ancient, rich, renowned land. Behind it lay Italy, dismembered, and powerless. Now that he was master of the high Alps, he had it in the hollow of his hand. Beautiful Castle Tyrol! Good, strong Castle Tyrol!

The noblemen in the antechamber listened in astonishment to the Emperor within singing in a loud, clear voice. "He sings songs like King David before the ark of the Covenant!" said the Bishop of Augsburg. But the Emperor, alone in his chamber, looked out on the white, clear country, smacked his thigh, and sang merry, coarse, bawdy little songs, such as they sang in the public-houses in his Bavarian villages.

## § 2

Two days later the Emperor himself solemnised the wedding
of Margrave Ludwig and Duchess Margarete, to the
great chagrin of the country and of all Europe.    On the
next day, in the city of Meran, he invested the newly-
married pair with the titles of Carinthia and Tyrol.    He had
donned his imperial regalia.    Konrad of Teck carried the
imperial sword, Arnold of Massenhausen the sceptre, the
Lord of Krauss the orb.    Margarete was heavy with pomp,
her robes stood out around her, stiff and loaded with jewels,
and she gazed rigid and motionless straight in front of her.

## § 3

In the Castle of Vienna sat Albert the Lame and John of
Bohemia in protracted conference.    The Wittelsbacher's
acquisition of Tyrol had completely united the Luxemburger
and the Habsburger again.    The Emperor had not only
stolen Tyrol, he had also invested his son quite shamelessly
with Carinthia, where the Habsburger sat fast, and which
the Emperor himself had helped him to acquire.    The
princes were less amazed and incensed over the Wittelsbacher's impudence than over his folly.

Albert had taken every precaution to defend his Carinthia
effectually.    The lame prince had even undergone the complicated rites of the Carinthian investiture, which were
doubly wearisome for him ; he was concerned at all costs
to assure his popularity.

The blind Luxemburger had greater imagination and
more comprehensive plans.    This Tyrol, this lovely fruit
which the bold, rude Wittelsbacher had plucked, bore a worm

at its heart.    The lame Albert with his rather untidy clothes and hair gazed with interest, with a faint, reluctant admiration at the blind King, who, upright, elegant and faultlessly dressed, sat before him, and softly and warily outlined his incredible and daring plans.    No, the Emperor would not have much joy of his new country.    He, John, was at heart an accommodating man.    Hitherto he had opposed Ludwig when he had had to, when his interests demanded it, but without passion or hatred.    From now on it would be different.    He was filled to overflowing with disgust and indignation at this last clumsy, shabby trick, at such stupidly arrogant greed and impudence, wearing a mask of hypocrisy before itself and the world.    The resentment of the cavalier and adventurer against the small huckster flamed out.

The new Pope, Clement VI, no theorist such as the deceased Benedict had been, but a man of the world, a splendid prince and ruler and politician, was on terms of great intimacy with himself and his son Karl, was Karl's tutor and bosom friend.    The Brandenburger's marriage had excited ill-will on all sides against the Emperor.    If the new Pope were now to launch from every pulpit an edict of excommunication against the Emperor, the curse would not be taken merely as a political move, but would receive approval and hearty applause from the whole of Christendom. Potentates, cities and peoples would renounce the Wittelsbacher; already they had refused allegiance.    Then if, with the support of Avignon, his son Karl should be elected Roman Emperor, he, John, could form with him an invincible league against Ludwig.

Albert rubbed mechanically his ill-shaven cheeks and listened attentively to the other's disquisition.    These were plans with a more solid foundation than most of the Luxem-

I

burger's ; but they meant violence, unavoidable war. He, Albert, was not willing to involve himself. He was no longer young ; he had been taught wisdom by experience ; and he only drew the sword in the last resort.

So they sat together, the two powerful princes who ruled over more than half of Central Europe ; the blind prince pressed the lame as far as he could, but he could only wring a defensive alliance from him.

Then, when the conference was at an end, John stretched himself, rose to go, and began to grope blindly along the wall ; but he could not find the door. Albert could tell him well enough where it was, but on account of his lameness was unable to go to his aid. At that they both laughed long and heartily, until one of the attendants outside opened the door at last.

## § 4

TERRIBLE calamities swept over the mountain country, the vengeance of God because the Duchess had so grossly violated the sacrament of marriage. " The plagues of Egypt ! " cried the Pope's supporters over all Europe. " The plagues of Egypt ! " repeated the blenching people, sighing, beating their breasts and fasting.

First as a renewed punishment for the sins of mankind the windows of heaven were opened, a second deluge descended.

" Alas, Deucalion's day returns ; Aquarius drowns us in water,"

quoted Abbot Johannes of Viktring from an old Latinist. As if the massed rivers of Europe had been poured out over the land, trees, meadows, villages and human beings were torn from their bearings ; the Inn bore down with it bridges, towers and houses ; the lower valley of the Adige resembled a lake ; from Neumarkt people went by ship down to the farms which lay below Tramin.

In the same year, in rapid succession, great fires destroyed the cities of Meran, Innsbruck and Neumarkt.

But the strangest and most terrible calamity of all, paralysing the people with fear, was the gigantic swarm of locusts which in this summer ravaged the country. They came from the East. After they had eaten bare Hungary, Poland, Bohemia, Moravia, Austria, Bavaria and Lombardy, they spread themselves over the fertile Tyrol. They flew so thick that they hid the sun. They flew both day and night, and yet they took twenty-seven days to follow up the course of the Adige.

The horrified people bore holy images through the streets, prayed and stretched their hands towards Heaven. The priests of Kaltern had the vermin condemned by a formal declaration of an ecclesiastical jury, and excommunicated them from the pulpit. They were gigantic in size, had teeth like glittering precious stones, and the housewives ornamented their dresses with them. The swarms that devastated the valley of the Inn were doubly remarkable. The leaders with a few of the rest flew about a day's journey in front of the host and sought the places that would be most suitable for the whole swarm. They broke up again into squadrons with almost military discipline. They devoured bush and tree, they devoured every green thing, they devoured the green blade, the corn, the millet, root and stalk. The earth was black and grey as if withered up, when at last they flew away.

## CHAPTER II

### § 1

The Duchess Margarete journeyed over the Arlberg. In St. Anton a little girl of eleven or twelve stood with her mother among the gaping crowd. As the procession went past the child cried eagerly and importantly : " Mother ! Mother ! which is Her Grace the Duchess ? The long, thin one or the other, the Maultasch ? " *

The mother, a stout, comfortable young woman, grinned, reddened, and aimed a blow at the child : " Will you shut your meat-trap, you little brat ? "

The people around laughed, the child blubbered, the expression caught on. It flew through the country, it flew farther ; soon the ugly Duchess was known to all Christendom only as the Maultasch. Margarete heard of it and wore the nickname with a certain quiet, bitter deliberation. What should her new castle be called ? Bruneck ? Neugrafenburg ? She called it Castle Maultasch.

### § 2

Margrave Ludwig sat with his friend, Duke Konrad of Teck, over bills and receipts. The stiff young Margrave gave a dry summary of facts and figures ; the massive,

* Translators' Note.—We have thought it best to leave this well-nigh untranslatable word in the original. " *Maul* " means " maw " or " muzzle "; " *tasch, tasche* " means " sack, bag, pouch." " *Maultasch* " might be rendered as " sack-mouth."

126

soldierly, somewhat older Duke of Teck listened attentively. He was in his armour and made no movement ; whereas in spite of his businesslike lucidity the Margrave could not refrain from striking the table and the rustling papers. His firm, lean face with the hard, lustreless blue eyes, the brown, weather-beaten skin, rather sparse, fair hair and fair moustache cut short in defiance of the fashion, was angry and exasperated. He had always held the Tyrolean barons to be a malignant, treacherous rabble. But that they should dare to cheat him so openly and impudently under his very nose, that they should snugly and ingenuously stick in their pockets not a half merely, but nine-tenths of his revenues, and in their accounts hardly take the pains to conceal it ; this was an arrogance of greed that he had not expected. Moreover, the barons had strengthened their position beforehand. Amnesty was assured them for their administrative offences ; further, they could not be controlled except by the native nobility, and as they were all related by blood this control was only a matter of form.

The massive, beardless, soldierly Konrad of Teck let the Margrave finish what he had to say. Then he said : " Act ! Agreements, amnesties ; these are only the gilt on the gingerbread. Lay one of them by the heels. Let the others protest and exclaim. When they see that it's no use, they'll soon become tractable."

With a half-smile the Margrave pushed a document over to his friend ; a warrant for the arrest of Volkmar of Burgstall. But it was not signed. " My father certainly would not have done it," he said. " God only knows how badly it may turn out. I have no security."

Konrad of Teck looked at him out of his dull brown eyes and growled : " Then get yourself a security."

Ludwig returned his glance, rang, and commanded :
" Her Grace the Duchess."

The two men remained silent until Margarete came.
Ludwig had no secrets from his friend, who knew well
enough how things stood between him and Margarete. It
had come about that out of their mistrust and aversion a cool,
friendly comradeship had slowly grown up. Margarete was
clever, was not importunate, and neither gave nor asked
for sentimentality. This seemed very right and proper to
the Wittelsbacher ; and this stiff and prosaic relationship
was the only kind where a man was concerned that in these
years did not get on Margarete's nerves. He accustomed
himself gradually to her strange numbness and immobility
as to her ugliness, and there was no contemptuous undertone
in his words when sometimes in conversation with Konrad
he called Margarete the Maultasch, just as the whole
country did. Some time passed before she came, for she
never appeared except in ducal pomp. She wore a dress of
a heavy, brown material, with much gold on it ; her face
stiff and masklike with rouge and powder, her hands painted
too. The Margrave laid the document before her, then
indicated in a few words how complete the case was
against Volkmar of Burgstall. Margarete saw before her the
dull, heavy Volkmar, naked, brutal greed on his face. With
his clumsy hand he had struck wherever he could ; in the
struggle against the Luxemburger he had put young Rottenburg and her merry, harmless brother Albert in the forefront
and concealed himself, the malicious coward, in some cellar-
like, dingy corner of his castle. Under the rouge her face
remained stiff and expressionless. " Arrest him ! " she said.
Even the inflexible Konrad of Teck looked up surprised.
" You are a gallant woman, Your Grace ! " he said.

" Since that is your advice, Margarete," said the Brandenburger, " your countrymen will have to bear with it peacefully if I follow it." He begged her also to sign the warrant of arrest. She did so.

Burgrave Volkmar was arrested and tried. These proceedings against the first aristocrat in the country caused an immense sensation. The barons, each trembling for himself, closed their ranks ; from the south Nikolaus, Bishop of Trent, stirred up trouble, and from the west the Bishop of Chur. Konrad of Teck, who had charge of the prisoner, would not retreat one step. Impeachment, confiscation of property, judicial examination, torture. It did not come to a verdict. Before that the Burgrave died unexpectedly in prison. The country muttered, threatened to rebel, did not dare, knuckled under, and was silent.

Margarete was sitting at her toilette table when she received the news of Volkmar's sudden death. Fraülein von Rottenburg, who was combing her hair, drew a shivering breath, trembled, and let the comb fall. " Go on," said Margarete, and her full, deep voice was calm and without a tremor.

§ 3

THE Duchess looked out from the loggia of Schenna Castle at the sunlit land. Jakob of Schenna sat opposite her. On the walls beside their heads stalked the gaily-pictured knights.

It did her good to hear Schenna's tired, clever voice. His clear, succinct sentences were like a warm bath. The Margrave had wished to draw him into his service. But Herr von Schenna had left the diplomatic dignities, the golden chains of honour, to his brothers, Petermann and Estlein ; he himself was ever ready to advise ; but he would not accept a post.

He was speaking of the Margrave, as often before. " No,"
he said, pointing to the pictured knights, " things like that
mean nothing to him.    When he sees a forest he does not
think of the dragon that may be there, nor of the lady kept
imprisoned by a giant, who must be delivered.    He considers
the value of the wood in the forest, and whether it would
repay him to send it to the nearest town to encourage house-
building.    The Margrave has never seen the gnomes ;
they will not return, either, while he reigns.    Nor will he
try to rival King John.    He will not lay much weight on
winning in the tournaments eighteen or twenty times a year,
or having the most fashionable armour, or being in Paris as
often as he can.    But against that, he will see that his name
does not appear often in the correspondence of Messer
Artese of Florence, that the tradespeople are able to come
and go with their goods in security, and that firm and honest
magistrates sit in the towns."

He stuck to his favourite theme.    The old days were
gone.    Knighthood and knightly customs had become cheap
and shoddy.    One could not any longer simply march out
into the world and flourish one's sword ; the police
would come up.    Just now, in this colourless age, neither
honour nor property was to be won by adventure.    Perhaps
in earlier days life had been more beautiful, gayer, more
honourable.    But the world had become more complicated.    The castle had been replaced by the town, the
powerful individual by the organisation.    When the knight-
errant asked for meat and drink and shelter, zounds, they
demanded payment from him !    The future did not belong
to him, but to the burgher ; it was not to be won by arms,
but by goods and money.    Knights like King John might
sweep ever so splendidly over the earth ; but what they did

would have no durability.    The infinitesimal, slow, painful, calculating works of the towns—these had durability.    They built small, they built anxiously, but they built cell by cell, set stone on stone, without stopping.

Margarete was convinced of the truth of these axioms. Had she not experienced it profoundly and terribly in herself ? What was love ?    What was adventure ?    They hollowed you out, ground you down, made you empty and sore. Thoughts which she had had earlier took deeper hold on her, became essential, mingled with her blood.    Her ugliness was a gift, the finger-post by which God showed her the right way.    Knight-errantry, adventure, these were bright-hued bubbles, illusion.    Her task was to build for the future. Cities, the trades and handicrafts, good roads, law and order. Her business was not with festivals and pilgrimages and love ; her work lay in peaceful and sober politics.

These axioms appealed strongly to the Margrave.    She knew well enough, she felt, she divined, how narrow and pedantic he was.    But she respected his capability and dependableness, was accustomed to it as to something friendly, hard to give up.    The couple were much together; ate together, slept together, worked together.    There was a good understanding between him and her.    Their thoughts were knit together.    Margarete was the moving spirit, but her ascendancy was so unnoticeable that one could not distinguish who was the leader and who the led.    Often in conversation with Konrad of Teck the Margrave would say appreciatively : " My wife, you know, the Maultasch."    Through all this Margarete remained closed up within herself ; her icy exterior could not be pierced ; she treated him with great and honourable politeness, but that was all.

In the second year of her marriage Margarete became

pregnant.  Her nature became more free now, her deep voice sounded warmer ;  but that remoteness and rigidity never quite fell from her.  She remained free from violent or excessive desires, calm, without the stronger emotions. She saw that the child, a girl, was neither beautiful nor ugly. It had the hard, angular brow of the father, and, thank God, his mouth and not hers.  She tended the child carefully, maternally, conscientiously, but without affection.

§ 4

THE Pope drew the arm of the young Margrave Karl of Moravia-Luxemburg within his own, and led the prince up and down the luxurious room, talking enthusiastically and persuasively.  Outside, in the white town of Avignon, burned a clear, bright sun.  In the Papal palace it was pleasantly dark, not too hot.  The sixth Clement with his dark, strong, strikingly typical face, the contours emphasised by the bluish shadows made by shaving, had a tender, paternal feeling for the young prince, his apt pupil.  Karl had predicted the Tiara for him :  he predicted the crown of the Holy Roman Empire for Karl.

Yes, and now it had come almost to that.  The Wittelsbacher, the clumsy bear, had snatched too greedily at every booty.  His last bite, Tyrol, was too big for him ;  he would choke on it, he would suffocate.  However cautiously and uneasily the Electors and the cities of the Empire might kick against the control of the Curia, yet the evil odour that went up from the Tyrolean business stank so much in everybody's nostrils that they could hardly remain faithful to the person of the usurper, Ludwig of Bavaria.  Yes, now he had come creeping here, the Wittelsbacher.  He had whined humbly before the Papal stool, acknowledged the long inventory of his crimes, pledged his submission. Clement smiled, and clasped his young pupil more firmly round the shoulder. The Bavarian had come too late. Already he, Clement, had pronounced excommunication on him in solemn conclave ; already he had instructed the Electoral College to proceed to the election of a new Emperor. When his dear pupil Karl of Luxemburg journeyed to the Rhine to-morrow, to Rhense, for the election, he would take with him the certainty that the Pope had done everything he could by means of his blessing and his curse to make true his prophecy regarding the Imperial crown.

A few days later, in fact, the majority of the Electors gave their votes for the Luxemburger. Of the five princes who voted for him the first was his father, the second his uncle, the third an archbishop without bishopric or land, the fourth and fifth were bought with much money.

After the president of the college, the Archbishop Baldwin of Trèves, had announced the result of the vote, Karl received the embraces of his father and the good wishes of the Electors, and despatched an express courier to the Pope. Then, in private, the long, lanky man stretched his arms and breathed freely. Chosen German King, presently Roman Emperor. He was not like his blind father, the knight-errant. He would not glitter merely, and throw everything away as soon as he had gathered it together. He would have, hold, own. But he was not like the slow, pedantic, bourgeois Bavarian either. Castle *and* town, that was it ; soldiering *and* administration. Not to amass territories merely : what was great about that ? But to cultivate them, to knead them into shape. Church, art, science, town-building. Gather, amass, foster. Gather and foster them all : lands, cities, titles, castles, scholars,

relics, objects of art.  Was he vain ?  Was he avaricious ?
No :  this was his long thought-out, clearly-recognised duty
as a prince.  The lean, sinewy gentleman seated himself at
the writing-table.  He noted definite lines of action, sketched
out a scheme, a canon for his administration.  Arranged
scientifically duties, exigencies, plans.  Classified them ;
number one, two, three.  Worked for many hours, deep into
the night.

He read over what he had written.  Did not a little touch
of vanity cling to all of it still ?  He was a pious man ; vanity
was a sin.  He would atone.  He collected relics passionately :
thorns out of Christ's crown, robes, skulls and arms of saints.
Someone in Pavia had offered him the remains of the holy
St. Vitus.  The saint was much too dear.  In expiation he
would buy these relics now, although he was being cheated.

§ 5

A TINY, fat, fidgety man stood before Margarete.  He was
very obsequious, and spoke in a guttural voice.  His name
was Mendel Hirsch, and he was a Jew.  During the persecution of the Brothers Armleder he had fled from Bavarian
soil to Regensburg, where the burgesses had protected him.
Out of the hundred and twenty-seven communities in
which the Jews had been butchered at this time, he was one
of the few people who had escaped.  Now he carried
a safe-conduct from the E peror, and for prudence one too
from the rival Emperor Karl.

The Duchess had never seen a living Jew at close quarters.
Attentive, slightly repelled, she regarded the thickset man,
who in his brown cloak and peaked hat strutted up and down,
pouring out a stream of guttural words, striking droll atti-
tudes.  So this was how they looked, these people who

defiled the sacrament and cruelly tortured innocent children :
the race who were cursed by God and who had crucified God.
She had often heard of the strange, uncanny people, and had
not long ago—on the occasion of the last Jewish massacre—
discussed them exhaustively with Abbot Johannes of Viktring. He had neither approved nor condemned the persecutions. That ancient curse which their own lips had
called down was being fulfilled on this stricken people.
" His blood be on us and on our children ! " The Abbot
shrugged his shoulders, and cited an ancient classic :

" Wretch that I am, my fears are great, for great my
offences."

Margarete found this solution a little too simple. Of
course a man who fanned one of these persecutions into flame
might be acting from zeal in the cause of God. Perhaps. It
was certain that he gained much by it. For was there a more
approved way of getting rid of Jewish creditors than by
killing them ? Why, if it was expedient and fitting to
exterminate them, did just the wisest princes, spiritual and
temporal, use their influence in favour of them ? The laws
of Friedrich II of Hohenstaufen, the bulls of the fourth
Innocent, betrayed an outlook very different from the valiant
abbot's. And the reigning Pope Clement—he was her
enemy, but diabolically clever. Why did he stand in front
of them so solidly and protectingly with his bulls and severe
ordinances ?

She looked at the little man who gesticulated restlessly
before her. He told of the sufferings he had gone through.
How they had driven his people into their houses of worship
and burned them, how they had stuck others in sacks weighed

down with stones and miserably drowned them in the Rhine, how they had mutilated, tortured and strangled them, defiled women before the eyes of their pinioned husbands, and hung their children, spitted on spears, like flags, out of the windows of burning houses.    He related this hurriedly, with many a graphic detail and gesture.    His vivid guttural words stumbled over one another ; he smiled apologetically, was accusing, resigned, strewed his narrative with jesting phrases, called on God, ran his fingers nervously through his discoloured beard, shook his head.    The Duchess heard him in silence : Herr von Schenna slouched in a corner, awkward and ungainly, and regarded attentively the zealous, odd-looking little man.    Mendel Hirsch begged to be allowed to settle in Bozen.    He was on his way to Leghorn to some of his co-religionists.    But just now at the sight of the flourishing cities and markets of Tyrol it had occurred to him that here was a better and newer field.    " The carrying trade, Your Grace ! " he said.    " The carrying trade !  The fairs !  The markets !  The great routes from Lombardy to Germany, and from the Slavonic countries to the Roman used to pass through here.    Why should Trent, Bozen, Riva, Hall, Innsbruck, Sterzing and Meran be less than Augsburg and Strassburg ? "    The Bishops of Brixen and Trent were already inclined to give protection and privileges to the Jews.    With the gracious permission of the Princess he would soon make trade flourish here.    Bring money into the country, much money, big money.    He could dispose of capital to any extent they liked.    Gave more liberal terms than the gentlemen in Venice and Florence.    He would export wine, oil, wood : import silk, furs, swords, Spanish wool, jewels, Moorish gold-work ; pelts from the Eastern Slavonic states, above all, slaves, too.    They were not needed

here on the land ?   There were sufficient serfs ?   No ?
No.   But then glass, that would be needed, Sicilian
glass ;   he had an excellent connection.   And coloured
fabrics, of course, would be needed.   And cinnamon, pepper,
spices.   He would soon arrange all that.   They had only
to let him arrange it all.

Margarete said she would take his request into consideration.   When he was gone she talked it over with Schenna.
He was greatly attracted by the Jew's projects.   Of course
they should let him settle, and try to keep him.   He was of
the new age ;   he would bring life into the country.   At the
tournament, certainly, Herr Mendel Hirsch would not
make much of a figure ;   the barons, even the burghers,
would frown on him.   But just because of their lazy
arrogance the indolent populace should have this mobile
flea of a man dropped down their back.

So the Jew Mendel Hirsch came to Bozen.   He came
with a swarm of sons, daughters, sons-in-law, daughters-in-
law, grandchildren ;   there were three babes at the breast
and an aged, mumbling grandmother.   Almond-eyed,
nimble-footed, talkative, they thronged the streets of Bozen,
regarded the bright, stately houses, walls, gates, squares,
people ;   appraised them, judged them with quick decided
words and gestures.

It could not be said that the Bozen burghers took up the
Jew Mendel Hirsch with enthusiasm.   On the contrary
the Margrave—who like his father the Emperor prized the
Jews and showed them favour as promoters of prosperity
in the towns—had first to make his wishes strictly known
before Hirsch was even accorded shelter.   And even then
they treated him with the utmost surliness and suspicion ;
called the children from the street when he went by, wiped

their sleeves if they brushed his, shouted curses and insults after him, pelted him with mud when his back was turned. The fat, active, little man went on as if he saw or heard nothing, wiped off the mud when it struck him, smiled, ran his fingers through his discoloured beard.   If they carried it too far, he would shake his head and say : " Now, now ! " He always remained obsequious, and after being turned away came back again.   He bought a house for himself, another, a third.   Wares arrived for him, piled themselves up, of all kinds, beautiful, in an abundance such as they had never seen, not too dear.   He bought whatever was offered, estimated it quickly and exactly, always had money, and paid cash.   The resident tradespeople made wry faces ; the other burghers got used to the Jew, cursed him still perhaps, but more out of habit than conviction.

When Mendel Hirsch had anything particularly fine and new to sell, fabrics, furs, jewels, he brought them first to the Duchess and Herr von Schenna.   Both enjoyed talking with the widely-travelled man, who knew routes, goods, men and affairs so well, and saw them from such a different and such an unusual angle.   When in serious conversation big words were used he made a wry face ; for knighthood, tourneys, banners and such things he had a good-natured, jeering contempt, which captivated and exhilarated Schenna.   He said : " Why always rattle a sword and be in the right ? A little reasonableness and everything goes better."   He became nervous and anxious at the sight of lances, spears and armour.   Once when he was summoned by the Duchess he did not come, because there were soldiers about the roads. " He is a coward," said Margarete.

" Of course he is," said Herr von Schenna.   " At best he would only cut himself with a sword.   But he goes about alone and unarmed among people who hate him, and his only armour is the Margrave's safe-conduct."

Margarete learned that every evening he read out of his intricate Hebraic books and taught them to his children. She heard of his strange customs, of the prayer-mantle, the phylacteries, the special food. She asked him for details. He evaded her politely and firmly. This pleased Margarete. He was ugly and different. He wore a mask. She was the Maultasch, he the Jew.

Little by little more Jews came into the country. To Innsbruck, Hall, Meran, Brixen, Trent, Rovereto ; all with a horde of almond-eyed children ; about twenty families. Money flowed in, the towns became greater, more luxurious, the streets better ; new strange fabrics, fruits, spices, wares, poured in. The mountain land lived more richly, more comfortably.

All week from early morning till deep in the night the Jews pushed their business. No affair was too small for them ; they would wait for hours, indefatigable, for any-thing. They accepted every humiliation, bent before it, and when someone pushed them out of his way or spat on them, they did not defend themselves. But on Friday evening they closed themselves within their houses, and while their Sabbath lasted they would give heed to nobody, not even to the greatest noblemen, nor for the sake of the most important transactions. The people stood before their barred doors, threatening : " There they're at their witch-craft and cursed trade. Wizardry, impious, damned, black arts." But the Jews did not let the threats bother them, and kept the doors and windows firmly closed.

On this day Mendel Hirsch was accustomed to kindle a great many festal lights, and exchange the brown cloak and

K

the peaked hat for a beautiful robe of old cloth and a splendid
cap ; his wife, his daughters and daughters-in-law too attired
themselves with splendour.   Then in his ugly guttural voice
he sang psalms and prayers and his children sang along
with him.   He went and sat about in his house, ate well,
drank well, rejoiced in his children and his wealth.   Read
out an extract from the Word, accompanied it with ingenious
exposition, applied it to the events of the day.   The house
glittered with ornaments and was fragrant with costly per-
fumes.   He laid his hand on his children's heads and blessed
them, praying that they might be as Manasseh and as
Ephraim.   He took his ease in his house, stroked his beard,
nodded his head, and said : " On Sabbath all the children of
Israel are princes' children."

The Margrave said to Margarete : " It is good that the
Jews have settled in the country.   They bring money in,
make things stir.   All the same there is good enough reason
for the people not standing them.   There's that Jew Mendel
Hirsch.   He has no church, no vestige of religion !   He's
worse than a heathen, or a brute beast."

Herr von Teck said in his discordant voice : " The most
offensive thing of all is that a creature like that has no sense
of dignity.   How he crawls !   How he fawns like a dog !
Vermin !   Lice ! "

Margarete was silent.   " He is the Jew," she thought.
" I am the Maultasch."

# CHAPTER III

§ 1

BLIND King John sat in the wretched, bare, peasant room; his barber combed his hair and beard. Yesterday had been oppressively hot, but now a fresh wind came from the north-west. It was half-past three in the morning; the sun was not up yet; the sky was clear. With the king there were two of his officers already in their armour, his high chamberlain and adjutant, and two pages. Despite his sixty years and his blindness the Luxemburger laid the greatest weight on being correctly clothed and armed. The chamberlain and the pages rubbed his white, wrinkled skin with essences; and put on ceremoniously his shirt, his clothes, and his silver armour.

The king had only slept for a few hours, but he was fresh and in radiant spirits. In front of him was a large wood; behind it stood the English. To-day, then, at last, they would fight. It would not be a mere skirmish, it would be a great and arduous battle. The English had everything at stake.

The elegant, blind man standing there, washed, armed, enjoying the summer morning air, had forgotten all the faint, melancholy thoughts which in the last years had risen out of his wasted and vanished life into his darkness. Like an animal that after long confinement in his winter stall sniffs the spring, he savoured greedily the scent of battle which was in the air around him.

He went outside, breakfasted before the house, and joked

with his gentlemen.    A faint, pure wind was blowing.    In
a moment the sun would rise.    His father had been Roman
Emperor, omnipotent over all Christendom.    He, John,
was fighting now for French pay ; there was really no
sense in his mingling in the great dispute between England
and France : he had done it out of simple pleasure in fighting.
Besides he had squandered the money that he had received
from France for recruiting, and now he was driven to pretty
miserable subterfuges.    Seen truly, nothing, absolutely
nothing, had come right with him.    And what if it hadn't !
Now he did not care a button.    Now he was going to fight.
He was very happy.

They gave him slices of white bread, butter, honey,
a cup of mead.    Bees hummed around him.    He stroked
the soft hair of his pages.

He had squandered the money intended for the mercenaries.    He smiled.    Well, well, if his son Karl was German
King to-day, that money had had a good deal to do with it.
Karl must never know.    He guessed probably, but he must
never know.    He was so correct.    No matter.    He himself
loved France, he had rendered her many good services, and
besides to-day—he felt it—he would make up abundantly for
the squandered money.    He shook himself, straightened
himself, and asked if the sun was up yet.

They mounted their horses and set out.    Their way was
through a large wood ; behind that, in a wide, dusty field,
stood the enemy.    They had not let their visors down yet ;
birds sang, twigs brushed their faces, they could smell the
leaves.    It was beautiful to be alive ; it was beautiful to
ride through the woods in the morning ; and behind the
woods stood the enemy.

Ah, now the birds fell silent.    Clattering, shouts, roars, pounding, trampling horses, clear trumpets, dust, everywhere dust. They were at the end of the wood. The king kept with his gentlemen. " How does the battle go ? " he asked with the excitement of the born gambler. His attendants had to describe all the fluctuations of the struggle. He gave commands, threw his troops here and there. But the blind king's strategy remained perforce theoretical ; his officers corrected his orders at their pleasure, and without making any bones about it, or did not carry them out at all. Dust lay thick on the field, lay thick and grey on stalk, blade, corn-ear, on the horses and the coats of mail. The battle had broken up into countless bitter skirmishes. Then the old king was not to be held back any more. Did he guess that his commands were mere empty sound, respectfully received, but ignored and disregarded ? Suddenly he raised himself high ; his good, brown horse reared and neighed ; he sent a clear, joyful cry into the tumult, and broke away. His officers tried to hold him, but the pages pressed on, burning with ardour. So, in spite of all restraints, he came into the thickest of the fight ; his jewels, his valuable armour attracted opponents. He was encircled, extricated, encircled again. Two Scottish knights in particular, two penniless younger sons, had their eyes on his jewels and his magnificent breastplate. The blind old man talked, shouted, laughed, struck around him. He was separated from his officers ; the pages had kept beside him. He talked jestingly, now grim, now inspiriting, now cynical, to one of them, the fair, delicate Jehan, his darling. Jehan was already hewn down, dead, but the blind king went on talking to him. At last his wounded horse threw him, buried him under it. They pressed in on him, tore off visor and helmet, dashed in his skull. There he lay still and pitiable in the dust, the most vivacious man and prince of the age. His beautiful beard was badly torn and clotted with blood ; the shabby knights tore the silver breastplate from his breast ; the ring would not come off his hand, as it lay stiff and cramped in the dust, so they hacked the finger off. Then the battle drew away, and the French, for whom the blind man had fought without aim and without object, were scattered and beaten.

The dead king lay alone. Huge, glittering blue flies settled on his face.

§ 2

KARL OF LUXEMBURG, the German King, had escaped, wounded, from the battle. The King of England, always pleased and proud to demonstrate how chivalrously he conducted war, sent him his father's body with a respectful escort. Karl stood now before the horribly mangled corpse. He had never loved his father. The aged spendthrift who had run such a wayward zig-zag course over the earth, who had played so madly and arrogantly with his crowns instead of defending and establishing them, had heavily compromised his heir. Yet rights, titles and lands had been acquired on every side. He would not squander his powers ; he would not try to do the impossible and keep everything ; he would consolidate, and round out what he had, regarding only realities, not outward splendour. There, now, lay King John, his father. He had been a great knight, the first knight in Christendom ; he had tasted great glory ; now he lay there, a heap of horribly mangled, decaying flesh. He had lived in vain, he had died in vain. He had laughed at Church, priests and saints, and yet had not set the world under his feet ; had won neither Heaven, nor the world. "Sleep in peace, father ! I will be different from you."

King Karl had the heart taken out, and the flesh separated from the bones in boiling water. He conveyed the bones to their native Luxemburg, and had them buried beside holy relics. Then—Aix-la-Chapelle having closed its gates— he had himself crowned in Bonn as King of Germany, in Prague as King of Bohemia. Now that the French were defeated, Emperor Ludwig held that the right time had come to direct an emphatic protest to the rival king. He summoned him in high-sounding terms to relinquish his pretensions and submit to him as the stronger. Karl replied in the same style ; his strength did not consist in embattled hosts, but in the aid of his great ally : God.

For a start, however, he looked around him for earthly allies. He negotiated with Hungary, with lame Albert. On his side Karl had legitimacy, the title, the Church, religion, everyone's sympathy ; Ludwig had the power. Their lands adjoined ; but both were prudent and cautious, and took care that war should not break out there. The ingenious, resourceful Karl imagined he had found the Wittelsbacher's weak spot in a very different quarter : in Tyrol.

There the Bishops of Trent and Chur, who hated Margrave Ludwig, had been agitating and intriguing without ceasing. The feudal barons, gnashing their teeth at the Wittelsbacher's brutality and avarice, only awaited a chance to recall the Luxemburgers. The lords of the great Lombard cities too, the Carrara, the Visconti, della Scala, Gonzaga, regarded the menacing proximity of Emperor Ludwig with deep anxiety.

They sent an embassy to King Karl. Couriers, ever more urgent. The troops of the bishops stood at his disposal, the Lombard mercenaries, the barons' levies. Karl came to a decision.    The opportunity could not be better.    Margrave Ludwig was fighting away in the north, in Prussia. Let him win renown against the heathen !    Tyrol, at any rate, had neither troops nor a ruler.

Something of the adventurous spirit of his father came over Karl.    He set out secretly, accompanied by three trusted friends, all in disguise travelling as merchants with Lombard passports.    They journeyed in severe frost, over snowed up mountain paths.    Arrived unexpectedly in Trent.    Solemn high-mass in the cathedral.    Karl in imperial regalia.    The insignia, to tell the truth, sceptre, sword and orb, were, alas, only substitutes ;   the Wittelsbacher had the real ones in safe keeping.    Bells ringing, incense.    " Gloria in excelsis " sang the gloomy Bishop Nikolaus in his fanatical voice, the boys singing after him.    Karl held a review ;   the troops of Bishop Nikolaus, of the Italian cities, of the Bishop of Chur, the Patriarch of Aquileia, countless south Tyrolean barons, and of his brother Johann, panting for his revenge. He set out in his might, took Bozen, took Meran.    Sat down in great force before Tyrol Castle.

Margarete was thrown on her own resources.    The Margrave and Konrad of Teck were far away in Prussia. The subordinate leaders hesitated, referred the matter to God, when they were asked, Can the castle be held ? and continually shuffled all responsibility on to Margarete's shoulders.    Ever thicker and narrower closed in the ring of the besiegers.

Margarete went around in grim calm.    Her husband Johann, the malignant little wolf, had stood before the barred door, and she had not let him in.    Now he had come with armed men and regiments and all the pomp of war to force an entrance.    After her humiliation she had pieced together the fragments of her ruined life well enough, had achieved a marriage, had brought her land and her life into some kind of order and decency. It was nothing great or beautiful or splendid. It was a poor, mutilated remnant of life, patchwork here, imitation there, riddled with gaps and makeshifts. But it had been well-won, it had been salvaged out of the mire and the void, it was a reclaimed and consolidated possession. And now came this contemptible creature a second time and wanted to tear it from her! Oh, she would show the smooth, cunning Karl, and Johann, too, the malicious, watchful wolf!

She knew that the important thing was to hold out for the first few days. She had few, but trustworthy, troops. She organised the defence herself. She was no coward, and did not hesitate for a moment—they all saw this—to expose herself. Her will, her imperious yet prudent energy, permeated all the garrison. The first assaults were driven back efficiently and without great sacrifice; among the troops in the castle a certain grim jocularity prevailed; the Margravine enjoyed a sort of familiar reverence and admiration. " Our Maultasch! " said the soldiers.

Among the officers was a Bavarian, a repulsive young man, an albino, Konrad of Frauenberg. The others avoided him because of his repellent, insolent and sullen disposition. For the very same reason Margarete was attracted to him. She transferred the command of the defence to him; they understood each other excellently. Where the others saw nothing but sullen arrogance, she found him brief of speech and energetic in action. He in return croaked his grudging and pert recognition of her energy, her arrangements.

The besiegers became more annoyed every day. It was clear the country could only be taken by a sudden swoop or not at all. There they were sitting before this unexpected obstacle, besieging a woman, the ugly, despised Duchess, the Maultasch, and making no progress. Karl tried to swallow the unanticipated check, pressed his lips, choked down his fury. It was unaccountable that his well-equipped army should go to pieces against these walls. Where did this woman, this ridiculous Maultasch, get the strength ? He was profoundly disturbed, prayed, searched his conscience. In Trent he had been shown a finger of Saint Nicholas. He had wanted to acquire the precious relic—he possessed a hand of the saint already—but they would not part with the finger. He could not withstand the temptation, and on the spur of the moment had drawn his knife, cut off a joint of the finger, and taken it with him. Perhaps that had annoyed the saint, perhaps that had diverted luck from his banner and given it to his enemy ? Karl sent the finger-joint back with a diffuse and apologetic letter.

But it was of no avail now ; his repentance came too late. The Margrave was approaching. If he once accepted battle the great danger was that his line of retreat towards Italy might be cut. Karl lifted the siege and left Tyrol Castle. Began to retreat towards the south in sullen rage. Johann howled, the Italian nobles raged. Karl's road was marked by pillage, burning, devastation. Meran in ashes, Bozen in ashes, all down the valley of the Adige fields wasted, vines uprooted, houses destroyed.

Meanwhile the Margrave rode clattering into Tyrol Castle. Embraced Margarete tempestuously, respectfully. Never had he been seen to display such affection. She, she alone, had saved Tyrol. " Our Maultasch ! " said the Margrave to Konrad of Teck, clapping her on the shoulder. " Our Maultasch ! "

## § 3

KONRAD OF TECK made use of the opportunity to degrade the native nobility to complete impotence. Margarete guessed the full, deliberate ruthlessness of his measures. But she let him do as he pleased, and made no objection. Since she had saved Tyrol for the Wittelsbachs she had felt herself warmly and intimately bound to her husband. She felt herself to be one with the land ; her own physical well-being demanded that the country should be ruled according to Wittelsbach axioms : the nobility brought low, town and burgher exalted. Slowly she raised herself up together with the land, freed from the oppression of the barons.

She sat in her Castle Maultasch. She bored, she burrowed into the land. She had three children now, two girls and a boy, Meinhard. She looked after them faithfully, but she had nothing in common with them. The land was her flesh and blood. Its rivers, valleys, towns, castles were part of her. The winds of its mountains were her breath, its rivers her arteries.

Once she went walking at midday by the bank of the Passer, lay down under some rocks to rest and nodded to sleep. Presently a delicate, echo-like voice wakened her : " God be with you, Your Grace ! " She started up and saw a tiny, little, hairy, bearded creature standing in a cleft of rock, bowing to her over and over again with quick, confiding, droll gestures ; then vanish. A gnome ! The gnomes were in the country again ! The gnomes who only came when they felt they were safe, who only showed themselves to real princes and princesses, were visible only to them ! Now indeed she was the mistress of the land in the mountains.

# CHAPTER IV

KING KARL left the land in the mountains soon after he gave up the siege of Tyrol Castle. With sundry relics, but otherwise with little gain. All the same he did not fail while retreating to inflame the Counts of Görz against the Brandenburger, nor, following his father's example, to bestow on various lords and princes a number of Tyrolean towns and jurisdictions which he did not possess ; thus stirring up ever new enemies for the Wittelsbacher.

On his return to Germany he was soon richly indemnified for his failure in the Tyrol by an unanticipated development in the struggle for the empire. Quite suddenly at a bear-baiting in the neighbourhood of his capital at Munich, Emperor Ludwig, the Wittelsbacher, died. The full-blooded man fell from his horse in an apoplectic fit ; an old peasant woman closed his huge, frank, blue eyes ; monks bore the corpse away secretly to give it consecrated burial in spite of ban and interdict.

There stood Karl of Bohemia now, and his foe, who had had great countries under him and cities depending on him, was dead. Yes, the saints had helped him. He, Karl, was now, at the turning point of the century, undisputed German King without a rival.

He was weary of his dispute with the Wittelsbachers, they of their dispute with him. Lame Albert mediated. Karl and his brother Johann gave up all claim to Tyrol and

Carinthia, invested the Margrave with these states, and promised to make his peace with the Curia. The Wittelsbachs in return recognised Karl as German King, rendered him homage, and delivered up the crown jewels.

The crown jewels! Karl had longed with anguish for them. He possessed so many valuable relics, and yet not the precious symbols of power, which should belong to him. He had felt himself and his dignity naked and defenceless so long as he did not have them, so long as he had had to put up with shoddy imitations. Now he bore the sweet and precious things in solemn procession to Prague and placed them in his treasure chamber. The sacred spear was there, also a nail from the cross, not to mention an arm of St. Anna. But best of all was the antique sceptre, the orb of clear pale gold, the spiked crown, and the sword brought by an angel to Charlemagne when he fought the heathen. The king had the jewels consecrated in the cathedral of Prague. Then he carried them himself into his treasure vaults. There they lay now among the white bones of martyrs, among jewels, precious books and pictures, among deeds and treaties, among sacred spears, thorns from Christ's crown, splinters from Christ's cross. The gaunt king stood before them, smiled with his thin lips, stroked with his lean bony hand the spikes of the crown, the curious dents in the irregular, by no means round orb, and the blunt rusty sword of the great Karl, the first of his name.

## § 2

AGNES OF TAUFERS-FLAVON came seldom to her Tyrolean estates. Her younger sister, had been married meanwhile to a lord of Castelbarco, a man very suspect politically, who played off against each other the Bishop of Trent, certain

Italian city magnates and the Tyrolean court, and for the
rest possessed enormously rich domains and privileges.
Agnes travelled a great deal, living now with her elder sister
in Bavaria, now with the younger one in Italy.   After
Duke Johann had been driven out she had not been further
troubled ; on all questions which might have caused any
dispute between her and the authorities, she advised her
officials, shrewdly, to give way before a dispute could arise.
She did not go to court oftener than propriety demanded
and carefully avoided any appearance of importunity.

She was now of a disturbing, conscious, almost disquieting
beauty.   In Italy men laid cities and principalities at her
feet, killed themselves for her ;  even the boorish Bavarians
clicked their tongues, smacked their thighs and declared :
Yes, one would lick the dust and commit stupidities for her.
She walked amiably with a tiny ambiguous smile through the
homage, the combats, the suicides.

If she appeared seldom at the Tyrolean court, yet she
showed, wherever she was, the most burning interest in
Tyrolean affairs.   With parted lips she listened greedily
to accounts of Margarete's activities.   Her measures against
the nobility, for the cities, for the Jews, her defence of the
castle against the Luxemburgers ;  every tiny detail of Margarete's life Agnes had reported to her and repeated, on her
request, again and again.   She never interposed with a word
meantime, or even with a gesture.   If one demanded an
opinion of her she turned the question aside, and, with a
smile, made some trivial remark.

She loved to show herself to the people.   She was arrogant ;  she never responded to their greetings.   She never
gave money to any of the benevolent institutions in the
villages and towns ;  the peasants on her estates, too, were

badly treated.    Nevertheless the people loved to look at her.
They stood in her way when she passed, admired her, cheered
her, loved her.

Often she received a visit from Messer Artese of Florence.
Agnes lived very prodigally ; she needed ever and again
the help of the insignificant Florentine banker, who
bowed so continually and had a mortgage already on all her
property.    Messer Artese told her a great deal about the
Tyrolean court.    He had little good to say of the Margrave
and the Maultasch.    Certainly Ludwig was always in
financial straits, for his wars had swallowed up mighty sums.
But he borrowed from his Bavarian and Swabian lords, and
anxiously avoided the help of the good, willing Messer
Artese ; yes, he even redeemed at a sacrifice the mortgages
which the Italian still held.    The violent manner, too, in
which the Margrave's viceroy, Konrad of Teck, was
accustomed to bring in money and property—these confisca-
tions and executions—went sorely against the grain of the
quiet and polite Florentine.    One should acquire money,
certainly ; money, so long as it wasn't stolen, came from
God.    The tardy debtor should be shown no consideration,
overdue mortgages should be called in ; certainly.    But all
with decency, politely, in good form.    Dungeons, cutting
heads off—pah, that was not done ; it was unseemly.

But Messer Artese was bitterest of all over the preference
shown to the Jew Mendel Hirsch.    What ?    Before him,
the quiet, modest, cultured Italian gentleman and good
Christian, they put that stinking, gurgling, strutting,
impudent, importunate Jew, that filthy devil's spawn ?
Was it not enough that this people cursed by God, this
people who had tortured and crucified our beloved Lord
and Saviour, defiled the German and Italian towns ?    Had

the unholy Maultasch to throw them the land in the mountains as well, so that they might creep in like worms, devour
everything, and no more be got rid of ?   There they sat
now, the loathsome vermin, cropping up everywhere,
pressing their money on everybody unasked, and had the
audacity, the wretched, pestilential rabble, to ask for a lower
rate of interest than he, the highly-respected and honoured
Florentine burgess, liked by all the princes and lords !   His
face, usually so gentle, polite, and controlled, was distorted
into a grimace of boundless rage.

Agnes listened to him quietly.   She listened to it all,
inscribed it on her memory, stored it safely away, and was
extraordinarily amiable to Messer Artese.   He closed up,
excused himself many times, and glided again into obscurity.

§ 3

AFTER the agreement with King Karl Margarete and the
Margrave were left indisputably in secure possession of
Tyrol.   Through the death of his father the Emperor,
Ludwig was involved in complicated and difficult disputes
with his brothers over the inheritance.   At last it was
agreed that out of this inheritance he should hold Upper
Bavaria *de facto*, but of Brandenburg only the title and the
electoral dignity.   Freed of his cares for Brandenburg, he
reigned in his established Tyrol ; his power stretched from
Görz as far as Burgundy, from Lombardy to the Danube.
He called himself Margrave of Brandenburg and of Lausitz,
first Chamberlain of the Holy Roman Empire, Count of the
Palatinate, Duke of Bavaria and Carinthia, Count of Tyrol
and Görz, suzerain of the bishoprics of Agley, Trent and
Brixen.

Margarete's relations with him were cordial, almost

maternal.   It had become a certainty to her now that God
had deprived her of feminine charm so that she might
sink all the woman in the ruler.   This knowledge had
satisfied her.   Her life lay as tranquil as a still lake.   In her
decisions there was a large, straightforward frankness.   The
woman and the regent were one.   What she advised, what
she did, was never wire-drawn or evasive.   It was of an open,
mature, warm, maternal quality, which often ignored the
letter and precedent of the law, but always had its inner,
salutary justification.

It was a hard and stony course she had to follow.   Continuous war ; with the Luxemburger, the bishops, the Lombard cities, the refractory barons.   Time and again the
structures she built up so painfully were torn down, destroyed.
In addition to that earthquakes, floods, fires, pestilence, the
plague of locusts ;  the finances badly crippled by the steady
military expenditure.   It was not easy to make the land
flourish under these drawbacks.   But her full womanhood,
breathing and giving confidence, streamed into the land,
supported it, gave it ever new growth and sap.   She made
allowances, released from their taxes cities which had
suffered from war or fire, forced the stubborn barons in spite
of their grumbling to pay at least a part of their tribute.   All
this happened as if by a natural law, without outcry or
violence.

When she had difficult financial questions to solve, she
sent for advice to the Jew, Mendel Hirsch.   He appeared
forthwith in his brown coat, fat, fidgety, and officious, heard
Margarete out, wagged his head, smiled, said it was quite
simple, and spluttered in many roundabout words an unforeseen solution.   The little overdriven man, hounded over
the earth, was very grateful to the Duchess for the good-will

L

which had given him a fairly secure resting-place and a roof
over his head.    He loved her, he felt with her, he exerted
all his ingenuity for her.

For it was hard to keep one's head above water in the
chaos of Tyrolean administration.    True, they had bridled
the headstrong feudal lords and ejected the calamitous
Messer Artese.    But the Margrave thought nothing of
borrowing the great sums he needed from his Swabian and
Bavarian lords.    In return they were unscrupulous in
their demand for pledges and securities, and kept on snatching
more for themselves, so that in the end nothing was gained.
On the contrary :  it had been at least natives who bled the
country formerly, but now foreigners, Bavarians and Swabians, battened on it.    They sat in all the important positions ;
the avaricious and violent Konrad of Teck had laid hold of
monstrous possessions for himself, Hadmar of Dürrenberg
had seized the salt revenues of Hall, certain Munich gentlemen, Jakob Freiman, Grimoald Drexler and other citizens,
the mines in the district of Landeck.    Moreover, the most
important duties and taxes were farmed out to Bavarians,
Swabians, Austrians.    On this point the Margrave would
not listen to a word of advice.    He trusted his Bavarians
and Swabians ;  they exploited his trust to the full.    Nevertheless, Mendel Hirsch, who, protected by Margarete, kept
prudently in the background, managed to insinuate into
the agreements with these gentlemen clauses which saved
the prince from being completely at the mercy of their
caprices.

Margarete always remained distant towards the Bavarian
friends of her husband.    Only with one did she become more
intimate, with the officer by whose help she had held Tyrol
Castle against the Luxemburgers, with the white-haired,

thick-set, red-eyed Konrad of Frauenberg. He was so hideous, so unpopular, so lonely. She felt an affinity between herself and him, she spoke more familiarly with him than with the others, picked him out. The croaking, morose man rose rapidly, acquired administrations and domains. She even managed to arrange that he should be made High Steward.

One other thing she achieved, the promulgation of a code. Tariffs were fixed, the discretion and jurisdiction of the feudal lords further straitened, the central authority strengthened, burghers, trades and handicrafts encouraged. The gay, many-coloured towns blossomed, expanded, became great and luxurious. The castles of the barons no longer shaped the land's destiny ; the magistrates decided it, and the great fairs in the towns. Even the small towns woke up, Bruneck, Glurns, Klausen, Arco, Ala, Rattenberg, Kitzbühel, Lienz. From the great exchanges and markets, from Trent, Bozen, Riva, Brixen, routes and traffic branched all over the world. What Mendel Hirsch had sown was blossoming richly.

The Duchess loved the gay, noisy towns ; the handsome, busy settlements were literally her very own work. What did men matter, or love ? Could one have a richer life than hers, blossoming, expanding, and multiplying itself in all directions ? Was not this ebb and flow, this living, purposive flood, a part of her ? She surrendered herself completely to it, grew into it. Must not the land feel that, respond to so much love, let her become a part of it ? Yes ! Yes ! Yes ! The houses in the towns looked at her with living, understanding eyes, the streets rang differently, with a more intimate echo, under the hoofs of her horses. Her frozen impassivity melted, she surrendered herself, streamed out towards others, was appeased and happy.

§ 4

HERR VON SCHENNA and Berchtold von Gufidaun rode easily
in the warm evening on their usual road to Schenna Castle.
They were coming from Meran, where with great ceremony
Margarete had instituted a smaller council in addition to the
great council, and had substantially increased the liberty of
the burgesses. This was a gift of great value, on the Duchess's
side sealed by sacrifices in money and influence. The people
had thanked her duly and respectfully, had cheered, had said
with respect, " Our Maultasch."

The gentlemen had to dismount, and make way for a small,
elegant procession. They greeted it very politely. Agnes
of Flavon sat in the litter. People pressed round her :
" How beautiful she is ! An angel from Heaven ! "
They raised a shout, and it sounded very different from the
applause at the ceremony, enthusiastic, rapturous.

Herr von Schenna whistled an Italian air. Berchtold von
Gufidaun stared reflectively straight before him ; the blue
eyes in the masculine, keen brown face had a strained look.
He was not very quick in drawing his conclusions.

On their road, just outside the town, a troupe of tight-
rope dancers were displaying their tricks to a handful of
people. A fiery-hued buffoon brought out a big monkey. It
crouched melancholy and grotesque inside a hoop, and sprang
for an apple. Then a girl appeared, danced, juggled with
balls. Then came the monkey again. They had stuck
him now into a dress of blue silk and clapped gold tinsel on
his skull. He sat there, long-armed, squat, very ugly, sad,
malignant, and showed his yellow teeth in his powerful
out-jutting jaws. The people stared for an instant. Then
it burst out from all sides, making them roar and double

up and split their sides with endless, breathless laughter. "The Maultasch! Yes, it's the Duchess! The Maultasch!"

The gentlemen rode further. Berchtold drew a hissing breath through his teeth, deeply disturbed. A vintager, a young girl, barefooted, brown and pretty, passed them, with a smiling, modest greeting. Berchtold did not look at her, Schenna threw her a passing jest. But his gaiety did not ring quite true. Soon it sank too; and silent, like Berchtold, he rode on, crouching on his horse in his usual ungainly posture, his long, wrinkled face twisted with somewhat wry reflection.

# CHAPTER V

## § 1

In Ala, while two noblemen, Azzo and Marcabrun of
Lizzana, were negotiating with a canon from Trent, in the
middle of a sentence Baron Azzo, the elder of the brothers,
reeled ; his face became yellowish, then black and blue ;
he collapsed.    In the soft parts under the armpits and under
the thighs there were black, suppurating boils, as big as an
egg.    He rattled in the throat, did not return to conscious-
ness, and died in a few hours.    The gentleman from Trent
rode back horrified to his city as fast as his horse could carry
him.    So the plague had arrived.    Now it had broken into
the land in the mountains.    It had been no fable that four
or five had already succumbed to it in Verona.    And so now
the Black Death was in the mountains.    And now God
help us all !

The pestilence had come from the East.    It raged first
of all along the coast, then passed into the hinterland.    It
killed in a few days, often in hours.    In Naples, in Mont-
pellier, two-thirds of the population died.    In Marseilles
the Bishop died, the entire Chapter, and all the monks and
minorites.    Large  districts  were  without  inhabitants.
Great three-deckers tacked about the sea with all their cargo,
and nobody at the helm, the whole crew having perished.
The plague raged terribly at Avignon.    The cardinals
succumbed, the matter oozing from their boils defiled their
magnificent vestments.    The Pope closed himself into his

innermost chamber, let nobody in, and kept a great fire going
the whole day in which he burned aromatic herbs and frankin-
cense to purify the air.    In Prague, in the treasure vaults
of his castle, Karl, the German King, crouched among his
heaps of gold, curios and relics, fasting and praying.

Like a fury the pestilence burst into the valleys of Tyrol.
Of the inhabitants of Wipptal only a third were left, of the
populous monastery of Marienberg only Wyso, the Abbot,
Rudolf, a priest, a lay brother, and Brother Goswin, the
chronicler.    There were valleys in which but one in six
survived the plague.    Because one's breath and sweat,
clothes and eating utensils carried the sickness everyone fled
from his fellows, hostile and suspicious.    Friend fled from
friend, bride from bridegroom, children from their parents.
People expired without the sacrament ;  in the towns many
houses stood empty with all their furniture, and nobody
would trust himself within them.    Masses were not read,
processes were not decided.    The doctors suggested many
reasons, but in the end could find no better one than that it
was God's will.    They could do nothing.    Mad with fear
men mortified themselves, scourged themselves ;  women
bound themselves into sisterhoods.    Processions of Flagel-
lants, fanatics, prophets.    Others drank themselves dead
drunk, and practised every kind of gluttony and debauchery.
The bleeding, emaciated, flagellant brethren encountered
gay and drunken processions holding carnival.

Of Margarete's three children, Meinhard, the son, remained alive ;  the two girls died.    They lay hideously
bloated with enormous black ulcers.    Margarete thought :
" Now they are as ugly as I."

She had no time to brood long over this.    She worked,
and went about, fearless, clear, and calm.    In the monstrous

confusion only a few of her commands were obeyed and that badly ; all the same, she kept her land more firmly in control and order than in the universal dissolution other rulers had been able.    When the pestilence exhausted itself, she tightened the reins at once, and accommodated the complete administration of the country to the new and more elastic circumstances created by the depopulation.    She took precautions, too, against the dissipation of the countless vacated properties, and used the opportunity to bring many lands and properties into her hands cheaply, but not dishonestly.

Messer Artese was very busy ;  it was a good time for him.    All over the world houses and estates, rights and privileges, had fallen to heirs who did not know what to do with them.    He acquired and accumulated.    But in Tyrol he encountered resistance.    Restrictions that hemmed him in, rights of pre-emptor by the court and by the authorities, obstinate clauses.    In Taufers Castle, before Agnes, he let himself go, broke out, and raged.    That Jew, the sly Mendel Hirsch, was to blame for it all !    He obstructed him, the good Christian financier, in his business.    He had contrived all these impudent, diabolically sly clauses and difficulties just to trip him up.

Agnes let the Florentine rave till he was tired, listened quietly, and gazed at him steadily with her deep blue eyes. Then in a calm, exasperating voice she began to relate things. She had been on the Rhine.    There in countless towns they had seized the Jews and burned them.    For the Jews had created the pestilence, they had thrown poison into the wells. She knew it for a fact.    In Zofingen they had found poison. In Basle she had been present herself when they had driven the Jews into an island in the Rhine, into a wooden house, and burned them.    They had shrieked horribly, and the stench had remained for a long time in the air. They had done rightly. The cursed Jews were really guilty of the pestilence. Lame Albert of Austria, it was true, the Bishop of Mainz and the Maultasch protected their Jews. Agnes added slowly and calmly, her eyes steadily on the Florentine : " No doubt they have their own good reasons."

Messer Artese listened but did not reply. Returned to his native Florence without having finished his business.

Soon from Italy the rumour came creeping through the valleys of Tyrol, slimily, making headway until it became a firmer and firmer certainty : the Jews had made the pestilence. The pestilence would not cease so long as they let the Jews stay in the country. Suspicion came to a head. Persecution, violence.

Meanwhile, the Jews went about their business. They had much business, great business, they were very important. Little Mendel Hirsch ran about fidgeting and sputtering ; his countless children ran, olive-eyed and important ; even the aged mumbling grandmother revived, and enquired anxiously : " How does business go ? " It was going excellently, thanks be to God. The pestilence was slackening of itself. There was much to do, to sell, to buy, to negotiate, contracts to be made. In a few weeks now they would be able with God's will to hold their first great market in Bozen after the pestilence. Her Grace the Duchess— God shield her !—needed Mendel at every turn.

Meanwhile the menace drew near, dangerous, snarling, senseless, and ever blacker. The Jews recognised it. It had been like this twelve years ago at the great massacre prompted by the Armleder brothers. It came this time from the south-west. In vain the Pope, the wise, kindly, worldly Clement, set his face against it, and sent out his papal bulls, pointing to the fact that the Jews had been struck down by the plague like the others ; why then should they help it on ? It was not the poisoned wells, it was their ready cash and the written claims on their creditors that caused their undoing. The Jews were robbed and murdered in Burgundy, on the Rhine, in Holland, in Lombardy, in Poland. In twelve, in twenty, in a hundred, in two hundred communities. The Tyrolean Jews waited, fasted and prayed. There was no need to give huge presents to the authorities here. That the Duchess would protect them to the utmost of her power was certain. Also that the Margrave was their well-wisher, like his father, the Emperor, the encourager of trade and the towns, who had always held his shield over them. But it had become evident that against a maddened populace who scented blood and money neither Emperor, nor Pope, nor prison was of use. One could only wait, pray, and go about one's business.

And then suddenly, on one and the same day, it broke out in Riva, Rovereto, Trent, and Bozen. At Riva the Jews were drowned in the lake ; at Rovereto, amid great hubbub and rejoicing, they were made to leap to their death from a precipice ; at Trent they were burned. In Bozen people paid more attention to pillage, and the killing was badly organised. They went about it unmethodically, and thus the mumbling grandmother, a daughter-in-law, and one of the small children remained alive.

The Margrave had not been able to protect his Jews in Munich : in Hall and Innsbruck he interposed energetically between them and the violent mob. He was for justice and commonsense. If he could not help the dead any more, at least he could chase the pack of pursuers off their booty. The murderers had little joy of their deed. Bavarian and

Swabian lords in place of the dead now exacted their dues on behalf of the Margrave, and far more harshly than the Jews could have done. At last King Karl, too, got his finger in the pie. He demanded his share in the property left by the murdered people, from Ludwig, as well as from all the municipalities in which Jews had died. Sharp haggling began over this.

As soon as she heard of the atrocities, Margarete hastened to Bozen, horrified and downcast. She arrived at night. Saw by flickering torchlight the house brutally torn down, the cherished little rooms, once crammed full of the most varied belongings, now empty, plundered, defiled. She saw the corpses of the sons, daughters, sons-in-law, daughters-in-law ; of the swarm of quick, almond-eyed children ; the first horribly mangled and mutilated, the others without any obvious wounds. They lay there very still, who had been so brisk and agile, and very still too lay Mendel Hirsch. He had on a prayer mantle, and phylacteries on his arm and forehead ; no wound could be seen ; in the torchlight it looked as if he were smiling, obsequious, important, officious, mild, and shrewd. Margarete almost believed that in a moment he must shake his head, and gurgle, that it was not so bad after all, it was quite simple ; the people were not really wicked, they were only exasperated, and a little slow and dull in the understanding ; what they needed was merely good guidance. But he said nothing ; he neither fidgeted nor gurgled ; he lay quite still. He had meant well, by himself chiefly of course, but also by her and the country, and he had been wise and very capable, and had brought great profit to the land, and to her beloved towns. Now they had slaughtered him, stupidly, senselessly, bestially. Why, why had they done it ? She turned to one of the bystanders with the stern, imperious question. "Well, he made the pestilence ! " said he, bashful, stupid, and a little defiant.

In a corner the surviving small child wailed softly ; the mother, strangely arrayed in all her finery, tried to sing it to sleep in a broken, discordant voice ; the grandmother mumbled. Margarete went nearer, and raised her hand to stroke the child. She felt weary and wretched. She saw her hand in the torchlight ; it was large and shapeless, the skin was dull and yellowish ; she had forgotten to paint it.

## § 2

In Munich, in one of the spacious rooms in the new residence which his father had begun and which he was zealously extending, Margrave Ludwig gazed coldly at the Baroness of Taufers, Agnes von Flavon. She begged permission to sell certain parts of her property. A Tyrolean appeared as buyer. But in the background lurked Messer Artese. The Margrave was not sympathetic to Agnes ; he had heard many rumours of her slovenly, haphazard management ; his lean, brown face with the short, fair moustache remained impassive ; his grey, rather piercing eyes regarded her mistrustfully.

Agnes sensed very well his hostile vigilance ; but she did not allow herself to be put out in the least. She moved gracefully to and fro, regarded him with her deep, blue eyes, smiled with her delicate lips, very red in her pale face, was dignified, gay, and not exaggeratedly amiable. Cautiously, dexterously she began to lure him on, twitting him gently on his surliness.

He gazed at her. They had done her an injustice, after all. His friends expected every woman to stick day and night to the house, run after the servants and look after the kitchen and the linen cupboard. She was a fine piece of womanhood, undeniably. Tender and delicate and well-cared-for in every fibre, and yet lithe and strong. He dismissed her more courteously than he had received her Sent for her a second time. Followed her a long while with his eyes. Sighed. Thought of Margarete. She was pregnant again. No, she was certainly not beautiful. When one looked at the other and then thought of her— a kind of horror might well come over one. She was clever, our Maultasch. The people had a respect for her, but they did not like her. When the other appeared, then they cheered.

Both his daughters were dead now. Among the people they said : a judgment from God. He was guilty, naturally ! Because the Pope would rather see Tyrol in the possession of his pampered pet Karl, his, Ludwig's, marriage was a violation of the sacrament, and his children were bastards. The bells did not ring, and for fires, floods, locusts, and plagues he was blamed.

The fools ! The pedantic asses ! The dolts ! Was it such a great pleasure to be the husband of the Maultasch ? Long since he had ceased to notice her appearance. Now he suddenly saw it. He was the laughing-stock of Europe with such an ugly wife. Here he was, a great prince and ruler, the most powerful man in Germany. Cities and fruitful places blossomed where he smiled ; or fell into ruins where he showed his anger. He had not achieved this easily. Had worked conscientiously day and night. Known no fear except the fear of God. Done his duty, sternly and in spite of all difficulties, day by day. And what was his reward ? The mockery of Europe.

Below him Agnes stepped into her litter. People stood

around, bareheaded, admiring. Were she in the Maultasch's place they would not cry, " The judgment of God ! "
even if the locusts or the pestilence came.

Was she not looking up ?    He turned quickly away like
a stripling caught peeping.


§ 3

A few weeks later Margarete bore a dead child. The
Margrave withdrew into himself, and became colder towards
her.   No, his marriage was not blessed.   Now all his hopes
must be set on his only son, Meinhard, a fat, harmless lad,
mediocre and weakly, who appeared to take little after his
grandfather Ludwig, and much more after his grandfather
on the mother's side, the good King Heinrich.

After a week's time Margarete was already going about
her work.   She worked with the same industry and conscientiousness as before.   But the pleasure had gone, the
towns were no longer her darlings.   The officious little
Jew, who had been so successful in bringing life into the
country from every quarter, was slain ;  the children she had
borne were dead.   Wherever she went everything went to
pieces.   Nothing succeeded, nothing blossomed.   The
Margrave ?   A conscientious arid prince.   Her son ?   A
thick-set, stupid, ordinary youth.   What remained ?

During this time she drew closer to Konrad of Frauenberg.   This repulsive man with the red eyes and the white
hair was the fifth among the six sons of Trautsam of Frauenberg, a not very important Bavarian knight, who in a former
battle, however, had earned the gratitude of Emperor
Ludwig.   So young Konrad had come as a page to the
Bavarian court, and then had gone in the Margrave's train to

Tyrol, where he remained in the background for a long time as a subaltern. His ugliness and his rough, sullen, bitter ways isolated him ; he had no prospect of ever becoming anything more than a subordinate officer, until his bold and impetuous audacity during the siege of Tyrol Castle brought him to the front.

All that was still romantic in Margarete, all her longing for colour, movement, adventure, all the remnants of what Herr von Schenna called the earlier time, she showered on the hard and ugly Frauenberger. This albino with the wide, froglike mouth, the croaking voice, the stubby, coarse hands, appeared to her a kind of enchanted prince. It was with him as with her ; under the rude exterior there was certainly a fine and gentle spirit. One had, of course, to become rough and boorish if one was stuck in a body like that. The poor lonely, misunderstood man ! She was especially kind and motherly to him.

In his harsh youth, when he had received many knocks, Frauenberg had learned a sort of cold, hard cunning. He knew he was ugly ; and he took it as a matter of course that everybody should push him down. If he had been higher up he, too, would have trampled on others. He believed in nothing in the world. Money, power, possessions, pleasure were the aims of all men ; greed, ambition and lechery their motives. There was neither reward nor punishment, neither justice nor virtue. The whole business was without meaning. There were only clever men and dolts ; and bad luck and good luck besides. He subscribed to that song which with prosaic conviction praised seven things as worthy to be striven for and sung. Eating was the first, swilling the second, relieving oneself of what one ate the third, of what one drank the fourth, lying with a woman was the

fifth, having a bath the sixth, but the seventh and the best
of all was sleeping.

When the Duchess openly let her interest in him be seen,
he never thought for an instant that this interest was more
than a sensual titillation.    It was not to be wondered at,
moreover, that the ugly woman should hit upon him, the
ugly man.    He had resigned himself to his fate ; he was
reasonable, sensible.    He had told himself that as a fifth
son and with such a face it was impossible to come to the
front.    Yet he had never ceased to lie in wait, sly, hard,
sharp-eyed, and ready to spring.    Now it had paid him
magnificently.    It was a devilish fine piece of luck that the
ugly hag should burn for him.    He would exploit it.

Before his valet he let himself go, triumphing loudly,
with obscene eulogies on the Maultasch and her eagerness.
Greedy as he always was, he stood the fellow an extra jug
of wine.    By one candle's light, alone with his attendant,
he boozed all night.    Bawled his song about the seven
pleasures worth striving for.    Croaked that he would know
how to make this Maultasch serve him.    Stretched himself
comfortably then, and prepared to sleep.    Yes, this was the
best thing of all.    He felt his limbs sore with over-fatigue.
Cracked his joints.    Stretched his gaping jaws.    Turned
on his side, yawning voluptuously.    Slept.

He made for his goal with cautious cunning, and never
too openly.    The Margrave, he divined, did not like him.
He kept out of his way.  Never pushed himself forward.  But
he was always there, and with impudent familiarity took
advantage of every available moment when Margarete was
alone.    So he annexed castles, estates, jurisdictions, domains,
and became at last High Steward.    No one, not even himself,
would ever have predicted such a rise for him.    He pocketed

everything, with an impudent and greedy grin. Remained as High Steward what he had been as an insignificant officer. Had respect for nothing and nobody, believed in nothing but power, money and lust. Now, as before, Margarete hung all her dreams on the albino. His loathsome appearance singled him out, gave him an affinity with her. In that gross, fleshy, repulsive clod there must, there must be a soul hidden. No radiation came from him to her ; all that connected them was at most an occasional vulgar, sneering, evil familiarity. She did not see or she interpreted his emptiness as bitter resignation, or as deliberate silence, which modestly concealed and belied his gentle and noble self.

Herr von Schenna was troubled to see Margarete slipping further and further away from the Margrave, for no more vaild reason than she that was letting herself drift, and half against her will being drawn to Frauenberg, whom he disliked intensely. It offended him that the fastidious Margarete should choose precisely this confidant to keep him company. Had he then something in common with that fellow ? Was it possible that she put his fine, cultivated scepticism in the same class with the crude, vulgar futility and cynicism of the Bavarian ? It pricked his vanity that Margarete should give him this partner in her confidence.

Otherwise things were going very well with Herr von Schenna now. The plague had not touched him. He had inherited lands, he had also utilised the period after the pestilence to give the finishing touches to his magnificent estates. He lived in his castles delicately, and comfortably, among pictures, books, works of arts and peacocks, declined as before to hold any office, gazed happily and reflectively over his spacious fruit gardens, fields and vineyards, grew daily milder and wiser, and was as serene and self-contained

M

as a well-tended and ripening fruit. Abbot Johannes of Viktring, now Duke Albert's secretary and getting gradually very old and shaky, could apply almost the whole of Horace to him.

From his peaceful retirement he would have gladly helped Margarete. He attempted to draw closer the relations between her and the Margrave His efforts were seconded by the fact that the weight of the Church's excommunication on Margarete's marriage began to be lifted.

Duke Johann, the Luxemburger, had been long tired of being a married man in the eyes of the Church, while in reality a bachelor. His position had been much bettered through the acute policy of his brother, King Karl ; he thought of completely establishing it by a judicious new marriage. But to do this he must first be divorced legitimately and with all formality from Margarete. He asked her for an interview. He desired to find in common with her a formula which, acceptable to both, would neither humiliate him nor her. Their interests were the same. All that was obvious, and Margarete was ready to receive him. So Duke Johann appeared as a guest at Tyrol Castle. This time the doors opened for him. Drums, trumpets, every mark of honour. Johann's long face still looked boyish. He blinked at Margarete without any embarrassment out of his small, deep-set eyes. Fell into a tone of grim banter, a certain ironical camaraderie, which rather pleased her. They sat together, hatching grounds for the divorce, eagerly turning them this way and that, moulding them, forging them. Came to a satisfactory agreement. That although she was related to him at the fourth remove, Duke Johann had married Margarete without being aware of such kinship. That although both of them had taken honest pains to consummate the marriage, they had, doubtless because Johann was bewitched, not succeeded in achieving this. As, however, Johann could very well consummate a marriage with another lady, and desired to perpetuate his illustrious line, he entreated the Pope to annul his marriage with Margarete. The Pope, friend of the house of Luxemburg-Bohemia, would doubtless accede to the request. This decided, Johann breakfasted once more with Margarete. Both were in good spirits. " You have not grown any older, little wolf," said Margarete.

" And, by God, you are a stateswoman in spite of everything, Duchess Maultasch," replied Johann. Each felt superior to the other as well as to the situation ; everything had solved itself perfectly ; on this basis they found their relations really quite pleasant. They parted on good terms, with a grim, mutual confidence.

# CHAPTER VI

## § 1

THROUGH the death of these two children of Margarete's, the succession to the land in the mountains had become as precarious as in good King Heinrich's time. The sole heir to the country was the boy Meinhard, whose health was delicate, and whose sisters had both died in childhood. So once more the powerful German princes turned their eyes towards Tyrol, and stretched out their greedy hands. The Luxemburgers were rounding off their possessions on the Rhine and the Moldau, and had withdrawn from the struggle in the south ; but Wittelsbach and Habsburg sat tight on their formally precise and documented claims, eyeing each other and waiting.

The Habsburger especially, Albert the Lame, had sown the seeds of a far-sighted and clear-headed policy, which he had little hope of seeing ripen in his time. But the cripple, whose lameness had made him bitter and sagacious, had long since relinquished immediate success in favour of future advantage ; and for him it was a question either of securing Tyrol, the road to the West, the bridge to his Swabian possessions, or of renouncing all dreams of empire for ever.

He set out first to win over the bishops. Trent and Chur had had short shrift from the Wittelsbachs, and were well inclined to attach themselves to the Habsburger, who had pampered them. He showed himself gracious and open-handed also to all the nobles who were influential in Tyrol.

On the Schennas, on the governors von Matsch, on the Frauenberger he bestowed titles, dignities, and sinecures which brought in much money and carried no responsibilities.

From the Margrave himself he sought in every way he could to win confidence and friendship. He did not fall on his exposed flank during the Luxemburger's attack ; on the contrary, he reconciled him with his adversary. Soon matters had gone so far that Albert the Lame was able to marry one of his daughters to Ludwig's son, Meinhard, the small, thick-set, inoffensive, delicate heir to Tyrol. Besides this Albert, who usually kept a strict enough eye on his accounts, was exceedingly liberal to the Margrave, always sore-pressed for money, and so made him more and more dependent upon him.

Then all at once, when Ludwig again applied for a considerable loan, the Austrian's financial advisers explained that this time, unfortunately, it was impossible to grant his request. Their coffers were exhausted ; yes, they were even regretfully compelled to call in the sums which had formerly been lent to him. Deeply concerned, embarrassed, furious, the Margrave was on the point of turning on them with angry looks and words, but controlled himself, bit his lips, and went away in silence.

He thought of a personal application to Albert. But he could not subdue his pride to such a course. On a second encounter between the Habsburg financial advisers and his own, the former announced very innocently that they had thought of a just and admirable settlement. As security for the old loans and the new one which he was asking for the Margrave should hand over to Austria for a few years the government of Upper Bavaria. By administering it along with his other provinces, Albert would be able to economise, so that in a short time he would certainly recover the whole of the debt.

The Margrave's cheek paled when his officials informed him of the Austrian offer. His hard, piercing blue eyes looked keenly at them. No, they were not smiling. Their faces were sober, serious, official. He gulped, said he would think it over, nodded, and dismissed them.

His spirits sank when he was alone. But he straightened his massive neck. The request was sheer insolence. Still, Albert was clever, and his friend ; he certainly did not intend it as an insult. So apparently there was no other means of raising money : that was the position. And in giving up the revenues, he was not giving up the land. None the less, if the head of the Wittelsbachs handed over to a Habsburg the government of his native land, it was, in spite of every assurance, an affliction, a bitter, bitter affliction hardly to be borne.

When he brought the matter up in council, he did so quietly and objectively, treating it as if it were not very important. Eyed his barons suspiciously, to see if they would dare to show visibly their secret glee. Ah, if only his friend Konrad of Teck had still been alive ! He would not have needed to be suspicious of him. Everything would have been easier to bear. But a truce to sentimentality ! He outlined the problem briefly ; expressed no opinion ; requested their advice. The Frauenberger was the first to speak. Like all the others, of course, he saw that the Austrian proposal amounted to simple extortion. He had not the slightest preference either for Ludwig or for Albert, for Bavaria, Tyrol or Austria. The Habsburger was the richer and cleverer of the two ; therefore he would probably gain his point. Besides that, he himself, the Frauenberger,

had already been bribed with huge sums of money and offices
of honour, so that he was bound to secure Ludwig's assent
to the proposal. But if he advised compliance, Ludwig,
who disliked him in any case, would become suspicious. On
the other hand, whether one advised for or against, there
was nothing left for the Margrave to do but to grind his teeth
and sign the humiliating contract. So he, Konrad of
Frauenberg, knowing that the Habsburger would never find
it out from the result, could cheerfully allow himself the
amusement of being a Bavarian patriot, and dissuade his
prince from agreeing to the degrading Austrian demands.

Margarete was wildly enthusiastic about the Habsburg
proposals. There would be money in abundance and the
oppressive debts which still lingered on from the time of good
King Heinrich would be discharged at last, at long last.
With this pressure removed, how her beloved cities would
blossom ! Bavaria had always been for her merely an append-
age. She would gladly exchange it for money. She had
learned from Schenna and Mendel Hirsch what money meant.
What was the use of having a huge body and too little blood ?
Now the land would have enough blood ; now it would be
restored to health. Her good land ! Her dear, flourishing
cities ! The Margrave listened with a gloomy brow. It
was clear enough now how little she had ever understood
him. He was a Bavarian, a Wittelsbach, the son of an
Emperor, habituated to the idea of empire and to think in
terms of countries. She was a Tyrolean ; her thoughts
went no farther than her frontiers. Her thoughts stopped
at the lowlands, and went no farther. She was the daughter
of a petty Count of Tyrol, narrow-minded, thrifty, com-
mercial. He was the first-born of the Holy Roman
Emperor, made for universal dominion, responsible only to

himself and to God.    No, between him and her there stood
more than her mere ugliness.

The subtle Herr von Schenna spoke next.    Ludwig
detested him for the time being.    Of course he was on
Margarete's side ; he was a Tyrolean, not a Bavarian.    He
said it was unfortunately impossible to nourish the finances
of both countries from their own resources.    So it would be
convenient to entrust the noble race-horse of Bavaria to his
Habsburg friend for a short period of fattening in his stables.
Thus one would get at last sufficient fodder for the good
horse of Tyrol.    And in any case, what other solution was
there ?

Yes, what other solution was there ?    There was the rub.
However clearly one stated objections to the plan, it was
of no avail.    The Habsburger's bait would have to be
swallowed.    The Margrave bowed his head, bent his massive,
threatening neck, and thanked his advisers curtly and sulkily.
Said he would take their opinions into consideration.    They
all knew what his decision would have to be.

§ 2

IN heavy dejection Ludwig rode away from Castle Tyrol
with a small retinue and headed for the north, towards
Munich, to make the last trifling arrangements before
transferring the administration of the country to the
Habsburger.

A sad October day.    A thin, desolate, drizzling rain.
What did he get out of life ?    He was a ruler, he was a
powerful prince.    But the greater part of his duties, the
greater part of these solemn ceremonies, proclamations, and
engagements, was nauseating and burdensome.    To hand
over the government of his native land to the Habsburger,

and to do it with a friendly face, to say "God reward you
for it!" He ground his teeth. He felt the enormous,
blank, blue eyes of his father upon him. What would he
have said to this?

Those he had left behind him were delighted. That
disgusting Schenna, too clever by half, making a mock of
everything, with his insolent, vacant, soft smile. The
Frauenberger, the shameless mutton-head, croaking about
the Wittelsbach dignity, about the bond between Wittelsbach
and Bavaria, and all the time secretly hugging himself; for
the poisonous toad knew very well that there was no other
way out. The Maultasch, thinking of nothing but her pet
Tyrol, looking on Bavaria merely as something to bargain
with, something to fling away gladly in return for gulden
and Veronese marks. Hideous creature, making him the
laughing-stock of Christendom! How repulsive she is!
Sitting there, craning her neck to hear the croaking of the
Frauenberger, the albino, the monstrosity! His wife!
His Duchess! Ugh! The Maultasch!

Truly, in Christ's name, what did he get out of life?
Could he not find something to do while on the way to
Munich to take his bitter medicine, something which would
have a less bitter smack? Suppose he were to turn aside
at Taufers and see for himself how matters stood there?
It would not take up much time, and at any rate the longer
he put off the other thing the better.

In Taufers Agnes was by no means so surprised as he had
expected. When the porter announced that the Margrave
was approaching with a few gentlemen, she drew a deep
breath, it is true, stretched out her arms, and let a satisfied
smile play over her bright red lips; but she received the
prince with courteous indifference, not at all as if she were

specially honoured.  The meal, too, which she ordered for him, and all the other arrangements for his visit, were tasteful enough, and not unsuitable, but far removed from that ostentatious luxury which rumour attributed to her, and with which she had entertained much less important gentlemen, even small Italian barons.

Ludwig looked at her.  Candles were burning and on the hearth was a small fire of sweet-smelling woods.  Fruit and comfits were being served.  A dainty creature, by our Lord's Passion and Death !  No wonder that tongues were busy about her.  But she didn't make it easy for a man.  Her conversation was cool and a little mocking ; she kept one at a distance.  The serious, awkward Margrave made a few helpless attempts to say something gallant to her.  She looked at him quietly and uncomprehendingly.  No, she was actually a prude !

All the more unexpected on the morrow was her calmly proffered request to be allowed to join the Margrave on his journey to Munich.  She wanted to visit her sister, and had other business as well in Bavaria.

Embarrassed and hesitating, the Margrave made no reply. This request was most inopportune.  It would give rise to gossip.  He was a serious, solid man, and no longer young enough for such adventures ; it was quite unfitting that he should become a subject for gossip.  But it was impossible for him to refuse this small favour to the lady—for after all she was that—whose hospitality he had claimed.  Somewhat grumblingly, with ungracious reluctance, he answered at last that he would be delighted.

On the journey she was very conventional in her behaviour, reserved and retiring.  Secluded herself most of the time within her closed litter.  But there, alone behind her curtains, she rolled her triumph on her tongue. That other woman, her enemy, sat in Castle Tyrol, the acknowledged Margravine of Brandenburg, Duchess of Bavaria, Countess of Tyrol. Had a solid, honourable husband. Had borne him children. Had knit him to herself, and herself to him. But now she, Agnes of Flavon, was travelling around with that same Margrave in her enemy's hereditary country.

In Munich Ludwig, proud and constrained, accomplished his vexatious duties. As soon as they arrived, Agnes had taken leave of him with courteous and not excessive gratitude. Now he was glad of her occasional company to brighten his depressing evenings. The first time she excused herself, but the second time she came. He grew accustomed to her. She went into the country to visit her sister. He put off his return journey until she was able to join him again.

On this return journey through a brilliant late autumn Agnes no longer secluded herself in the litter. She rode sparkling on a gaily-caparisoned horse by the Margrave's side, her head proudly uplifted.

§ 3

MONEY flowed into the land : the huge sums for which Bavaria had been pawned. Industry breathed freely. The mines, the salt works. Streets were widened, trade was encouraged and regulated. The cities stretched themselves, expanded. The citizens strutted, gravely swaggering. Their houses grew higher, and were filled with fine furniture, works of art, utensils. Walls, towers, town halls, churches sprang up. Spiced wine and game appeared even on week-days on the well-appointed tables of the burgesses. More gorgeous than the wife of the small country squire, the citizen's wife sailed in silks, enormous caps, noble ribbons, trains and jewels.

Since when had this happy change taken place? Since the Margrave had become friendly with the lovely Agnes of Flavon. Agnes von Flavon, the beautiful, the blessed. She it was who had had the happy idea of renouncing Bavaria, so that all the power and wealth were diverted into Tyrol. The grace of God upon our lovely Agnes von Flavon! One could see that she was set apart. On her heavenly face there shone visibly all the blessings of Our dear Mother of God. But as for the other, the Maultasch, she was branded. The wrath of heaven was upon her. Whatever she did was accursed. Her children died. Plagues fell on the country, pillage, floods, vermin, whenever she lifted her hand. All that she counselled or did was accursed. Was it not she who had brought about the union with Bavaria, the root of all evil? Was it not she who had called in the hard and greedy Bavarian nobles who drained the country dry? Did she not cleave still to the Frauenberger, that monstrous mass of deformity? Had not she made him Lord High Steward? It was a piece of luck that the Duke had turned away from her. He had found out at last where the right woman was. Good times were coming now. God bless our lovely and beloved Agnes von Flavon!

Agnes looked at the people who thronged to see her as she looked at trees and houses, and needed their applause as she needed jewels. She smiled. Went through the gaping, admiring crowds without looking to left or right, her head held high, with small, audacious, arrogant lips. And the people cheered.

# CHAPTER VII

## § 1

ESTRANGED from her husband, estranged from her son Meinhard, Margarete went about sunk in melancholy self-absorption. She was obsessed by Agnes and her triumphs. She looked at Schenna, at the Frauenberger. She watched her cities growing, expanding, breathing freely. Her sowing ; her work. She was a mere wretched, empty shell, denied the commonest satisfactions, but this at least she had accomplished. This only, but this at least was hers enduringly.

Schenna felt her position all the more acutely. He saw how the people ascribed to the beautiful woman every benefit conferred by the ugly one. This realisation, this painful awakening, he wished to spare her. He saw, too, that Ludwig was becoming more and more involved in Taufers. He was still putting up an astonished and hard-pressed resistance, the stolid, helpless man, for this was his first experience of such entanglements. It was still only an adventure, transient and delimited. But soon, perhaps in a very few weeks, it would be too late to extricate him, soon he would be voluntarily and irremediably bound.

Schenna wanted to bring him back to Margarete. He wanted to bring the people back to her. The people were stupid and had no instincts ; what they thought was of no importance at all ; every brute beast was shrewder and

more instinctive than they ; but he could not suffer that
Margarete should see her last support giving way.

He would have to bend all his energies, then, to get the
idiotic ban of the Church removed from her.   The taint
of excommunication scared the people away, and scared
away her husband.   For though her marriage with Johann
had been formally dissolved, so that the Church no longer
regarded her as an adulteress, still the Pope had not yet
given any sanction to her cohabitation with Ludwig.   The
Church considered their marriage as a concubinage, and
Meinhard, their son and heir, as a bastard.   She and her
husband were still under the ban, and their country under
the interdict.   The Margrave had sent ambassadors to
Avignon, offering to give the Holy Father every satisfaction
he could wish ; but the Pope, egged on by the Emperor
Karl, had refused to be won over.

Clement was now dead, and his successor, Innocent VI,
was strongly under the influence of the Habsburger.   It was
to lame Albert's own interest to see that his daughter married
the ecclesiastically acknowledged heir of Tyrol and not
a bastard.   Schenna set to work with unwonted energy.
Went from Ludwig to Albert, from Albert to Margarete.
From Munich to Vienna, from Vienna to Tyrol.

Albert laid down conditions.   He was sowing for the
future.   Through her marriage with Meinhard his
daughter would have a claim to the land in the mountains.
But young Meinhard was a Wittelsbach.   So, in certain
circumstances, the Wittelsbachs would also lay claim to it.
Now it had been shown that the refractory country could
only be held in the long run by one whom the people accepted
as their rightful ruler.   The Maultasch was not loved, but
as the sole legitimate representative of the old Counts of

Tyrol she was religiously regarded by the people as the rightful owner of the country. It was hers to dispose of ; the man to whom she bequeathed it would have the people on his side. Albert, therefore, asked nothing from Ludwig of Wittelsbach ; but he demanded a binding testament from Margarete. In case she, her husband Ludwig, and her son Meinhard, should leave no lawful heirs of their bodies, the land was to pass to the Dukes of Austria. A formality. Purely a formality, he insisted to Herr von Schenna. And only valid in an extremely improbable and unlooked-for contingency. But he was after all a bit of a pedant ; and he wanted Margarete's signature. In return, he guaranteed to extract from the Pope the removal of ban and interdict upon Ludwig and Margarete.

Schenna thought this proposal very advantageous. He had always preferred the gay, affable Austrians to the heavy, violent Bavarians.

§ 2

MARGARETE sat alone over the document ; it was late in the evening.

So she was to make over her country to the Habsburgs. Well, she had brought it first to Luxemburg, and then to Wittelsbach ; why not now to Habsburg ? Albert the Lame was undoubtedly the cleverest and most reliable of the German princes. And Rudolf, his son, was bold, resolute and sagacious. Efficient people, the Habsburgs. They would be sure to rule Tyrol efficiently too. They had Austria, Carinthia, Carniola, the Swabian border lands and Görz, and governed Upper Bavaria. They would not govern Tyrol less well.

Tyrol ! Her Tyrol ! She had only just pried it loose

from the grip of Bavaria. Now she was to add it as the seventh state to a group of six. An administrative job for foreign princes. Her Tyrol !

But not so fast ! That was looking very far into the future. Meanwhile her son was still there. He was not so bold and clever as Rudolf, or Albert's other sons. He was, admittedly, a youth of not much account. But he was her son. The great grandson of Count Meinhard. What could Tyrol mean to the others ? Even if her son were a complete idiot, he was Tyrol.

Gently, gently. No one was trying to oust him. In case he should die without—— He looked far into the future, that shrewd Albert, lame and bitter man. Really strange, that it was precisely her signature he wanted. There was her husband, the Margrave, the Emperor's son, the Wittelsbach ; but the shrewd Albert would have none of him, only her signature.

What did Ludwig think about it ? He was efficient too, and on good terms with the Habsburger. Curious, that his opinion had not been asked for. Was the acute Albert already aware how far apart they had drifted ? Formerly he would have consulted with her about it ; but now he was away. In Bavaria. With Agnes. She stared fixedly before her, her broad shapeless mouth twisted in sorrow, but not very bitter. Why should not Ludwig take his pleasure with Agnes von Flavon ? She was very beautiful. He was no longer so young as he had been. He had worn himself out. Now he was rid of Bavaria and could relax himself. She was very beautiful. Why should he not take his pleasure ?

She rose heavily, groaning a little. Read the proclamation over once more. It was long and circumstantial.

' We, Margarete, by God's grace Margravine of Brandenburg, Duchess of Bavaria and Countess of Tyrol, to all
Christian subjects now and for ever who at any time see,
read or hear this document, give Our Greeting and the
following, to wit : Should it happen, which God in his grace
avoid, that We and the illustrious Prince Our Well-Beloved
Spouse, Margrave Ludwig of Brandenburg, should depart
this life without heirs of our bodies jointly begotten, and
should Our dear Son, Duke Meinhard, depart this life,
which may God forbid, without heirs of his body, then shall
our aforesaid sovereignties and counties, lands and domains,
together with the castle at Tyrol, and all other castles, passes,
fortresses, cities, markets, villages, serfs and jurisdictions
whatsoever, be delivered wholly as a lawful inheritance and
legacy to Our dear Uncles, the Dukes of Austria——"

She let the document fall awkwardly, so that it rolled
itself up with a crackling noise on the table. She left the
room, and with heavy, shuffling steps began the round which
she was accustomed to make every night before going to
sleep. Solitary, in her magnificent robe, which hung with
strange lifelessness on her body, the ugly woman trailed
through the halls, the sitting-rooms, the corridors, preceded
by the uncouth shadows cast by her candle.

She came to the spinning-room. The heavy door opened
without much noise. The maids had finished their work ;
a couple of serving-men had joined them. They were all
clustered in a knot round a young, thick-set girl who stood
there sturdy and bewildered, with an, amused grin on her
face. Shrieks of mirth around her, loud guffaws. What ?
She really didn't see it ? Then she was the only one in
Tyrol who didn't. Try again. Now then ; the Ugly
Sister was foul and hideous ; wherever she set her foot

N

everything shrivelled up and died.    The Lovely Sister shone like an angel from heaven : whatever she touched burst into flower and wherever she set her foot there was the chink of gold.    Now, who was the Lovely Sister ?    A—Ag—    At last a broad flash of comprehension lit up the maid's face.    Agnes von Flavon !    Of course.    And the Ugly Sister ?    Ah !    Great bewilderment.    And then it dawned upon her too, and she doubled up with laughter.

There was so much shrieking and sniggering that no one remarked the Duchess.    She stood perfectly still with her candle in the shadow of the half-open door.    Then slowly she shut it, and trailed away down the corridors.    Back to the document.    She spread it out before her.    " We, Margarete, by God's grace Margravine."    The parchment crackled.    She dipped her quill in the ink ceremoniously and appended her signature.

## § 3

ALBERT THE LAME sat in his palace at Vienna, wrapped in his dressing-gown and a blanket.    On a table beside him among other papers lay Margarete's deed.    His son Rudolf was present, the Bishop of Gurk, and the aged Abbot Johannes of Viktring.    The Duke himself, stricken in years, had received extreme unction ; he knew that he had but a few hours to live.    Shivering in spite of the blanket and the over-heated room, he sat in his easy chair, and noted with a pang that was almost pleasant how slowly the life ebbed out of him.    His mind, as usual, was clear and placid, with a kind of gay cynicism.

Rudolf enquired for the third time whether he should not summon his other brothers.    His firm face, fair and tanned, with its square, low forehead, hook-nose and strongly-developed under-lip, was serious, self-conscious and unsentimental. The paralysed man for the third time refused. The boys had plenty to do ; his death was not to disturb them.

He breathed quietly ; his sound hand opened and closed and opened again. He had lived a good life, in so far as a human life can be good. There had been toil and trouble in it ; there had been success. He had advanced his own fortunes and those of his lands. He was at peace with himself, with men, and with God.

His son Rudolf had a good inheritance. It was pleasant, and a mark of God's favour, that he had lived to see the document which assured him Tyrol. Now everything was rounded off ; from Swabia to Hungary it was completely rounded off, all Habsburg land. Governed well and in a Christian manner, with order and justice. His sons were sound, sensible men. He knew very well why he did not wish them to be inconvenienced by his death.

So he, too, is passing away, the last of the three. John of Luxemburg died a fool's death, a stupid, chivalrous death in a battle which did not concern him at all. Ludwig of Bavaria died a frivolous, unexpected death, on a hunting expedition, leaving his affairs chaotic and unsettled ; an indecisive death, a vague and featureless death, a death which was as half-baked and stupid and inarticulate as his whole life had been. He, Albert, had never called himself Roman Emperor, had never striven for the Roman crown, had neither won it nor wanted it. But on any just computation —he smiled a gentle, guileful smile—he had always been the most powerful of the three, the real arbiter of Christendom, and things had always fallen out as he wished them.

Now he felt dreadfully tired. He called for Rudolf in

a voice which died away hoarsely. Rudolf came quickly
towards him. The lame man's sound hand groped for that
of his son, but fell before it touched him. His head sank
forward on his breast.

Rudolf was firm and collected. He was now the head
of the Habsburgs, the most powerful of the Germans. The
Bishop of Gurk offered up a prayer. The aged Abbot
Johannes of Viktring slid his withered brown hand over
Margarete's parchment. " More enduring than bronze,
this my memorial," he murmured, quoting an ancient classic.
Then he shuffled over to Albert. Saw that he was dead.
Gathered his energies together, drew himself up, swayed,
stood firm. Made his voice as steady as he could, and after
several attempts announced, " Defunctus est Albertus de
Habsburg, Imperator Romanus." The Bishop and the
new Duke stared at each other : the dead man had never
held this rank, nor desired it. The aged man repeated with
emphasis, faltering, but solemn. " Now Albert of Habsburg,
the Holy Roman Emperor, is dead." Then he shrank into
himself again, shuffled back to the table and crossed himself,
mumbling.

§ 4

THE little chapel dedicated to Saint Margaret in the ducal
residence at Munich is crammed full of magnificent potentates. Outside is a clear, ruddy harvest day. Within, the
coats of mail of the lords temporal chafe the pompous robes
of the lords spiritual, so closely are they packed together.
The Dukes of Austria are there, Rudolf, Leopold and
Friedrich, their Chancellor and Marshals, Johann von
Platzheim and Pilgrim Strein, the Bavarian and Tyrolean
nobles, the Margrave's Marshals, Burgraves, Chief Huntsman
and High Steward, Schenna, the Frauenberger, Konrad

Kummersbrücker, and Dipold Häl.   The vestments of the
spiritual peers are violet and salmon-coloured.   The Bishops
of  Salzburg,  Regensburg,  Würzburg  and  Augsburg ;
Deacons,  Provosts,  and  Canons.   The  vicars of Tyrol,
Teisendorf and Pyber.   Ensigns, papal and military.   Incense.   Outside, swarms of people, held back by the military.
In every window, on the sunny autumnal trees, on every wall
and balcony, swarms of people.

Within, Ludwig and Margarete knelt before the Papal
Commissaries, Bishop Paul of Freising and Abbot Peter of
Saint Lambert.   Yesterday their marriage was formally
annulled, and they were enjoined to live apart from each
other.   To-day the Bishop solemnly read the Papal Decree
of Absolution ;  since Ludwig of Bavaria, eldest son of the
late Ludwig of Bavaria, who had claimed to be Holy Roman
Emperor, had performed everything laid upon him by the
Pope, and since he had acknowledged in person his offences
against the Church, he, the Bishop and Abbot Peter, as
Papal Commissaries, granted the said Prince and the Princess
Margarete a dispensation on the score of their blood relationship, and permitted them to solemnise their marriage anew,
recognising as legitimate their previously-born son, Prince
Meinhard.   Removed from Ludwig and Margarete all
taint of sin, pronounced them capable of holding their
privileges, fiefs, estates and rights.   Received them once
more into the bosom of the Church.   Freed their lands from
the interdict.

Then the church doors all over Bavaria and Tyrol were
thrown open, doors which had been shut for many decades.
The bells, which had been dumb for so long, began to swing,
and rang out.   The people, starving for spiritual nourish-
ment, streamed into the churches.   Men and women

who had grown up without having once seen a church service or heard a peal of bells listened to their first Mass, and were uplifted in wondering happiness on the waves of the resonant, dazzling, magnificent liturgy of adoration to the Triune God.

# CHAPTER VIII

## § 1

" I WILL have nothing more to do with the Habsburgs ! " cried Duke Stephan of Lower Bavaria, angrily, in his hard military voice, and threw his steel gauntlet with a clatter on the table. He started from his seat and strode up and down. His cold, suspicious eyes glared from his angular skull wrathfully and contemptuously at his brother the Margrave, who remained seated, his head wearily bowed over the table so that his neck bulged more massively than ever. The great hall in the Munich Residence was not properly warm in spite of all the heating ; outside a disagreeable compound of snow and rain was falling.

" Very well," said the Margrave, and his voice sounded weary and depressed. " Then, brother, I shall leave you to prepare the other document we agreed upon."

Duke Stephan compressed his lips beneath his thick, wiry, dark brown moustache. He came forward and explained his outburst. " We have all treated the many unpleasant problems of our inheritance in our different ways. We have not bullied each other. We have, each of us, defended our own interests, clearly and practically, without juggling or trickery, and not interfered with each other. All six of us have felt it keenly that we had to break up and divide our lands, and make Wittelsbach small ; yet there was nothing else to be done, and we haven't said much about it. But, brother," and he raised his voice till it rasped accusingly, " that you should have consented to the Testament bequeathing Tyrol to the Habsburgs, you, the head of the Wittelsbachs, forces me to speak. I know it's a purely Tyrolean affair, and not my business ; and I have never meddled in your affairs. But that hits me too hard, it rankles in my blood, and I cannot help telling you so."

The Margrave made no answer. His hard, piercing blue eyes were fixed dully on vacancy ; he looked much older than his brother, who was very little his junior. When he persisted in his silent dejection, he who was usually so quick in retort and so ready of tongue, Duke Stephan said in a milder voice : " You can say that it was your wife's business, not yours ; and you can say that the lifting of the Pope's ban and interdict was good payment for a mere scrap of paper ; and you would be justified. But all the same, I should never have consented in your place, nor would any of our brothers, nor our father, if he had been still alive." The Margrave sat on wearily, huddled up, curiously effaced. This forlorn helplessness on the part of a man usually so hard and overbearing made his brother uneasy. He said, in an almost apologetic tone : " I know it can't be easy to have the Maultasch for a wife and Frauenberg for a High Steward."

When he was alone the Margrave fell into a fit of dull, paralysing, helpless exasperation, such as he had never experienced before. What kind of a situation was this ? There he was in his Residence, and his younger brother, Stephan, the cipher, the mediocre good-for-nothing, with his wretched, little Lower Bavaria, had stood before him and given him a dressing-down as if he were a brat of a boy. And he—how in all the wide world had that happened ?—

he had sat still and suffered him to go on. Was he so far gone as that? Was he so powerless?

Stephan had been right; that was the explanation. The Habsburgs ruled jointly, leaving the shrewd Rudolf to be their leader. He was their head, they were a whole body; their huge agglomeration of land was guided as a whole. Wittelsbach was split and broken into six fragments. He had allowed it to break up, he, the eldest. And not only that. He had helped the Habsburgs to get their hold. With the massacre of the Jews. That had been his first mistake. If he had protected his Jews, as Albert the Lame had done, his purse would never have become so empty and moth-eaten. He would never have had to hand over Bavaria to the Austrian treasury officials. Now they were scattered thick over the land, controlling and directing as they pleased. Everywhere, below, beside, and above the Wittelsbach standard, flew the red lion of the Habsburgs. He felt his father's huge staring eyes upon him. He blew his nose. His brother had been right.

But it was no use brooding over it. The mistake was made. The Jews were dead; and those who were still alive would be induced by no promises to come back. The land was bare and penniless, and the Habsburgs governed it.

Stuff and nonsense! That wasn't really the root of the trouble. It wasn't that that had been flung in his face. It was the Testament. The Testament signed by his wife, the hideous Maultasch. That was the point to get hold of; that was the problem to grasp. It was a relief to shift his self-accusations on to her shoulders. What was it his brother had said? It can't be easy to have the Maultasch for a wife. No, by God's Passion, it wasn't! He lashed himself into a sullen rage against his wife. She was to blame for everything, including the Bavarian contract with the Habsburgs. There she sat, the hideous Maultasch, with her ridiculous lover, the Frauenberger, that croaking monstrosity. There they sat together, hatching ruin for Bavaria. The laughing-stock of Europe. Oh, his instinct had been sound that day when his father had walked him up and down, and he had rebelled against marrying the woman. He stared into vacancy. Blew his nose, ground his teeth and groaned.

Betook himself to Agnes. She was lying on a sofa, her falconer standing before her. She had on her hawking gauntlet and was playing with her latest falcon. She saw at once that the Margrave was burning to speak to her, but she let him wait. Busied herself with the falcon, showing him off, and making no attempt to send the falconer away.

Ludwig growled out that to-day he had little interest in sport and falconry. Oh, the Margrave was out of spirits? Had been having trouble? She was sorry for that. With Duke Stephan? Dear, dear. But the Duke was quite a pleasant gentleman. He had been speaking about the Margravine's Testament? And about the Bavarian-Habsburg contract? Not about that? Oh well, only a passing reference.

If she would only send away the fellow with the falcon! But she showed no intention of doing so. Did she think it of such small importance that Stephan had been insolent? And was it a matter of indifference to her that he had come straight to her from his brother? The falcon opened its wings and shut them. She fondled it and called it pet names. She was filled with secret triumph. Had the moment come? Were the barriers down at last? Was the house of her enemy, so painfully erected, on the verge of collapse at last ?

So Duke Stephan had mentioned the Bavarian-Habsburg contract ? Well, she knew nothing about politics, of course, but, quite frankly, she had wondered at it herself. Such a great and wise prince—and to give the administration of his country to another ! She said it quite casually, hooding and unhooding her falcon, and immediately began a dispute with her falconer about the length of time the bird should still be kept fasting. Secretly she was gloating ; now was the time to squeeze the strength out of Tyrol, and divert it to Bavaria, or anywhere else. To ruin the life work of her enemy.

Ludwig sat oppressed with a great bitterness. What a fool he had been ! The very children had clearer insight. He should never have given up the administration of Bavaria. Even if he had had to pawn all his towns and revenues to Messer Artese. Margarete's Testament, that couldn't be revoked. But the administrative contract would expire in a few months : he would terminate it, come what might !

Agnes lay on the sofa, scarcely attending to him. The falconer was still there. If she had been alone he would have flung himself on her and shaken her : " Listen ! Don't you laugh at me ! I'm going to repudiate the contract ! I'm going to kick out the Habsburg officials ! Don't you laugh at me, you hussy ! " And he would have handled her in such a way that she would have forgotten her smiles and her preoccupation with the falcon. But the falconer stood there with his stupid, respectful air, and Agnes did not even look at him.

§ 2

KONRAD OF FRAUENBERG was negotiating with the Bishop of Brixen's advisers.    The bishopric was in complete subjection to the Margrave ; Konrad made that very clear to them. He sat croaking in high satisfaction, looking at the sweating men, and bullied them violently and at his ease.    Then finally, with contemptuous and gruesome joviality, he tossed the poor wretches a crust or two.    His secretary, an unobtrusive cleric, silently took notes of the proceedings with anxious conscientiousness.

When the gentlemen had gone, the Frauenberger gave directions to his secretary for several letters to officials on his own domains.    They always had to be screwed up to the same pitch.    They were not to be so slack—Satan of the nine tails fly off with them !    Not always to be remitting taxes.    Not always to be postponing the terms for socage and forced labour.    And not so much stupid sentimental slush about the infliction of penalties.    Only to punish a thief with the whipping-post and prison, because he stole " from necessity," what nonsense !    Everybody was driven by necessity.    The scoundrel was to have his hand hacked off as usual.    And to let off a poacher, because he had a family ! The deer had families too, and did he let them off ?    The fellow was to be hunted to death.    That was a good old custom.    There was to be no beginning made on his estates with modern humanitarianism.    The Frauenberger croaked on, the silent secretary wrote.

When he was alone the ugly man pushed back his colourless hair, relaxed himself, laid himself down on his pillow, cracked his joints, and yawned with lazy enjoyment.    It was a well-ordered world, and he knew how to deal with it.

God's Passion, he had gone far. The Margrave was nearly always away on his travels, visiting Agnes, or somewhere else. Why not ? Why shouldn't he prefer the lovely Agnes to his Maultasch ? What though he, the Frauen- berger, had a great deal to see to while the Margrave was absent ; the Maultasch, and Tyrol ? A great deal of work, ugly work. But profitable, that could not be denied. And Ludwig could not be easier to get on with. His Prince spared him the trouble of quarrelling with him.

He regarded his thick, red, fleshy hands. Obviously he had undervalued his virility. One had only to believe in it oneself to make all the women believe in it too. Nowadays any woman he wanted would come at his nod. He stretched himself, whistled and grinned. Rose lazily. Brought out ink, brushes and parchment. A pastime for vacant hours, when one wasn't sleeping. To-day he felt like it. Schenna thought him a dull fool : believed he had no eye for beauty. Schenna was no ass, but if he thought he had a monopoly of appreciating delectable roundnesses, smooth and pleasant to the touch, he made a mistake, the finicking fop ! He arranged his sheet of parchment. Oho ! He knew very well what was what in beauty. He grinned, whistled his favourite song to himself, the one about the seven joys of life, and set to work. His broad mouth hung open con- tentedly, he smacked his lips, clucked, gurgled, croaked, hiccuped, outlining and filling in with the brush. Bright colours, well laid on. Women's clothes, breasts, a face. He was deeply absorbed in his occupation.

He lifted his eyes. Margarete was standing behind him. Her shapeless face was distorted in a queer, ridiculous way, Obviously she had seen the thing ; so there was no sense in concealing or denying it.

He looked at her coolly, pursed his broad mouth, and croaked lazily : " An amulet."

" An amulet ?    That ?    That careful and pretty portrait of the creature ? "    He, ingenuous and bold : " Yes, of course."    She knew well enough that he had a boundary dispute with the lady.    There was, besides, her evil political influence over the Margrave.

Margarete looked at him darkly with her full, strong eyes.    He bore her gaze with cool indifference.    She ordered him finally to give her the picture.

" Why not ? " he croaked.    It wasn't exactly a pious amulet.    One could conjure into it one's own wishes and desires.    Her wishes for the lady he dared say were just as disagreeable as his own.    He grinned, and with a deep, exaggerated bow handed her the picture.

When she was alone she looked at it for a long time, and examined it closely.    The hair was golden, the eyes stared, two stupid blue specks, out of the crude painting.    With her painted fingers Margarete drew a pin from her hair.    Slowly, carefully, she stabbed it through the blue spots.    The parchment was stout ; she bored, bored more fiercely, and slowly pierced it through.    The parchment crackled.    There were two small, frayed holes in place of the eyes.

§ 3

THE Margrave rose, the interview had lasted barely ten minutes.    They had discussed nothing but business, and both question and answer had been icy in their precision.    " There is still the Taufers affair," said Margarete.

" Later," said Ludwig, waving it away.

" It has been dragging on for nearly a year already," said Margarete.    " It must be settled finally."

" What do you want to do, then ? " asked the Margrave, resentfully

The Taufers affair was a dispute concerning boundaries which had broken out between Agnes of Taufers and the Frauenberger. Agnes sheltered herself behind the see of Brixen, which had endowed her, and not the Frauenberger, with the disputed lands. He was right in fact, she in law. Only the Margrave's insistence was needed to make Brixen abandon its pretexts, and Agnes lose the properties. But since the Bishop's advisers assumed that this was not Ludwig's wish, they plucked up courage to resist the Frauenberger stoutly on this point.

Margarete, in hostile mood, recapitulated the evidence against the bishopric. The Margrave, as sullen and stiff-necked as she, enumerated the political grounds for not annoying the Bishop at the moment. They eyed each other darkly and obstinately. If it had been a question of their own possessions, they would never have opposed each other with such bitterness.

Hitherto, in spite of their growing alienation, they had never come to a serious quarrel. Not a word had the Margrave uttered about Margarete's Testament, not a word about her relations to the Frauenberger. Nor had she mentioned the name of Agnes in his presence. Now they quarrelled hotly, throwing out threats and insults far more violent than the trivial occasion warranted. They confronted each other, raging. The Margrave's quiet, manly face was twisted with passion. She retorted with forced composure, wounding and contemptuous.

Till at length he could contain himself no longer, and in open, jeering wrath flung at her : " All this is only for your pet baboon, the Frauenberger ! "

She went quite grey, gasped, and cast a look of hate upon him. Then she said, hoarsely : " Yes ! Yes ! I won't allow justice to be prostituted for your harlot ! "

He clenched his hand to keep himself from striking her. Abuse was not his usual weapon. But now he fell upon her with vile terms : " You hag ! You abomination ! You stinking slut ! Is that what you fabricate, you and your baboon squatting together ? Is it not disgrace enough for me to have a wife like you, branded by Heaven ? Will you drag my name further into dishonour ? Are you out for men, you, with a face like that ? You're a fine match for each other, the Maultasch and the baboon ! " He broke off suddenly, and made for her with swollen veins and a face so distorted that she retreated behind the table. " I won't stand it ! " he screamed. " I'll strike him dead ! I won't be made a fool of ! "

# CHAPTER IX

## § 1

MEANWHILE the Frauenberger sat in Taufers Castle blinking at Agnes from his reddish eyes. "We'll soon come to an agreement," he croaked. "You are rich, I am not so poor. Do you set much store by these farms? I don't. To me they're only an excuse for seeing you." With his blunt red hand he caressed hers, long and white. Agnes smiled. Here was a man; he had force, will, shameless directness. "The world is stupid," he croaked. "Stupider even than one thinks." He sat there, with his wide mouth in his clean-shaven, rosy face, broad, solid, shameless and ugly. "It seems to me that for miles around we're the only sensible people." And his short, hard, aggressive fingers slid further up her arm.

But all the same he had no intention of yielding a jot to her in the dispute between them.

## § 2

AGNES went about with a light, dancing smile on her lips, draining to the dregs her triumph over Margarete, rolling it on her tongue. Bound the Margrave closer and closer to her, cold-bloodedly, imperceptibly; undermined him, insinuated herself into him, took possession of him.

He was a sober, thrifty man, not at all inclined to extravagance. She asked him, casually and over her shoulder, for

gifts which usually would have caused him years of deliberation.    If he made the slightest objection, she did not insist,
and dropped the matter at once.    But she had a way of
turning her back with an air of sneering surprise, scarcely
discernible, but profoundly contemptuous, which disturbed
him more than tears and prayers and railings could have done.
So she gradually turned the solid, calculating man upside
down, drove him into luxury and extravagance, rotted away
and pulled to pieces what Margarete had created by decades
of work.

All at once Messer Artese reappeared.    He was everywhere, in ten places at once, with three brothers who were
very like him, insignificant and unfailingly courteous.    Before
anyone was aware of it he had his hands again upon the
taxes, the salt revenues, the mines.    Margarete's icy contempt he met with countless bowings and scrapings, and with
the greatest readiness released the Margrave from his liabili-
ties to the Habsburgs.    Ludwig could now terminate that
contract if he wished.    True, what he paid to the Florentine
was three times as much as the Austrians required.    Messer
Artese vanished again, like a shadow, as he had come.
Appeared at Taufers Castle.    Who that saw the polite little
man would have thought that he could ever rage as he had
once done before Agnes ?    They sat facing each other,
Agnes and he, and smiled to each other with faint, knowing
smiles.    Ah yes, a fine country, a rich and blessed country.
Wine, fruit and grain.    Flourishing, well-regulated, in-
dustrious cities.    He pulled, she thrust.    She struck the
Duchess, the ugly creature, when she thrust.    He was already
less fascinated by the pleasure of making profits ; he was
goaded by the desire to wreak destruction on the work of his
enemy, to rend it asunder, to annihilate completely the work

of the dead and defeated Jew.    She thrust at the ugly woman
he tore at the dead foe.

Sleek in his fat sat Konrad, the Frauenberger, and plumped
himself out ;  his clean-shaven, wide-mouthed face shone
rosily.    He lay among cushions in the elegant little salon
at Taufers ;  Agnes sat beside him.    The sun came into
the room, he blinked, stretched himself lazily, yawned, and
cracked his joints.    Agnes begged, commanded, threatened
and cajoled ;  he must accompany her to Trent.    He said
he wouldn't think of it.    The Margrave could dance
attendance on her.    She turned away, flicking him with that
light, surprised air of contempt which was so successful
with the Margrave.    He laughed heartily, keenly amused,
and turned over on his other side.    As she remained obstinately silent he began to yawn.    Laid himself out, his joints
cracking, and fell asleep peacefully and comfortably, snoring
loudly.    In an hour's time he woke up ;  evening was
setting in, and she still sat sulking in the opposite corner.
He roused himself lazily, went over to her, seized her with
coarse joviality, and pulled her down on the cushions beside
him.    She offered no resistance.

He treated her according to his mood.    Let her fawn for
a caress like a dog.    Soothed her with promises which he
broke, as a matter of course, with a laugh.    Send him away ?
How could she ?    He would laugh.    And it would be
ridiculous too.    Who else was there so ugly ?    So impudent ?
Had such a hard grip ?

There was no second Frauenberg.

She lay relaxed under his coarse caresses, and looked up at
him obliquely.    Saw his sly, satisfied, fleshy, grinning face.
How ugly it was !    How full of strength, how mean !    She
was curious.    Was it impossible to get at him, was it possible

to make that impudent and confident visage shrink and blench
with fear ?

She began to incite the Margrave against him. Quite
unobtrusively, apparently in jest. The seed fell on good
ground, which had for long been prepared. Germinated,
budded, grew. What was it Duke Stephan had said ? It
couldn't be easy to have such a wife, and the Frauenberger
for one's High Steward. He would put an end to it. He
had had his bellyful. The laughing-stock of Europe. He
would make an end of it. In Munich. Make one clean
sweep. First of the filthy Habsburgs, and then of the
Frauenberger, the misbegotten obscenity

§ 3

" TAKE a good look at me," said the Frauenberger to
Margarete, strutting with grotesque and exaggerated importance. " Take a good look at me. Perhaps you won't
have many more chances." As Margarete looked up in
amazement, he went on croaking : " I know I'm no beauty,
but I'm certainly unique. Anyone who's interested in me
had better have a good look at me now, to keep me fresh in
his memory. For I won't be there to look at much longer.
Something is brewing against me. The Margrave looks
daggers at me. Unluckily there are plenty of real daggers
behind him. He has ordered me to accompany him to
Munich. There he'll relieve his feelings. Gufidaun,
the good, honourable young man, who can't stand me, and
Kummersbruck haven't been able to keep their mouths shut.
So take a good look at me, Margarete. When I'm gone,
fill yourself up with wine and dream of me. You don't
need to have any masses said. You're a good fellow, Duchess
Maultasch," he laughed and clapped her on the shoulder.

Then he whistled his song about the seven joys, blinked at her, and went out on his straddling legs.

Margarete had not uttered a word. Now she sat alone before the massive table, stately in bright green damask, and stiff with paint. Deeds and documents were piled in front of her. The room was dark and gloomy ; in her ears rang the Frauenberger's song.

He was quite right. What else was there in life but the seven joys of his song ?

She had never given up the struggle. She had been beaten and brought low once, but she had not given up. Out of wreck and ruin she had built up her life anew, the land, the cities, her gay, noisy, populous, striving cities, her work. And now the blood which she had painfully guided into them was to be tapped, drawn off, into Bavaria, some-where or other, to please the harlot ; uselessly wasted. The Margrave had said nothing to her, but she had been assured of it from various sources. The administrative contract with the Habsburgs was to be terminated. Her towns, her Tyrol, to be left naked, empty, drained dry, cast off.

And that wasn't enough. The other thing. The Frauen-berger. The ugly, solitary man. Who belonged to her. Whom she had raised up. Maybe he was evil, despicable, a scoundrel. But he belonged to her. He, above all men. And he, too, was to be taken from her. Ah, she had not forgotten how he had cried at that interview : " I'll strike him dead ! I won't be made a fool of ! " She heard his voice, hoarse with hatred, and saw his burning eyes. Yes, Konrad's instincts were sure ; there was murder in the air. If he went to Munich, he would not come back.

Her withered old Fräulein von Rottenburg appeared in the room, and coughed. The Italian dealer had come, the

man from Palermo whom she had sent for. She was glad
of the diversion, and ordered him to be admitted. He stood
before her ; a round, olive-skinned face, quick, brownish
eyes. He had all kinds of things. Gaily-coloured birds,
fine shimmering cloths and stuffs, precious stones, rare
essences, quaint comfits. Helped by his assistant, he spread
his wares out before her with quick and supple movements.
She lingered over this and that. Asked to have things
explained to her, forgot to attend, and then spoke more
eagerly than ever. What was that thing ? A vial, a tiny
vase made of a dull-coloured, semi-precious stone, beautifully
shaped, firmly closed and sealed. That ? Oh, Her Grace
was a connoisseur, Her Grace had excellent taste. That
was certainly a great rarity. Cut out of one piece, and how
noble in shape, in moulding ! The work of a great master,
certainly. Would she have the goodness to consider the
pictures cut on it ? Here the Hohenstaufen Emperor,
Friedrich the Second, and here the Jewish King Solomon,
and there the Queen of Sheba, and on the fourth side the
Sultan Boabdil, a mighty and cruel prince of Barbary. Its
contents, too, were a great rarity ; a subtle fluid, odourless,
colourless and tasteless ; and whoever drank but one drop
of it lived no more than an hour, but expired like a wick
without oil. A precious, noble vial.

The Duchess bought a great deal, at random, without
bargaining, which was unlike her. Cloths, spices, many
jewels, two of the gay birds, and also the vial.

Then she sat down to table and ate. Ate quite alone,
magnificently arrayed. The table, too, was sumptuously
bedecked with ornamental vessels, golden dishes and plates.
Music in the anteroom. Footmen, pages, and carvers ran
to and fro. She ate enormously. The Frauenberger was

right.    This was one of the seven joys of life.    Around her
were piled the purchases she had made, the jewels, the stuffs,
and also the vial.    With her painted hands she carried the
food to her mouth ; soup, fish, roast meat, and the precious,
quaint comfits which she had just bought.    She swallowed
them and tossed down the wine.    The twilight fell ; huge,
solid candles were lit.    She sat alone, stiff, heavy, pompous,
and ate.

§ 4

So there it lay.    He had not dared to bring it himself.    He
had sent it by a messenger.    A short, courteous note accompanied it, in which he asked for her signature.

She had summoned Schenna immediately.    Before him
she let herself go and burst into tears.    The Habsburg
contract really terminated ?    Blocked and abandoned the
fine, skilfully made channel through which sap and
vigour was flowing into her cities !    And she was asked
further to lend her signature to it !    The ground under her
feet was crumbling like sand.    Her life-work undone,
slipping away from her like flowing water, not to be arrested.
Everything ruined, senselessly, stupidly destroyed.

Schenna listened quietly, his long, faded face strangely
puckered ; her tears, her breakdown touched him more
closely than he cared to admit to himself.    Poor woman !
Poor Duchess Maultasch !    Had your mouth been a finger's
breadth smaller, the muscles of your cheeks but a little tauter,
your life would have been contented and happy, and Tyrol
and the Roman Empire would have worn another aspect.
He chid himself.    Foolish sentimentality !

When at length he answered her, he had himself well in
hand again.    In his high, weary, frail voice he pointed out

that she had nothing to gain in refusing to sign ; formally her signature meant nothing, and the Margrave was only requesting it for reasons of prestige. But if she did sign, at least they could not prevent her from having her say when the contract was liquidated.

But as she sat crouching there in silence, broad, heavy, forlorn and despairing, he was moved again. He said he would like to help where he could. He was a Tyrolean ; it irritated him that alert, living, cultivated Tyrol should be sacrificed to sleepy, stolid, brutal Bavaria. He gave himself an impatient shake ; it was a weighty decision to take, and one really should not be so soft-hearted. But then he stood up and said, and in his earnestness there was a spice of irony, that if she still valued his services, he was willing, in order to save what could be saved, to take over the chief office in the mountains, the office of Burgrave. With her plump, painted hand she pressed his, long, thin and loose-jointed.

Then the Frauenberger appeared to take his leave. He stood clanking in his armour, and over the bright steel there grinned rosy, bare-cheeked and smooth, his impudent, wide-mouthed face. All that was left for him, he said, was to plunge into obscurity, into the world of underlings, where the Margrave could not find him ; for he was not at all minded to die. So at the right moment on the journey he would disappear. One had to be a man, and take the ups and downs of life lightly. She was a good sort ; he had had more fun with her than with many a doll face. It had certainly been more interesting. And so God be with her.

She said he had given her an amulet with evil wishes for a certain person. It was her turn now. She handed him the dull-coloured vial. The liquid was odourless and taste-less ; but whoever drank of it was in hell or in Paradise within an hour. Before he vanished into obscurity, into the underworld, he should consider that well.

He seized upon it, and grinned that she was the devil of a woman. Odourless, tasteless ; well, that was certainly to be considered.

She hastily replied that she had said nothing. But the Sicilian had sworn it was so. And since she supposed she would not see him again, she was giving it to him. It was entirely his affair, she had said nothing.

Extraordinarily massive in his armour, he croaked from his many layers of steel ; he gave her many thanks. As he had said, a devil of a woman. He lifted cumbrously his mail-clad arm, clapped her on the shoulder, croaked : " Our Maultasch ! " Clattered off, cased in metal, unwieldy, grinning with his frog-mouth. Whistled his song.

From below sounded the horns and trumpets of the departing company. The Margrave had not taken leave of her. Should she go to the window ? Her limbs refused to obey her. She leaned against the table, ashy pale, like a painted corpse.

## § 5

THROUGH the golden-brown September landscape trotted the Margrave and his gentlemen. For a while they rode beside the pale, wide waters of Chiemsee. There was a strong wind, the mountains, a velvety blue-grey, fell behind.

Ludwig was in the best of spirits. He wore a light breast-plate, and had given his helmet to a page, so that the wind blew pleasantly round his short-cropped head. He felt very youthful ; his hard, blue eyes were brighter than usual in his brown, masculine face. It had been a good decision to get rid of the Austrians. Now he was riding into his

country as its real master.    Down with the arrogant red
lion of Habsburg, away with it from beside the blue lion of
the Wittelsbachs !    He rejoiced in the prospect of reinstating
his own officials, and making a clean sweep.

Yes, a clean sweep.    He had made up his mind exactly
what to do with the Frauenberger, too.    That very night
he would seize him and settle the matter with him, honourably, by the sword.    He had no doubt of the outcome.
Then he would have room to breathe.    He would see very
little of Margarete.    Let her sit in her castle at Tyrol ;  he
would live in Munich, Innsbruck and Bozen, and govern
as he thought fit.    If she consented, well and good ;  if she
didn't consent, well and good too.    Agnes would not be
able to find any further reason for turning her shoulder on
him in that pert, airy manner which so annoyed him.

The fact that he had thrown off his dejection and knew
so exactly what lay ahead of him stimulated him to greater
freedom and light-heartedness than he had known for years.
He cracked jokes with Berchtold von Gufidaun, and with his
faithful Kummersbrucker.    He even regarded the Frauenberger with a certain grim benevolence.    He was riding
along, broad and rosy in his shining armour, humming discordantly, blinking with reddish eyes at the sunny, contented
world—and yet was as good as dead already.    The Margrave
called to him, and rode beside him.    The Frauenberger
retailed smutty jests and made impertinent remarks.    Ludwig
laughed heartily and adopted the same tone : they exchanged
coarse and pungent soldiers' gossip, and enjoyed themselves
amazingly.

Then they had an early mid-day meal.    They ate in the
open air, plentifully, drank, and lay down for a while.    Then
after another drink they mounted their horses again.    Ludwig

had his helmet open, he would not close it until they reached Munich. The Frauenberger kept close beside him ; the Margrave openly sought his company. They set off. They were now in the plain ; the mountains faded away behind them. The plain was vast and monotonous ; sometimes a small, insignificant country gentleman's seat flickered by in the sun, or a farm, or a tolerably wretched village. They rode on briskly ; they would be in Munich before evening.

The conversation between the Margrave and the Frauenberger became halting, and then stopped. Ludwig felt extraordinarily tired, his breath came heavily, his light armour oppressed him. Had he drunk too much ? To the right of the road there appeared a village ; its houses had a strange, round appearance, were a dirty white in spite of the bright sunshine, and leant queerly towards each other. Somebody said : " That place is called Zorneding." Was it Gufidaun's voice, or Kummersbruck's ?

Suddenly he plucked at his helmet, at his breastplate, and pitched forward on his side from the horse, his half-unloosed helmet hanging down. Kummersbruck and a page galloped up and lifted him. The helmet clattered into the dust ; his face was ashy-pale, but not distorted ; his lower jaw hung down. The massive neck of the dead man did not look threatening now, only fat and stupid. They rubbed him, and prayed. Into the silent bewilderment of the others broke the Frauenberger's penetrating, croaking, vulgar voice : " A strange thing to happen. In the open, near Munich. Just like his father." Berchtold von Gufidaun looked him up and down, his face dark with menace. Blinking impudently the Frauenberger stood his ground and croaked : " Do you want anything ? " Gufidaun slowly turned away, and said nothing.

In the Chapel of St. Margaret in the Munich Residence
the corpse was laid in state.    Many candles burned.    Ulrich
von Abensberg, Hippolt von Stein, and five other barons kept
the death-watch.    The Frauenberger too was among them.
But he soon began to yawn and withdrew.    Stretched himself on his bed, whistled his song, cracked his joints, hiccuped,
clucked, and fell into a peaceful sleep.

BOOK THREE

# CHAPTER I

## § 1

In Landshut in his palace Duke Stephan had just given directions which of his gentlemen should accompany him to Munich. He wanted to greet his eldest brother, the Margrave, who had made the happy resolution to drive the Habsburgers out of his country. Duke Stephan proudly congratulated himself that it was really he who had precipitated this decision. He held higher his head, with the short, thick, nut-brown moustache ; certainly his recent protest had stiffened Ludwig's back. And now he would go to Munich and see if he could not effect a closer unity among the Wittelsbachs. Damn it all, if Ludwig and he were firmly resolved, why should they not succeed in bringing the Wittelsbachs under one roof, and in welding them together like the Habsburgs ? Of course the Habsburgers fought like turkey-cocks when they held counsel in private ; but when they showed themselves in public they stood as one man, and nothing but honeyed words passed between them. It was a good thing that Ludwig had roused himself at last. He would not rest now until the torn house of Wittelsbach was patched together again.

They brought his armour, and began to arm him for the journey. Then a courier arrived from Munich and announced the Margrave's death. Duke Stephan stood motionless, his mouth half-open, his fingers strangely rigid. Then with a violent explosive command he dismissed his attendants, strode to and fro still only half-clothed, and made sudden imperious gestures. His face worked; it knotted menacingly, and became smooth again; the short, thick moustache jerked with the trembling of his lips.

He saw possibilities, manifold, iridescent. They started up on all sides. Young Meinhard was a boy, weak, stupid, good-humoured, and moreover was at the beck and call of his own son, Friedrich.

Yes, in Stephan's hands lay now the destiny of Wittelsbach. To unite the two Bavarias. To force unity on his hostile brothers, the Hollander, the Brandenburger, the Counts Palatine. They must be made to see, they must knuckle under. Who were they, anyhow, Ludwig, Albrecht, Wilhelm, and Ruprecht? In themselves they were nothing; but Wittelsbach was a great deal, was everything. A potent influence would go out from him; his faith, his honourable, upright, disinterested will would overflow into them; they would let themselves be persuaded.

He sat down heavily; his face lost its conventionally stiff, military expression, his shoulders grew slack. Ah, nothing of all this would happen. His hopes were feverish, deceitful. He was not the man to carry this through. Certainly the opportunity was good; but the burden was too heavy for him. His father before him, the Emperor, who was much more robust, had been a temporizer and had had to leave his work lying half-finished; how should he, the weaker man, bring that botched and mutilated project to a conclusion?

His brother had died on the road. A bad omen. He had not liked Ludwig particularly; and he had never been intimate with him. The brothers had, all six, avoided close contact; each had kept a strict and suspicious eye on the others to see that none seized too large a portion of the

inheritance. But Ludwig had been an honourable man ;
life had not been easy for him ; he had married the Maultasch and made a great sacrifice for the House. Now he
was dead in the prime of his life. Clouds were gathering
round the Wittelsbachs ; their glory was departing.

He remembered how he had heard the Papal bull which
proclaimed his father's excommunication : " May his sons
be accursed : may they be driven from their houses, delivered
into the hands of their enemies and utterly destroyed." He
had been a small boy at that time ; the resonant, menacing,
heroic phrases had conveyed nothing definite to him ; but
they had filled him with fear, and had always haunted him.
Things had not gone well with the Wittelsbachs since then.
Their lands falling to pieces. The brothers destroying one
another. In the north-west, in the Flemish provinces,
their mother the Empress had reigned along with Wilhelm,
the most gifted of the brothers. They had come into conflict, and Wilhelm had defeated his mother in that wild
and bloody sea-fight in the estuary of the Maas ; she had
fled to her brother-in-law, the King of England. She had
been an overbearing woman, gloomy and distant towards
her children ; yes, one had to put up a resistance against her,
one always felt oppressed in her presence. Now she was
dead, wearied out with splendour, suffering and care, and
Wilhelm, the most frank, talented and lovable of the brothers,
had fallen into raving madness, made a sick man through his
conflict with his mother and his exile in a foreign land. No,
things did not stand well with the house of Wittelsbach ;
that curse had reached its bitter fulfilment, if not literally
at any rate in spirit. He stared in front of him. His
brother's death left him the chance and the obligation of
riveting the mountainland more firmly together, of retaining

P

the Southern marches.   He looked at his hands ; they lay heavy, slack, and powerless.   How should he with these hands——— ?

Nonsense !   He had taken too much heavy spiced wine with his breakfast, that was all.   It made the blood heavy, the mind dull.   Were his prospects not excellent ?   The boy Meinhard was weak and easy to guide.   'Zounds, he would be able to maintain an ascendancy over him, at any rate.   He straightened himself ; above his compressed lips the short, thick, nut-brown moustache stood out resolutely. He would weld Wittelsbach together and make it great in the world.

He bade them finish arming him.   Now he had double occasion to ride to Munich.   He spoke in his old, rasping, military voice.   He commanded his son Friedrich to come.

Prince Friedrich had heard already of the Margrave's death.   He was almost bursting with plans and energy. Meinhard adored him, and followed him about devotedly. Through Meinhard he was now more powerful than his father.   The young man, slender and elegant, his dark hair falling low over his broad, angular, self-willed forehead, had from his earliest youth regarded his associates with contempt.   He alone was the real descendant of the Emperor. He had gnashed his teeth to see Wittelsbach splitting into ever smaller units.   He had rebelled haughtily against all that his father said and did, his father who had neither the wrist nor the thighs to curb this noble, sensitive, unruly steed of Wittelsbach.   Oh, he, Prince Friedrich, had the capacity and the knack for that ; he would tame the steed.

So he came into his father's presence, slender, proud, hostile, and full of secret contempt.   Duke Stephan considered this son of his to be more gifted by nature and more fortunate than himself, saw in him his own fulfilment, and loved even his rashness, his quick anger, his arrogance. Yet when Friedrich asserted himself too impudently he could not control his temper, and it always came to wild outbursts between them.

Curtly, in a brusque and military tone, Stephan informed the Prince that Margrave Ludwig had died suddenly ; he was going to ride to Munich now for the funeral, and contemplated staying for some eight to ten days. In the meantime Friedrich was to take control at Landshut, and send a courier to him in Munich if anything of special importance should arise. Friedrich reflected. Never yet had his father left him so much responsibility ; what lay behind it ? He measured his father mistrustfully. Ah, the Duke feared his influence on Meinhard, and wanted to go to Munich alone so that he might detach Meinhard from him, and supplant him.

He threw his head back, shot a quick look out of his brown eyes at his father, and said insolently that he could not think of staying away from his friend Meinhard on such a sad occasion ; he would ride to Munich too, of course. There were two or three other gentlemen in the room, also a page. Duke Stephan swelled with rage and asked hoarsely whether the boy was out of his wits. The others stood wide-eyed, tense with expectation. Friedrich replied that he was quite in his senses ; every honourable prince and gentleman must understand him and agree with him. The Duke advanced upon him menacingly in his clattering armour. The youth stood his ground at first, then turned and fled. Threw himself on a horse—no one dared to stop him—and spurred on towards the south, towards Munich.

The Duke laughed, at first angrily, then appreciatively.

Relieved at this outcome, his gentlemen laughed with him.
" A young imp, Friedrich ! " said the Duke.    " A young
imp, His Highness the Prince," repeated the gentlemen.

But then slowly Stephan's gloom returned.   He could
not control his own son.   How would he ever be able to
master the refractory Wittelsbachs ?

He mounted his horse.   With a great cavalcade he rode
heavily along the way over which Prince Friedrich had
galloped before him.

§ 2

THE Master of the Hounds, Herr von Kummersbruck,
informed Meinhard of his father's death.   He broke the
news very gently, in roundabout phrases.   It was lost labour.
The eighteen-year-old lad understood not a word, so that
at last Herr von Kummersbruck had to say plainly and bluntly
that the Margrave was dead.

Meinhard gazed at him dumbfounded out of his round,
candid eyes ;   turned the news over in his good-natured
thick head ;   and broke into a sweat.   He had no idea what
effect this event might have, or what he was to do about it.
He was Duke now.   That would be a great strain probably,
and would bring labour and inconvenience.   He would have
felt much more comfortable as a small country squire.
Really it was very unfortunate for the country and for
everybody that his father was dead.   For he had been
capable and energetic, whereas his mother, as his friend,
Prince Friedrich, had pointed out to him, was licentious
and repulsive.   God knew that in reality neither his father
nor his mother had troubled about him.   His father's death
was a matter of indifference to him except for the fact that
it cost him vexation, exacted care and thought.

He drew out of his pocket the tiny rodent he always carried

about with him, the little, long-tailed dormouse that by
patient labour he had trained, so that it answered to the
name of Peter and at his whistle would come and eat with
him, and sleep with him. He contemplated the little beast
with great, aggrieved, unhappy eyes, and stroked it.

Little by little he freed himself at length from his confused,
awkward embarrassment when he saw that people accorded
him a quite different importance from that he had held
before. From the generals and the highest officials down to
the humblest lackeys their faces were more devoted, more
discreet, and more servile. As he slowly became aware
of this, he had great sport in testing and corroborating it
continually. He kept on giving chaotic and contradictory
orders, and with amusement watched his subordinates busily
executing them ; he made his people skip, and thought it
funny that their faces always remained submissive and
unresentful.

There was only one man who openly refused to be
impressed by Meinhard's new dignity, the Frauenberger.
Whenever he saw his formidable bulk, Meinhard had an
uncomfortable feeling ; his fat, bare face with the frog's
mouth, the whitish hair, the reddish eyes, had always seemed
dangerous to him ; his jovial manner, too, filled him with
apprehension. Now Frauenberg came up to him, blinked,
and croaked familiarly, paternally : " Well, my young
Duke ! It isn't easy. But don't lose your head. We'll
manage all right." He took the young man's fat, good-
natured hand in his own fleshy, menacing one, blinked at
him, not at all respectfully, not at all submissively, rather
with a jocular, mocking superiority, turned his back, and
went off whistling his ditty.

Then Prince Friedrich arrived, tempestuous, covered with

sweat, and burning with ardour. Rushed at once to the young Duke. The cousins embraced ; Meinhard felt released in the presence of his friend. Friedrich related his encounter with his father ; Meinhard was enthusiastic. The dark, slender prince, overflowing with youth and the desire to achieve great deeds and win honour, poured out his soul and carried away with him the fair, stout, unresisting Meinhard, who with his simple, round, blue eyes looked up at him entranced, and congratulated himself on having this splendid friend He unbosomed himself completely, and told about the Frauenberger's disagreeable, presumptuous manner. Friedrich foamed and stamped. Declared that he would soon put that right. He commanded the Frauenberger to come. Said insolently over his shoulder that the Duke did not need his presence in Munich, and desired him to go to meet the Dowager Duchess, who without doubt was already on the way to Bavaria. Smiling, impudent, with good-humoured mockery, the Frauenberger gazed for a long time at the two young gentlemen, said he would have liked to assist at the obsequies of the late Margrave, who had been so gracious to him, but felt himself honoured that they had entrusted him with the escort of his equally gracious Princess. He only hoped, he added with paternal anxiety, that the young gentlemen would manage all right in Munich without him. He blinked from the one to the other and went.

Friedrich had come with an impetuous political programme and exerted himself to win his cousin's allegiance to it before anyone else, his father, the Maultasch, or the Habsburger, could intervene. He did not agree at all with the Wittelsbach tradition of government, which played off the burghers against the nobility, and advanced the towns at the expense of the castles. This hesitating, cautious, bargaining and chaffering policy, which accepted and respected the commoner as a full-fledged human being, was antipathetic to his very soul. The world was upheld—he took this to be axiomatic —by the Christian knight, by the prince who knew no restrictions save the self-chosen laws of chivalry. But the knights of to-day had no pride, made all kinds of concessions and compromises, and let their power diminish rather than increase. The nobility should be strengthened, the commonalty humbled, so that it should be only a footstool for the feet of princes. What was money! Or trade! Or the towns! They must burnish up again the old, shining laws of chivalry, and base the land and the Empire on them.

Young Meinhard listened with enthusiasm to the other's extravagant speeches. His friend came now to practical proposals. Meinhard should bring these ideals to fruition in his lands. In Bavaria there were still noblemen of the old school, who had treated the burgher vermin all their lives with fitting contempt. Along with him and a number of these aristocrats Meinhard should found a hunting and jousting brotherhood in accordance with the strict statutes of earlier knightly orders such as the Round Table and similar noble companies. But this league should not merely serve for sport and play ; from it should go out a renewal of the whole nation. And instead of a cabinet of old, dried-up theologians and officials—this was most important of all— the league would be the real ruling authority.

Meinhard was for it with all his soul. He had felt anxious about ruling ; now he was relieved and happy that it promised to be so pleasant, that he would be able to discharge it in co-operation with a joyous, gallant company of cavaliers and comrades, under the direction of the gifted and amicable Friedrich.

They laid their heads together, and made a list of the noblemen who should be taken into the league. Ulrich of Abensberg, Ulrich of Laber, Hippolt of Stein first of all. Then Höhenrain, Freiberg, Pinzenau, Trautsam of Frauenhoffen, Hanns of Gumppenberg, Otto of Maxlrain. Several names sounded not quite unobjectionable, and demanded long and careful consideration. The young Duke had taken his dormouse out of his pocket ; it sat on the table, its eye peeping from its blunt head at them as they wrote, and whisked its tail to and fro. The two youths worked until their heads perspired.

When Duke Stephan arrived in the evening the administration of Bavaria was as good as disposed of. Friedrich had urgently warned his cousin to be scrupulously on his guard before Duke Stephan. So the Duke found his nephew shy and stubborn. He wanted his signature on certain crucial questions, frontier concerns, and matters relating to the customs. Meinhard evaded him, saying, on Friedrich's advice, that he wanted to wait first until his father was under the ground. Duke Stephan knew very well that Friedrich was behind this opposition. He raged, but was proud of his son.

Then Margarete arrived, and on the same day, very magnificent, Duke Rudolf of Austria. The Margrave was buried with tremendous pomp. Agnes of Flavon found again that black suited her best. People looked at the catafalque of the dead man, at the Dowager Margravine, at the Counts Palatine of the Rhine, at the Dukes of the two Bavarias and of Austria, but their eyes constantly returned to Agnes again.

Margarete of Tyrol, Duke Stephan of Lower Bavaria, and Duke Rudolf of Austria were all tugging at young

Meinhard, asking for ordinances, agreements, ratifications, signatures. Under Friedrich's influence the good-natured, easily-led youth remained firm. On the third day after the Margrave's funeral the Arthurian Order of Bavarian Chivalry was founded. Meinhard and Friedrich were the commanders, the lords of Abensberg, Laber and Stein the lieutenants. Membership, fifty-two barons from Upper and Lower Bavaria. When pressed by his mother and by the Dukes, Meinhard responded that he was bound by his knightly oath not to say or do anything vital without consulting his trusted friends, the members of the Arthurian Order. Stephan, Margarete and Rudolf stood dumbfounded. What was this aristocratic clique which had laid hold of the youth? They eyed each other mistrustfully. Only Stephan divined the hidden hand straight away. "That young imp!" he burst out, highly gratified.

Ulrich of Abensberg was married to the elder sister of Agnes of Flavon-Taufers. Through him Friedrich came to know Agnes. He was captivated. Agnes looked graciously on the young, slender, turbulent prince. She became the patroness of the Arthurian Order. Was present when the banner of the Order, which bore her colours, was consecrated. She said to Friedrich: "One can embrace your politics, Prince Friedrich, with one's whole heart." As the banner was lowered in front of her he declaimed the formula from his very soul: "*Pour toi mon âme, pour toi ma vie.*" She went about among the clanking warriors, dispensing gracious words appropriately chosen for each. Her long, blue eyes, filled with understanding, lingered often on the slender, dark Prince; her small, daring lips smiled to the Abensberger; with her long, white hands she stroked Duke Meinhard's dormouse. All were filled with enthusiasm and elation.

# CHAPTER II

## § I

" MAY I report to Your Grace," said the Frauenberger to Margarete, " how the Margrave died ? "

Margarete had become very corpulent. The slack skin hung down in hideous folds from her apelike out-jutting jaws ; on her cheeks it was covered with furrows and warts, which the rouge could no longer conceal.

" Yes," said the Frauenberg, grinning, " the Margrave was unusually pleased when we rose from table. We had been drinking, he and I. I always kept beside him. He fell sideways from his horse. He was not very much disfigured. It was odd that the stroke should have taken him near Munich. Just like his papa."

Margarete said nothing. Her eyes, usually so expressive, were staring and vacant. " Well, Duchess Maultasch," croaked Konrad, " we won't have much difficulty with Meinhard. A bit shy, but a good lad. The Bavarian keeps stirring him up, black Friedrich, the stupid lad. Just wait ! There's nothing to be afraid of. Surely I've earned a kiss," he grinned. But as the breath of his wide mouth came near her she recoiled in horror. " No ? All right then," he said good-naturedly.

The very aged Abbot Johannes of Viktring had come to Munich too with Duke Rudolf of Austria. He had now become quite shaky and decrepit ; he trembled and most of the time kept his eyes closed, mumbling occasionally unintelligible things to himself. He patted Margarete ; his skin was still more dried up than hers ; he called her " My good girl."

Later she begged him to come to her.  Told him about the dull-coloured vial, and related her conversation with the Frauenberger, word for word.  It was not a confession and more than a confession.  He crouched there, shrunk, lifeless ; she did not know whether he understood her or not, but that did not matter ; the only thing that mattered was to unburden herself to a human being.  But when she had ended he quoted an ancient classic :  " Much that is dreadful is there in the world, but nothing more dreadful than the human heart."

Agnes evaded the Frauenberger, treating him with cold sarcasm.  He said good-humouredly :  " You are in a bad mood, Countess ?  My face does not please you any longer ? " Then he clapped her on the shoulder, grinned, and croaked : " But you are a goose, Agnes.  You are pinning your faith to the young fellows, the coxcombs.  You think the old ship is leaky.  You are a good, stupid goose, Agnes." He caressed her and pawed her all over.  Seeing that she still evaded him, he laughed good-naturedly, stretched himself on the couch, turned over, and yawned noisily.

§ 2

DUKE RUDOLF, the Habsburger, greedily snatched the documents which his Chancellor, the clever Bishop of Gurk, handed to him with significant solemnity.  He buried himself in them, and read them repeatedly ; although usually so calm and self-possessed, he was feverishly excited.  He caressed the papers as he listened to the exposition delivered to him by the Chancellor, this Bishop of such unusual juristic attainments.  What tremendous consequences the discovery

of these documents would have !   He read them once more.
With pious solemnity kissed the papers, knelt down, and
prayed.   Filled with passionate and uncontrollable gratitude,
he wrung the hand of the Bishop, who stood cool and collected
and did not permit the slightest smile to escape him.

Duke Rudolf had inherited from his father his hard head
for facts, his clear eye for realities and possibilities.   He
knew that Habsburg was not yet strong enough to bear the
obligations of imperial dignity without sustaining the most
vital internal loss.   The maintenance of imperial authority
dissipated one's power, sucked one's marrow.   Wittelsbach
and Luxemburg had been forced to feel it.   There was only
one course ;   for the moment to renounce prudently this
outward and supreme glory, but internally to make oneself
so strong that at last the imperial crown would have to fall
as a natural perquisite to Habsburg as the strongest.   This was
the policy which Albert had practised already with such
great results.

Rudolf saw clearly and soberly that there was no other
way for him.   With iron resolution he forced himself to
keep within these limits.   But he did not possess the calm
spirit of his lame father, who was satisfied with the con-
sciousness that he had the real power.   It chafed him to
have another set over him as his liege-lord, with every right
to the title of Holy Roman Emperor.   Who was this Karl,
after all, this sneaking, lean, hollow-cheeked fellow with the
long, dirty, curled beard ?   He, Rudolf, possessed territory
like him, had like him founded universities, cathedrals, and
palaces, the university of Vienna, the great cathedral.   But
the other at the right moment had seized a favourable
opportunity of securing the crown, and now it would be
madness to squander one's strength and power for the sake

of that outward symbol. Still, not even Rudolf's reasonable arguments could keep the knowledge that another was over him from gnawing at him, from rubbing, chafing, and tormenting him.

He was too proud to betray these thoughts to his Chancellor. But the astute Bishop had divined them, and pondered within himself how he might concoct a cooling salve for his master's fever.

Suddenly, one evening, he saw the way. Abbot Johannes of Viktring, whose company he liked, had just said goodnight to him. The Abbot had retired, as he did every evening, to work at the comprehensive chronicle on which he had been busied for an endless time. He was extraordinarily close about it, and kept the manuscript locked up and concealed. Lately, seeing that he could not write any more, the old man had brought in a brother of his monastery, to whom he dictated. This man had been made to swear a sacred oath never to divulge a syllable. Whenever there was a conflict of opinion, people enquired of the Abbot. What stood written in his chronicle was accounted as final truth, like the Gospel.

When the Abbot retired the Chancellor said to himself : " Whatever the Abbot writes counts as history, and is history. And yet it is only paper. All actions, all rights and privileges are paper. And will be acknowledged ; one can count on that. Seen rightly, the world is founded on paper. Karl of Bohemia has astute, learned theologians, who have built round his crown a wall of privileges in paper. Are we in Vienna less astute and learned than they are in Prague ? "

He interviewed the Abbot. He recalled to his memory the death of Duke Albert, and how the Abbot had then proclaimed : *Defunctus est Albertus de Habsburg, imperator*

*Romanus.* This sentence, said the Chancellor, continued
to burn in Duke Rudolf's mind ; it burned like the ever-
lasting light on the altar, it burned day and night.   The old
man listened with lifeless eyes.   The Chancellor spoke on
in veiled hints, the old man mumbled.

All at once the papers were there.   The learned Abbot
had lighted on them during his researches in the archives of
the imperial palace.   They were covered with dust, they
had lain forgotten in a corner, the precious documents.
Incomprehensible !

Yet, as the Chancellor was explaining now to the Duke,
they were far more than mere trifles for the historian.
They were of tremendous and vital importance, capable of
planting Habsburg on a new, lofty, powerful pedestal,
immediately beside the Roman Emperor.

Feverishly excited, Kudolf examined the papers.   There
were five charters.   They had been granted by Roman Em-
perors, by the first Friedrich, the fourth Heinrich, and went
back to Cæsar and Nero.   They ordained that the house of
Habsburg should be singled out from the other German
princely lines, freed it from burdensome obligations, endowed
it with peculiar rights, and constituted the Habsburgs the
chief, most exalted and most authentic Princes of the Empire.

Rudolf looked up slowly and reflectively at the Chancellor.
Serious, candid, and cool, the latter gazed back at him.   Then
Rudolf lifted the papers from the table, pressed them to his
breast, and said firmly, he was resolved to accept the dignities
and responsibilities which in these papers God had laid upon
him.

With tremendous ardour he announced to the whole of
Christendom the discovery of these great privileges.   Large
embassies to the Pope, the Emperor, to all the courts.   Solemn

masses in all the churches in the Habsburg territories.
Prodigiously exalted, Rudolf had the room in which he was
born—he, the head of the Habsburgs, to whom God had
granted the favour of bringing these charters again to light
—transformed into a chapel.

There were dumbfounded faces in the chancellories of
the German Princes. The jurists of Bohemia, of Brandenburg, of the Palatinate, wrote to one another, met together
personally, carried on cautious and inconclusive discussions,
looked at each other : a word was on the tip of all their
tongues, but no one dared to speak it out. At last the word
was spoken in Italy ; it was passed on by the chronicler
Villani ; Petrarch, who had been applied to for his opinion,
had uttered it clearly and unequivocally. The privileges
of the Austrian House were a swindle, a lame forgery. But
yet they could not trust themselves to make use of the
Italian's decision.

With deep displeasure Emperor Karl contemplated the
doings of the Habsburger. It almost spoiled his pleasure in
his relics that his rival should possess such precious documents.
He doubted very much their genuineness ; in particular the
charters from Cæsar and Nero, in spite of their unexception-
able Latinity, seemed to him suspect. But all the same,
even after Petrarch's pronouncement, he hesitated and did
not dare, even to himself, to regard the manuscripts simply
as forgeries.

Duke Rudolf sat over his precious documents, read them
again and again, buried himself in them, stamped every line,
every flourish on his heart. The Chancellor and Abbot
Johannes looked on. With mutual understanding and
satisfaction they saw that the Duke was incorporating the
privileges more and more fundamentally in his Credo.

## § 3

AFTER her return to Tyrol Margarete remained sunk in her vacant, strange apathy. She let the business of administration look after itself. Proclamations had to be sent by couriers to Munich for the young Duke's signature; they remained lying for weeks, for months. The councillors ruled on their own responsibility with hesitating half-measures, for they did not know definitely who would eventually prevail, Wittelsbach, Habsburg, the Maultasch, or the Munich Arthurian Order. The weightiest matters dragged on without being settled.

Margarete was completely exhausted. She had raised herself up with such incredible exertion, had been flung down in the mire, and had gathered herself together again. It had all turned out to be mere talk; everything was stupid, false, brazen; purity, virtue, strength, order, significance and meaning were silly phrases just like royalty or chivalry. The Frauenberger was right; there were these seven joys over which his lewd ditty chuckled, and nothing else in the world.

With almost pedantic eagerness the ugly ageing woman turned to these. Her board groaned with dainties; she sat for hours at table; Burgundian, Sicilian and Bohemian cooks vied with each other in her kitchens. Out of great beakers she drank heavy, ardent wines. She insisted on having everything; she had to taste everything. Rare fish, fowl, game, shell-fish, prepared always in some fresh way, boiled, roasted, baked, in milk of almonds, in spiced wine. Insatiable, she was always asking them to produce something new; greedy, full of apprehension lest she should overlook something, miss something. She went early to bed, rose late, and slept for long spells during the day as well.   For sleep was the best thing of all.   She had adopted the Frauenberger's custom of stretching, yawning noisily, and cracking her joints.   So the corpulent, ageing woman would lie, snoring, repulsive and hideous.   Her harsh, copper-coloured hair hung in unruly strands.   Over her face she had a mask made of a paste prepared from ass's milk and powdered cyclamen roots ; for this kept the skin younger.

The Frauenberger was pleased with the Duchess's development.   Yes, the Maultasch was a sensible woman, had recognised that his view of the world was the right one. He clapped her appreciatively on the shoulder.   Took over the organisation of her pleasures.

Strange rumours flew secretly through the town of Meran, through the Passeier.   It was whispered that to make nocturnal communication easier, the iron basketwork at the oriel window of Castle Tyrol had been reconstructed so that it could be lowered into the courtyard to receive visitors and wound up again.   In the prison tower of the Castle, it was said, rotted the favourites who had become embarrassing to the Duchess.   People sneered knowingly at the privileges granted to the Passeier valley, its royal manor farms, its exemption from taxes, its special dispensations for the chase and the cutting of timber.

The Duchess went farther into the south.   Her little pleasure house gleamed all white ;   dark blue beneath it, the broad lake quivered in the mid-day sun.   Ruined stone steps led downward between pomegranate trees.   On a long, gay, decorated bark the ugly woman glided festively over the dark blue water ;   before the prow fishes leapt and skimmed ;   the white spray from the oars flew rhythmically. As she lay on the poop, music rang out of the belly of the ship.

Q

Wherever she went she found little Aldrigeto of Caldon-azzo. The impetuous, violent youth, with the golden-pale, passionate face, the short nose under quick, large, dark eyes, seventeen years old, had seen her in Verona, then in Vicenza, where Can Grande the younger, the most powerful lord in Lombardy, had prepared a solemn reception for her. Little Baron Aldrigeto was the only bearer of his proud and powerful name who had survived the ferocious and bloody wars with the Castelbarchi. He had himself fought furiously in several engagements. Now most of his castles and estates were in the hands of the enemy; he had fled to the court of the great Veronese prince, demanding almost with threats help for a renewal of the feud. He was the last scion of his ancient house; was measurelessly spoilt, following every impulse to its extreme limit. The women loved his keen, golden-pale boyish face.

He saw Margarete. He saw her, the great della Scala by her side, ascending the steps of the palace, between reverential files and dipping banners, amid the ringing of bells, stiff with paint, in superb state robes covered with gold and precious stones, magnificently ugly. He felt her long, strangely apathetic gaze resting on him. Naturally, like all the world, he had heard of the sinister and wild legends which surrounded her; how this insatiable woman had driven out her first husband, had poisoned her second, and had spent countless lovers in her boundless lust. She was called the German Messalina in Italy. It flattered him that she should look at him. He was attracted by her power, through which, perhaps, he might be able to crush his enemy. He was attracted by the dangerous reputation which surrounded her. He was young, a late descendant of an ancient race. He was attracted by her ugliness.

The Duchess spent two summer months on the broad lake
with the boy Aldrigeto. It was swelteringly hot ; at night
too they were almost always in the open. She had had tents
set up on the south-eastern shore, on a small peninsula, amid
the ruins of Roman villas, between ancient olives. They
lay on hammocks under mosquito nets. Dark blue, bronzen,
slept the lake.

The incredible happened ; the wild, golden-pale boy began
to fall in love with the ugly woman. He was beautiful,
slender, golden-pale like the broken statues which stood here
and there among the olive trees. She was a great, mighty,
impassive, hideous idol, full of magical power. What to
him were the young, slim, ardent girls, who breathed more
quickly when he came near ? They were geese, they were
empty and stupid and silly, and all as alike as peas. The
Duchess was something apart, unique, full of timeless knowledge, ruler of the mountain lands, imprisoned in her enigmatic, omnipotent, lonely apartness. He hung all his
dreams on her. Soon it was not any longer ambition, self-
interest, and curiosity that bound him to her. Sometimes
when he talked heroically to her of the mighty empire,
stretching from the Po to the Danube, which he would weld
together, she would slowly turn on him her sorrowful,
impassive, unspeakably ugly face, and in the middle of a word
he would break off and founder. Something in that face
gripped him with panic, terrified him, bound him mysteriously
and indissolubly. Thus they would be together in the brooding mid-day, the Duchess, a great, sorrowful, ancient,
legendary monster out of a sunken age, encrusted with the
scars of countless battles, languid with endless experience,
and the boy, slim and supple as a palm, late descendant of
some rude conqueror, looking out of the hot, dark eyes in

his pale face into a future which for the other was the
past.

She divided a pomegranate. The blood-red juice spurted
over her painted fingers. Her wide, coarse mouth drew in
the glass-clear seeds ; they splintered under her large,
irregular, champing teeth. " How strange ! " she thought.
" This boy regards me and is not disgusted. It almost looks
as if it were not self-interest that attached him to me. I
have grown old, empty, dried up, and now comes someone
and loves me." She thought of Chretien de Laferte ;
with her fat hand she stroked Aldrigeto's shining black hair.
With a sudden movement the boy twisted his head round,
and bit her in the hand. Then he laughed, but not maliciously. Silvery white stood the olives, in the noon-day the
still, languid lake shores quivered and swayed.

While the Duchess was in Italy, in Tyrol the rumours
about her became ever thicker and more sulphurous. She
was a witch, it was said ; nightly she sucked the blood of
men ; she could be in two places at the same time ; while
she was present in the flesh in Verona a woman had seen
her in Tramin riding through the air on a chestnut horse.
More and more frequently the authorities had to have people
scourged for speaking disrespectfully of the Duchess.

Flaccid and idle Margarete lay on the shores of the lake
Hour, day and month stood still. When the bark shot
under the trees then suddenly the lake was blotted out, and
the shadows awakened her coldly and menacingly out of her
sultry twilight dreaming. So the boy Aldrigeto loved her.
He was slender, beautiful, women's eyes grew moist with
longing when they saw him, and he loved her ; but she was
too spent, too empty, to take pleasure in the fact. Moreover,
she remembered the Frauenberger : sleep is the best thing

of all. With a dull yearning she desired only one thing : always to remain like this, always to dream on like this in the brooding summer, slack, breathing out her soul in peace like the sunny lake.

## § 4

THE noble company of Munich, the Arthurian Order, had meanwhile been constituted. With great ceremony the inauguration had taken place ; acceptance and dubbing of the members, consecration of the banners, coronation of Agnes of Flavon as queen of the Order. Then a great tournament, splendid banquets, extensive hunting.

Prince Friedrich's principles pleased the young, violent knights of the Order extraordinarily. They were there, they were young, they were the lords of the world. They were filled with a boundless arrogance, bursting with a need to lay about them, to shout, to yell, to make an endless, joyous hubbub. To fill the world with their youth, which did not know what it would be at, with their strength, which was without direction or goal, with their thirst to undertake something, to act. Now Prince Friedrich had given this vague, violent impulse a beautiful and sonorous name, and something that resembled a meaning, an idea, an ideal. The young, insolent, swashbuckling lords felt suddenly that they were bearers of a mission ; they had God, justice, power on their side, and were happy.

Where did one eat and drink so mightily as at the Munich Court ? Where was there better hunting ? Where were more knights killed at the tourneys, or so much festive noise ? The scraps for the fools and dwarfs who crawled about among the guests' legs were richer than the whole table of many a small prince. The young barons were so swelled up with

pugnacity that they assailed utter strangers with the demand :
" Is there a nobler lady than Agnes of Flavon ? " and if the
other responded that he did not know the lady, fought with
him to the death. After their hunts they burned peasant
houses, burned down whole forests, as festal illumination
for their nightly camp in the open.

The court dances were too refined and ceremonious for
them. There was the droning of bagpipes instead of the
flute, in place of the harp rattled the tongs and bones. They
danced clumsy country dances, the Ridewanz, the Hoppeldei,
and other heavy boorish hops, and accompanied them with
bawdy songs, smacking their thighs. They stamped around
like wild bears, tossed the women up till their skirts flew
over their heads, and banged them down again in no very
respectful manner, amid universal laughter. They played
dice, madly and excitedly ; played away farms, castles, and
estates ; sometimes gave them back, and occasionally struck
their opponents dead. Among them reeled those who were
drunk, and who could not retain their wine. They sang
rude and filthy songs ; at night Frauenberg's song of the
seven joys was bawled and hiccuped through the streets of
Munich in a squalling chorus.

Young Duke Meinhard went about in this roaring tumult,
stout, good-natured, stupid and pleased, and felt proud to be
the centre of the festive and renowned organisation which
was carried out in his name. He smiled amicably at everybody, and said that to-day everything had gone particularly
well again. Gazed up adoringly at the slender, dark Prince
Friedrich. Stroked his little dormouse Peter, and told the
attentively-gazing little beast that he was very happy, that
ruling was an easy, simple affair, far pleasanter than he had
anticipated.

Lazily and with satisfaction Agnes let herself be surrounded by the veneration and extravagant spirits of so much youth.   In private she began to note here and there a hardening or a slackening in her skin, a tiny, dry fold on her lip or beside her eye, a white hair ; she felt that her movements were becoming just a little more laborious, heavier, more comfortable.   She needed the tumultuous adoration of this host of young men as an acknowledgment of her power ; she needed their noisy deification, she bathed in it, she allowed the boundless worship of Prince Friedrich to flow pleasantly over her.

Amid the hubbub the Prince of Bavaria-Landshut did not forget his political plans.   It was not mere noise and violence that he saw around him, but power ; not mere drunkenness and gluttony, but lordliness and splendour. Along with the leaders of the Arthurian Order, Abensberg, Laber and Hippolt of Stein, he arrogated to himself the complete direction of affairs.   The young Duke entrusted to them whatever they wanted : powers of administration and advice, office and seals.   They governed while dining or hunting.   Between two beakers of wine towns were insolently deprived of their privileges, peasants were pressed into senselessly harsh forced labour.   The ancient decree which forbade wild game and fish to appear on the peasant's table and reserved them for the nobility was strictly reimposed. Meinhard's household, the amusements of the Table Round, were extraordinarily expensive.   The domains were dissipated, the dues, taxes and moneys of the towns were withdrawn from necessary objects and squandered for the uses of the Arthurian Order.   The taxes were raised.   The damage done by wild game rose till it could not be computed ; the peasant who tried to help himself was hunted to a horrible death. Certain lords of the Arthurian Order even fell upon the transports of the merchants ; at first it was a jest, later a welcome addition to revenue. Trade and business stagnated owing to the insecurity of the roads.

The towns murmured, the peasants groaned. The Tyrolean lords stood at the frontier, together with Duke Stephan and the Habsburger, inactive still, but with menacing brows. From time to time the Frauenberger appeared in the Arthurian Order as a guest ; he was not invited to become a member. This did not annoy him in the least ; he made jokes and jeered ; it could not be gainsaid that he knew how to put the knights in high spirits. Duke Stephan sent a sharp message to his son ; he would lose his inheritance in Lower Bavaria if he did not return to Landshut. Prince Friedrich did not reply and cast the messenger into fetters.

The Habsburger fared little better in Munich, either, although he sounded his way more cleverly and prudently. Duke Rudolf had cemented an alliance against Emperor Karl with the King of Hungary. In a confidential note he invited Meinhard to come into this alliance, stigmatising the Emperor as the natural enemy of the Wittelsbachers. But Prince Friedrich, as the result of an infinitely obscure policy of prestige, considered no prince of the Empire except the Roman Emperor himself as of equal birth with the Wittelsbachers, and would make no alliance with any ordinary territorial ruler, certainly not with the presumptuous Habsburger. No, even if political and economic reasons were against it, Wittelsbach would stand, proudly and nobly and on idealistic grounds, beside the only German of the same rank, the Roman Emperor.

At dinner a hump-backed, parti-coloured court jester stuck on his bauble the confidential letter of the Habsburger, the chief, most exalted, and most authentic prince of the Empire. From guest to guest ran the variegated dwarf, with innumerable profound obeisances, displaying on his bauble the Austrian letter which traduced the Emperor so maliciously behind his back. Then in Meinhard's name Friedrich despatched the torn and soiled letter to the Emperor in Prague, with a bombastic covering note written as from equal to equal.

# CHAPTER III

## § 1

ON a skiff there arrived at the peninsula on the south-east of the lake the aged Johannes of Viktring. He was attended by two brothers from his monastery and bore with him in a locked chest " The Book of True Histories," which he had brought to a close at last.

The ancient was now quite dried up and very wise. He had seen so many things, had found polished couplets to suit all men and all happenings, had weighed all things and recorded them in his book. What was still to happen could only be fresh variations on what he had described. Moreover, he had learned that an Italian, a certain Giovanni Villani of Florence, was working on a chronicle as wide and soundly planned as his own. High as he might stand now above the ebullitions and vain agitations of the heart, it had yet annoyed him to hear the Italian's work highly lauded by clever and judicious men. Greedy for approbation, the Italian literary man wrote facilely ; he operated with sensational descriptions, touched up to produce a strong effect, while he, Johannes, the responsible scholar, filed and rounded, solidly verified dates and facts, always keeping in mind the work as a whole. So now he had decided to put the finishing touch to his work. He dictated to his secretary : " I leave it, however, to later writers to make a better record of future events, and here end my account, doing so in a manner which, or at least I should like to think so, is sober and worthy of history." He mumbled for a little, sniggered, laid his withered hand on the shoulder of his secretary, and full of false, assumed humility, dictated the final sentence : " But should it be adjudged less excellent than I think, yet may it be forgiven me as undertaken to the glory of the holy and indivisible Trinity, to which be honour, laud, praise and worship to all eternity. Amen."

And so now the ancient sat among olives and walls a thousand years old, and handed his work to the Duchess, hoping for appreciation from his diligent pupil. Margarete lay in a hammock, pouring cooled orange juice into her large mouth ; indolent, slender, and white, the boy Aldrigeto lounged beside her, languidly amused at the toothless old sage.

When evening came and it grew cooler, she had the secretary read it aloud to her. The cleric's practised, deep, uniform voice recited the Abbot's dedication and introduction. With a great command of quotations the Abbot showed how life and reality became history, how nothing remained of life and existence but history, and how history was the final goal and the best basis of all action. What remained of great men but their memory, which was like the fragrance left by apple-laden ships on our shores when the ships themselves were already far away on the shore of the beyond ? In this sense he began to unroll the picture of the last hundred and twenty years ; a picture of the brevity of human life, of the transience of nature, the inconstancy of fortune, the swift and fickle changes of earthly fame.

Margarete thought : " All this I know, but it does not move me any more. My programme lies behind me." But gradually, as the deep, uniform voice of the cleric proceeded with these manifold occurrences, as the histories, gay, simple,

sly, impudent, tender, great, and small succeeded each other,
all dispassionately and skilfully set down, each one introduced
and disposed of exactly as the one which preceded and the
one which followed it, gradually they bore her on with them,
and she glided into the pictured stream of Time.    Meinhard,
the great Count of Tyrol, strong, sly, unhesitating ;  she
was part of him.    These lands which for so long had been
divided : she had done her part to weld them soundly together.
These towns which had begun as ridiculous little settlements :
she had done her part to make them great and flourishing.

And now she was separated from the main stream, stranded
in a brackish, dead backwater.    Her life in the little peninsula appeared to her all at once unspeakably fatuous.    The
olive trees, the old walls, the orange grove—what were they
more than an empty, stupid, showy facade ?    How was it
possible to bury oneself in this dead, brooding, remote
summer, while outside violent, wild, and destructive things
were happening in her land, while the German princes were
fighting over her poor, smiling, stupid son ?    What had she
in place of all that ?    The boy Aldrigeto, a pretty little lad.

All the next day she read " The Book of True Histories."
The ancient beamed, against his usage drank wine, the larger
half of which was spilt by the trembling of his hand, and
wagged his head.    Then she dispatched an express courier
to Can Grande at Vicenza ;  she must speak to him urgently.

With a deep, indulgent smile she took a light farewell of
the boy, stroked his shining black hair, and caressed his
golden-pale, passionate face.    Said she would be back in
three days.    The boy suffered her endearments with languid
pleasure, playfully seized her wrist in a painful grip with his
strong fingers, and smilingly let her go.

In Vicenza she had a brief interview with Signor della

Scala. The astute, energetic nobleman felt friendly towards Margarete ; one could discuss things quickly and sensibly with her. She said that the episode with little Aldrigeto was now ended ; she had good and kindly memories of the boy. That she might continue to hold him in such good remembrance, would Signor della Scala do her the favour of taking care that he disappeared ? Can Grande's strong, fleshy face with the brown, arched eyes was turned on her with attention and understanding ; he bowed courteously.

## § 2

MARGARETE emerged from her brooding, stagnant summer dream into the fresher air of her native mountains. She was greeted without enthusiasm. The land was suffering. The Munich regime of the Arthurian Order, torn perilously hither and thither by Agnes's caprices, exerted pressure experimentally at various points in Tyrol, and made the land sick. The towns declined, the peasants growled, at breaking point. "The Maultasch is ruining us," they said. "She is sucking our blood dry. Now that the Margrave is dead, it is clear enough that all the good came from him, and all the bad from her."

With a strong hand Margarete drew the reins tight. Rooted out the worst abuses. Softened the rigour of the decrees which came from Munich. The people breathed again : " Ah, now Agnes of Flavon has interfered at last ! The beautiful, blessed Agnes ! Our guardian angel, our saviour ! "

In the loggia of Castle Schenna Margarete sat with the master of the castle. On the walls walked the gay knights, Garel of the Vale of Flowers, the Lion Knight. " How good it is that you have awakened again ! " said Herr von

Schenna. The mountains lay bright and friendly, shouldering each other, undulating. A fresh wind blew ; fruit and vineyard lay sunning, almost ripe.

"Why did you not waken me sooner ?" asked Margarete.

"You needed to have all this summer to yourself, Duchess Margarete," said Schenna.

The Frauenberger croaked : "What a shame that you have ended it already, Duchess Maultasch ! He was a pretty lad, golden-pale, southern. And so boundlessly devoted to you. That can't be found every day. What is there for you here ? Work, dirt, and filth. You should have left the Munich oafs to come to the end of their carnival. They would have hanged themselves in their own folly."

The Duchess journeyed with difficulty in a snowy January to Munich, to see the doings of the Bavarian Arthurian Order on its native heath. She was received in the capital with suspicion, constraint, and frigid politeness. When she pressed him more closely, requesting explicit information, Meinhard hedged, and said, smiling fatuously, that he ruled along with his knightly comrades, stammered something about petticoat government, slapped himself finally on the chest, and declaimed a few phrases of Prince Friedrich's on the principles of aristocracy which must be substituted for the modern huckstering rule of the mob. She had an interview with the Prince of Landshut. Slim, courteous, and arrogant, he pointed out to her that so far as he knew Duke Meinhard was of age. It was his affair to whom he should entrust his seal. Her maternal advice would always be listened to.

This was all the satisfaction she could get.

Everywhere she came up against Agnes. Her colours,

her manners, her moods, fashions, and tastes gave the court its tone, and determined the government of the land.

Agnes paid the visit to the Duchess which etiquette demanded. Simple and slender she sat before the ugly, coarse, painted, magnificent Margarete. Her deep blue eyes smiled politely in open triumph into the conscious, urgent, menacing eyes of the other. On the hearth blazed an abundant fire ; the fragrance of burning sandal-wood filled the great, dark room.

" You are permanently settled in Bavaria now, Countess Agnes ? " asked Margarete.

" Not at all, Your Grace," replied Agnes, and her some-what sharp voice was hard as a knife after Margarete's warm, rich tones. " I intend in the course of a few weeks to go to Taufers. Though, of course, my presence there is not neces-sary. I have capable officials ; and Herr von Frauenberg, too, has had the goodness to take over the management of my lands."

The Duchess regarded Agnes with quiet attention. She had filled out ever so slightly, but her skin was quite smooth. She sat lightly and buoyantly ; soft and unfurrowed her neck rose out of her dark dress. The adoration of all these lads was obviously a fine fountain of youth to her, better than baths and rouge. She sat so secure, so full of triumph, that her small lips hardly showed disdain any more.

" You have occupied yourself a great deal with politics lately ? " asked Margarete.

" No, Your Grace," said Agnes ; she was very vigilant now and on the watch. " His Grace the Duke and Prince Friedrich ask me now and then for my opinion. I do not keep it back then ; why indeed should I ? But it is the

opinion of a foolish woman, and does not pretend to be more."
She spoke with extraordinary politeness.

"I do not hold your opinion always to be the right one,
Countess Agnes," said Margarete. "Yes, quite candidly,
I am convinced that it is sometimes harmful to the country.
I will make you a proposition," she said cheerfully, almost
jestingly, "How would it be if you confined your opinions
to Bavaria?"

Agnes responded with great animation in the same light,
cordial, and lively vein. "You are my sovereign, Your
Grace. But is not Duke Meinhard my sovereign too?
Now if he should absolutely insist on having my opinion about
some Tyrolean affair? Glad as I would be to follow every
wish of Your Highness, can I refuse the Prince when he
demands my views, silly as they are? And I am sure it
costs you only a hint to have my stupid words blown to
the winds."

The two ladies regarded each other, and both smiled. The
triumph round the lips and in the eyes of the beauty was
perhaps just perceptibly heightened. Then they talked of
other things. Of the building alterations to the Munich
Residence, of the hair-nets, which were now coming in
again from Prague. Margarete had laid a heavy, golden
web over her stubborn, harsh, dyed, copper coiffure. Agnes
passed a lazy hand over her own rich, shining hair; she
could not reconcile herself to the new fashion.

§ 3

EMPEROR KARL resided in great pomp in Nürnberg. Held
banquets and tournaments. Received the councillors of the
city; foreign artists and scholars. Had long, comfortable
and interesting discussions with them. Rested here from

his state labours, far from his capital. Took part in the great carnival celebrations which the rich city prepared in honour of his Roman Majesty.

The Emperor's beard, a docked wedge, was beginning to grey, his lean face was becoming pallid and wrinkled. But above his rather flat nose his brisk eyes blinked, sly and very vigilant ; his long, bony frame was quick and sure.

The Emperor was pleased. He had waited until he was firmly seated in power. Not until then had he begotten a child. God had blessed his prudent delay ; it had been a son, a healthy, substantial boy, to whom he could well bequeath the Empire. The lucky father had sent the child's weight in pure gold as a votive offering to Aix-la-Chapelle ; then he had knelt among his relics and announced to the bones : " I, Karl the Fourth, Roman Emperor, have a son and heir. Ye beloved, adored saints, ye noble martyrs, pray for Wenceslaus, my son ! "

Now he sat cheerfully in Nürnberg, enjoyed the company of his poets and architects, avoided politics, conversed lightly and freely with his Chancellor, the widely experienced, world-travelled theologian, about things human and divine, increased his hoard of relics and other valuables, and diverted himself with sledging, masquerades, and tournaments.

Unexpectedly into these days of relaxation burst the Duchess Maultasch. The Emperor and his gentlemen were deeply astonished. Since Karl had besieged her in Castle Tyrol, Margarete had maintained only the coolest and most formal relations with him. Her arrival, wrote the Chancellor to his friend, the Archbishop of Magdeburg, was one of the fifteen wonders that were to be fulfilled before the Judgment Day. He made very merry over the German Messalina, this modern Kriemhild who paid her court now after having

R

all her life plunged land and people into sorrow and misery for the sake of her private loves and hatreds. He described how she sat on the balcony at the tournament next to the beautiful Princess Hohenlohe, this coarse woman, covered with warts like a toad, fat as a brewer.

The well-disposed Emperor received his former sister-in-law with ironical good-will. Oh yes, they had been a good deal together in their young days. At the time when he was liquidating his father's Italian adventure, he had had many a good talk with her. She had been a clever princess, but all the same without enough ballast. Insatiable, she had wanted to have everything, so in the end everything had run through her fingers. He had skilfully curbed his temperament ; and he was Roman Emperor and had a son to whom he would be able to leave a firmly-cemented kingdom. She wandered about the world, and a weak, ill-advised, young boy, a plaything in the hands of any clever adventurer, was squandering her lands. On the other hand, she had ignominiously and insultingly locked his brother Johann out of Castle Tyrol, and then before the Curia they had had to twist and turn the affair as if the marriage with Johann could never have produced a right heir. The Emperor could not resist presenting Johann's spruce and well-grown son to her. Who had the right heir now—she or Johann ?

Ancient history. Ancient history. Margarete quietly accepted the irony and the humiliation with a businesslike calm which she had probably learned from the Jew Mendel Hirsch, with an equanimity which let the preliminary formalities pass quietly over her head, if only she might reach her object. Then she entered her complaint. Complained of the insane outrages of the Arthurian Knights who

were ruining the land.   The Emperor listened ; inwardly
he was grinning like a mischievous boy who puts out his
tongue maliciously.   He assured her of his personal interest,
but emphasised the fact that after so many years of the strain
of government he was now taking a few weeks' holiday.
Ultimately, the matter concerned only the House of Wittelsbach.   However, in spite of that, he would take it into
favourable consideration after his return to Prague.   Even
on a second attempt Margarete achieved nothing more ;
she had humiliated herself in vain.   Obviously, Karl was
firmly resolved to regard the internal degeneration of Wittelsbach with complacent neutrality.

Otherwise the ageing Emperor treated the Duchess with
an amused gallantry, almost a parody of gallantry, which
formerly would have exasperated her beyond endurance.   It
gave a spice to the high-spirited enjoyment of his holiday,
his carnival, to have his good fortune and his achievements
thrown into strong relief by the folly of this ambitious
woman whose frustration was so complete.   He joked
almost good-naturedly about the Maultasch with his
Chancellor.   She showed herself without diffidence, in the
clearest light, blazing with jewels like an idol, by the Emperor's side.   The people stared at her in great astonishment.
She kept her eyes only on her goal : Tyrol, the towns.   To
drive out Agnes, to tear the land out of Agnes's hands.   So
filled was she with this idea that she never had the slightest
inkling of what she was to the court and the city : the
grotesque crown of this carnival.

§ 4

AGNES was very exhilarated by her interview with Margarete.   The Duchess had suggested an agreement, and

renounced further war    Had, in indirect ways, admitted her defeat.

Agnes knew that the Arthurian Order by itself could not hold the land permanently.   The towns, all the nobles who did not belong to the Order, were in revolt.   On the frontiers the Habsburger stood watching, the Wittelsbacher threatening.   If now the Maultasch as well were to press in from the south, it would be folly to think of holding the country without allies.

Prince Friedrich would not see the truth of this.   Slender, dark, and haughty, he made sanguine speeches about the power of his sword and the justice of his cause.   Agnes was very fond of him.   But she thought of the Frauenberger, and how merely with his jovial, menacing smile he reduced all this boyish exuberance to empty vapour.   She heaved a weary little sigh, stroked the Prince's dark hair, and began cautiously to recommend a reconciliation with his father, Duke Stephan ; so that Wittelsbach could show a united front against Habsburg, and against the Maultasch.   The Prince jumped up as if stung, deeply hurt, his pride up in arms that she should expect that of him.   Agnes was silent, her keen lips smiled, she continued to stroke his hair.

A few weeks later Stephan of Lower Bavaria and the Counts Palatine, Ruprecht the Elder and the Younger of the Rhine, concluded an alliance with the councillors and burghers of Munich and eleven other Bavarian towns, as well as with twenty-two Bavarian barons, against those who called themselves Arthurian Knights and alienated Duke Meinhard from his lands and people.   They refused recognition to the ministers who had taken over Meinhard, his authority, his voice and office, declared the government seal of the Arthurian Order to be invalid, the laws and regulations, which it had issued, to be null and void. They pledged themselves to rescue the young Duke from the discredit into which the Order had plunged him, and to endeavour to give him a better control and management of his sovereign powers.

The Arthurian brotherhood talked and threatened largely, took a few Munich burghers as hostages, and declared that they would string up the rebels by the heels like mad dogs. Meanwhile in several towns in the mountains the troops of the Arthurian Order were disarmed and imprisoned, and customs officers who tried to raise money were flogged. The Munich Table Round considered the hostages forfeit, mishandled them, ordered them to lick the floor clean with their tongues, and ignominiously hanged two of them. This did not prevent the barons' troops from becoming fewer day by day, while in the North Duke Stephan was assembling a horde. The haughty lords would not hear of dissolving their Order voluntarily. In Munich, in the great salon of the Residence, with crossed swords, they took a solemn oath to remain united and to resist until the end. Duke Meinhard hovered about, shy, exalted, stupid and superfluous during this performance ; unobserved he stroked his dormouse Peter, then joined fervently in the chorus when the others swore that they would never submit, never, never, never !

There began now for the Duke a wild life of wandering, of whose significance he was only partially aware. He was trailed around the castles of the Arthurian Knights, passing from one to the other. Was at Castle Laber, Castle Pinzenau, Castle Maxlrain, Castle Abensberg. They hunted and caroused. Stormed the castle of a rebellious baron here and there  Conquered Castle Wörth, and two castles of the Master of the Hounds, von Kummersbruck, the old Margrave's intimate friend. The measures to which the Duke gave his signature became ever more wild and senseless. A small market town whose total of taxes fell short of expectation was razed level with the ground ; Kummersbruck, who had declared himself neutral, was beheaded without trial. This execution drove all the neutral nobility into the camp of the enemy.

Meinhard, never very robust, was hardly equal to these perilous hunted journeys. While the others caroused, he sat melancholy and apathetic, and slept sometimes where he sat. More and more his travels began to resemble a flight. In all the south the Arthurian Knights no longer possessed one town, or one castle. They were being driven back step by step to the Danube, where their most impregnable fortresses lay. But still they issued haughty edicts, and threatened rebels with the most horrible penalties. They fled to Neuburg, then to the See of the Bishop of Eichstätt, who was devoted to them. Duke Stephan's troops occupied the whole of Upper Bavaria, and finally besieged Meinhard with the last of his supporters in Castle Feuchtwangen in the valley of Altmühl. The Bishop of Eichstätt suggested that he should try to get through with Meinhard, disguised. The young Duke entered into the plan enthusiastically ; he had much amusement out of the dressing up and no conception what it was for. But they had only reached Voburg when they were recognised by the peasants, detained, and delivered over to Duke Stephan in Ingolstadt.

Feuchtwangen fell. Prince Friedrich and the last of the Arthurian Knights were captured.

In the palace at Ingolstadt the Duke and Prince Friedrich confronted each other. In the presence of Agnes of Flavon-

Taufers. The Duke in his armour, foaming with rage. Towns and villages ruined, men lost, money squandered. All on account of the stupid lad. He growled martially through his thick moustache, his face like iron. The slender youth stood with dark, wild eyes, his arm wounded and in a bandage, his face grey. " You will humble yourself, you will do penance in the church before all the people ! " commanded the father. The son only laughed scornfully. " I'll let you rot in my filthiest dungeon ! " the Duke raged.

Agnes glided from the one to the other. " The bandage must be renewed," she said anxiously, and thereupon began to rearrange it.

" These doctors ! " the Duke cursed. " A set of bunglers ! " He ran himself for a doctor and dressings. " The devil's imp ! " he swore.

Slowly, wrangling hard, while Agnes acted as mediator, they came to an agreement. About each separate Arthurian Knight, whether he should be pardoned or suffer the extreme penalty, there was a bitter struggle, outbreaks, railing, raging. Twice Duke Stephan directed the hangman to hold himself in readiness. At last they found a peace tolerable to them both. Munich was fixed on as Meinhard's permanent residence ; Prince Friedrich was still to keep his seal, but his edicts would require the counter-signature of a Lower Bavarian or Palatine counsellor. Agnes was to be the intermediary between Munich and Landshut-Ingolstadt.

Duke Meinhard laughed softly and thankfully. He was glad to be able to rest after these wild weeks, and stroked his dormouse.

# CHAPTER IV

## § 1

Margarete held counsel with her ministers. There were present, Ulrich of Matsch, the provincial governor, Heinrich, the Vicar of Tyrol, Count Egon of Tübingen, Commandant of the German Order in Bozen, Jakob of Schenna, Berchtold of Gufidaun, and Konrad of Frauenberg.

Now that Duke Stephan had seized power and sway in Upper Bavaria, what was to be done?

They could come to an agreement with the Wittelsbacher. If Bavaria was not to be ruled from Tyrol, they could accommodate themselves to Tyrol's being ruled from Bavaria. For, seeing that the real regent, Duke Stephan, did not have his seat in Munich but in Ingolstadt or Landshut, his centre of government was far enough from Tyrol to make centralisation and unification more difficult, and to guarantee to the mountain land a certain degree of autonomy.

But they could also call in the Habsburger against Duke Stephan. He was only waiting for this. Certainly dependence in some form or another could not be avoided there either. But a strong and stable regime would be assured.

Stubbornly and wearily the argument dragged this way and that. Margarete listened in dull vexation. Did the obvious idea occur to nobody, then? Had she acquitted herself so badly? She gazed at Schenna, at Gufidaun. They were staring in front of them with troubled, vacant faces.

Strangely enough it was the Frauenberger who proposed the plan which she awaited. With a broad, complacent grin he expounded it. If the young Duke was really so incapable of standing by himself and needed guidance, why not entrust the guidance to his legitimate guardian, his mother, the Duchess, who in many more difficult situations had conducted herself so splendidly? They should bring Meinhard to Tyrol. If the Bavarian lords had been able to allure him into their stinking, forsaken holes and corners, surely by God's help or the devil's they would manage yet to get him into Tyrol, his native country. Once they had him in the country, they would rule Bavaria from Tyrol. Duke Stephan would think twice before he ventured on a military adventure into the mountain land from the Danube. And even then they could always fall back on the Habsburger as a natural ally. In the worst event they could formally renounce, against an indemnity, their claim to Upper Bavaria, and restrict themselves to a great, autonomous Tyrol.

Yes, an autonomous Tyrol. That was also Margarete's idea. Bavaria as a dependency; or in the last resort not even that. But Tyrol for the Tyroleans.

The next thing they had to consider was how to withdraw Meinhard from under the influence of Duke Stephan, and to get him out of Munich and into Tyrol. Since the beginning of his reign the young Duke had never yet set foot in the mountain land. It was only reasonable that the people should at last demand to see him.

At the instigation of Schenna and Gufidaun a great assembly was called at Bozen. There came to it strong, fair-haired men with short, broad noses and sly, lazy eyes, and lean, tanned, black-bearded men with keen, arched noses and sharp, quick eyes. There came the three chief men in the mountain lands, one from Tyrol, one from the Adige, one from the Inn ; there came the High Steward and provincial governors and burgraves. There came barons, great and small, and representatives of towns, districts and jurisdictions. There were altogether a hundred and fifty-three nobles and commoners. On two radiant late summer days, under dark-blue skies, they assembled in the gay, chattering market-place of Bozen. They considered, they deliberated carefully, thoroughly, cautiously, in guttural, harsh, explosive voices. Their eyes sought each other slyly or honestly ; they made ceremonious, angular, naïve gestures ; with their heavy cloaks they wiped the sweat from their faces. The mountains stood round russet and violet, snowy-white on the summits.

They decided to send a letter to the young Duke. This letter was signed by seven of the barons, the elder Ulrich of Matsch, Schenna, the Trostberger, Heinrich of Kaltern-Rottenburg, Gufidaun, the Frauenberger, Botsch of Bozen ; and was sealed by four of the towns, Bozen, Meran, Hall, Innsbruck, in the name of all the others.

The letter was as follows : " Beloved and gracious Prince ! We beg to inform Your Grace that we have assembled in Bozen and agreed to beg you for your own honour and good as well as for that of the land, to come to us, seeing that we have for so long wished to see you, as was but reasonable ; for you are our beloved and rightful lord. Also with us you will be better appreciated and honoured and be less subject to wrong guidance than has been the case, as we have been told, in Bavaria ; and also your land and people here will remain free from the miseries which exist there. Among us in the mountains everything by God's grace is quiet and settled, as prosperous as ever it was in your father's blessed

time ; and peace reigns in the land and on the frontiers.
Gracious Prince ! We beg you to put your trust in us :
we mean well by you. Rely upon us, we will give up our
lands and lives for you ; but trust nobody else at all."

The Frauenberger brought the letter to Munich. He
came with a stately escort, and delivered the note in solemn
audience. Did not anticipate the slightest success, all the
same ; was certain, rather, that other means would be
necessary.

At table Prince Friedrich related that his dear cousin
Duke Meinhard had received a very curious document from
his province of Tyrol, which he really could not withhold
from the noble company. The letter was read out. They
sniggered at first, then they exploded. Laughter, mounting,
tempestuous, caught them all up. Agnes smiled, the ladies
laughed, the gentlemen roared till they split their sides,
the lackeys tittered obsequiously, the pages giggled, Meinhard's dormouse squealed.

"These Tyroleans ! " they said, breathless, with shaking
sides. "Yes, our Tyroleans ! " said the Frauenberger,
good-humoured, rosy, fat, and winked his reddish eyes.

## § 2

" Do you, too, find the letter from your land in the mountains so comical, Your Grace ? " asked the Frauenberger.
Although his business had really been completed with the
delivery of the letter, he had remained in Munich and kept
Meinhard company a great deal.

In the presence of the stocky, fleshy man with the frog's
mouth and the bare, rosy face the young Duke had always
an uncomfortable feeling ; his jovial ways frightened him.
But he could not very well get away when Frauenberg

came ; the massive, hoarse, laughing man impressed him ;
he talked so differently from everybody else, without respect,
bluntly, nakedly.    One had a not unpleasant feeling of
helplessness before him, felt carried away by him.    Full of
unsatisfied curiosity mixed with repulsion the mild, thick-set,
stupid Duke fluttered around the albino.

His Tyroleans' letter had in reality not appeared at all
absurd to Meinhard ;  on the contrary it had sounded very
kindly and pleasantly in his ears ;  it was only because the
others had laughed so terribly and found the letter so silly
and presumptuous that he had had to laugh with them.    But
now the Frauenberger, that great, talented man, seemed to
take the Tyrolean manifesto very seriously, and this was
extremely pleasant and comforting to the harried and hedged-
in Prince.    Something simple and peaceful had spoken to
him out of that confiding letter :  for a couple of minutes
it had been as if there existed no Munich and no burdensome
knightly ceremonial and no Arthurian Order and no
Wittelsbachs.    It must be lovely to lie on a mountain
meadow among great cows, to hear nothing but the soft
wind and the faint, snuffing sound they made in cropping
the grass.

The Frauenberger stood before him blinking.    Meinhard
was compelled to draw nearer to him.    " How glad I am,"
he said, looking up at him with his vacant round eyes, " that
you don't find the letter from my Tyroleans stupid."

" Stupid ! " croaked the Frauenberger fervently.    " Every
word is in its right place !    Every letter makes itself felt !
Those who have laughed over it are the dunces !    Otherwise
would I have signed it ?    To-day, at any time, I would sign
it again, with both hands ! "

Meinhard took another tentative step nearer the fat

Frauenberger. "I'm so tired and bothered," he complained. "Friedrich, too, is not so friendly to me as he used to be. I had thought at first that ruling was easy. Now I am dragged this way and that way, and everybody nags at me."

The albino laid his enormous fleshy hand on Meinhard's shoulder, and croaked : "My lad, don't let yourself be put upon !"

Meinhard trembled under the big man's hand, tried to evade it, and then submitted to it.

"You have friends, my young Duke," the Frauenberger croaked, blinking honestly, smiling comfortingly.

The day after that he asked : "Really, why do you stay here, my young Duke ? If the letter from your Tyroleans is not displeasing to you, why don't you follow its advice ?" They were taking a run on their horses ; it was early morning ; beneath them, among countless spits of gravel, rushed the Isar, fresh and green ; a great raft was being steered cautiously amid the cries and shouts of the boatmen. The pace of the horses slackened, Meinhard slouched limp, stout and embarrassed on his light bay.

"No, that wouldn't do," he said. "I can't do that."

"Why can't you ?" persisted the Frauenberger. He rode up quite close to him, and raised his chin with his hand as if he were speaking to a child. "Who is master here," he asked, "Duke Stephan or you ?"

"Yes," said Meinhard, "who is master here ?" But he did not sound defiant, rather brooding and troubled. All his trust in the Frauenberger was gone ; the Isar fretted beneath him, how sad it was ! He felt shy of the Frauenberger, and that afternoon was on the point of begging Prince Friedrich to send him away.

Next morning the albino spoke no more about the plan of leaving Bavaria. He lay with Meinhard in the grass among ripening fruit. He sang his ditty of the seven joys, adding a paternal, benevolent, juicy commentary. The young Prince was very sympathetic to this view of life ; he stroked his dormouse Peter and was happy. The Frauen-berger stretched, cracked his joints, turned round on his side, yawned, and slept, snoring lustily. Yes, sleep was best of all. Attracted, but still with shy and timid eyes, Meinhard regarded his unconcerned, fleshy, snoring companion.

Agnes said to him : " You have been a very long time in Munich, Herr von Frauenberg. And you have such im-portant duties in Tyrol. Do they not miss you there ? "

The Frauenberger grinned, looked her over with his reddish eyes, so that she breathed more quickly, and croaked : " Naturally, I am only here for your sake, Countess Agnes."

They came together, he lay on her couch ; it was an oppressive summer day ; the air in the room was heavy and dreadfully hot. She stroked his smooth, fat, rosy skin. " Now," she smiled, " have I chosen the wrong path ? I have provided for myself pretty well, it seems to me."

He grinned : " We'll see, my chicken, we'll see."

That was what she called well provided for, he thought. It was he who was well provided for. If he took the boy with him to Tyrol now, he could hold the mother through the boy, the boy through the mother. He was the real regent of Tyrol. Oh yes, if one were ever so ugly, what could one not make of oneself with a little sense, intelligence and luck ?

In his broad, pleasant, hearty way he continued his bullying of the youth. Enticed him, spurred him, drove him on. Gripped him roughly in his stubby, red hands. To Tyrol !

Now at last Meinhard must go to Tyrol, and show himself to his earldom. "It's flight then?" ventured Meinhard fearfully. Eh? Who was thinking of flight? Only they need not make too much ceremony about the journey. They would simply set out, Meinhard, himself, and two or three attendants. Without too much talk. There was too much chattering in Bavaria and Tyrol: it confused the simplest things. At the end of the week Prince Friedrich was to journey to Ingolstadt to see his father. They would ride away at the same time. In the opposite direction, towards the south, towards Tyrol. The dormouse Peter would see his mountains again.

## § 3

"My son is coming, Schenna!" said Margarete, and her dark eyes were filled with animation. She had had a messenger from the Frauenberger, saying that he would bring Meinhard.

"How glad you are, Your Grace!" said the tall noble, bending forward and looking at her with grey, friendly, very old eyes. "I had given up hoping that you would ever be so happy again."

Margarete did not listen. "I know," said she, "that he has no gifts. There are thousands up and down the land who are more gifted. But he is my son. He is made of the soil of this land, of its air, its mountains. Believe me, Schenna, he can see the gnomes."

Yes, Margarete had hoisted again the lowered and tattered banner of her hopes. All her will, all her life was concentrated on the expectation of her son's coming. With her pudgy, painted hands she stroked the portrait of the mild, thick-set, stupid youth.

§ 4

WITH a servant in front and one behind Meinhard and the
Frauenberger rode southwards at a rapid trot. It was
raining, and the indifferent track led often through thick
woods, and was completely smothered in mud for long
stretches. It was not easy to discern the right road in the
wet and gloomy darkness ; there was too much rain to
permit of torches.

The gentlemen wore no armour. They steamed in
their wet clothes, and from their soaking leather caps and
jerkins a strong odour arose. They rode in silence ; from
time to time as they trotted through a sleeping hamlet a dog
barked at them.

A halt was made in the village of Lenggries. After
a few hours the Frauenberger was for pushing on again, but
Meinhard was tired and miserable, more from nervous
tension than from the long ride. The more difficult part
of the journey still lay before them ; for they thought it
advisable to avoid the more populous districts and to penetrate
into Tyrol by the wilder passes. So in deference to Meinhard's wishes they turned aside into the inn at Lenggries.

In the dark and narrow room the Frauenberger and Meinhard slept on sacks of straw. The roof was low, and the
fire smoked without warming the foul atmosphere ; rain
and wind blew in through the window opening. The
Frauenberger snored noisily ; the gnawing of a rat sounded
in a corner. Meinhard lay there, all his limbs aching with
weariness, but he could not sleep ; his skin itched and his
eyes burned. He felt cramped and unhappy ; he felt
suddenly that it was senseless to go to Tyrol ; he would have
preferred to turn back again to Munich. He shrank from

meeting his mother ; she was so fat and ugly and domineering. He turned a furtive eye on the albino, who lay massive and peaceful, snoring in his sleep. He was afraid of the Frauenberger, but there was no one else who could help him. Taking an uncertain gulp from the coarse jug of stale beer which stood beside him, he gazed at a fly which was crawling over the Frauenberger's face without apparently disturbing him. At last in a low tone he called : " Herr von Frauenberg ! "

The other awoke immediately, and croaked in his flat voice : " What's the matter ? "

" Nothing," said the boy ruefully. " Only it's so uncomfortable. I can't sleep ! "

" Then let's go on ! " decided the Frauenberger, getting on his legs as he spoke.

" No, no," implored Meinhard. " It's only that I'd like to talk for a little. I'll be sure to lie quiet afterwards."

" Stupid boy ! " growled the Frauenberger.

" Did my father really care most for Tyrol or for Bavaria ? " asked Meinhard.

The Frauenberger blinked. "For Tyrol at first and then for Bavaria," he said.

" And then he died ? " questioned the young Duke.

" Yes," replied the other, " then he died."

When Meinhard awoke after a few hours of uneasy sleep, his little dormouse Peter was gone. The young Duke and the servants sought for it, while the Frauenberger growled at the delay. At length the little creature was found dead among the Frauenberger's straw. It must have strayed from its master's side, and been crushed by the heavy man in his sleep. Meinhard was paralysed by the shock, overwhelmed with inert and numbing sorrow. He stared

S

with dull and helpless horror at the albino as the latter took the quaint little creature which he had loved out of his hand, held it up by the legs, and then, whistling, threw the tiny corpse into a corner. " And now to horse," he croaked.

They rode farther up the river. The valley became narrower and more tortuous ; the wretched little track followed the endless windings of the rushing, greenish-white stream. Thick forest, dripping trees. Below them, foaming, green as glass, cleft by countless spits of gravel, the brawling, rapid water ; above them through the fir tops a dejected, dirty-grey sky. The walls of rock in many places closed in upon the path so narrowly that the horses shied, and could be urged on only with difficulty.

Then the track forked, and they plunged into dense, endless forest. They followed the dwindling stream, which chattered noisily as it cut its way clearly and blithely through the dusky woods. It was a silent region, uncannily solitary. The rain fell monotonously and hopelessly ; even the Frauenberger's whistling lost its freshness in such wet, grey, melancholy surroundings, slackened and died away.

At length a high mountain barrier shut off the river valley which they had followed so far. They were in a semi-circular arena of gigantic, whitish-brown cliffs, awesome in their bleakness. Behind these lay Tyrol. They spent the night in this upper valley. The Frauenberger and the servants disposed themselves as well as they could in the open. A microscopic ruined hut served to screen the Duke from the rain.

There he cowered in the hut, half crouching and half lying, the boy Meinhard, Duke of Bavaria, Margrave of Brandenburg, Count Palatine of the Rhine, Count of Tyrol. He peered and peeped to find out if the others could see him, or if they were already asleep.    When he was sure that he was alone, he let himself go.    He was terrified, he felt battered and unspeakably wretched.    Slow tears dropped from his vacant round eyes down his fat, stupid cheeks.    He wept because the Frauenberger had suffocated his dormouse Peter ;    he wept because the cliffs which he would have to cross to-morrow were so high.

## § 5

AGNES was astounded at the masterly ease, the boldness and directness, with which the Frauenberger had kidnapped the Duke.    He impressed her ;    he was a man ;    that was not to be gainsaid.    Listlessly, without conviction or belief in their success, she organised counter measures.    She would have liked best to leave everything in Prince Friedrich's hands, but he was in Ingolstadt.    She had to make arrangements for the pursuit by herself.

She sent couriers to the frontiers, small bodies of armed men.    They had to act warily, without exciting attention ;    it would never do to prevent the Prince by open violence from setting foot in his Earldom of Tyrol.

The Frauenberger believed that once he had the little shooting-lodge of Karwendel behind him he would be out of danger.    But a few hours before they reached the easy pass by Achensee, they met the transport waggons of a timber merchant, who had been working in that district, and whom the albino had once had flogged for daring to object to some rather too high-handed transactions.    The Frauenberger's first thought was to attack the merchant and get rid of him ;    but then one of his six carters might get clear away, and the Duke would be still more endangered.    So he decided to let the timber merchant go, and in spite of the qualms of the servants, who knew the passes, to abandon the easy climb over the Plumser Joch and try the difficult and unusual path over the Lamsen Joch down to Schwaz or Freundsberg.

They left the horses behind, and when almost under the cliffs turned aside into a smaller glen. The streamlet which had formed this glen was a sluggish trickle, and often disappeared altogether, flowing underground. The servant who knew the way went on ahead. They stumbled over willow brush and boggy ground. It was still raining. Then the glen widened unexpectedly, and oddly enough all at once a maple tree loomed out. Then more maples. A whole grove of them. Old trees, which stood tall and motionless in the rain. Only dimly behind them could one discern through the veils of rain the gigantic white cliffs which as far as one could see shut in the glen irrevocably and were so high that their summits were invisible through the trees. There was no wind ; with regular monotony the rain could be heard dripping from the leaves of the solemn, dun-coloured old trees.

Meinhard could go no further. They called a halt in the pouring rain, and ate of the food they carried. Meinhard could not eat. The fact that the tops of the cliffs could not be discerned terrified him. He would never be able to get up there and over ; they were imprisoned in the glen under the spectral, uncanny trees as if the world ended there. They began the ascent. At first it was not difficult. They climbed gradually, following the tiny turns and twists of a mountain torrent. The servants were in front, looking for the easiest path. Meinhard had climbed more difficult places before, but he seemed to be paralysed. His legs were like blocks of wood, he sweated with fatigue, and laboured in his breathing. He slipped on the wet rock, the Frauenberger held him up, he winced at every contact. The farther up they climbed, the higher, more mocking and unsurmountable frowned the cliffs before him.

Fading rhododendrons, dwarf brushwood, snow. The servants marched on with even strides. Uncertain, puffing, slipping, faltering, the Duke followed. Suddenly one of the men stopped, listened, and looked at the Frauenberger. He had heard it already, but there was not a flicker on his smooth face. Obviously the timber merchant had given the alarm. " Either men or grazing cattle," he said coolly. Pushed on further. The servants, too, quickened their pace.

Meinhard had hoped for a rest. He was exasperated because they showed no signs of stopping. Then he relapsed into dull lethargy, and let himself be dragged on limply by his sturdy companion. If they paused to recover breath for a moment the sharp cold stung them. The snow became deeper, the young Duke broke through the crust clumsily at every step.

The Frauenberger reviewed the situation with clear incisiveness. If there had been no snow they could have got him across. As it was, to get over the ridge with the weak-kneed creature was impossible. Besides it looked as if Meinhard were turning refractory. He was letting himself become heavier and more inert.

The servants were a good way ahead. The Frauenberger halted : " Well, young Duke ? " he croaked. " Tired, are you ? " Meinhard sank exhausted in the snow and panted. The Frauenberger whistled his little song. Thought everything over sharply. This attempt had failed. He had already faced that fact. What was to be done next ? Let Meinhard fall into the hands of the Wittelsbachs again ? They would have a stronger hold than ever on the boy after the unsuccessful flight. It would have been a good thing to play Meinhard off against the Maultasch ; but that was out of the question now. It would be better to deal with the Maultasch alone then, and with all excuse for the troublesome interference of the Wittelsbachs once and for all removed.

He kept on whistling. Took a drink of wine from his flask. Offered it also to Meinhard. "We have to go on further, young Duke," he said, and gave him his hand to help him up.

"I can't," whined Meinhard, getting up with difficulty. "And I don't want to," he added, sulkily.

"Is that so ? " grinned the Frauenberger. "All right, then, my boy, you won't," he said. He croaked the sentence out as genially as usual, but something in the tone of his voice made Meinhard look up. The albino had completely stopped blinking, he turned a hard and watchful eye first on the servants and then on him. Meinhard's vacant, round eyes grew glassy with terror ; only a small, hoarse noise came out of his throat. He twisted his short, fat, childish hands into the woody undergrowth of the rhododendrons, and braced his feet well into the ground. Calmly grinning, the Frauenberger said : "Come along, young Duke ! " with his fleshy, red hands slowly prised open the stiff, clinging fingers of the boy from their hold on the rocks, lifted him high, held him over the precipice, croaked : "Adieu, my boy ! " and let him drop. The body rebounded several times, did not fall far, and lay still.

With a shrill, piercing whistle the Frauenberger called back the servants, and silently pointed over the edge. They scrambled down ; the corpse was terribly battered ; the thick, feeble skull was split open in two places. They waited for their pursuers. Two officers with several men. The Frauenberger said he had been trying to catch marmots with the young Duke, and the boy had missed his footing. He stood plump and fleshy in his wet, reeking leather jerkin, and blinked out of his reddish eyes. Large flakes of wet snow drizzled down on the body. A faint, cold wind had begun to blow. They all removed their helmets and caps, standing mute in the snow around the disfigured corpse.

# CHAPTER V

## § 1

Through the halls and corridors of Castle Tyrol reeled a woman, crying out brokenly, falling, rising up, stumbling on again. Her monstrous, misshapen lower jaw hung slack, her hair was matted in strands, some of an ugly, dull copper colour, and some faded to a yellowish white. A kind of voluminous nightgown fluttered about her puffy, thick-set body, over her large, sagging breasts, and trailed on the ground behind her. The servants took the raving, howling, reeling figure for a drunken woman, and only gradually recognised the Duchess.

The courier with the report of Meinhard's death had arrived very early in the morning, and Margarete had received the news in bed. She had risen without undue haste, and then with a shriek had passed the bewildered, embarrassed maids and lackeys blindly, stupidly, trailing her nightgown behind her.

Schenna led her back to her bedroom. Now she was crouching there with vacant eyes, thinking fragmentary thoughts.

Her path was lined with corpses. The head of Chretien de Laferte ; the odourless, tasteless poison of which the Margrave had died ; her daughters, with the great black festering swellings of the plague ; the Jew Mendel Hirsch in his prayer-mantle, smiling ; the boy Aldrigeto ; Meinhard. It was all because she was so ugly ; that was why Death stalked at her heels, that was why from every corner empty, bony skulls stared at her. She crouched there without

274

stirring.   Noon came, and evening.   The wizened Fräulein
von Rottenburg asked her if she did not want to eat, or to
dress herself.   She did not stir.   Her path lined with corpses.
It was because she was so ugly.

Meanwhile the Frauenberger escorted Meinhard's dead
body into Tyrol by way of Mittenwald.   He grinned to
himself ; it had been uphill work that had made him the
escort of his dead sovereign.

The mountain land received its Prince with dejection.
In solemn session it had invited him to come.   Now he
came in this fashion.   The people stood by the roadside as
the procession wavered past in the rain and snow.   Bells
were rung, the clergy came in full robes, the feudal lords,
the judges, the officials bare-headed.   Past them went the
bier, up the Zirler Berg and down into Innsbruck, up the
Brenner and down again, by the Jaufen Pass, and the Passeier.
While they crossed themselves and gazed after the bier, the
people had slow, heavy, uneasy thoughts.   This was the
last Count of Tyrol.   Things had not gone well with the
Maultasch.   Her first husband driven out, her second
dying such a queer death, her son dead before he saw his
own country.   Besides that, war, revolution, flood, fire,
pestilence. No, Tyrol had not done well under the Maultasch.

At the castle gate the rigid Duchess awaited the procession.
Her white paint showed crudely above her black clothes.
So she crossed the courtyards alone, beside the bier.   Behind
it, massive in his armour, loomed the Frauenberger.

§ 2

IN Munich people were deeply affected by the news of
Meinhard's death. Not a soul believed that it was accidental ;
at the most they were doubtful whether the Frauenberger

had done it on his own account or by order of the Maultasch ;
but no one dared to venture this opinion aloud.  Only
Giovanni Villani, the sensation-loving Florentine chronicler,
honest Johannes of Viktring's rival, who was then staying
in Munich for the purpose of tracing certain documents,
asserted it as a fact that the young Duke had been violently
done to death  He assembled in careful order and with
cumulative effect all the reasons which might and must result
in such an act ; he made them the subject of a polished
and eloquent chapter in his chronicle, and read it aloud to
everybody who cared to listen.

Stephan, Friedrich and Agnes were filled with rage and
dismay.  Not one of them had reckoned on a solution of
such simple and cynical brutality.  For the first time in
their association Agnes and Friedrich turned on each other.
He should have sent the Frauenberger away, she said, and
had no business to leave Munich so long as the man was there.
He said she should have had Meinhard more carefully
watched ; hardly had he been gone a day before everything
was in confusion ; nobody was to be trusted.  Duke Stephan
stood wretchedly enough between them.  Fate was not
kind to him ; he had feared as much ; it was not to be
granted him to make the house of Wittelsbach a power
again in Christendom.  When they had wrangled themselves
weary they agreed to concentrate on securing Bavaria ; they
did not feel strong enough to leave its frontiers unprotected
and make a dash for Tyrol.  On the other hand, Agnes
wanted to visit Tyrol and sound the situation there.

With quite a small retinue she arrived at Tyrol Castle,
and was received by Margarete on the very same day.  She
sat there looking rosy, smooth, young and fair, in a very
simple black dress ; the Duchess, painted a staring white,

her hands and her shapeless neck heavy with gleaming jewels, was stately in satin and brocade. In a somewhat stiff and formal tone she remarked that it was very kind of Agnes not to have shrunk from the hardships of a journey in winter in order to pay her last respects to her son. Looking at her with sweet composure, Agnes replied that of course it was no more than her duty to do so, after the many favours she had received from the House of Tyrol. Besides, she had been so intimate with the dead Duke. She could not describe to the Duchess how terribly the dreadful news had upset her. Margarete stared at her fixedly, her broad, powerful, painted, chalk-white face like a mask, and asked if she would care to see the Duke. Agnes, a little reluctantly, for she did not like looking at the dead, said that she would. Both women went to the Chapel, the one in brocade with heavy, dragging steps, the other lightly and proudly. The young Duke was laid on a magnificent bier, with thick clouds of incense around him and men in silver mail keeping the death watch. At a sign from the Duchess the enormous coffin lid was swung open, and there lay the young Prince, his fat, amiable face, shockingly battered, fixed in a distorted stare above his armour. The body was far gone in decay ; and in spite of balsam and spices an evil stench arose from the shining metal. Agnes swayed and lost her colour. Margarete led her back.

When they were both settled by the hearth again Margarete said lightly : " Our last conversation has become quite pointless now, Countess Agnes. My son is here again, not in Munich."

Agnes, perturbed by the lightness of her tone, and ignorant of her purpose, made no reply, but opened her eyes wide and waited.

Always in the same terrifyingly casual and conversational tone the Duchess continued : " You married Chretien de Laferte, and then he died. You reduced my beloved towns to a state of dependence on Bavaria, and they are almost ruined. You attached yourself to the Margrave, and then he died. You made yourself my son's intimate friend, and now he is dead. Was it not rather bold of you, after all that, to come to visit me in Tyrol ? "

This was all said quite cursorily ; with a smile on the hideous, ape-like protruding mouth, and a contorted pretence of geniality on the corpse-like, painted face. She even leaned over and laid her hand with horrible familiarity on Agnes's arm, a thing which she had never done before.

Agnes sat pale and numb. " I don't know what you mean," she stammered.

" It was kind of you," went on Margarete, " to come of your own accord. Otherwise I should have had to invite you ; and, believe me, I should have invited you in such a manner that you would have come."

" I don't understand you at all," said Agnes with blenching lips.

" Yes," Margarete stood up, suddenly breaking off the conversation. " You will be my guest then, until the Duke is buried. That may not be for some time ; the preparations are rather involved."

" I had really intended to spend the interval at Taufers," said Agnes. She was shrunken with fear, her voice trembled.

" Not at all, not at all ! " said the Duchess warmly. " You will stay here. Have not you and yours often been the guests of Tyrol ? "

" You must not think of leaving us," she concluded, escorting Agnes to the door. " You would find the journey very uncomfortable." A footman brought the tottering Agnes to her room. Pikemen were standing before the door, and presented arms as she crossed the threshold.

### § 3

MARGARETE, left alone, walked up and down with a strangely elastic step, a kind of uncouth dance.

What a pity it was that the creature had surrendered herself so simply ! It would have been stimulating to inveigle her with cunning, to knead the dough before eating the cake. But all these smooth puppets were like that. Beautiful and stupid.

Margarete went out into the open, alone. She trudged and clambered about on the snow-covered vine terraces. Sat down in the snow. Sank her hand into its soft coldness, made a snowball, let it drop and made another.

To bring the creature low, to destroy her, pulverise her, annihilate her, crush her until nothing was left of her but the poor mouldering clay. To grow fat on her terror, her wretchedness, her despair, until her beauty lay low, a vile stench like the boy yonder in the chapel.

When the withered Fräulein von Rottenburg came after a time, she heard what she had not heard for years. The Duchess was singing. With her dusky, warm, full voice she was singing. She sat in the snow and sang ; full and vibrant tones rang from her ugly throat.

### § 4

HER next move was to summon Schenna. She expounded to him that the fall which had precipitated Meinhard to his death was unquestionably to be laid at the door of the Countess von Flavon-Taufers. She was not disposed to gloss over this crime. Rather her intention was to visit it with exemplary punishment. Schenna, deeply perturbed, urgently dissuaded her. Whether she liked it or not, the populace felt for Agnes a sympathy as passionate as it was unreasonable. To proceed against her would be dangerous. Her possessions, power and influence could be curtailed ; but political expediency forbade anything further.

Nervous and irritable Margarete returned that she was quite aware of her own unpopularity. It could not be any worse than it was. So she would be risking nothing.

Schenna contradicted her with unusual bluntness. She would be risking everything. Candidly, she would be risking nothing less than a revolution, which would let in the Wittelsbachs. She burst into a flood of tears ; in no circumstances could she endure any longer the rival pretensions of that creature. She would rather throw up the sponge. She stared angrily into space, inaccessible to all milder persuasions. Schenna wandered uneasily to and fro with his long, irregular strides. If she absolutely insisted on it, he recommended after a while with a curious spasm of ill-humour on his face, then in God's name let her appoint a public Court of Justice. For no consideration in the world should she proceed against Agnes without a trial and a judicial verdict.

She sent for the Frauenberger and the various influential barons. Clearly and incisively she recognised that they were all for Agnes and against her. But with a few exceptions they were willing to sell her their adherence. They regarded her prosecution of Agnes as a caprice ; well, they were willing to back up that caprice ; but they thought it fitting that Margarete should pay heavily for their indulgence.

They all put forward claims and demands. It wrung Margarete's heart, and made her grind her teeth. Loyal

and submissive they stood before her, full of patriotic scruples.
Underlying all that was a grin of mockery; pay nothing,
and you get nothing

The barons settled things among themselves, and balanced
their claims. The Frauenberger delivered their joint
demands to the Duchess. These were barefaced and shameless. Margarete was to form a Cabinet of nine Ministers.
Those proposed were the Frauenberger, Schenna, Berchtold
von Gufidaun, the two Herren von Matsch, the Military
Governor and the Provincial Governor, Egon von Tübingen,
Commander of the German Order, Heinrich von Kaltern-
Rottenburg, Diepold Häl, and Hans von Freundsberg.
These gentlemen, who were also to act as judges in the prosecution of the Countess von Flavon, were to constitute the
chief justiciary and administrative power of the country.
Margarete was to pledge herself to undertake no business
of government, to appoint or discharge no officials, to enter
into no negotiations, alliances, or contracts with foreign
rulers except with their consent. Moreover, she was not
to have the power of dismissing any of the Ministers; if
one of them was removed by death or any other cause his
successor was to be appointed by the Cabinet itself, not by
the Duchess.

Margarete sat alone over the document. She wrinkled
her forehead so deeply that the paint cracked. To sign this
meant to leave her towns defenceless, to throw the land to
the insolent barons for them to sink their greedy teeth into,
and tear out each a piece for himself. To sign this meant
to let the land of Tyrol lapse into a congeries of petty feudal
baronies, to undo disgracefully the work to which her fore-
fathers and herself had devoted for hundreds of years their
wealth, their energies and their lives.

Into her thoughts came suddenly the bearded little creature which she had once seen among the rocks of Castle Maultasch. It bowed repeatedly, looked at her with grave and ancient eyes, opened its mouth.

Violently she drove the gnome away. Down with the land ! Down with the cities ! Let her own neck be humbled ! Let it bow to the arrogance of her vassals ! There was no escape. The issue had to be fought out between her and that other. It would be senseless now to reject the demands of the barons and save that creature. She would gnaw again at Margarete's work, hollow it out, destroy it. That beautiful woman was the worm at the heart of the country ; all its troubles sprang from her impudent lascivious beauty. She must be stamped out, exterminated, blotted out from the light, swept from the earth. There could be no peace for the mountain land so long as the woman existed.

When she stood before God she would be able to plead that for hours, days and weeks at a time she had harboured not the smallest selfish thought, nothing but the pure and simple will to submit herself and do her duty. And again and again that vain and empty creature had smashed with an idle hand all that she had constructed amid hardships, humiliations and sacrifices, the agony and terror of which that woman was not in a position even dimly to comprehend. Was that just ? Was it just simply because she had a skin-deep beauty, that the stupid, empty, wicked, base creature should spread herself abroad, should overshadow and leave no room for her, with her teeming burden of painful knowledge ? That could not be the will of God. The fight must be fought to a finish. With a welcome spasm of pain she felt how closely she was linked to the beautiful woman, how clearly it was her destiny to decide the issue. There could be no evasion, no shutting of the eyes, no concealment, no shrinking from the mighty task, no compromise. It had to be fought out to the bitter end. The Frauenberger came for her answer. Her hand lay heavily on the document containing the barons' demands. She looked up, regarded the Frauenberger, and said quietly, without raising her voice : " Scoundrels ! Blackmailers ! "

The Frauenberger replied coolly and jovially : " Yes, Duchess Maultasch, we're not exactly cheap."

Then she signed it.

## § 5

WHEN she was alone Agnes sank down in cowed exhaustion. What on earth had she done ? Handed herself over to her enemy with a friendly smile. What had she been thinking of ? Of course Meinhard's death was a loss and a blow to the Maultasch, but it was a still worse blow to herself. With Meinhard out of the way, and after her bold, unexpected renunciation of Bavaria, the Maultasch had come off victorious. She did not understand, considering the situation, how she had let herself enter her enemy's house, to crown her triumph.

She was quite alone and forlorn. The room was badly warmed ; she shivered. Was it really only cold ? A feeling crept over her which she had never known in all her life, constricting her and making her shrink. She had always been pert and assured, she had always been mistress of the situation, had always shuttlecocked men about at her pleasure. Now she was quite helpless, her enemy could wreak her will upon her. Terror and cold overwhelmed her. Her deep blue eyes were not daring now, but blank and extinguished, her elastic figure sagged, her white hands

T

showed wrinkles, her smooth face was broken up into small, stiff, dry creases. She stayed like that until evening. Then lights were brought, the fire made up again, and food set on the table. She pulled herself together, ate, grew warm, and recovered her spirits. Bah! that was just what the other wanted, to see her brought low, whimpering and frightened. She would certainly not dare to do her any serious harm. Was not the whole country on her side? The other, just because she was ugly, wanted to see her proved a coward. She wouldn't dream of giving her that satisfaction. She stiffened herself, her eyes became cool and daring as usual. She ate with a good appetite, asked for second helpings, and jested with the servants. Slept well, peacefully, and long.

When the Frauenberger came next day he found her contentedly munching bon-bons and tinkling a frivolous song on the lute. She made fun of the old-fashioned furniture in her room. He grinned, it was true the Maultasch didn't provide such modern and comfortable lodgings as she did. He caressed her. He blinked at her and remarked paternally that he had warned her in plenty of time not to have anything to do with the young fellow, for it wouldn't succeed. She asked casually if the Maultasch had sent him. She wasn't to be scared. What were their real intentions? And how long was the farce to go on? The albino croaked out that she was to be arraigned before a Court of Justice. She returned that she wished they would be quick about it, for she was bored in Castle Tyrol. Also she wanted her maid and her dressmaker, so that she could appear in a fitting costume before the Court. He said she had only to command. When she was alone again she munched bon-bons and tinkled on the lute.

# CHAPTER VI

THE Duchess made it her business to see that the high and secret Court which was to condemn Agnes should be constituted with due pomp and ceremony. The three surrounding chambers were guarded by men-at-arms to ensure the secrecy of the proceedings. The nine gentlemen sat in gloomy silence. Margarete herself was heavily laden with the magnificent insignia of her rank.

Agnes wore a simple, salmon-coloured dress which had been designed for a reception or some lesser function. Her bearing was light and assured. She was convinced that the Maultasch would not dare to lay a finger on her, and that the solemn formalities of the Court were intended only to frighten her. All this was arranged only to make her, the beautiful woman, shrink into insignificance before the ugly one. No, she was not at all disposed to give the Maultasch that satisfaction.

The Vicar of Tyrol, who acted as prosecutor, read the charge sheet. The Countess von Flavon-Taufers had always endeavoured to influence Meinhard for evil, and in a direction harmful to Tyrol. When the young Duke was in the very act of entering Tyrol, to escape from her influence, and when his association with his true and faithful subjects threatened to undo her plans, she had attempted to seize him by force, as a result of which the Duke met his death.

Agnes said she was amazed to see how the wise and powerful gentlemen could put such an evil interpretation on

such clear and simple facts.   Yes, she had been on the best
and most intimate terms with the young Duke, who, like
his father, had honoured her with his friendship and confidence.   To the best of her feeble feminine abilities she had
from time to time given this or that piece of advice as a loyal
Christian subject for the glory and benefit of her sovereign
and his lands.   When the Duke was on his way to Tyrol,
Duke Stephan unexpectedly announced his impending
arrival in Munich, and so she sent couriers on horseback
after Meinhard with a letter advising his return to Munich
in the circumstances.   Her couriers, unfortunately, had
found the Duke already dead.   That was all clear and
unambiguous.   She was a great sinner, she concluded with
a smile, but in her humble feminine opinion there had not
been the slightest word or action in her relations with Duke
Meinhard which she would not venture to acknowledge
boldly before God and man.

She offered this explanation in a casual manner, without
rising from her seat, and in hard, clear tones.   Young, fair,
serene and engaging, she sat in her simple, salmon-coloured
dress before the gloomy judges.

Margarete said that in Munich she had ordered the
Countess von Flavon not to meddle in Tyrolean affairs, and
the Countess had refused to promise.   Agnes replied that Her
Grace had misunderstood her   The Vicar of Tyrol read
a sworn affidavit to the effect that the Countess's couriers
on their own admission had been charged to bring the Duke
back to Munich by force.   Everyone looked at the Frauenberger, who must have been the source of this information.
He maintained an air of detachment.   Agnes declared that
this statement, if it really emanated from the couriers, was
sheer calumny   The Frauenberger grinned.

The Duchess sat there, her robes of black brocade sweeping round her in stiff, projecting folds, the golden insignia of her rank glittering on her bosom. Unexpectedly, without looking at Agnes or anyone else, she began to speak, breaking into a pause of silence. In an even voice she revealed everything, in plain, unadorned language. That wherever she had laboured for the mountain country, by the Adige and the Inn, from the Italian lakes to the Isar, this Countess von Flavon had followed, preventing and undoing her work. She spoke slowly, without raising her voice. She spoke of her cities and the measures for their welfare, and how this Countess von Flavon had opposed them. She spoke of her financial arrangements, and how this Countess von Flavon had recalled into the highlands the Italian banker, Messer Artese, whom she had expelled. She spoke of the independence of Tyrol, and how this Countess von Flavon had persistently sacrificed the land to Bavaria, which sucked its blood. She spoke of the Arthurian Order, of Ingolstadt and Landshut. Slowly from her broad, misshapen mouth dropped the bare and telling facts. They fell evenly and monotonously, trickling like heavy sand, irresistibly, till they shrouded the brilliant Agnes from head to foot, making her colourless and pitiable and commonplace. There was complete stillness when the Duchess had finished ; one could hear the logs crackling on the hearth ; the barons sat drooping in grey dejection.

Agnes said she had never sought to be influential. She had given her opinion when she was asked, and even then with hesitation ; she had never thrust advice upon anyone. She saw that her words fell on deaf ears and carried no conviction. Then she rose, stood there with gay, frank, light-hearted pride, looked at the gentlemen one after the other, and said that if she had committed a sin, it was only that of being in the world at all. God had made her as she was. So long as she did not efface herself she could not prevent people from turning their heads to look at her, and finding pleasure in the sight.

They all stared at her ; even the rapid quill of the Vicar of Tyrol ceased its scratching. With his tired, grey eyes Schenna looked her up and down ; the lean, upright Egon von Tübingen gazed as if obsessed into her deep blue eyes ; the honest, good-natured Berchtold von Gufidaun blew his nose and sighed ; the Frauenberger blinked at her with his reddish eyes. These words of hers, Agnes felt, had not missed their mark. She had laid bare a part of her nature, had held it up proudly in both her hands before their faces and before her enemy, saying : " There you are ! Look ! That is what I am ! " She enjoyed the effect of her words, breathing deeply, drinking it in.

Then she noticed that the Maultasch was looking at her too. The blue eyes of the beautiful woman plunged their gaze deep into the brown eyes of the ugly one. And Agnes saw that Margarete was smiling. Yes, a little smile cracked the crude, white paint on the Duchess's face, and it was not a feigned smiled ; it was genuine. Then Agnes knew that the other had laid her plans deeply ; that her own triumph was poisoned in advance, and that she was undone. She began suddenly to tremble, she paled, her limbs gave way, and she had to sit down.

§ 2

INTO the condemned woman's chamber, unannounced and unexpectedly, came the Duchess. Agnes had received the verdict with great composure, lightly and proudly. And when she was alone she had reassured herself that the Maultasch would never dare to proceed further. But then she had remembered that small secret smile of Margarete's, and that distressing, shivering feeling which she had never known before, crept up her spine again. Now, when the Duchess appeared, she pulled herself together at once, and rising courteously, not too hastily, begged her to be seated.

Margarete said : " You have suggested, Countess, that between you and me there is something more than a sovereign's severity towards a rebellious subject who harms the country. I beg you to understand that I can be nothing but the sovereign ; for the injured country is part of me, and when I act it is the country that acts through me." She said this lightly as if it were a matter of course, but with conviction and great dignity.

Agnes listened with attention and courtesy. She did not understand what the other meant. She thought only : " Ah, she wants something out of me. She wants to talk it over, to justify herself. How weak her position must be ! She feels she is the underdog, and she wants to bluff me. I mustn't let myself be caught. I must say no. Whatever she promises I must say no."

Margarete saw that she was not understood. She tried another tack. Wearily, a little impatiently, but yet kindly, she said : " You have had successes, Countess. I do not grudge you them. I hope you will yet enjoy many. My aims and ambitions are set in an entirely different direction ; try to believe that. All I want is a guarantee that you will not harm Tyrol any further. Nothing else. Acknowledge before witnesses and by affixing your signature that your influence has been harmful to my country. Swear on the gospels to refrain in future from any political activity. If you do that I shall quash the death sentence. Your fiefs shall revert to my jurisdiction. You shall be set free, and leave the country."

There it was, the trap ! Agnes sneered inwardly : "She will never dare to have me killed. And she thinks I am stupid enough to pay for her cowardice."

She said : "I cannot sign any such document. My sole political activity has consisted in being alive, in being in the world. You can have me swear to anything you please. But neither you nor I can prevent any man who looks at me from following my opinions and not yours." She looked Margarete up and down without flinching ; her blue eyes ran over her, summing her up contemptuously. They jeered at the misshapen jaw, protruding like an ape's, at the flabby cheeks, the monstrous chin settling into fold upon fold, the squat, solid body. Those eyes searched out everything, pierced through the paint, and mockingly noted the dry, warty, scaly skin.

More deeply wounded than ever the Duchess controlled with an effort her boundless exasperation and distress. She said, and her contemptuous tone sounded false : "Leave it to me, Countess, to decide whether it is necessary or not to have you put out of the way. I think you rate yourself too highly. But I shall be satisfied if you sign the required declaration."

How lame and halting her retort was ! She felt it herself. And Agnes felt it, with high exultation. She was now quite certain that the other would never dare to let the sentence be carried out. Make admissions to her ! Make a confession to her ! She wouldn't be such a fool !

"I am very sorry I cannot comply with your wishes," she said, drawing its full value from this honeyed, malicious expression of conventional regret.

The Duchess rose to her feet. Her resolution was taken ; to blot the creature out. The country required it. It was God's will. She must be swept out of the light, off the face of the earth. The air was defiled, the ground burned, so long as she moved and breathed. Heavily she trailed to the door, like an ailing, wounded, hideous, sorrowful animal. Lightly and courteously Agnes escorted her.

§ 3

The Ministers pressed Margarete urgently to reprieve the Countess. After such a trial she would take good care not to intrigue further against Tyrol. In no circumstances should the Duchess venture to take any steps against Agnes while affairs in Tyrol were so precarious. The Ministers also prevented the slightest whisper about the whole proceeding, the arrest, the trial, and the verdict, from penetrating into the country.

Schenna represented to Margarete that the populace would never believe any evil of Agnes, and that if she laid hands on Agnes she would draw down on herself the most fanatical hate. No verdict and no dissemination of evidence by the Ministry would prevent them from prating of blood-guiltiness and murder. Every cloud, every thunderstorm, every disease of the cattle, would be interpreted as an omen from Heaven against the Duchess. Insistently with his shrewd, grey eyes, he implored her and conjured her not to do anything rash, to postpone action at least until after Meinhard's funeral.

She said quietly : " It won't do, Schenna. The fight must be fought to a finish, Schenna."

The Frauenberger sat alone, carousing. It was night. In a corner lay his attendant snoring. He kicked him, and

bade him make up the fire, then gave him some wine.
Whistled and sang to himself. Reviewed the situation
sharply. Logic, logic ! If Margarete achieved her purpose,
if Agnes was branded as a traitress or executed, there would
be a revolution, and it was very doubtful, as matters then
stood, whether the barons would be able to maintain their
ascendancy. If they thwarted the Maultasch, she, stubborn
as she was, would recur continually to the subject, and they
would never be able to enjoy their triumph in peace. What
was to be done ? Logic, logic ! He reflected, drank and
reflected again. Then his face lit up and he grinned. He
gave his attendant another drink. Croaked and fell asleep.

Next day he visited Agnes. Found her in excellent
spirits and delighted to see him. She said she could not
complain of boredom any longer. At least she had plenty
of visitors. To-day him, yesterday the Maultasch. Yes,
he lied—for Margarete, of course, had told him nothing—
he had heard that the ladies had come to a perfect understanding. She looked at him with a slight air of suspicion.
He blinked and began to make fun of Margarete. He had
brought perfumed brandy with him. She drank some of it.
She lay among the cushions ; her fine white throat rose and
fell with laughter. He paid court to her. She felt pleased
and stimulated. The brandy he had brought was certainly
a very special kind, and went quickly to one's head. He
had overreached her, had the Frauenberger, yes, and whisked
Meinhard away from under her very nose. But she would
not have missed her defeat for anything. He was a man,
the only one who had ever impressed her.

She lay among her cushions, pleasantly exhausted.

How low the rooms were in Castle Tyrol. The ceiling
was coming down on her. Lower and lower. Push the

ceiling up again, Konrad! It suffocates you. It presses down on you. She laughed hysterically. Or was it a a rattling in her throat?

The Frauenberger blinked at her and waited. Watched her with an expert eye. Nodded his head as he saw how she rolled over on her side and then on her back again, how she laughed, panted, gasped and contorted her face, fighting for air with her arms; and then slid sideways from the cushions.

Slowly he summoned her women. Informed the other members of the Cabinet that their dispute with the Duchess touching the reprieve of the Countess von Flavon had now no object, since the Countess had just died of a stroke, obviously brought on by excitement.

## § 4

WHEN Margarete heard that Agnes was dead she felt a dull and numbing void. She had been filled with the thought of Agnes, and now that had vanished, leaving only an empty husk.

Slowly from holes and corners she collected her scattered senses. Should she not be feeling free, light, happy and exalted, now that the destroyer was dead and out of the way, and the land no longer in danger? Not a bit of it. More and more a dull and senseless rage gathered within her. She had wanted to see her enemy humbled. Led solemnly to execution, she should have admitted: "I am defeated. I am nothing but a contemptible, beaten little scrap of humanity, and you are the Princess, high and unattainable, chosen by God." Her death was not important, but this admission was important. And now she had been cheated out of her hate, her revenge, and her triumph;

the woman she hated had been spirited away from under her nose to a shore whither she could not follow.  Miserably, cruelly and crudely swindled, she was left behind, while the other flew aloft, light, smiling and inconquerable.

Margarete raved.  What was the good of all her sacrifices ?  She had thrown away the country, thrown away her forefathers' work and her own, submitted disgracefully to the greed and shamelessness of the wolfish barons.  And now the other had escaped with a mocking smile.

She overwhelmed the Frauenberger with vile abuse.  The solid man stood his ground, cool and unmoved.  Her curses flowed off his clean-shaven, rosy face like jets of water.

She summoned the Cabinet.  With barely controlled passion, her voice, usually so measured, coming in hoarse, spasmodic gasps, she demanded the immediate publication of the trial and the verdict, and the dead woman's ignominious burial as a criminal.  If that were not done, she would be held guilty of this sudden death.  The Ministers opposed her unanimously, with all their strength.  Most of them, like the rest of the country, believed that Margarete was really guilty of Agnes's mysterious and unforeseen death. They were honestly indignant at the frivolous and godless claim of the Duchess to have the assassination of her hated rival represented as a righteous and patriotic deed.  They even felt that their own extortions from the Maultasch were retrospectively justified by this attitude of hers, morally and in every other way ;  it was clearly evident that one could not have too many safeguards against such an immoderate and criminal woman.  Besides, they were greatly relieved at the lightning solution of the conflict, and were unwilling to have matters complicated anew by anything whatever. In his croaking voice, incisively, clearly, and without reserve, the Frauenberger summed up the position. What on earth was the Duchess after? God had taken into His own hand the punishment of the crime; and now the criminal was dead, out of the way. That was all the Duchess had wanted, or could have wanted. It was unchristian to pursue the dead with hatred. If the people were to break out into violent protest one could hardly blame them. Von Matsch went on: Of course the people indulged in disrespectful remarks about the Duchess. And he knew there had even been demonstrations in several places after the Countess's death. But since the Ministers were closely ranked behind their sovereign, such small revolts would be easily stamped out. Several agitators had already been arrested and would be publicly whipped; that would stop the mouths of the others. But if the dead woman were to be dishonoured, public indignation would be so general that he would not answer for it. The honest Gufidaun, who after a long struggle had convinced himself that the Duchess was not guilty, laboriously clothed his thoughts in speech: The criminal was dead. Before earthly judges one could pay no higher penalty for sin than one's life. To calumniate the memory of the dead did not befit such a high and noble lady as the Duchess. He sat down in embarrassment, for he seldom spoke. The others all associated themselves with his words.

The Duchess looked at Schenna. He scratched on the table nervously with his lean fingers and said nothing.

Margarete stuck to her point. In feverish, stammering, disjointed phrases she kept on repeating that she would not give it up, she owed it to her prestige, she insisted upon it.

But the Ministers remained firm. They entrenched

themselves behind the agreement, showed their teeth, and declared that they would never give the requisite consent to measures taken against the dead woman. Margarete raved about mutiny and rebellion. The Ministers retorted that they could afford to ignore such a reproach. Their consciences assured them that their opposition was in the best interests of the country and of the Duchess herself ; and in defending the dead woman they were aware of the approval of the whole of Christendom. Margarete had to give in.

She raged until her voice and her strength failed her. These Ministers, these scoundrels and cowards ! How glad they were not to have to carry out their verdict ! How shamelessly they had overreached her ! Cheated her out of the country, and then with vile sophistry backed out of the contract. Villains, swindlers, blackmailers ! She thought of applying for help to some foreign country, but the Wittelsbachs were sworn adherents of Agnes, and the Habsburger was too clever to make himself unpopular beforehand by taking steps against the dead woman.

She made one last desperate attempt to get the better of the dead. At the eleventh hour she arranged Meinhard's funeral so that it fell on the same day as Agnes's. Whoever went to Taufers to honour Agnes would have to absent himself from the burial of his sovereign Prince. Stubborn and desperate, she challenged the country to decide between her and Agnes.

Silent, in vacant obstinacy, and with wild looks, she sat in Castle Tyrol and waited to see who would be on her side and who on that of Agnes. Deep within herself she knew as well as anybody that Agnes had triumphed in her death, that the battle was over, and the dead woman beyond the reach of all force and guile.

# CHAPTER VII

## § 1

THE members of the Cabinet discussed who should attend the burial of the young Duke, and who should go to Taufers. They agreed to leave each individual free to decide on his own responsibility. Most of them decided to go to Taufers. Were not their hands clean of Agnes's blood? Why should they not show it? The Frauenberger, Egon von Tübingen, the Commandant of the German Order, and the honest, ponderous Gufidaun decided to stay at Castle Tyrol.

Jakob von Schenna sat awake late into the evening. But he was not reading the scroll which lay on the table. He paced up and down with his stiff, irregular gait. He had intended at first to plead illness and go neither to Tyrol nor to Taufers. The political aspect of the affair did not matter to him. The rumours and agitations of the populace troubled him not at all, and he had far too little ambition for himself to take his personal safety into account. But the tension between the two women had always stirred him; it moved him more deeply than ever now that it vibrated between the living and the dead. Margarete had appealed to him for help, and for the first time in his life he had refused her. He did not want to be drawn into this struggle, he did not want to take sides. He simply did not want to.

Once more he was perhaps the only one who saw the connecting links. Margarete the Duchess was in the right. Agnes had been the destroyer; it was a blessing for Tyrol

that she was gone.    But was it Margarete the Duchess who
had struck the blow, or Margarete the woman ?    Was
Agnes doomed to die because she harmed the country, or
because she was beautiful ?    He did not venture to decide.
One thing was certain :    Agnes had been the loveliest
woman between the Po and the Danube.    He was an
ageing man.    Was that perhaps his sole reason for not
venturing to decide ?

He did not want to be old and accommodating.    It had
not been fair of the Maultasch.    He had accepted her
misshapen mouth, her flabby cheeks, all her wretched
ugliness.    But he could not accept her hatred for the dead
woman.    A simple, straightforward emotion prevented him.
One must bear witness on beauty's behalf.    He would go
to Taufers.

§ 2

FROM Pustertal over Bruneck people poured into the valley
of Taufers.    Never had these mountains seen so many
people.    They trudged painfully through the deep snow,
and soon there was a trodden road.    They passed the night
under the open starry sky, in the clear, sharp frost.    A whole
town of canvas tents sprang up.    They pressed on in thousands, and in thousands again ;    even women and children
were there risking the hardships and dangers of the winter.
The snowy air resounded with curses against Margarete,
the witch, branded by Heaven.    Foully and treacherously
had the ugly she-devil murdered the sweet and gentle Agnes,
who now lay in state in the Chapel of Taufers, waxen-white,
an angel of God, a bright and lovely saint.    In an endless
train they streamed past her, very different in rank, age and
appearance ;    barons, peasants and townsmen ;    but all

devout, moved and sympathetic, all full of wild and abusive indignation against the Duchess.

Meanwhile in the chapel of Castle Tyrol lay the dead Meinhard, the last Count of Tyrol, in solitary state. Only those Court officials and officers had stayed behind whose duty compelled them to remain in any case.

With icy and taciturn reserve Margarete moved among the whispering mourners, noted the gaps among her guests, and coldly made the last arrangements for the funeral. Was Herr von Schenna not there? No, he had not yet arrived. In the afternoon, still not come? No, Herr von Schenna was not there. She sent a courier to his Castle. Herr von Schenna had gone away to Taufers.

Schenna too.

The strong stench of decay emanating from Meinhard's corpse overpowered all the spices and essences. The people in the chapel almost swooned; the officers who stood on guard had to be relieved every hour.

At about the third hour after midnight Margarete went into the Chapel. She knelt in silence beside the putrefying body of her son; the foul stench did not scare her away. The guards were changed, twice, three times, and still she knelt there without stirring.

Schenna too.

She called on her dead enemy, summoning her imperiously. The dead woman came. She pleaded with her. The other smiled and said nothing. She held up to her all the crimes she had committed, senselessly, idly, impudently trifling with the power of her smooth, vain, shamelessly voluptuous beauty. Here in the chapel where lay the dead Counts of Tyrol who had shaped and moulded the powerful, rich, storied mountain country, she reproached her dead enemy

U

with all that she had destroyed, ruined, and disfigured. The
other hovered to and fro, unattainable ; the odour of
corruption melted around her. She smiled and hovered
and said nothing.

Schenna too.

The other had triumphed. Margarete was in the right,
yet the other had triumphed. Margarete had annihilated
her, and yet she had triumphed. She was annihilated, dead,
and yet triumphant. They all sided with her. Schenna too.

On the next day the incense fumed, the choirs sang, the
coffin was lowered and the slabs of stone heavily shot into
place to close the tomb. But the ceremony awakened no
inner response. The choral songs did not blossom from
the mourners' hearts, the solemn gestures remained sterile,
the few participants stood stiff and ill at ease, shivering.

In the canvas town beside Taufers a great funeral feast
was celebrated. People warmed themselves at huge open
fires, and seethed and roasted meat. The sharp distinctions
between the classes were obliterated. The peasant regaled
himself on game and fish which were forbidden him by law,
instead of on his usual roots and pickled cabbage. The
burghers contributed sausage and roast pork. In the
exhilarating frosty cold there began a measureless and lugu-
brious orgy of eating and drinking. In blissful intoxication
the people recalled with extravagant phrases the angelic
beauty, gentleness and goodness of the dead Countess von
Flavon ;  and wild execrations were hurled against the
Maultasch, the devil's mistress, the assassin. The dead
Agnes was transfigured for the populace in a festal cloud of
flowing wine and savoury roast meat such as they would
never again enjoy.

Alone in Castle Tyrol Margarete held the magnificent

funeral banquet. She sat there alone, stiff and painted, among banners, sashes and standards, at the table which glittered with festal plate, gold and precious stones. The Frauenberger, secretly grinning, Gufidaun, and the Commandant of the German Order, took the dishes from the carvers and pages and laid them ceremoniously on the table. Margarete sat stiff and rigid. The courses arrived in unheard-of abundance, and were removed again untouched. So she celebrated the funeral feast for three long hours.

### § 3

THE Frauenberger's secretary, that quiet, humble cleric, was overwhelmed with work. The Ministers exploited with bare-faced shamelessness the agreement they had extorted from the Duchess, and shared out the land among themselves. The sky showered deeds of gift, bequests, prerogatives, privileges and pledges. The government of the Bavarian Arthurian Knights had been moderation itself compared with this grandiose pillaging of Tyrol by the Maultasch's Cabinet.

With a broad grin the Frauenberger pocketed Agnes's estates, as well as the Castle and district of Pergine, and the Castle of Penede to the east of Riva ; Heinrich von Kaltern-Rottenberg the stronghold of Cagno on the Nonsberg and the village of the same name ; Hans von Freundsberg the stronghold and district of Strassberg, near Sterzing. The brothers von Matsch helped themselves with great liberality. They accepted Nauders, the town and district of Glurns, the prefecture of Eyers and Castle Jufal at the entrance to the Schnalser Valley.

Berchtold von Gufidaun and Egon von Tübingen, the Commandant of the German Order, looked on disapprovingly and kept their hands clean, although ridiculed by the others for their simplicity.

Schenna shook his head in perplexity over the greed of his colleagues. Ended by saying : " Rather myself than someone else," picked out for himself with a sorrowful and expert eye the district and jurisdiction of Sarnthein, pocketed also the Castle and manor of Reineck, the fortress and district of Eppan, and finally, deeply troubled by so much weakness and lack of restraint, Lugano above Cavalese.

Rigid and speechless Margarete signed whatever they presented. In the course of thirteen days half the country was mortgaged or given away.

## § 4

THROUGH the wild January weather five men struggled over the Krimler Tauern. They floundered into snowdrifts and fought their way out again, and bruised their hands and faces on ice and rocks. Death, silently and in a hundred guises, stalked them from crevasses and treacherous slopes of snow. Two bears followed them at a distance, fled, and nosed after them again. For three days they laboured on, until they came again to human habitations at the village of Prettau.

They were Rudolf, Duke of Austria, Herr von Rappach, his High Steward, Herr von Lassberg, his Treasurer, and two servants.

While in Styria, in Judenburg, the Habsburger had received an express dispatch from his Chancellor, who was then in the Swabian provinces which bordered on Tyrol. Bishop Johann of Gurk reported the confusion which had arisen in Tyrol as a consequence of Meinhard's death and pressed him, urgently and respectfully, to make for the land in the mountains with all possible speed.

Rudolf briefly reviewed the situation. The Wittelsbachs were certainly quarrelling among themselves over Meinhard's Bavarian inheritance and had no time to spare for Tyrol. The Chancellor was in the right ; it was most important that he should take the shortest cut and appear unexpectedly before Margarete. Go back to Vienna first ? An army ? No ! He rode straight from Judenburg to Radstatt in the Pinzgau, turned a deaf ear to all the entreaties of those who said that he should not think of crossing the Tauern in winter, and fighting for his life pushed stubbornly over the pass till he reached Prettau and Ahrental. Slipped into Taufers unrecognised amid the stream of mourners. Heard about the Ministry, its incredible plenary powers and its oppressions. Came to Bruneck. Arrived in Bozen on the twentieth of January on the fourteenth day of Margarete's independent reign.

So there he was now. The land, his land, for the possession of which he and his father had laboured for decades, was in the hands of the violent barons, and was being more hopelessly torn to pieces from day to day. He was quite alone, his forces consisted of two officers and two men. True, he had left orders in Austria for troops to be concentrated on the Tyrolean frontiers. But the mountain land could be divided up before these measures were carried into effect. He recognised quite well that his position was full of danger. It was possible that the turbulent, unbridled barons might not hesitate to seize his sanctified person, to hold him prisoner (even though such a proceeding could have only temporary success) and extort guarantees and confirmations from him. But, as usual, he was incapable of waiting. He was full of enthusiasm for his mission and of confidence in himself. Everything depended on his appearance in person.

The Frauenberger announced himself. He came as a delegate from the Ministry. Stood before the Duke, watchful and expectant. The Duke was very cool and reserved. The Frauenberger proceeded cautiously. Blinked confidentially at Rudolf and said genially that the Cabinet was by all means ready to recognise Margarete's testament in favour of the Habsburgs, provided that Rudolf guaranteed a continuation of the Ministers' powers and privileges for at least twelve years.

Rudolf regarded the broad, massive fellow, who stood before him solid and repulsive. The Frauenberger blinked at him impudently and knowingly as one scoundrelly trader might look at another over a profitable and dirty bargain. The Habsburger replied loftily that these were extraordinary customs and strange ideas which had invaded Tyrol. In the Habsburg lands no one who valued his neck would dare to make such proposals to his ruler. As far as he knew a German Prince was responsible only to God and the Emperor ; but a Habsburg, owing to the special privileges of that House, was not even responsible to the Emperor. With a good-humoured air the Frauenberger waited to see if this general and theoretic preamble were to be followed by some particular and practical suggestion. The Duke concluded frigidly that he was willing to examine the privileges of the barons and to determine their validity. At this the albino opened his frog-like mouth and croaked with easy and satisfied assurance that on such a basis they would certainly be able to come to terms. He counted on the Duke's examination being a generous one. In Tyrol they had always been generous enough never to cavil at the house of Habsburg's special privileges, although these had been unearthed late in the day and in very peculiar circumstances.

Then a remarkable thing happened. Slowly and quietly the young Duke lifted his slim, hard, bony hand. With his tanned knuckles he smote the other twice, right and left, on the fat, bare, rosy face.

The Frauenberger remained quite still. His slapped face did not show any mark of the insult, only a boundless astonishment. His lidless reddish eyes stared at the Duke, noted his low, angular, purposeful forehead, his hook nose, his underlip protruding above the strong chin. The albino blinked, blinked more rapidly, shook his head, shrugged his shoulders as if apologetically, bowed and went out.

Rudolf, left alone, breathed deeply, stretched his arms, smiled, and laughed outright.

The Frauenberger said to himself : " He could be put out of the way. But it wouldn't come off so easily as the other times. Besides, he has certainly taken precautions and has a good force at his back. It's cleverer to keep out of his reach. It's a pity for our fine government. But a fellow with a neck and a chin like that ! Well, I have raked enough together, anyhow. Who would have prophesied such a career for me ? We'll have to look into it and keep hold of all we can. What's the good of this eternal greed ? I am not a fool. I can draw back when the risk is too great. All the same it's a pity. But with a hook nose like that ! "

He whistled his song, stretched himself, yawned noisily, cracked his joints, and fell asleep.

## § 5

YOUNG, firm, with composure, but not without respect, Rudolf appeared before the Duchess. He greeted the stiff and taciturn woman and assured her of his personal sympathy. Then, in precise and courteous language, he went straight to his point. She was acknowledged by all the courts as a shrewd and strong ruler. It was all the more astounding that the brief space of her independent rule should have proved so bad for the country. Obviously her grief for the loss of her son, following so quickly on the loss of her husband, had upset her, and rendered her incapable of employing her great gifts. But the mountain country needed a strong hand more than ever at this time. Bavaria was threatening it on the frontier, nor would the nobles of Lombardy be likely to keep quiet in the event of a Wittelsbach invasion ; and internally the land was a prey to the shameless greed of the barons. He asked Margarete to consider whether she would be willing now to confirm that confidence which she had in the House of Habsburg, according to her testament, by making over the government of the country to him.

The ponderous old woman sat motionless before the young Duke. Her broad, misshapen mouth did not twitch, her enormous beringed hands lay as if dead on the heavy black damask of her robes.

Rudolf fixed his hard, clear grey eyes on her and waited, then continued that he did not want to entice her by vague promises. The Habsburg government had shown itself hitherto to be just, strong and vigorous. Tyrol would have no preference over the other Habsburg possessions, but he would answer for it as one sovereign to another, that it would be ruled in exactly the same manner, with strength, justice, and efficiency. As for her personal interests, he was sure that her requirements would be provided for in a more lavish and princely style than under the domination of her barons.

Margarete still made no response, and stared into vacancy with a dull and hunted look. Rudolf concluded by saying that he would not press her. It was a matter to be decided between herself and God. He begged her to have confidence in him, and to reflect without prejudice on his words.

Margarete said in a hoarse voice : " No further reflection is needed. I have confidence in you. I am fully aware how consistent your ideas are."

She rose and with a quiet, singularly lifeless gesture held her painted hands out, palm upwards, and then let them sink. Let everything drop, let it fall. All dropped from her, Tyrol, the towns, her work and the work of her fore-fathers, of Albert, of Meinhard the strong and impetuous, Heinrich's work and her own. Now she was quite stripped and bare.

Rudolf was not in the least given to sentimental or grandiose gestures ; but he was profoundly and strangely moved to see the ugly woman standing there so defenceless and humble, so weary of grandeur and destiny. He sank on one knee and said he would take the country only as a trust from her hands ; he would never forget that he was only its governor

§ 6

In all directions couriers spurred bearing letters and decrees from the Duchess. Margarete proclaimed that in conse-quence of special circumstances and the weakness of her sex she was not in a position to administer the country as its welfare demanded and to protect herself and others as was fitting. On the advice of her Ministers and the people's representatives, therefore, she was transferring her honourable and noble earldoms of Tyrol and Görz, her lands and districts in the valleys of the Adige and the Inn, together with her castle in Tyrol and all other castles, passes, towns, valleys, mountains, markets, villages, hamlets, fiefs, farms, provinces, jurisdictions, mints, customs, tithes, tolls, rents, taxes, dues, timber, fields, woods, hides of land, vineyards, ploughed lands, lakes, running streams, fish ponds, and game preserves, in short, the whole of her ancestral inheritance, to her dear cousins and nearest relatives, the Dukes of Austria. And she earnestly and solemnly enjoined all her prelates, abbots and the body of the clergy, and thereto her burgraves, administrators, governors, and all officials in Tyrol and elsewhere throughout her lands, and thereto the whole populace, to swear fealty and allegiance then and for all time to the Dukes of Austria, as to their rightful lords and masters.

Within a very short time they had all taken without resistance the required oath of fealty and obedience. On the third of February Bozen swore allegiance, on the fifth Meran, on the ninth Sterzing, on the tenth Innsbruck. But among the feudal barons all had not come to such a shrewd decision as the Frauenberger. With little prospect of success, they yet tried to stir up opposition, intrigued with the Wittelsbachs, and set themselves to organise a revolution in the North against the Habsburgs. When Rudolf entered Hall to receive the town's allegiance, there was a public uproar, and the Duke himself was in danger of his life. But the burgesses of Hall stoutly resisted the barons' mercenaries ; the town of Innsbruck sent help to

Rudolf, and it became evident that the towns were determined to support him through thick and thin against the arbitrary domination of the native aristocracy, who were backed up by Bavarian agents. A few days later the Austrian was able to announce proudly to his ally Lorenzo Celsi, the Doge of Venice : " In a peaceful manner and without much resistance We have come into possession of the land in the mountains, which was assured to Us as an inheritance from Our father's time. Both noble and simple have sworn fealty to Us, and acknowledge Us as their overlord. All the roads and passes from Germany into Italy are in Our hands, thanks to the favour of Almighty God."

Margarete attended to the complicated and formal business of the transfer with scrupulous conscientiousness. But she received only the most necessary visitors, and confined her conversation strictly to business. Then she wished to slip unobtrusively out of the country, with only her faded Fräulein von Rottenburg and two lackeys. But Rudolf would not consent to her going in such an unceremonious and unconstitutional fashion. He decreed that every conceivable honour should be paid to the departing sovereign. At the boundaries of their fiefs the feudal barons received her, and on the outskirts of the towns the spiritual and temporal authorities. But the Duchess's litter remained closed She could be only dimly discerned behind the curtains, sitting rigid and motionless in the swaying horse litter. The people peeped in with timid curiosity, but saw nothing. So she departed, sick and broken, the corrupter, the witch, the murderess, the lewd, insatiable, ugly creature, the Maultasch. Behind her grotesque legends sprang up, wild, horrible and filthy. Did not the weapons left behind in her castles

give forth a ghostly clattering and clanking sound ?    Did
not the skeletons of her murdered victims rattle in the cellars
and dungeons ?    People avoided the places which she had
frequented ; they were uncanny.    She was made into a bogey
for the children, and people said :  " If you are not good,
the Maultasch will get you."    Cattle were not allowed to
feed on the fine lush pastures above Castle Maultasch.

When she had passed Innsbruck, brooding vacantly in
her litter, she heard a small shrill voice :  " Fare you well,
Your Grace."    She started up, and asked the faded Fräulein
von Rottenburg :  "Who's that ? "    The Fräulein had
heard nothing.    Margarete peered through the curtains.
Then she saw two infinitely tiny bearded creatures.    They
trotted on the edge of the road and looked at the Duchess
with ancient, solemn eyes, doffed their dirty, brown, old-
fashioned bonnets, and bowed respectfully many times.    At
that Margarete lost her rigidity, her shoulders drooped, and
the squat, ugly woman broke down painfully.

She reached the frontier at the Bavarian Chiemgau.
Here a guard of honour was stationed, and presented arms.
Banners were lowered, music played.    The curtains remained closed, the litter swayed over the frontier into Bavaria.
When she was out of sight the customs officers, in obedience
to instructions, hauled down the splendid, heavy banner of
the Countess of Tyrol, and lazily, yawning and whistling,
hoisted in its stead the new, clean, sober flag of the Habsburgs
with its red lion.

§ 7

SLOWLY the sturdy maidservant rowed the heavy, clumsy
boat away from the little island over the Chiemsee.    It
was midday and very hot ;  the wide lake lay pale and still

around them. Both the ecclesiastics in the boat, Bishop
Johann of Gurk, the Chancellor, and the aged Abbot of
Viktring, were in a bad humour. The Florentine chronicler,
Giovanni Villani, the Abbot's rival, had published the
sensational news that Margarete, Duchess of Bavaria,
Margravine of Brandenburg, Countess of Tyrol, had been
living since her abdication in the most wretched poverty,
and that the Habsburger was leaving her to endure hunger,
misery and deprivations of every kind. The two gentlemen
had been sent by Duke Rudolf to Frauenchiemsee, where
Margarete was living, to urge her to set up a court worthy of
her rank either in Vienna or in any other town she pleased.
Had not the Habsburger assigned her the richest of incomes,
the four manors of Gries near Bozen, Stein on the Ritten,
Amras, and Saint Martin near Zirl, the revenues of the Castle
of Strassberg, of the Passeier, and the town of Sterzing,
besides a yearly allowance of six thousand Veronese pounds ?
The Duchess could have set up a court to rival that of any
German prince. But neither the shrewd and courteous
arguments of the Bishop, nor the Latin quotations of the
Abbot and his precedents drawn from history had been able
to tempt her away.

" She is dead to every interest," complained the Bishop in
Latin. " It does not matter to her whether Tyrol has war
or peace. I told her of the Wittelsbach invasion, and the
brutal wasting of the Inn valley by fire and pillage. She
listened as if I were speaking about the weather." The
lake lay quite still, shimmering palely, the oars dipped
regularly. The old Abbot said nothing. " And besides,
her revenues are piling up," began the Chancellor again.
" They are punctually paid to her, and not a penny is touched.
The gold is accumulating in her castles. She must be

incredibly rich. By Hercules ! " he finished peevishly, " that Italian is a faithless slanderer and detractor, a vile lampooner ! "

The withered ancient's heart opened at this description of his rival. " Your Eminence is in the right," he mumbled toothlessly. "Whoever doubted that he was a petty, wretched tattler ? "

On the banks of the little island sat the Duchess, neglected, crudely daubed with white paint, among rank undergrowth and garish country flowers, gazing after the boat. It was quite still, gnats flickered and waterfowl called sleepily. A strong smell of fish, nets and water-weed hung in the hot, motionless air. The boat crawled very slowly, rounded the point of the larger island in front, and disappeared from sight.

From the humble, greyish-yellow, sunlit fisher hut came her withered Fräulein, and summoned the Duchess to dinner ; Margarete stood up, stretched herself languidly, and trailed up to the house with her heavy, dragging step. Her mouth thrust itself out like an ape's, her cheeks hung down flabbily, huge and shapeless, her paint could not conceal the warts beneath. The still and submissive Fräulein opened the clumsy door for her. The savour of fried fish came welling out in a cloud. Margarete sniffed it contentedly and went in.

### THE END

THE LONDON AND NORWICH PRESS, LIMITED, ST. GILES' WORKS, NORWICH

" The range and power of this book are astonishing." NORTHERN ECHO.

" Of absorbing interest. The book, helped by an irreproachable translation, is an excellent example of the really good historical romance." GLASGOW HERALD.

" Teems with life. The translation could not be bettered." NATION AND ATHENÆUM.

" We closed *Jew Süss* full of admiration for Herr Feuchtwanger's ability. No short summary can do justice to this book." ABERDEEN PRESS.

" This great book is one of the most remarkable historical novels published for many years. . . . No summary can adequately convey a sense of the beauty and terror, the vivid colouring, the tragic irony of this book, which places Lion Feuchtwanger in the front rank of contemporary novelists." DAILY HERALD.

" Of the fabric of history itself, immense with the immensity of a Titian or a Correggio." QUEEN.

" Indeed a masterpiece, the restoration before the eyes of our soul of a world." BRITISH WEEKLY.

" Epic in conception and achievement, *Jew Süss* is already acclaimed as a classic." ENGLISH REVIEW.

" Truly a great book." SHEFFIELD TELEGRAPH.

" A work of genius. . . . A magnificent historical romance. Its exploration of the hearts of men and women is profound." ILLUSTRATED LONDON NEWS.

" A very splendid romance. . . . A drama of extraordinary majesty and power." STAR.

" Finely conceived, and finely carried out to the end." SPHERE.

" ' Great ' fits *Jew Süss* as no other adjective fits it. It moves with the glamour and glitter of a superb pageant. Its stage teems with life and colour." SKETCH.

" A great novel, really great in the sense that the works of Shakespeare, Beethoven and Wagner are great." GLASGOW EVENING CITIZEN.

" A book of genius, a very great book." TIME AND TIDE.

" A book of the hour. . . . A very powerful historical novel." GRAPHIC.

" Herr Feuchtwanger's extraordinary and brilliant work. . . . One has an impression of a whole people in action." LONDON MERCURY.

" The triumph of the novel is its superb picture of Jewry. . . . It is the epic of the Jew. I have read nothing to equal it in passion, in imaginative intensity, in penetrating vision." SUNDAY EXPRESS.

" May be pronounced without hesitation the first great historical novel of the present century." JEWISH GUARDIAN.

" A most exceptionally powerful story, glowing with colour and life." GUARDIAN.

" A really fine historical novel, at once an admirably done canvas of history and an admirable personal narrative." CHURCH OF ENGLAND NEWSPAPER.

" So instinct with truth, so vital, so ruthless, and done in so grand a style as to make of it great literature." REVIEW OF REVIEWS.

" An astonishing work, and one of the finest historical romances of recent years." DUBLIN REVIEW.

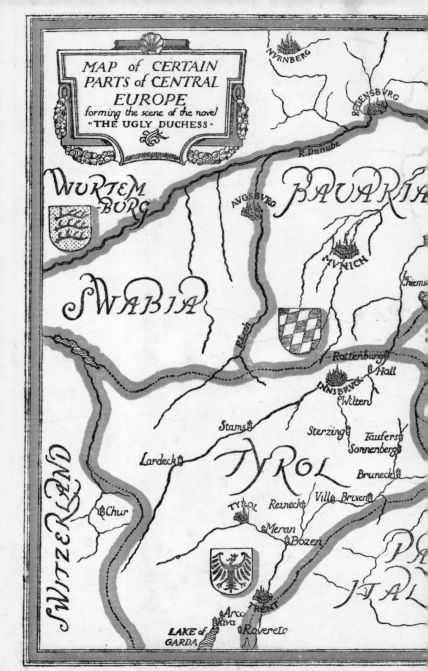

MAP of CERTAIN
PARTS of CENTRAL
EUROPE
forming the scene of the novel
"THE UGLY DUCHESS"

NVRNBERG

REGENSBURG

R. Danube

WURTEM-BURG

AVGSBVRG

BAVARIA

MVNICH

L. Chiems

SWABIA

Lech

Rattenburg
Hall
INNSBRVCK
Wilten

Stams

Sterzing
Taufers
Sonnenberg

Lardeck

TYROL

Bruneck

Villa Brixen

Chur

TYROL
Reineck
Meran
Bozen

SWITZERLAND

PA
ITAL

TRENT
Arco
Riva
Rovereto

LAKE of
GARDA